Scarlet

Jane Brindle

HEADLINE
FEATURE

First published in 1991 by
Sphere Books Ltd

Reprinted in paperback in 1995
by Orion Books Ltd

First published in this paperback edition in 1998 by
HEADLINE BOOK PUBLISHING

A HEADLINE FEATURE paperback

10 9 8 7 6 5 4 3 2 1

ISBN 0 7472 5751 5

Typeset by
Letterpart Limited, Reigate, Surrey

Printed and bound in Great Britain by
Mackays of Chatham plc, Chatham, Kent

HEADLINE BOOK PUBLISHING
A division of Hodder Headline PLC
338 Euston Road
London NW1 3BH

Scarlet

CONTENTS

AUTHOR'S FOREWORD

My gratitude and thanks to all the kind people who live in the beautiful medieval village of Dunster, situated on the edge of Exmoor and close to the west Somerset coastline in England.

When carrying out research in this lovely village – a perfect and lingering relic of times gone by – I was inundated with endless offers of help, and precious documents were put at my disposal.

I must make particular mention of Mrs Winter, who lives close to the old blacksmith's shop, and who very kindly loaned me a number of precious old books.

I would also like to stress that the evil and sinister blacksmith in this story bears no relation whatsoever to the kindly and well-beloved man who for many years was a blacksmith in Dunster. (The latter generated love and admiration; the former was a monster who created only fear and loathing.) Vincent Pengally and Greystone House were conceived in the depths of a dark and terrifying notion.

PART ONE

New York
1937

THE PAST

From childhood's hour I have not been
As others were – I have not seen
As others saw – I could not bring
My passions from a common spring.

Edgar Allan Poe, 'Alone'

CHAPTER ONE

For God's sake, Cassie help me! Come at once.
Forgive me, but I am desperate.

Scarlet Pengally

The letter trembled in Cassie's hands, and as she read the words over and over they seared her mind, shocking her to the very core of her being. Yet this letter from England was not the *only* shock Cassie had suffered recently and somehow, she had the awful premonition that it would not be the last!

The letter, though, had shaken her more than she realised, or was it the reading of her father's will earlier today that had devastated her? There was no doubt that, because of it, and now *this*, Cassie's whole life had been turned upside down. In the space of only twenty-four hours she was alienated from everything she had been brought up to believe. All that had gone before in her life was now meaningless. She was lost, adrift from all that was familiar, stripped of her identity, and left without a purpose. Cassie felt the room slowly spinning as her senses began to dim. 'It's alright, Cassie . . . you're only dreaming.' She heard her own voice, yet it was not hers, so strange did it sound. But, of course, that was it! She was only dreaming, living through a nightmare from which she would wake at any minute.

3

Crossing to the long casement window from which she gazed out into the darkness beyond, Cassie knew that she was *not* dreaming. The nightmare was real! As real as all the other nightmares that haunted her as a child . . . only this time it was different. This time her mother was not there to take Cassie in her arms, to gently stroke her hair and lovingly whisper words of comfort. Oh, how Cassie had adored that darling frail creature, with her pretty face and soft blue eyes, and how she had missed her during the two lonely years since the Good Lord had seen fit to take her. She was always Cassie's comfort, her peace of mind, and her friend. The only one who truly loved Cassie, who encouraged her in her art studies and her love of painting. Cassie's father, the respected and wealthy financier, had always been as ruthless and unfeeling with her as he had been in his banking transactions in the city of New York. He had been a big man in his own field, strong, demanding and always reluctant to give any quarter; he had never learned the art of compromise and it was his way to ride roughshod over anyone who displeased him. Cassie must have displeased him from the day she was born, because he had no love or regard for her . . . only suspicion and inexplicable animosity. For as long as Cassie could remember, he had kept her at a distance, always favouring her younger brother, allowing him the freedom and privileges Cassie had never known. In her heart she knew from an early age that he loathed her; that, for some reason she could never understand, he could not bear her near him. Cassie's brother followed his every example, spurning and despising her in the same way. Only her mother gave her the love she was hungry for: always there, always protecting, always guiding and encouraging, never failing Cassie when she needed her.

When, as so often, Cassie woke screaming with terror

and bathed in the sweat of the pursued, it was *she* who took Cassie in her arms and gave her solace, *she* who wiped away her tears and coaxed her from the nightmares that plagued her . . . terrible, violent nightmares, yet so vague and obscure that Cassie could never remember them afterwards. They were there, though, in Cassie's subconscious, only waiting for her to close her eyes and enter that terrifying world of darkness, and they would surround her, engulf her until the very breath was squeezed from her body. It was then that Cassie's mother would reach out her arms and hold her close, safe and secure – for a while.

Looking out of the window, Cassie noticed absent-mindedly how the big soft snowflakes were already beginning to settle on the ground. They made a deep white halo of light beneath the street lamps, glistening and sparkling with many dazzling facets, forming patterns which had a peculiar beauty of their own. It was sad that their lives were so very short, that with the touch of warmth they would simply melt away for ever, as though they had never existed.

Cassie felt like that . . . fragile and threatened, and now as though she had never existed. She could barely see for the rising tears which stung her eyes. Standing up tall and straight against the window, she swallowed hard and deliberately blinked back her tears: she would not cry; she must *never* cry! Somewhere, deep in her subconscious, every instinct warned Cassie against it and she recalled some years ago when her favourite doll was accidentally smashed, she wanted to cry then . . . Momma had told her, 'It's beyond repair. I'm sorry, darling . . . you cry if you want to.' She *did* want to. But the tears just would not come. They dared not.

Cassie didn't know how long she stood by the window, she only knew that she was desperately unhappy and afraid. Inside the room it was warm, but outside it was a cold February night, with the breeze cutting spitefully into the newly fallen snow, whipping it up and spinning it high into the air until it disappeared from sight. Soon, visitors were leaving: selected business colleagues of Cassie's father, various other beneficiaries of his will, and lastly the lawyer who had so sincerely expressed his heartfelt sympathy regarding Cassie's unforeseen circumstances. He was a kindly man, and Cassie believed him when he had told her after the reading, 'I begged your father to make proper provision for you in his will, Cassie . . . after all, you are the elder child. But he was adamant that everything he owned must go to your brother. He never gave me his reasons, but no doubt the sealed letters he left to both you and your brother will explain. I'm sorry, Cassie . . . so very sorry.' Then he smiled warmly, adding, 'Oh, but I'm sure your brother Edmund will do the right thing by you. Don't worry, child. If it should prove to be necessary, you do have the right to appeal.'

But Cassie had read the letter which Jonathan Thornton left to her, and she was convinced of three things. Firstly, Edmund would make *no* provision for her. Secondly, an appeal would be thrown out of any court on the grounds that her 'father', Jonathan Thornton, was in sound mind when he made his will, though there might be questions about Cassie's sanity! And, lastly, she had learned now without doubt that she had no right whatsoever to *anything* belonging to the Thornton family. She also knew, after all these years, why Jonathan Thornton publicly acknowledged his 'daughter' Cassie . . . while privately spurning her. It was all there, written in his own hand, and even through the written words Cassie could sense his repugnance of her, so much so that she could hardly bear to hold the letter in her hands long enough to read it. Afterwards she dropped it into the fire, where she watched the flames curl about it until it was engulfed, and reduced to blackened ash. There were things written in that letter . . . horrible things which she must forget if she was ever to know peace of mind. But the one staring fact Cassie could *not* forget was that *Nancy Thornton was not her real mother*. Jonathan Thornton was not her father and though he had taken her in and provided the *material* aspects of her upbringing because of his wife's pleas on Cassie's behalf, he had done so grudgingly, and had regretted it ever since. There was nothing in his letter to tell Cassie of her true background or to give her any idea of how she might discover her own identity. There was no remorse for his harsh treatment of her; no comfort of any kind, only hatred, and something else – something which permeated through his every word and turned her heart over. That something was *fear*. And, it awakened the same in Cassie. He wanted her to leave this house on Madison Avenue where she had grown up. He insisted also that she should change her name from Thornton, and never again contact his only child, Edmund. He concluded the letter by saying:

> I have done my duty by you, for the sake of my lovely Nancy, and now I owe you nothing!
> You will find enclosed a letter from England, which I purposely kept from you. *The letter is from your real mother. Go back to her, where you belong. And may the devil take you both.*
>
> Jonathan Thornton

Cassie watched as the visitors went into the night, tightening their coats and pulling up their collars as they climbed into their various carriages and motor cars. In the blackness of the window, the room was mirrored in its expensive detail, its deep plush carpets of red, and furnishings of velvet and silk. The furniture was grand and ornate, and there on the large marble mantelpiece was a photograph of Jonathan and Nancy Thornton, he still tall and overbearing in his early sixties, slightly balding and upright of stance, and she tiny, delicate, with smiling blue eyes and goodness shining from her. And there, in the window, was mirrored Cassie's own image and she looked nothing like either of them.

For long agonising moments Cassie regarded the image that was her with a great deal of curiosity . . . as though observing a stranger. The figure was not short, neither was it tall, but a pleasing height for a woman, being also slim and softly rounded, with square straight shoulders and an air of confidence which belied the inner insecurity. Soft wavy hair with tints of auburn and gold tumbled to the shoulders and framed the small oval face, giving it added loveliness and a peculiar innocence . . . almost vulnerability. The mouth was softly red and perfectly shaped, marred only by the lop-sided dimple in that fold of flesh below the bottom lip. The nose was trim and straight, with only the tiniest tilt to its tip, and the eyes, which were spaced a suitable distance apart, were not over-large but dark and attractive. They had an artist's way of seeing deeper than most, and they had a particular sadness about them.

Suddenly Cassie heard familiar footsteps approaching her room. It was Edmund, and the very thought that he was about to halt at her door and knock on it caused Cassie's stomach to churn and her heart to pound with fear. He knew she did not belong! He *also* had received a letter after the reading of the will, and there was no doubt in Cassie's mind that his father had told him how she was a usurper . . . a cuckoo in the nest.

The knock came, then, before Cassie could answer, the door was pushed open and there he stood, a handsome young man not yet sixteen years old, and almost two years younger than Cassie. She had often wondered at the stark difference in their physical appearance, for his eyes were vivid blue like Nancy's, and his hair was golden yellow like his father's had once been. Cast in the image of Jonathan Thornton, his son Edmund wore a permanent scowl on his face and he saw a potential enemy in everyone.

'You read my father's letter?' His voice was hostile as he came into the room, closing the door behind him.

Cassie could find no words to say to him, being both afraid and reluctant to enter into any kind of conversation on a matter that was so terrible to her. Drawing the curtains on the night, she turned to face him and was not surprised to see his gloating expression as the blue eyes raked her face. Then he smiled, an unexpected smile that straight away put Cassie on guard. 'I won't leave you penniless . . . even though you do understand that anything I do for you is out of the goodness of my heart. I am under no obligation, but I know how fond of you my momma was.' She was *my* momma too, Cassie thought, in spite of everything, and she would not let him take that away from her. She hated his voice as it went on, pompous and patronising. 'I've made arrangements for the sum of twelve thousand dollars to be deposited in your name at Central Bank.'

'I don't want your money.' The thought disgusted her.

'You'll need it to make a new life . . . use it wisely.' His eyes were cool and delighted. 'There'll be no more.' He turned away; then, as he opened the door to leave, he swung round, on his face a darker look, as he told her scathingly, 'I always knew you didn't belong! You have three days to leave this house . . . after that I never want to see or hear from you again.' He smiled once more, his face wreathed in pleasure as, gently laughing, he said, 'Goodbye, Cassie . . . whoever you are!'

For a long time after his footsteps had retreated and the room was struck with an eerie silence, Cassie made no move. Her mind was churning, agitated and confused. What should she do? Where would she go? Again the tears threatened and, as before, she suppressed them. Three days! The obvious kept pushing itself into her mind, and each time she fought it off, until there was no fight left in her. She had no friends, nowhere to go but in one direction: the direction in which fate was pressing her. England! She must go to England and seek out the woman who claimed to be her real mother; she must find Scarlet Pengally, and learn from her the truth about the past. Strange, Cassie thought: little more than twenty-four hours ago she was Cassie Thornton, residing on Madison Avenue, New York. She had a life, an identity, and a promising future as an artist. The name Scarlet Pengally was unknown to her and she had no aspirations whatsoever to go to England. Now she was nobody; she had no family or place, no future and no past . . . except through this woman. She had to find her! She had to know why Jonathan Thornton had allowed his wife to bring Cassie up as her own child, though he himself had never been able to love her. The more Cassie thought on it, the more she knew that her destiny was already written.

The letter from England was postmarked some six months ago, and the chilling thought struck Cassie that perhaps the fearsome thing which had made Scarlet Pengally desperate enough to write such a letter might by now have caught up with her. For both their sakes she hoped not. The letter was strangely disturbing, as though written under great duress by a highly imaginative and nervous creature, or by a madwoman! Either way, it beckoned Cassie to old England, and she could not resist. Something about that letter, about the woman who wrote it, and some dark curious instinct deep inside Cassie, compelled her to go!

The next three days went so fast that Cassie hardly had time to conclude all the arrangements for her trip to England. Once her mind was made up, though, she found a great energy for the task in hand, yet at no time did she feel excited, or look forward to the journey with any degree of enthusiasm. To her mind it was something that must be done, and the sooner the better! It was strange, though, she mused, how she went about the arrangements – almost as if it was not her but someone else. She felt apprehensive, unsure of herself, and always there was within her a murmuring sense of impending danger, a disturbing intuition of evil, which made Cassie wonder more than once whether she should leave the past undisturbed and go about her life as though she had never seen the letter from Scarlet Pengally. Yet, she *had* seen it, and it burned in her brain like a flickering beacon, guiding her constantly to its source, driving her on into the darkness, where she was convinced there would surely be light to shine into all the deep terrifying corners of her old nightmares, and only then would the truth be laid bare. And so with increasing urgency she planned everything, right down to the smallest detail.

The bank confirmed a deposit of twelve thousand dollars in Cassie's name, after which she was duly issued with all she needed for the trip. The withdrawal she made consisted partly of dollars and partly of English currency; there were also arrangements made, in the event that she might need to withdraw from the account during her stay in England.

'And have you any idea how long your stay in England might be?' The rotund and bearded desk clerk was sweating profusely, being unused to executing his duties with such speed. Impatiently he dabbed at his soaking brow with a grey and grubby handkerchief.

'I can't say,' Cassie told him, 'it could be days . . . it could be weeks.' She hoped it would be the former rather than the latter, yet suspected that the purpose of her trip would not be so quickly satisfied . . . unless of course Scarlet Pengally had perished in the time between her sending the letter and Cassie receiving it.

Within hours of leaving the bank, Cassie had secured a berth on the *Queen Mary*, sailing for Southampton in two days' time, and she had booked a room in a stylish hotel in Manhattan, within walking distance of Central Park. Her room being situated on the thirtieth floor, she could easily glimpse the Hudson River from the wide panoramic window. Madison Avenue and the Thornton residence seemed a million miles away.

As if to discard the ties with that part of her life, Cassie had left the house with only the clothes that were on her back, and a small golden locket given to her one Thanksgiving by the darling woman she had always known as her momma. It was a gift she would always cherish. She had no conscience about using the money put into her account by Edmund Thornton, because he was a very wealthy young man with a secure future and an even more secure past. She had *neither*.

The next two days sped by with alarming speed, during which time she haunted Broadway, spent an enlightening evening at the theatre, paid a few cents to cross over to Staten Island on the ferry, saw Central Park by horse and carriage, and browsed round the big department stores buying expensive clothes in warm soft colours, which belied the fact that she really ought to be in a state of mourning. Jonathan Thornton had disowned her. Now it was her turn to disown him!

When, at eight a.m. on Wednesday 17 February 1937, Cassie leaned across the rails of the liner *Queen Mary* and looked back to see the towering buildings of the New York skyline diminishing in the distance and the Statue of Liberty with her arm raised as though in farewell, something snapped inside and a great wave of sadness engulfed her senses, until she was forced to turn away from the sight of the land which was America, and her land, her home and her world. She was sailing for a new world now, a world away from all that was familiar. As the great liner carried her further and further away from the beloved shores of America, a wave of nostalgia swept over her, yet she knew there was no turning back. When she made her way along the deck, glancing behind her one more time before New York harbour had merged with sea and sky, Cassie was made to wonder whether she would ever return.

CHAPTER TWO

'That's right, dear . . . we *did* have a lady staying here by the name of Miss Pengally. Oh, but she's *gone*. Been gone these many weeks. I'm sorry, dear . . . and you all the way from America to find her!' The homely Mrs Grady had run a respectable boarding-house in Weymouth for many years, and she was proud of the fact that she never forgot a face. 'Striking handsome woman was Miss Pengally . . . had something about her that always made people turn their heads to stare after her. But she never encouraged them, oh dear me no . . . she was a woman who always kept herself to herself.' She might have added 'obsessed with her privacy', but thought better of it. She shook her trim grey head, folded her arms and creased her round bright eyes into a smile. 'I'm sorry you've had a wasted journey,' she said, simultaneously offering Cassie a china plate which was piled on one side with neatly cut sandwiches, and on the other with half a dozen tiny cakes, each with a cherry on top. 'Have another sandwich before you go, dear,' she urged.

Cassie gratefully declined. Her appetite had been quelled with the news that Scarlet Pengally was no longer at the address given in the letter. She felt disheartened and thoroughly drained by her long journey. Since arriving in Southampton on a cold windswept March day, she had wasted no time in travelling straight to Weymouth in the

15

south of England, by way of train and local bus. Victoria Street had been relatively easy to locate and now here she was, seated in the tiny welcoming parlour of the boarding-house named in Scarlet Pengally's frantic letter. The news that she had been gone these past weeks was a devastating blow for Cassie. 'No, thank you all the same, Mrs Grady.' She had to keep searching; she *must* find Scarlet Pengally! 'Did she leave any forwarding address? Did she say anything about where she was going?' For a moment it crossed Cassie's mind to go to the police with the letter. But her instincts warned her against it. After all, there was no real reason to . . . and she felt that Scarlet Pengally would not thank her.

Mrs Grady shook her head in a slow thoughtful manner as she returned the plate to the table. 'No, I'm afraid she didn't . . . and of course, it's my policy never to pry into the affairs of a guest. As I say, in the time she stayed here, Miss Pengally never socialised with any of the other guests. She spent a great deal of her time in her room . . . took all of her meals up there. She was a . . . nervous type, I thought. None of us ever knew where she came from.'

'Did she have any visitors?'

'None that come to mind.'

Mrs Grady regarded her visitor closely. It was plain to see that she was a wealthy young woman, but then, *all* Americans are wealthy, she thought wryly. She felt a pang of compassion for this one, though, because, in spite of her expensive blue two-piece with its beautifully tailored straight skirt and tiny nipped-in waist, there was a forlorn look about her face, an almost tragic loneliness in the lovely eyes, that no amount of money could erase. 'Look here, my dear,' she ventured softly, 'You've come a very long way and you're obviously exhausted. I know my little boarding-house probably . . . isn't what you're used to, but . . . I do have a spare room . . . a nice one overlooking the promenade. You're very welcome to stay the night . . . give yourself time to think, and to refresh yourself.'

Cassie considered for a moment. She *did* need time to work out her next move. Also it was getting late, and she had not arranged alternative accommodation. She had deliberately travelled light, bringing with her only one portmanteau and a smaller valise, both of which were standing in the hall. Mrs Grady's suggestion made sense, and so Cassie thanked her. 'I will stay overnight,' she said, feeling the weight of sleep on her, 'and you're right, Mrs Grady . . . I am very tired.'

'That's settled, then!' Mrs Grady was already on her feet. 'I'll fetch the key . . . and call Amy to take the cases up.' She made a hurried departure from the room, a broad smile on her face as she went. It was her *first* American guest, and she saw it as a real feather in her cap!

In a matter of minutes, the landlady was back. 'There you are, dear,' she told Cassie, handing her a small bunch of keys. 'Room Four, just at the top of the stairs. You'll find the bathroom at the end of the corridor . . . and there are clean towels on your dresser. Amy's taking your bags up right now.' She walked with Cassie to the door. 'If there's anything you need, dear . . . just ask.'

Cassie thanked her, saying there was nothing she needed apart from a good night's sleep, and made her way up the stairs to Room Number Four. She was pleasantly surprised to see a spacious room, which was tastefully furnished. There was a large brass bed with a deep floral eiderdown, wardrobe and chest of drawers in light oak wood, beige-patterned linoleum, pretty chintz curtains at the long casement window, and a small hand-basin tucked unobtrusively into one corner. Cassie had to agree with the delightful Mrs Grady. It was not the luxury she was used to, but it was clean and welcoming and strangely comforting, she thought, giving her the feeling that she'd been there before. But of course she had not.

Collecting her valise from near the wardrobe where Amy had placed it, Cassie swung it up onto the bed; all she wanted was to bathe and afterwards to climb in between the sheets and fall asleep. Tomorrow she must decide what to do. There must be *some* way she could trace the woman who claimed to be her mother, but for now she was bone-tired and couldn't think straight.

Some time later, after having soaked in a tub of hot soothing water, Cassie returned to her room and was about to turn back the bedcovers when two things happened. She noticed the three framed prints on the wall directly above the bedhead and, leaning forward to admire them more closely, it struck Cassie there was something not quite right about the manner in which they were hung. All three were small landscapes, probably not very valuable she guessed, but pretty and decorative all the same. Two were hung beside each other higher up the wall; the third was at odd angles to these, being much lower and curiously isolated, as though hung there as an afterthought. Instinctively Cassie reached out to touch it. It was then there came a sharp intrusive knock on the door, startling Cassie and causing her to swing round, accidentally knocking the picture from the wall and onto the bed. 'Who is it?' she called. For some inexplicable reason she felt afraid.

'It's only me, miss . . . Amy.'

'Oh, Amy . . . come in.' Cassie relaxed, retrieving the picture as Amy came into the room carrying a tray. 'Mrs Grady thought a cup of cocoa and a biscuit might help you to sleep better.' She was a bright little thing in a dark dress and white pinafore. Her small brown eyes smiled at Cassie. 'I'll put it down here, shall I, miss?' Without waiting for an answer, she came forward and carefully placed the tray on the bedside table next to Cassie. When she straightened up to bid Cassie goodnight, her eyes grew round with alarm as she saw that Cassie was preparing to replace the picture on the wall. 'Oh, miss . . . let *me* do that!' she urged. But it was too late. Cassie had seen the damage on the wall, and was already examining its peculiar shape.

Cassie's fingers traced the deliberate jagged shape which had been etched into the plaster, seemingly by a sharp instrument. Her eyes were not deceived. 'It's a *cross*!' she gasped.

'*She* did that!' Amy's face was drained of colour as she pleaded with Cassie. 'You won't tell Mrs Grady about it, will you? It'll cost me my job if you do.'

'What does it mean?' Cassie was both alarmed and intrigued. '*Who* did it, Amy? And why would it cost you your job?'

'I should'a told Mrs Grady . . . but I know *I'd* have got the blame. I'm responsible for these rooms being kept in good condition, but oh, she goes on when there's damage done and money to be spent. She *always* blames me! She'd blame me for *this* if she knew about it . . . that's why I put the picture over it . . . so as she wouldn't notice. But it weren't nothing to do with *me*. *She* did it!'

'Who? *Who* did it, Amy?'

'The one you were asking about. Miss Pengally . . . Scarlet Pengally. This was *her* room, y'see.'

A small hope was awakened in Cassie, but it was tempered by the strange discovery she had made. Why in God's name would Scarlet Pengally want to gouge the sign of a *cross* onto the wall? 'Sit down, Amy . . . *please*.' Cassie indicated towards the small wicker chair by the window. 'Tell me about Scarlet Pengally . . . tell me everything you know.'

Shaking her head, Amy began retreating towards the door. 'I don't know *anything*, miss. Honest, I just know that she was the one who put that on the wall. It wasn't there one day . . . then it *was* there the next, and she used to get these terrible nightmares. I sleep in the attic, over this room, and sometimes I'd hear her moaning and crying. I came down to her one night . . . but I were too late to stop her.' She pointed a shaking finger to the cross on the wall. 'Y'know, miss . . . she were still asleep. Even when she was *awake*, she'd sometimes behave in a funny way . . . whispering one name over and over. "Silas," she'd say . . . "Silas" . . . all quiet and spooky-like . . . as though he were whispering to her, and she were whispering back.'

'Are you saying she was crazy?' Cassie was deeply angered by such a prospect.

'No!' Amy appeared shocked. 'No, she weren't "crazy", miss. She were a lovely lady . . . kind and quiet . . . and oh, you could see that she'd been a real beauty . . . still was! But she *were* a little strange sometimes. Not "crazy", you understand. She'd just go off in a world of her own. She were *poorly*; that's what it was.'

'Amy, think very hard . . . did she say anything at all about where she was going when she left here?' Now, more than ever, Cassie felt desperate to find her!

'No, miss. She never talked about nothing like that. She were a very private sort of lady.'

'Are you absolutely certain that she didn't say where she was headed?'

'Yes, miss . . . she never told nobody where she'd come from . . . nor what her plans were. Not at all.' Amy watched as the American visitor sank to the bed. She did look tired, poor thing, and it would have been nice if she'd been able to tell her what she wanted to know. But what she said was the truth. Scarlet Pengally never told anybody *anything*! 'Goodnight, miss. Oh, you *won't* tell Mrs Grady about that damage to the wall, will you, miss?' Amy was anxious to leave.

'No, of course not. Goodnight.'

Cassie waited until the door was closed behind the departing figure before once more examining the marks on the wall. She felt oddly disturbed by them, even afraid, though she didn't know why. Who was this man Silas? Why was Scarlet Pengally so obsessed with him that she felt compelled to whisper his name, 'over and over'? And what had been her reason for carving a large cross into the wall? What did it all mean?

The questions spun in Cassie's mind even as she drifted into sleep, tormenting her dreams and causing her a fitful night. So much so that when she came down to breakfast, she felt no more rested than when she had retired. Yet, she looked deceivingly refreshed in a pretty green paisley dress, with her hair brushed loosely into natural waves. She put on a bright and cheery front, chatting to the other guests and passing the time of day as though there were no other issues on her mind; when all the time her mind was beleaguered by thoughts of Scarlet Pengally, by what had driven her, and by thoughts of what had become of her since leaving this house. She couldn't help but think of the letter and its desperate wording. And, for the first time, Cassie felt both guilty and moved with compassion. What *was* it that had prompted Scarlet Pengally to contact her after all these years, and in such a way? The letter had been a call for help. And no help had come! What had been the consequences, wondered Cassie, and, in wondering, her blood ran cold.

'Did you put the picture back, miss?' Amy lifted the portmanteau into the car. 'You didn't say anything to Mrs Grady, did you, miss?'

'No . . . I didn't say anything. And yes, I put the picture back.' Cassie smiled and handed the girl a half-crown.

'Ooh! Thank you very much.' Amy had never been given such a tip! 'Where will you go now? Now that you've not found who you were looking for?' she asked, as Cassie buttoned up her green fitted jacket and climbed into the vehicle.

'I think my next stop will have to be London . . . there

must be somewhere there where they keep records. One thing is for sure . . . I don't intend to give up!' Cassie had never been more adamant.

'That's right, miss!' The girl's face lit up with a smile. 'There *must* be a place in London where they keep everybody's records!' She prepared to close the door behind Cassie. 'They might *even* be able to tell you about "Greystone House!" . . . though I shouldn't think your friend would go back *there*, miss, oh no! She seemed too frightened of *that* place!'

'Greystone House?' Cassie grabbed the girl's fingers as they closed on the half-open window. 'You never mentioned that to me! When I asked you if Miss Pengally had said anything, you said she had told you nothing at all!' She clambered from the car, gripping the anxious girl by the shoulders and telling her impatiently, 'Amy! It's *vital* that I find this woman. You *must* tell me all you know. What about this "Greystone House"? What did she say . . . is that where she came from?'

'I don't know, miss . . . honest! I didn't tell you no lies . . . she never told me anything. But sometimes, when I took her tray up . . . she'd be snoozing, like . . . and she'd mumble all the time in her sleep. *That's* when she mentioned "Greystone House" . . . and if you ask me, it couldn't have been a very nice place . . . because she always woke up when she dreamed about it, and her black eyes were all big and frightened! She won't have gone *there*, miss, I'm sure of it!'

'What else, Amy?' Cassie knew the girl had not deliberately kept the information from her, but, if she had forgotten this much, it was likely there was something else as well. 'Think hard, Amy! She talked in her sleep, you say?' The girl nodded. 'You heard her mention this "Greystone House"?' Again the girl nodded. 'There *was* something else . . . *think hard* . . . what else did she say in her sleep, Amy? *What else?*' Cassie insisted.

'Well . . . she were always going on about that man . . . that "Silas" . . . oh, and *another* name . . . *Cassie*! And sometimes when she called the names, she'd cry like a baby. Once or twice, she'd say about that house, and it always seemed to frighten her, I know *that*, miss!' She paused, her pretty little face crumpled up as though trying hard to recall Miss Pengally's every haunted word. 'That were all, really. Oh! And there was one time when she mumbled about a place called Minehead . . . Minehead! Yes, that was it!' She gave Cassie a bright smile, seeming suitably pleased with herself.

'Nothing more?'

'No, miss. Like I told you, she never said anything to anybody about her business . . . but she had these awful dreams . . . day *and* night, when words would tumble from her, and sometimes she'd wake up in a terrible state . . . like something was after her! She got real poorly sometimes, and she wouldn't eat for days.'

'She had a doctor, then. What was the doctor's name, Amy?'

'No, miss . . . there weren't no doctor. She wouldn't have no doctor. Honest, miss . . . there's nothing else I can tell you.' She began to look distressed.

'Don't worry, Amy . . . you've helped more than you know.' Cassie fished about in her handbag before withdrawing a small notebook and pencil. She began scribbling into the book, quietly repeating those things which the girl had told her and which she felt would help in her search. 'Greystone House'. 'Minehead'. If Cassie had harboured any doubts about her journey to England, they were gone now, replaced by an even stronger compulsion, a feeling deep within her that drove her on; she would not rest until she had found this extraordinary woman who had sent her such a strange summons.

As the vehicle drove away in the morning sunshine, with Cassie gazing out of the window at the lovely crescent-shaped bay with its golden sands, and at the numerous people sauntering along the broad promenade, she could not dispel the disturbing sense of evil that continued to pervade her thoughts. She could not rid her mind of the cross that Scarlet Pengally had carved into the wall above her bed. Was it another cry for help, Cassie wondered . . . or was it something more sinister? Either way, its discovery only served to lend a greater sense of urgency to her search!

Cassie's destination was Minehead, which Amy had explained was in the West Country. 'How long will it take me to get there?' Cassie asked the ticket clerk at the railway station.

'Five hours and more . . . depending on whether your connections at Westbury and Taunton are on time, miss.' The thin-faced man pushed Cassie's ticket and her change under the counter window towards her, 'But it'll take a blessed sight longer if you don't get your skates on, luv. We've only two trains a day going to your destination . . . one leaves at five minutes to midnight . . . and the other's just about to pull outta the station!' Seeing Cassie scrambling her luggage together and hurriedly making her way towards the indicated platform, he called out, 'Enjoy your stay in England!' But Cassie was already out of sight. She wasn't looking forward to the journey which the clerk had described . . . five hours on a train and changing twice before she got to her destination.

It was four p.m. when Cassie alighted from the train at Minehead in Somerset. It had been a long slow journey but, strangely enough, she was not tired, only relieved at having arrived, and convinced that here, in this seaside town, she would at last come face to face with Scarlet Pengally.

There had been two taxis standing outside the railway station, both waiting for fares; Cassie took the first one.

'Where to?' The little man tilted his cap and gave Cassie a wide toothless smile, at the same time stowing her cases into the car.

'A decent hotel,' she answered. 'Which would you recommend?'

'Why, for a lady like yourself . . . American aren't you, miss?' When she smiled and nodded, he went on, 'The Wellington! You'll be comfortable there, I can promise.'

The Wellington Hotel was situated only a matter of minutes away, along the Parade and into Wellington Square. It had an impressive stone facade with an elegant and comfortable interior. In no time at all, Cassie was allocated a splendid room on the first floor. It had its own bathroom adjacent and featured two large windows which were draped with cool green velvet curtains. The room was immediately overlooking both the church and the square, with its handsome statue of Queen Anne. Outside the people bustled to and fro, all going about their business and occasionally stopping to pass the time of day with each other.

Cassie very carefully hung her clothes in the large wardrobe and folded the smaller items into the drawers of the regency chest. She noted that a number of her outfits would require pressing. Her four pairs of shoes she lined up on the top shelf of the wardrobe. Then, relaxing into a deep floral-covered armchair, she kicked off her blue ankle-strap shoes and stretched out her legs with a sigh. A feeling of contentment washed over her and, for a few precious moments, she laid back her head and closed her eyes. 'Dinner at six,' the man had said. Time enough to relax a while before getting ready.

As she drifted into a gentle sleep, Cassie's thoughts meandered, and always they were agitated by one name, that of the elusive Scarlet Pengally. Was she really as beautiful as Amy had described? 'Big black eyes' she had said. 'You could see that she'd been a real beauty . . . still was.' Cassie's fevered mind would not be stilled, and as she thought again on the cross which was branded as deeply in her own senses as it had been on the wall of the room where both she and Scarlet Pengally had stayed, the inexplicable feeling of dread permeated her dreams until, with a start, she was awake, beads of perspiration already breaking into gentle rivulets which trickled down her temples. Shaking off the morbid and disturbing thoughts which persisted, Cassie went to the bathroom, turned on the taps and began undressing. She felt uneasy, threatened somehow. Yet she convinced herself that it was all her own imaginings, together with the fact that the room had a chill about it, and possibly she might be catching cold. After all, she had travelled many miles since leaving New York, and there was no doubt that she was very tired.

At six p.m., Cassie entered the dining room, a pleasant room overlooking the square, with round tables covered in blue cloths; blue lampshades hung overhead, deep blue carpets lay underfoot and the long casement windows were dressed in soft blue curtains, with cream lace at the windows and large potted plants on the polished window ledges. All around the room close to the ceiling there were long stretches of polished shelving, filled with blue willow-pattern plates from end to end.

'Good evening.' The slim fair-haired head waiter smiled at Cassie, at the same time making every effort not to show his appreciation of the very attractive American, who was exquisitely dressed in a dark fitted blouse of silk and small dark neckerchief daintily knotted to the side of the neck. Her rich golden-brown hair was loose to her shoulders and her dark eyes were warm and friendly, yet touched with sadness, he thought, as he ushered her to a table by the window.

Cassie lingered over her meal of cod mornay with creamed potatoes and small fresh carrots. She was surprised to find that she was not very hungry. After a small glass of white wine, she returned to her room, collected her coat and went back down to the lobby, where she sought out the manager. He was a portly and friendly man, seemingly unaffected by his considerable duties and eager to be of every assistance to his overseas guest. 'I'm told that you intend staying with us for a month, Miss Thornton,' he smiled, suddenly feeling nervous in her presence. 'May I ask what brings you to this corner of our country?'

'I'm enquiring after . . . a friend, and I'm led to believe that I'll find her here in Minehead. Do you know the area well, I wonder? Have you any knowledge of a woman by the name of Scarlet Pengally? Or a place called "Greystone House"?' Cassie was dismayed to see a puzzled expression on his face. He must know! She felt suddenly defeated. 'Greystone House,' she repeated, 'do you know of it?'

He continued to frown a moment longer, before visibly relaxing and, bestowing a nervous smile on her, he said, 'Of course, miss . . . there aren't many people round these parts who don't know of Greystone House, or its inhabitants. The Pengally place is some two miles away on the outskirts of Dunster village.'

Cassie was greatly relieved. At long last she was near – so very near. 'Then you know of Scarlet Pengally? . . . She still lives in the house?' The questions tumbled out.

'I know only that there was talk of her coming back,' he said quietly, 'That she was ill . . . and since her return she has become somewhat of a recluse.' His manner was suddenly less friendly and it struck Cassie that he seemed very reluctant to continue the conversation. When she further questioned him, he murmured, 'I'll arrange for a taxi-cab to collect you. The driver will know the house.' He made a stiff little movement, and abruptly turned from her. In only a matter of minutes, the taxi-cab drew up at the hotel entrance. 'Dunster, is it?' asked the driver as she approached. He got out and held the rear door open for her. 'Whereabouts in Dunster, miss?'

Cassie clambered in. 'Greystone House, please,' she smiled, but her smile was not returned. Instead, the driver hesitated a moment before slamming the door shut. Then, returning to his own seat, he put the car in motion and headed out towards Dunster, his face quietly serious and his gaze constantly flitting to the mirror, where it surveyed Cassie with great curiosity.

As the car drove along the main road from Minehead to Dunster, Cassie's thoughts were in a turmoil. Now that she was so close, all manner of doubts and anxieties began to gnaw at her. What would she say to this woman who claimed to be her mother? Would she be forgiven for arriving so long after the letter had been sent to New York? And what of the fear contained in the letter . . . was it real, or imaginary? And, most of all, would they even *like* each other, she and Scarlet Pengally?

By the time the car had turned from the main road and was nosing into the narrow Dunster High Street, Cassie had almost convinced herself that she ought to instruct the driver to turn around. Her every instinct warned her to flee from there, to pack her bags and return to New York at once. But, if her instincts pulled her one way, her curiosity and sense of purpose insisted that she must see it all through to the very end.

'This is as far as I can go, miss . . . the road narrows further on, and I'd never be able to turn round.' The driver took off his cap as he waited for Cassie to climb out, before closing the door behind her. 'Would you like me to wait here for you, miss?' He took the fare which she handed him, and thought it was more than generous. 'It'll be dark in less than an hour,' he told her.

'No . . . don't wait for me.' Cassie had no way of knowing how long she was likely to be. Suddenly it occurred to her that, if she had any difficulty, or if after all she was not made welcome by Scarlet Pengally, it might not be so easy to locate a cab. 'How far is the house?' she asked.

The driver pointed down the narrow lane to where it became a footpath veering off to the right. 'Follow that path to the Packhorse Bridge. You'll see the house well enough. You can't miss it.' He shivered. 'Great ghost of a place it is . . . left to rot these many years.'

Cassie thrust two silver coins into his hand. 'Will this be enough to keep you here for ten minutes?' she wanted to know.

'Yes, miss . . . that it will.' He dropped the coins in his waistcoat pocket and slid back into his seat. 'Ten minutes, you say?'

Cassie nodded. 'If I'm not back by then, you can go.'

'Right, miss . . . do like I said, follow the path round to the right, and Packhorse Bridge is a short way further on.'

Following his instructions, Cassie came to a delightful old cottage with thatched roof and tiny leaded windows. The garden was just awakening from a long winter. Here and there patches of early flowering heather whispered of colour, and dormant plants twisted and climbed along the walls.

Unable, in the gathering twilight, to see either a bridge or what might be Greystone House, Cassie paused and looked about, wondering whether she should go back or knock on the cottage door to ask for directions.

'Lost are you, missie?' The voice was that of an old man, peering over the hedge and looking amused at her predicament. 'There ain't many folk as come this way . . . 'cepting them as live here. You shouldn't wander off the beaten track, girlie . . . it's so easy to find yourself on the moors an' hopelessly lost.' He nodded his head in the direction from which Cassie had just come. 'Go along that way, an' you'll come out on West Street. Anybody'll show you the way to the High Street from there.' He grinned warmly, before disappearing behind the hedge once more.

'Excuse me.' Cassie went over to the small wooden gate, leaning over it in order to see him clearly. 'I'm not looking for the High Street.'

Making his way towards the gate, wheezing hard and regarding Cassie with impudent eyes, he exclaimed, 'I'm blowed if you ain't *American*!' He laughed out loud. 'Well . . . you've come a bloody long way to get yourself lost, and *no* mistake!' He ambled towards her. 'Come in! . . . Come in an' set yourself down a minute.' He gestured for Cassie to follow him. 'The kettle's on the boil, I daresay you'd welcome a nice hot drink, eh?' When Cassie smiled gratefully, but preparing to decline his offer as she was impatient to find the house, he took her smile to be one of acceptance. 'Come on in,' he beckoned, scraping the mud from his boots and afterwards going into the tiny kitchen, where he put out two sizeable cups, and replacing the kettle onto the fire, he began the serious business of brewing a pot of fresh tea. 'Sit down, then,' he urged Cassie, who had been lingering by the door, not really sure whether or not she ought to take him up on his kind invitation. He was lonely, that was obvious, but she really ought to be getting on, she thought. She glanced around and her eyes alighted on the photograph of a young man. She could not tear her gaze away. Something in his warm, smiling eyes, and in the shock of earth-coloured hair, stirred dormant memories deep within her; and a strange sense of happiness, tinged with sorrow.

'That's my son, Trent.' The old man beckoned her to a chair. 'He's all I have left.' He seemed to sense her urgency to depart. 'We don't get many visitors these days . . .' Suddenly his eyes were sad, and Cassie was ashamed when he murmured, 'Not since my Ada passed on.'

A few minutes later both the old man and Cassie were seated round the small circular table by the back window. 'Now then, my dear.' He wrapped his gnarled old hands round the girth of his cup and began to slurp noisily from it. 'If you ain't looking for the High Street, and you ain't really lost as you say . . . then where *are* you headed?' he chuckled.

Cassie sipped the tea, hating it. 'I'm looking for Greystone House . . . for Scarlet Pengally.'

For a long awkward moment the old man gave no answer, other than to set down his cup, grab the cap from his head and to carefully fold it on the table, where it sprang open and fell to the floor. He made no effort to retrieve it. Instead he continued to look at Cassie in a particular fashion, at the same time rummaging about in his waistcoat pocket and withdrawing from it a short stubby pipe. After ramming it full with strings of tobacco from his pouch, he set a match to it and began puffing. 'What's your business with Scarlet Pengally?' His sharp blue eyes watched her with unnerving directness.

'She's . . . a friend.' Something inside her advised Cassie to be cautious.

'A friend, eh?' The words echoed suspicion, as he continued to puff on his pipe and consequently to be enveloped in great clouds of grey smoke. His round blue eyes were narrowed and stung by the burning vapour, but his inquisitive gaze never lifted from Cassie's face. 'You ain't her "friend",' he said suddenly, seeming relieved as the beginnings of a smile creased his face. 'You're *curious*, ain't you? You're a stranger to these parts, and somebody at Luttrell Inn has told you about Greystone House . . . and Scarlet Pengally. That's right, ain't it? You've heard enough to make you curious, and you've come a-looking? Well, you happened on the right fella when you came to old John Blackwood's door, and *that's* a fact!' He became quiet and thoughtful, and Cassie considered it best not to reveal her true purpose, becoming suddenly conscious that her enquiries had opened a door to the past that this old man, this 'John Blackwood', would prefer to keep closed. When he began talking again, with pain in his expression and, something akin to horror, she let him go on. 'Y'see . . . I worked at Greystone House for more years than I care to remember . . . man and boy! I know *everything* that went on there . . . that *still* goes on there.'

Suddenly, he pointed out of the window, to where the trees rose up at the fringe of the moors. 'Look there,' he told Cassie, 'beyond the trees. Look there . . . at the house itself.'

At first glance Cassie could not distinguish the tall gabled house from the trees which seemed to stand as timeless sentries all about it. But then it rose in her vision . . . the grey formidable shape looming sinister in the gloom, the yard overgrown and littered with old machinery and tumbledown buildings. It was a grim sight that sent a chill through her heart.

'I knew that house, *but the devil knew it better*,' the old man went on. Cassie could sense his fear, and it was just as real to her as they continued to stare at the house, his eyes misted by memories, and his voice barely above a whisper. 'If any room in that house could tell a tale, it would be the attic where, oh so many times, Scarlet was cruelly imprisoned; or the dark damp cellar . . . where her mammy gave birth to her all those years ago, with only Vincent Pengally to see his daughter into the world. Then there's a small frightened boy . . . who may or may not have done the terrible thing he was accused of.' He paused, then drawing his gaze from the house, he said, 'It's dead now! The house is dead . . . but not the evil. Not that!' He shuddered and sank deeper into his chair. 'I saw it all . . . *everything! But it ain't finished yet . . . not yet!* And, God help us all, there can be no happy ending to it. Some say it won't end in this life . . . *I say it won't end in the next either!*'

'Please go on.' Cassie sensed that he had paused in order to gauge her reaction. She knew also that he was sending out a warning. It did not deter her. How would it, when she herself was involved? Scarlet Pengally was her mother! And this old man, this 'John Blackwood', was probably the only key to her past. There was no going back now. She must know the whole truth, whatever the consequences!

PART TWO

England
1905

THE DEED

To know my deed, 'twere best not know myself.

Shakespeare, *Macbeth*

CHAPTER THREE

'You won't kill the child, will you?' she pleaded. 'Promise me you'll take care of him. He's your own flesh and blood after all . . . you can't deny that!' When the man hesitated to reassure her, she raised her head from the pillow, her vivid violet eyes belying the fact that she was close to death. Her voice was menacing as she warned, 'If you kill him, or harm him in any way . . . *ever* . . . I swear I'll come back and haunt you!'

The man reluctantly reached out and took her frail trembling hand in his in an effort to appease her. 'Haunt me?' he said softly, 'You would do *that*? *Yes . . . you would*! Do you know, Evelyn, my dear . . . I do believe you have the heart of a witch!' he smiled, and the smile froze on his face as he went on in a low chilling voice, 'Why should I want to kill the boy? As you say . . . he is *my* son, is he not?' There was antipathy in his expression, and doubt in his voice.

She looked at him, gently laughing, her abundant golden hair spilling like sunbeams over the pillow, and her pale beauty surprised him in the way it had done when he first saw her on a glorious summer's day some four years ago. She had journeyed from Taunton into the Somerset village of Dunster, near Minehead; apparently her husband was buying a pony for their four-year-old child. The attraction between them was instant. Within that year, her

37

husband had discovered their torrid affair and had issued her with an ultimatum: she must choose her illicit lover ... himself a married man ... or her husband and infant. When she confessed that she was with child, the scene that followed was ugly and violent, with the consequence being that she was thrown out onto the street. Her lover had then secretly installed her in a moorland cottage not far from his home. His frequent visits were both discreet and demanding. Lately she had come to regret her shame and would have pleaded with her husband for forgiveness, but he had long moved away, and both he and the child were lost to her for ever. Now she was wasting away and she sought no help or solace from anyone; no one would regret her passing, for there were those who claimed she was a witch. Her only wish was that her son should come to no harm at the hands of Vincent Pengally, for he was both a man and a monster, with little conscience and no compassion.

She gazed deep and searchingly into his grey expressionless eyes, then, giving a long, withering sigh, she shivered, gripped his hand in terror, and was gone, leaving him cursing her. As though the touch of her hand might burn his skin, he quickly withdrew it from her grasp. Reluctantly, he drew his gaze towards the open doorway, and there was the boy, Silas, small and dark-haired, with eyes as deeply violet as his mother's and possessed of the same virulent passion. His gaze fell briefly onto his mother's lifeless form and lingered there. Yet he showed no emotion and remained by the door, quiet and still. When he looked again on the man, he was not afraid, nor did he flinch when he was told, 'You are *not* my son. You never could be.' Yet when the man swept past him and out into the sunlight, the boy followed, keeping close like a shadow, determined that he *would* belong.

CHAPTER FOUR

'Thank God you found me, Vincent.' Hannah Pengally was lying at the foot of the cellar steps, one leg bent at a peculiar angle, her pretty face contorted with pain and her blue eyes moist with tears. 'I was on my way down to fill the coal bucket . . . the baby! You must hurry . . . get me to my bed. The baby's coming!'

'It's alright, Hannah. Don't worry . . . there'll be time to get the doctor.' Vincent Pengally was still disturbed by the recent scene in his lover's cottage, and even though she was gone from this world, her hatred still clung to him like poisonous vapour. But for now, with his wife's eyes on him, he smiled reassuringly, his sharp grey eyes taking stock of the situation. With a shock he suddenly realised that he was wrong – there would not be time to get a doctor. But then, out here in this isolated hamlet, their kind had little use for such luxuries. He was a blacksmith, and if he could deliver a foal or set an animal's broken leg, what need did they have for anyone else?

'Help me . . . get me to my bed!' Hannah pleaded, frantically plucking at his coat sleeve. The pain was unbearable, and she felt her senses dimming.

'There's no time,' her husband warned, a look of satisfaction creeping into his handsome face when he saw that she was no longer conscious. Gently, he removed the lower half of her blood-stained clothing, at the same time manipulating the leg that was horribly crooked. This he secured by means of two flat pieces of wood taken from a small crate and which he bound to the leg with strips of sacking.

The first child to be born was a girl, dark-haired like her father and perfect in every detail. 'You are mine!' Vincent murmured, holding the tiny infant high in his arms and seeming fascinated by her beauty. 'Scarlet!' he suddenly cried out. 'I shall name you after your late grandmother, my own dear mother . . . Scarlet Pengally.' His expression darkened when he added in a quiet voice, 'Nothing will ever mar your beauty, I promise you that . . . and no *man* will ever violate your innocence!'

The second child born to Hannah was a boy, with the same dark hair as his sister and a loud lusty cry to herald his arrival. When Vincent Pengally saw the child's deformed limbs and the twisted torso, he was shocked and repulsed. Recoiling in horror, he left the child where it lay, quickly going about the task of cleaning his wife and ensuring that the girl was warmly wrapped against the damp in the cellar. When, in due course, he had safely transported both daughter and wife upstairs to the bedroom, he stood at the top of the cellar steps and gazed down to where the infant was threshing its grotesque limbs in the air, its cries echoing round the damp walls and seeming more feeble in the half-light below.

For a long time he gazed down on that tiny deformed being, his piercing grey eyes devoid of any emotion. Only once did they flicker in astonishment when they were drawn by a slight movement over in the farthest corner and there, looking up with a bizarre expression on his face, was the boy. '*You!* . . . I'd forgotten about you,' Vincent Pengally exclaimed with a devious smile. Then the smile became a frown. He looked once more on the newborn, then again on the boy. '*She* did this,' he said, 'your mother's last curse!' He saw that the boy was crying profusely, yet making no sobs and he found that strangely offensive. He snuffed out the lamp, plunging the boy into darkness, and then closed and bolted the door. As he did so it struck Vincent Pengally that, since seeing his mother die, and hearing her unnatural threat, the boy had not uttered a single word, yet he *could* speak, there was no doubt about that, because he himself had heard the boy speak!

For the next three days, Hannah and the baby thrived. Vincent Pengally, however, was plagued with doubts and haunted by nightmares. The twisted torso of his newborn son was alive in his mind. He recalled the promise which the dying woman had extracted from him, and he was afraid, wary of the unknown. He had promised to look after the boy, Silas, and if he were to allow him to die, then who knows what other terrible things might happen?

Unable to sleep or to rid himself of the most disturbing thoughts, Vincent Pengally got up from his bed on the morning of the fourth day and, with the most awful trepidation, he unlocked the cellar door and, lamp in hand, peered in. The boy was seated cross-legged at the foot of the steps, his eyes raised and blinking in the sudden rush of light. Coming slowly down the steps, Vincent Pengally was astonished by the eerie silence. He was struck rigid when his fearful gaze alighted on the spot where the unfortunate newborn child had been left. Now there was no sign of it . . . only the congealed dark stain on the floor where Hannah's blood had been spilled . . . and a spattering of crimson spots on the bib of the boy's shirt.

The boy made no move as Vincent Pengally frantically searched the cellar, until the man turned to smile on him and to nod his head in approval. Then, like a shadow, the boy followed him up the steps and into the kitchen. When the sunlight streamed in through the window to settle on his face, it gave him almost an unearthly appearance. Only the violet eyes were untouched; darkly appealing they were, yet brilliant and hard as the most polished gems. Vincent Pengally was astonished at how handsome the boy was, more than any human had a right to be, he thought with some resentment.

CHAPTER FIVE

'Scarlet! . . . where are you, you little devil? . . . answer me this minute!' Hannah Pengally's thin angry voice carried on the gentle summer's breeze. 'Curse the girl!' she muttered, not unkindly, as, scooping her hand into the bowl which was lodged in the crook of her arm, she brought out a fistful of corn and cast it in a wide arc into the chicken-pen, afterwards lingering for a moment to watch the mad scrambling antics of the fowls.

'Ssh! Don't move, Silas!' In the darkest corner of the barn, the two small figures huddled together. It was the girl who issued a whispered warning, while the boy seemed agitated and would have fled from the barn, if only the warm closeness and the intoxicating smell of the girl had not kept him clasped tight in her arms. 'Keep very very still,' she whispered in his ear and, when her plump daring lips brushed softly against his skin, it was more than he could bear. All his boyish emotions became a tumult within him.

After a while they heard the slam of the kitchen door, as Hannah Pengally went back to her tiresome duties. At once the boy scrambled to his feet but, feeling his ankle tightly gripped, he bent his dark head to look upon the girl and, as always, his heart was filled with pain.

'We can hide here for ever!' she laughed softly, tugging mischievously at his leg. 'For ever and ever! . . . You'd like that, wouldn't you, Silas?' Her voice was taunting, teasing him beyond endurance. He struggled to free himself, but she would not let him go. In the pitch black of that farthest corner, Silas could not see the girl's face, but then he had no need to, for he knew every exquisite line of it. Her face was always in his mind's eye, that lovely laughing face with its black eyes and long flowing hair the colour of a raven's wing. No, he had no need to see Scarlet Pengally's face, he knew her only too well, loved her and loathed her, and feared her ever-changing mood. 'Why don't you speak to me, Silas?' The voice issued softly from the darkness. 'Why don't you *ever* speak to me? . . . I know you can if you want to.' There was a sharpness in her voice, 'You *can* speak! . . . I've heard you talking to the creatures on the moors!' She dug her nails into his flesh until he felt the blood trickling down his leg.

Outside, the August sun shone relentlessly, the tree-tops swayed in the warm breeze and the birds sang for the joy of it. Inside the smithy, the age-old grime which covered the windows rendered the atmosphere dark and gloomy; the heat was oppressive as Vincent Pengally worked over the forge. He had heard his wife calling Scarlet and was agitated. 'He's been gone long enough!' he muttered through clenched teeth, at once throwing down his hammer and storming towards the outer doors, snatching a leather harness from the wall as he went.

When the barn doors were flung open and the powerful frame of Vincent Pengally cast a formidable shadow over the ground, there was no escape route for the children. In a matter of minutes he had rooted them out, and swooped on them like a man demented. 'You devil!' He closed his fist about the boy's head, gripping it like an eagle with its prey and screaming obscenities as, with the strength of a demon, he lashed the boy to a length of wooden railings, then, ripping the shirt from his young back, and laying bare his shoulders, he raised the leather harness high into the air, intending to crash it down and split the soft flesh asunder. But there came into his fevered mind an image of the boy's mother, Evelyn, and of her dying vow. 'If you harm him . . . *ever* . . . I swear I'll come back and haunt you!' Vincent Pengally feared no man on earth; he would challenge any mortal being, but he was always wary of the unknown. He lowered the harness and went on slow determined steps to the far corner of the barn.

Scarlet was a child of exceptional courage, and when, growling with rage, her father plucked her from her hidey-hole, she made no sound. And when she felt the broad leather stinging her legs and buttocks she bore the punishment silently. Once, when Silas twisted his neck round and their eyes met, Scarlet was strengthened by the love and encouragement she drew from him. Afterwards Scarlet was returned to the house, her body bruised and throbbing, but her spirit never broken. Hannah Pengally took the child. She comforted and bathed her, before confining her to the small attic room where she would remain without food for forty-eight hours.

'Lock the door and stay well away!' instructed her husband, and he knew, weak woman that she was, Hannah Pengally would not disobey him.

'Why d'you goad him so, lad? . . . will you and young Scarlet *never* learn your lesson?' John Blackwood was a man in his thirties, a thin wiry fellow with a homely expression and a warm heart. He sighed when the boy gave no answer; then, dipping his cupped fist into the water bucket, he raised it to the boy's parched lips, watching with satisfaction when he eagerly supped it. 'That Pengally!' he muttered low. 'He can be a wicked bugger!' He saw how the boy was trussed so cruelly to the timbers that the ropes were digging deep and causing the skin to erupt in angry swellings. His legs were splayed and his arms were raised. 'The divil's bloody near *crucified* you!' he remarked under his breath, giving out a startled gasp when a trapped bird began fluttering in the eaves. 'But I can't let you loose, lad . . . you know that, don't you? . . . if I was to do that, like as not he'd stretch *me* to a frame and leave me to rot!' When he saw that the boy had taken his fill of the water and was looking at him with gratitude in his pained violet eyes, he nodded and gave a half-smile. 'That's it, lad! You be brave, young 'un . . . it's been four days now . . . he's bound to set you loose soon, on top o' which it's market tomorrow and I need you. But don't you let on that I've been giving you water!' he warned, before scuttling away at the sound of footsteps going by. 'My God!' he muttered as he slid away unobtrusively. 'I wouldn't treat a bloody *dog* like that . . . let alone a boy not yet twelve years old!' As on many previous occasions, John Blackwood was made to wonder at the strange relationship between Vincent Pengally and that poor wretched creature who hadn't spoken a word since the day he came to Greystone House some eight years back.

Inside the house, Hannah Pengally watched from the window as John Blackwood went about his daily tasks. When her nervous blue eyes flitted towards the barn door, her thoughts were much the same as the homely handyman's; only *she* had questioned the boy's right to live here at Greystone House, even though he had never been allowed to set foot through the door of the house itself. For a long time after giving birth to Scarlet, she had barely regained consciousness, and was at the mercy of her husband. Oh, he had cared for her, and he had taken tender loving care of their only child, but for some incomprehensible reason, since the day she got up from her sick-bed, Hannah Pengally had never really known a moment's peace. There was always the deep-seated feeling that something was being kept from her, and, even after unexpectedly stumbling over the small ragged boy in the barn, and being told by Vincent Pengally that 'he's nobody . . . I found him wandering the moors . . . deserted by his parents, I reckon,' the feeling persisted. Her own discreet enquiries revealed no more than her husband had already told her, and so she had to be satisfied with his explanation, yet she could not take to the boy and she was never sorry that he was confined to living in the barn. Vincent Pengally insisted that Silas would learn his station well and would become invaluable about the place. 'He has the makings of a good strong frame and, though he prefers to be dumb, he's no fool. I'll train him as a blacksmith. He'll cost no more than his food and board.'

Over the years, Vincent Pengally had been strict in his treatment of the boy. He had given him no better stabling than his own two horses, and he had dressed him in his own cast-off clothing, cut down and made to fit by Hannah. His food was the leftovers from the table, delivered by John Blackwood to the door of the barn twice a day. During his hard training in the duties of a blacksmith, the boy never complained, though he was often driven beyond endurance, and criticised for everything he did. Vincent Pengally's instructions were always by way of example. He made no attempt to converse with the boy, and belittled him at every opportunity. The first occasion when he had taken to punishing him was three years ago, at Scarlet's fifth birthday party. Silas was a fine strapping eight-year-old boy, his handsome physique and obvious strength belying the conditions of his pitiful existence, and owing much to the kindness of John Blackwood who, though he was careful not to incur the wrath of Vincent Pengally, kept an eye out for the boy.

On the day of Scarlet's birthday, when the special tea was over and her parents had resumed their respective duties, Scarlet remembered the little boy who lived in the barn and, clutching a small piece of her birthday cake, she went to him there, eager, in her childish innocence, to share her delight with him. At first Silas was shy and afraid, but he was soon won over by Scarlet's engaging personality, and together they laughed and played. When Vincent Pengally found them so charmed with each other's company, he was beside himself with fury. Although both children were severely punished after being made to feel like criminals and being assured that each was forbidden the other's company, it was *Hannah* who was to blame. She was never forgiven and, in turn, *she* never forgave the boy, and went out of her way to warn Scarlet away from him.

Hannah Pengally was not the only one to watch from a window as John Blackwood harnessed the bay shire in between the shafts of the flat-wagon. Up in the highest reaches of the old grey house, Scarlet rose on tiptoes on the upturned apple crate to see out of the tiny attic window. The whole aperture jutted from the outer roof at a sharp angle with small lattice windows on all sides; consequently Scarlet was afforded a generous view of both the yard immediately below, and the heart of Dunster itself.

Nestling in a corner of Somerset, the small town of Dunster had changed very little since medieval times. The skyline was a delightful confusion of slated and thatched roofs, with chimneys of varying heights and diameter, while a number of houses were ancient and bent, the black timber beams warped with age and the roofs dropping down to the many bowed windows like sleepy eyelids propped ever open. There was much evidence of Elizabethan influence, epitomised by a Latin inscription etched into a wooden beam in one house, which read:

> We are all worms-meat.
> Remember death shall be the end.
> God save our noble Queen Elizabeth.
>
> Amen.

At one end of the High Street was situated the quaintly

shaped medieval yarn-market, reminiscent of Dunster's past woollen industry. And, looming high above the trees, looking out over Dunster like a watchful sentry, was the magnificent castle which had survived savage and feudal times, and had belonged to the Luttrell family for generations. Closer to Greystone House was the humpbacked Packhorse Bridge, which spanned the River Avill, too narrow for the passage of a horse and cart, yet built above a shallow and negotiable point of the river, where a heavily laden wagon could easily cross when the river was low.

Greystone House stood on a high point at the farthest edge of the town, while behind and from both sides of the stout grey stone building, with its high reaching gables and formidable appearance, the wild primitive stretches of Exmoor rolled away as far as the eye could see. The path from the town to Greystone House was well trodden by the hooves of horses being driven to Vincent Pengally's blacksmith's shop. He was not a liked man, but his was the only smithy for many miles around, and he knew his own trade better than any man.

Scarlet followed John Blackwood's every move, her dark eyes stricken with compassion as she recalled how her father had strapped the boy up so spitefully. She knew that he was still there in the barn, spread out on the rough timbers, like a hide stretched out to dry. At least *she* had not been subjected to such hard-hearted treatment and, if only she hadn't foolishly taken to kicking at the door and screaming abuse, she might be freed herself! As it was, her father had issued instructions that she must stay 'locked up until she learns who's master!' At least she was fed and watered, and provided with a slop-bucket which her mammy changed daily. But Hannah Pengally made no attempt to speak to her rebellious daughter. Instead, when Scarlet ventured to address her agitated mammy she was warned to 'Keep your tongue between your teeth, child . . . or he'll make us *both* rue the day!'

Up there in the attic, with the powerful roof-trusses pressing down so low overhead, Scarlet felt threatened, ensnared like the rabbits that foolishly wandered into John Blackwood's traps. During these four long days when she had been entombed in that small airless space, where day and night had no beginning and no end, she had come to know every inch of every floorboard. She had counted the blocks of stone in the four walls and picked out the grey crumbling substance which oozed from between. She had studied the changing colours of the vast stretch of sky beyond the window, tracing the sun as it moved across her sight, and had been enchanted when the moon appeared in the shifting shadowy clouds like a strange glowing phantom.

Yet all the while there was something festering and growing in her heart, a kind of excitement which was mingled with fancy and fear. It was as though, in being so rigidly determined to suppress her mischievous spirit, Vincent Pengally had released a force within his daughter that was far more destructive and, like the most ominous storm whipped up by the elements, that same force would not be stilled until it had run its predestined course.

'John! . . . *I'm up here* . . . in the attic!' Scarlet punched her small clenched fist at the window, but it was jammed tight. 'Is the boy alright? . . . John!' Her frantic words went unheeded, as John's homely gaitered figure loaded up the last of the summer's apple crop, before clambering onto the wagon and seating himself onto the forward bench where he took up the reins. The horse lowered his great head and began pulling away in response to the gentle slapping of the reins against his back. Soon, the wagon had crossed the river and was lost from Scarlet's sight. She knew he would not be back for at least four hours, until early evening when he had sold most of her father's fruit crop in nearby Minehead. Tomorrow at the

Dunster market anything remaining would be sold, along with other produce from the smallholding. Scarlet felt guilty and saddened as, raking her eyes over the barn, she murmured, 'I'm sorry, Silas . . . truly sorry.' She slid down and settled into a corner, preparing herself for a long lonely vigil when the dark would eventually come and in the pitch black of the attic she would hear the night creatures scurrying about amongst the rafters and, just occasionally, brushing against her in their relentless foraging. Scarlet was not afraid of them, for she defended their right to be both inquisitive and resentful of the intruder who violated their undisputed territory. Yet, if the night creatures wished her gone, it was no more than Scarlet herself did. But, for now, Scarlet fidgeted on the hard unyielding boards as she endeavoured to make herself more comfortable. Several times she closed, then opened, her eyes. She thought about John on the road to Mine-head; she smiled as she imagined him cheerfully whistling as he went on his way. She thought about her mammy deep in the heart of the house, going about her domestic tasks. She even envisaged her father, stripped to the waist and bent over the fierce heat of his forge, while some patient and magnificent shire horse waited for the black-smith's attention. All of these familiar things brought a measure of comfort to Scarlet, but none so much as when she allowed her thoughts to dwell on the boy called Silas, an unfortunate creature who had the irritating knack of bringing out the worst in her. Even at the very minute when Scarlet was thinking of him and regretting the pain she had caused him to suffer, and though the recollection of it flooded her young heart with compassion, Scarlet *resented* him, and, if he was standing before her now, she would probably strike him for his part in it! He was too foolish, too trusting and she despised him for his weak-nesses. But then, she loved him also, and was suddenly overcome with remorse. His handsome face filled her mind, and the warmth it created in her spilled over to touch her heart.

Outside in the barn, the boy was also brooding on past events but, unlike Scarlet, his thoughts were dwelling on the haunting phenomenon which harked back to the time when he had first come to Greystone House, and in circumstances that, even now, he was uncertain of. But two things he did know, and they were, firstly, the depth of mutual loathing that existed between himself and Vincent Pengally, and the sure belief that that man alone knew the truth. The boy, Silas, fervently suspected that Vincent Pengally was his father, but his every instinct warned him never to betray that suspicion to *anyone*!

During these past days, when his discomfort had given way to intense pain and afterwards he had grown too numb to feel any sensation at all, Silas had been tormented by visions from his deepest infant memory. It was all a long time ago, and the memories had grown unclear with the passing of his earlier childhood. He vaguely recalled a woman, fiery and beautiful, whom he took to be his mother and who had been visited by Vincent Pengally on many occasions; the only one of which the boy could recall with any clarity was the last one. He remembered how the woman had grown still and quiet, and he himself had followed the tall dark figure that was Vincent Pengally, followed him to this house, to a cellar below, where he had seen and been part of such fearful things that haunted him still! Now the questions would not go away. Were these obscure memories *real*? Had those monstrous events in that darkened cellar really taken place? Silas was not yet a man and so these things were more awesome to his young impressionable mind. He dared not question too closely, for fear that he might expose a part of himself that was so obscene it must be forever hidden away. As it was, his sense of guilt and outrage forced him into a world of silence, a lonely painful world where only the creatures from the wild were made welcome. He had created a gentle, secret world where he could withdraw and remain sane. Only Scarlet threatened it. Only the lovely taunting Scarlet could throw it all into confusion and invade it in such a way that both excited and terrified him. He murmured her name now. 'Scarlet . . . Scarlet,' and the sound of his own voice startled him.

When, drawn by his soft calling, the huge grey gelding ambled across his stable towards the railings where he nuzzled his soft head into the boy's neck, Silas was comforted. After a while, his exhaustion forced him to close his eyes and long for sleep. When sleep came, it carried him far beyond all earthly pain and anguish, refreshing his mind and easing his body, renewing his strength for whatever lay ahead.

'Fetch her down!' Vincent Pengally had the look of a man wearied by his daily labours, with the heat and ash from the forge still on him. With Silas to help him, he would get through his blacksmithing at a faster pace, when the forge would be shut down before the hour of seven. These past days had been hard without the boy's help, but Vincent Pengally would not humble himself to admit it! He had strode into the kitchen on the stroke of nine, the exhaustion still etched into his grim face and his broad shoulders stooped as if beneath the weight of his work. He had washed, and afterwards eaten the meal of rabbit stew which his wife had put before him, and throughout it all he had not spoken one civil word to her. Now, though, he turned from the fire where he had been stretching his powerful frame and warming himself, and when he fixed his piercing grey eyes on Hannah's quiet anxious face, there was the semblance of a smile in them. A smile, yet *not* a smile, for it seemed to increase her anxiety. 'Did you hear what I said, woman?' he demanded, the smile still soft on his face, 'Scarlet . . . fetch her down. Now!'

Hannah made no move. 'Do you *mean* it, Vincent?' she asked gently, always unsure as to his mood; he could so easily change his mind, even before she had gone from the room.

He laughed, a low spiteful sound which caused her to cringe. 'Don't be so mistrusting, Hannah,' he chided, maliciously, 'I wouldn't *tell* you to fetch her down if I didn't mean it!'

She had to believe him as she hurried towards the door, the thought of Scarlet being let out of the attic lending wings to her feet. At the door, she turned. 'And the boy?' she ventured.

'Don't interfere in what doesn't concern you.' He watched her fiercely as she quickly nodded and scurried away.

On Hannah's return, some long moments later, her husband was seated in the horsehair armchair beside the fire hearth. When his wife and daughter came into the room, he got to his feet, collected a bowl from the table and, returning to the cooking pot which was quietly simmering over the coals, he scooped out a ladleful of hot stew and spilled it into the bowl. This he placed on the edge of the table, before gesturing to Scarlet to take up the place he had earlier vacated. 'Go on, girl!' Hannah sensed Scarlet's hesitation, as she pushed her forward, 'Do as you're told!'

Only when Scarlet was seated at the table and beginning to eat did Vincent Pengally return to his armchair. His wife sat opposite him and quietly took up her sewing, never once lifting her nervous blue eyes to gaze on either her husband or her daughter, yet concentrating on her work with such intensity that her knuckles were stiff as wood and drained white. The atmosphere was ominous, the silence broken only by the occasionally spluttering of the lamp which hung from the central ceiling beam, and the gentle scraping of metal against earthenware as Scarlet forced herself to swallow every mouthful of the piping-hot stew that had been put before her. Yet, although she was desperately famished and the juicy aroma from the thick rich broth assailed her nostrils and whetted her appetite, she was painfully aware that her father's stony gaze had rested on her downcast face throughout. There was a great need in her to glance up and meet his gaze with defiance, but she strongly resisted the temptation on account of her mother, who had pleaded with Scarlet to 'learn your lesson, child . . . don't dare put a foot wrong, and for God's sake, don't torment him with them black insolent eyes of yours!' Scarlet promised her mother that she would heed her warning because, although she despised such weakness, she deeply loved that poor wretched woman who had suffered the dark unpredictable moods of Vincent Pengally for too many years.

Pushing the bowl away and straightening into the hard upright chair, Scarlet asked demurely, 'May I please leave the table?' Even now she did not lift her gaze, although she sensed that he was willing her to do so. A long poignant moment passed, while both mother and daughter anxiously waited for his answer. After a while he rose from the depth of his armchair and went on slow heavy steps to where Scarlet was seated. He looked first at the empty bowl, and then, bending his considerable frame towards her, he put his two large, coarse hands onto her small shoulders and, giving a low satisfied chuckle, he lowered his head to put his half-open mouth softly against her forehead, keeping it there until Scarlet wanted to scream out, his touch reviling her and sending ugly shivers to every corner of her being. At last he straightened up, saying in a warm, self-satisfied manner, 'There's no reason why you can't leave the table, my dear. There's no reason why you must ever be punished again either . . . unless of course you *still* refuse to learn your lesson.' He caressed her face with the tips of his fingers, a note of anguish creeping into his voice as he murmured, 'Oh, Scarlet . . . lovely girl. Don't you realise that punishing you hurts *me* even more? *I love you!* Whatever I do is only for your own good. I've told you before, child . . . the boy, Silas, is a bad lot . . . he *eats* little innocent things like you! I'm only trying to protect you . . . you do understand that, don't you?' He waited, but when Scarlet made no response, he angrily flicked his fingers from her face, his roughened leathery skin having made an ugly imprint on the milk-whiteness of her delicately chiselled cheekbone. 'Leave the table and get ready for your bed.' Before storming from the room, he cast a cursory glance over his wife, who began quickly clearing away the dishes and instructing Scarlet to 'Give me a hand to fetch the tin bath in from the scullery, child. Then you must get undressed for your wash.' She nodded impatiently towards the big blackened kettle standing on the trivet in the hearth. 'There's plenty of hot water.'

In a surprisingly short time the table was cleared and the tin bath brought in, to be positioned on the rug, close enough to the fire for Scarlet to be pleasantly warm, but far enough away to prevent her from being scorched. Scarlet loved the feel of the warm soapy water running against her skin, and as her mother vigorously soaped and scrubbed her, the dirt, and the awful experience of being shut away in the attic seemed to fall away, leaving her deliciously clean and refreshed.

'*I hate him!*' The thought burst from her with venom.

'No, no child . . . you must *never* think that; you must never *say* that!' Hannah was horrified; supposing he should overhear?

'I *do* hate him! And I don't care if he hears me say it, either. He's wicked and spiteful. *You* didn't see what he did to Silas!'

'And I don't *want* to see. John Blackwood won't let the lad come to any real harm, you know that, Scarlet. He's been in and out of that barn ever since your father found you and that boy together.' She shook the girl. 'Whatever came over you, child? You *know* you're to stay away from him . . . and yet you will persist in defying your father. It must stop! Because I fear that, if it doesn't . . . then, one of these days, that wretched boy will come to real harm.' She had said too much and now regretted it.

'What do you mean, Mammy?' Scarlet was fearful for Silas who, after all, was not really the guilty one. 'Will he *kill* him? . . . Will he, Mammy? . . . *Will he kill him?*'

'Don't be ridiculous!' Hannah's hands were trembling as she went on soaping the girl's slim body. 'Don't you ever say such a thing again! *D'you hear me, Scarlet?* . . . you're never to say such evil things again!'

'Don't! You're hurting me!' Scarlet winced, pulling away as the hitherto gentle soaping became a frenzied onslaught against her bare skin, and causing such pain that the tears sprang to her eyes.

'Oh, I'm sorry, child . . . I didn't realise.' Hannah was mortified to see the abrasions rising beneath Scarlet's tender skin. At once she pacified the girl and began whisking the soap into a lather in the palms of her hands. This she gently laid onto Scarlet, soothing the skin and regaining the girl's confidence. 'There . . . no harm done. It's the soap, dear . . . see.' She tilted the block of green soap to an angle as Scarlet's dark eyes examined it. 'It's got such rough edges . . . I just forgot to be careful, that's all.' She gently stroked the girl's long blue-black hair. 'I really am sorry, Scarlet . . . are you alright?'

Scarlet nodded. She loathed it when her father touched her, but she normally liked her mother's hands on her, because they could be so gentle. 'Will he untie Silas soon, Mammy?'

'Soon . . . yes, child, I'm sure of it.' Hannah hoped so, because she never liked trouble, any kind of trouble. It played on her nerves so. 'Stand out of the tub, child,' she instructed Scarlet. 'Let's dry you off and get you to bed, before he finds his way back, in a temper about something or another!' Hannah had long admitted it to herself. She was frightened of him, but apart from Scarlet and the Good Lord above, Vincent Pengally was all she had.

The ritual was always the same. Scarlet would stand perfectly still, often shivering while one by one she extended her limbs to be towelled dry. Finally, her hair was rubbed, strand by strand, through her mother's strong capable hands, before it was painstakingly brushed to hang loose and damp down her back. Hannah often made the remark, 'It's growing too heavy, child . . . too long. I've a mind to take the shears to it.' But she never did, because, being cursed with thin fine hair herself, the thick black and magnificent mane that was Scarlet's inheritance from her father filled her with both envy and pride.

Scarlet would laugh at her mammy's impatient remarks. 'You *always* say that,' she would point out with a smile, 'but you won't cut my hair.' Then the smile would slip from her lovely face as she warned, 'I won't let you.' At first, when her mammy threatened to 'take the shears to it,' Scarlet was horrified. But then she began to realise that her mammy could never bring herself to do such a vile thing. And it would be vile, to cut away those long beautiful locks which were praised and admired by all who looked on them. Without them, Scarlet would feel naked and ugly. She would never again want anyone to look on her.

Yet, at that very moment, someone's hungry eyes *were* feasting on Scarlet's young body, and believing it to be the most exquisite sight his senses had ever beheld. Vincent Pengally's face was flushed with pleasure as he drew closer to the warped plank in the sturdy kitchen door which had created a small slit, through which he could enjoy the clear view beyond. He could see the huge oak dresser, bedecked with meat plates, and the big square table which had been his father's before. There were two comfortable armchairs, and the dark engravings on the wall. And there were the two females! His wife was engaged in gathering up the towels and other oddments, before hurrying them away, at the same time reminding Scarlet, 'Get into your nightshift, girl! Your father's only next door in the parlour . . . he snoozes very lightly, and if he were to come back and find you still not abed . . . well! It won't do his temper any good, I know *that* much!' She made herself breathless from rushing around and there was a real look of fear in her face, that gave the silent watcher a rush of satisfaction. Then, she was gone, and only the girl remained.

On long slim legs that moved seemingly without effort, Scarlet went nearer to the fireplace. Here, she stretched her arms high into the air and gave a low pleasant sigh. She liked the feel of the warm fire's glow on her naked skin. Now, she ran her two hands through her hair, lifting and fanning it around her pretty shoulders, until it lay like a flowing black mantle, reaching down her back and over her smooth buttocks, and following the young vigorous curves of her body, as water in a brook might wash over the gently undulating stones embedded there.

Now, when Scarlet swung round from the fire, Vincent Pengally's excited heart turned. He gasped aloud, quickly retreating a small distance when Scarlet startled and brought her dark gaze to rest on the very door behind which he was hiding. For a long moment they were both very still, the one softly listening within, yet uncertain as to whether she had imagined that low quick hiss, which might have been the evening breeze forcing its way through the aged walls. And the one also watching without, waiting with baited breath until it was safe. He saw how Scarlet was satisfied that it must have been her imagination, and his delight in her was all the richer

59

because, in her innocence, she had afforded him a while longer in which to enjoy her. His lascivious eyes raked her small virgin form. He coveted its shapely thighs and gently rising nipples that pushed hard and thrusting against the small mounds that would all too soon be the firm young breasts of a woman. He let himself covet it all a while longer, until the fever within him raged to such a pitch that he must either tear down the door that separated him from her, or take himself down to the river and offer his vile body to its murky depths.

He chose to do neither. He felt the desire ebb from him and all that was left was the fervent resolve to save Scarlet from her own bewitching beauty. As he went from there on quick silent footsteps, Vincent Pengally vividly recalled in every detail what he had been privileged to see. He was never more convinced that he must remain ever vigilant because, like summer fruit, the girl was beginning to ripen, and there would be those who were eager to taste of it. The thought was so repulsive to him that he was driven to seek solace outside, in the dark night, until the fury within him subsided.

Presently, Vincent Pengally moved away towards the house, and in a minute had gone softly inside, unaware that he *also* had been secretly observed.

Under cover of darkness, John Blackwood had crept back to the barn from his nearby cottage, bringing with him a scoop of milk from the urn and the leg of a small chicken which, with a bit of help, the boy might chew on. He had hidden the lamp he carried, while waiting beside the shrubbery, until the blacksmith's tall and formidable figure had exhausted its frenzied pacing.

Now, as he woke the boy with a warning to 'be quiet, young 'un', he wondered about Vincent Pengally's sanity. Almost without being conscious of it, he spoke his thoughts aloud. 'Is he a divil, or a man?'

'He's a *devil*!' Silas had also heard the footsteps stamping across the yard, haunted footsteps which sent ripples of fear through him. John Blackwood had made no mention of what he had seen, nor whom the footsteps belonged to. But Silas knew. They had belonged to Vincent Pengally and, as John Blackwood had intimated, perhaps to the devil himself!

CHAPTER SIX

The pony moved like the wind across the moorland. Laughing, Scarlet spurred him on relentlessly, her face upturned to the cutting breeze and her raven-black hair flowing behind her. As the pony carried her dangerously close to the steep slippery face of North Hill, his instincts caused him to pull back. Still laughing, and breathless from the wild flight over the moors, Scarlet brought the pony to a halt and dismounted, a little shock rippling through her when she saw how close they had come to tumbling over the precipice.

'Good boy . . . you're a clever boy.' She patted his thick muscular neck and nuzzled her face to his. 'It's a good job *one* of us is blessed with common sense,' she murmured, looking into his large brown eyes and thinking how beautiful they were.

Having escaped the confines of Greystone House without her father's knowledge, Scarlet treasured her forbidden freedom, when she need not be afraid that he would suddenly discover she was gone and track her down. Today was the last Friday in March and, as always on the last Friday of every month, Vincent Pengally would travel to the more remote hamlets hereabouts, attending to those animals who, for various reasons, could not be brought into the smithy; some were extremely valuable and were understandably cosseted; others might be old mares, or blue-blood stallions with fierce and dangerous tempers. Their owners knew that there was no finer blacksmith than Vincent Pengally. He handled these animals well, and was handsomely paid for his trouble.

Sinking into the long grass, while the pony contentedly grazed beside her, Scarlet gazed out towards the turbulent sea which stretched before her like a silvery sky speckled by sunbeams, and she thought there could be no lovelier place on God's earth. Here, in this corner of Somerset, where the town of Minehead had nestled and grown since medieval times, all of nature's elements had come together. Beyond the coastline lay the sea, and the land of Wales was clearly visible in the distance. Directly behind the town of Minehead, and all around, the green hills and valleys provided a natural protection from adverse weather conditions, and spreading away beyond the wooded areas where the vast lands of Exmoor, interspersed here and there with ancient little hamlets and isolated farmhouses. The moors were bleak and primitive, wild and terrifying. They had swallowed up many an unwary traveller who had innocently ventured into their uncharted territory, never to be seen or heard of again. Yet, though they were savage and merciless, the moors were also magnificent beyond description, glowing with life and splendid with colour, their beauty unsurpassed. They were vivid and alive, abundant with wild and exquisite creatures; they created the breath of life itself. Meandering brooks of pure shimmering waters ran through their very heart, nourishing and reviving the age-old landscape, ever tireless, always moving.

The moors sang and talked; they chuckled and moaned. They were never still or silent. To some they whispered a warning, but to others they beckoned. They beckoned now to Scarlet, just as they had always done and, if the light wasn't already beginning to fade, she might have

answered their call, for no one knew the moors as intimately as did Scarlet. And no one revered them with
greater passion.

Reluctantly Scarlet got to her feet and, gathering the
reins into her hands, she would have mounted. But, when
the bracken split beneath the heavy tread of approaching
footsteps, she glanced towards the spinney where the
sound was made, and there, striding towards her, was the
slim fair-haired figure of young Garrett Summers. Dressed
in dark green cords and a thick roll-neck jumper, he might
have been a fisherman's son. But, on closer examination,
the cords he wore were beautifully tailored, the jumper of
finest lamb's wool. His hands were slender and smooth,
and his pale handsome face had the elegant chiselled
structure of a gentleman. His father, a retired doctor, was
one of the richest landowners in Somerset.

'Scarlet!' His hazel eyes lit up as, slightly limping, he
hurried to her side. 'What are *you* doing so far from
home?' He was astonished, but then he remembered. 'It's
the last Friday of the month . . . of course! Your father's on
his rounds.' He bent over her, touched her arm boldly.
'Don't go, Scarlet. Stay a while.' Her dark beauty took his
breath away.

'I must go,' Scarlet protested, pleasantly surprised by the
touch of his hand. 'If my father returns before I do,' her
black eyes bored into his face and he felt her fear, '*Mammy*
will be the one made to suffer . . . she begged me not to
stray far from the house, and I disobeyed her.'

'Well, then . . . let me walk a short way with you?' The
relief flooded his kind features when he saw her gentle
nod, before she turned the pony and began leading him.
'Why doesn't your father make you go with him on his
rounds, if he's so concerned about you wandering the
moors on your own?' Like most people thereabouts, he
was aware of Vincent Pengally's obsession with keeping
his daughter hidden from prying eyes. He did not judge

that too harshly, believing that if *he* had a daughter as devastatingly beautiful as Scarlet, then he might behave in just the same way.

Scarlet laughed. 'He wouldn't do *that*, silly!' she scorned him, 'because then all the men might want to run away with me, and all the wives beat me black and blue out of spite.' The laughter slipped from her face and her voice became more serious. 'Besides . . . taking me with him would mean I might have to travel in the cart with Silas . . . and that would *never* do!'

'I should hope not!' exclaimed Garrett Summers, himself appalled at the idea. 'What a morose and moody fellow he is . . . like as not he'd burn you up with those sultry eyes of his.' He gave a small nervous laugh. 'There's something . . . frightening . . . about him.'

'Nonsense!' retorted Scarlet, amused by this conversation, 'you're just a coward at heart!' When he fell silent and appeared to be deeply wounded by her thoughtless words, she brought herself and the pony to a halt. The young man stopped and turned to see her smiling up at him, a devious delightful little smile, and her dark eyes alive with mischief. Reaching up, she kissed him full on the mouth. 'Don't mind me, Garrett,' she murmured, taking pleasure in the soft pink blush that began in his neck and swept slowly over his amiable features. 'If you knew me better, you'd know how I love to tease.' Scarlet's generous kiss had compensated for the hurt she had inflicted on him with her callous remark. Inwardly she chided herself for such thoughtlessness, especially when she had only recently overheard John Blackwood describing to a fellow market-trader how 'young Summers is home from the war . . . had his leg shot through. They do say as how he's desperate to get back . . . keen to be thrust into the front line. Bloody young fool!' Garrett Summers had returned from France some months ago, in December of 1916, and still he was not well enough to return. There were those, John Blackwood included, who predicted that he never would.

'Was it really awful?' Scarlet felt the need to know. 'Were there other men falling dead all round you . . . like John described? Was it so bloody and terrifying? Tell me, Garrett . . . I want to pretend I was there. Oh, if I'd been born a man . . . what glorious adventures I'd have!' Her voice trembled with excitement. Gripping his arm with her long slender fingers, she urged him 'Please Garrett . . . tell me about it!'

'No, Scarlet.' For a moment he hated her. He was repulsed by the excitement in her voice and horrified to see how vitally alive and glowing her black eyes were and how, in their hunger, they seemed to swallow him whole. 'I won't describe the terrible things I've seen, not to anyone . . . and certainly not to *you*, a girl of such tender years.' The small spiral of disgust he had felt crumbled away beneath the contrite and loving smile she now bestowed on him. 'Let's walk on, Scarlet. Soon it will be dark.'

'I'm forgiven, then?'

'How could you *not* be?' He laughed aloud. 'I can't imagine anyone not forgiving you . . . *whatever* you did,' he said. Certainly, *he* could never stay angry with her for long; she was too lovely, too alive, and too captivating. He adored her. When, as a young boy, he would go with his father to the blacksmith's, he had first seen Scarlet as a toddler, carrying the dolly-pegs while her mammy hung out the washing. She couldn't have been more than three years old, because he himself was only in his tenth year. But that first sighting of the little girl with the melting dark eyes and long black hair had haunted him ever after. He had seen her on only four occasions since: twice when he had gone with his father to the blacksmith's shop, once at the market in Dunster, and once on the fringes of the moors, when he had been rabbiting and she was sitting on a grassy bank, with her bare legs dangling into a fast-flowing brook. That last occasion was over two years ago, just before he had gone to be a soldier. She was the same age then as *he* had been on that first wonderful day when he had seen her in the garden with her mammy. She had made no protest when he also took off his shoes and socks, to sit beside her and dip his feet into the cold running waters. Straight away she was warm and friendly, and it thrilled him to discover how she remembered every detail of their previous meetings, when he had always believed that she had not even noticed him! That meeting by the brook was the most precious of all, although she seemed nervous and afraid in case her father should come searching for her. He recalled how, being startled by a noise in the undergrowth, Scarlet had sent him to investigate. When he came back to assure her that the noise was no more than a roebuck foraging there, Scarlet was gone; taken flight with the same terror as the roebuck had done on sighting *him*! But he kept close the memory of her; took it to war with him, cherished it and fell even deeper in love with her. Time and again he reminded himself that, in spite of her mature ways, she was only a child. And he suffered all the more because of it.

'Do you hate your father?' Scarlet's question broke into his quiet thoughts and split them asunder.

'No. I love and respect him.'

'How fortunate you are, then,' she said in a quiet, smiling voice. But then it was tinged with bitterness when she told him, '*I loathe my father . . . I'll always loathe him.*' She viciously flicked the horse-whip against her leg, wincing when it lacerated the skin there.

Garrett's gentle soul had been alarmed at her remark. He was mortified when he saw that she had cut herself. 'We're close to the river, Scarlet . . . let me wash the wound clean for you.' He put the pressure of his hand on her shoulder, willing her to stay.

'Don't be silly!' Scarlet shrugged away his touch and hurried her footsteps towards home. 'It's just a scratch,' she laughed. 'The dog will lick it clean when I get home, and nobody will be any the wiser.' She laughed again and, not knowing whether to take her seriously, Garrett laughed also.

Some distance away, the old woman paused in her herb-gathering, disturbed by the sound of passing feet and the echo of laughter. Looking up, she saw the young people and waved to them. 'Twilight's coming,' she called, 'get yourself off home.' The fair-haired young man returned her greeting, but the girl only looked, her black eyes raking the bent and shawled figure, and only the flicker of a smile on her bewitching face.

The old woman watched as they went on their way: he, the hopelessly smitten and gullible young man of nineteen tender years and she, not yet thirteen, but already aware of the power she had over him; not really *wanting* it, but not ready to relinquish it either. The sound of their gentle laughter lingered as they went on their way, too far off to hear the old woman's warning. 'Laughter doesn't come *free*, y'know,' she had called after the departing figures. 'There's always a price. It has to be paid for . . . *with tears*!'

At the top of the rise, Scarlet eased her mount to a halt, thankful that she had persuaded Garrett to leave her some long way back, he to his path, and she to hers. He was a nice enough young man, but not one whose company she would deliberately seek out. Besides which, the last remnants of daylight were rapidly fading, and she feared that her father would arrive home before her. From this peak she could just identify the narrow winding lane along which Vincent Pengally would travel back. Her dark eyes anxiously swept the snaking lane below, but there was no sign of any approaching cart. Scarlet breathed a sigh. 'Oh, but . . . what if he's *already* home?' The thought was so terrifying that it voiced itself aloud. Straining her eyes, through the growing shadows, Scarlet peered towards Greystone House. It stood out in splendid isolation, a grey awesome spectacle, with its high gable and many chimneys reaching upwards against the sky and making a formidable silhouette. In spite of much disrepair, the house was proud and its character old. Owned by the Pengallys for successive generations, it had been to each Pengally a host of a different kind. Over the years it had taken on the role of gentleman's residence, a farmer's house, a magistrate's quarters, a doctor's abode and, for the past fifty years, for Vincent Pengally and his father before him, the outbuildings housed the tools of a blacksmith, and the grounds were given over to a smallholding. The four acres of garden produced a reasonable crop of fruit and vegetables to be sold in the Dunster Market.

Scarlet continued to rake her eyes over the scene below, scouring the yard for any sign that her father had returned. If Vincent Pengally had already made his way home, the cart would be standing by the barn, and, like as not, the lamp in the smithy would be lit. Her father was always particular to put away his tools and to leave his workplace meticulously tidy. Scarlet could see no sign of the cart, and the smithy was in darkness. She was greatly relieved that her escapade would go undetected. 'Come on, boy . . . let's put Mammy's mind at rest.' She patted the pony's neck and coaxed him to lower ground, where they followed the narrow fern-strewed trail which led towards Packhorse Bridge and the approach to Greystone House.

As she neared the valley, Scarlet could see her mammy's small nervous figure walking up and down in the yard, and occasionally glancing towards the rising hills, a look of anxiety pinching her tired face. On seeing Scarlet approaching, she plucked up the hem of her skirt and ran forward, the relief sweeping her pretty blue eyes. 'Thank God you're back before he is!' she cried, catching at the pony's reins and gripping them tight in her fist. 'Where have you been all this time, child?' she demanded. 'Have you no thought for your poor mother? You *know* what he's like . . . and *still* you defy me!' She fumbled in her hasty steps but never once took her eyes off her daughter.

'It's alright, Mammy.' Scarlet stopped the pony and dismounted. She had no wish to see her mammy so distraught and it touched her conscience. 'I'm back now, and he'll never know I was even gone.' She slipped her hand into that of the woman, and together they hurried towards the barn. 'I'm sorry . . . really,' Scarlet affectionately rubbed Hannah's frail hand against her face, 'but I *had* to go. I can't stand being cooped up . . . it drives me mad!'

'Alright, child,' Hannah could see the genuine remorse in her daughter's dark eyes and she cursed the monster who kept them both prisoners. 'You go on, quickly, and see to the pony . . . groom him well, just in case your father takes it into his mind to examine him. Don't leave any traces of the moors on him . . . or on yourself. D'you hear me?' The fear had returned to her voice.

'Don't worry.' Scarlet swung open the big barn door and led the pony inside. 'He won't catch me out,' she promised.

'Let's hope not!' The thought was too much for Hannah to dwell on. 'Just be quick, child. Be quick as you can.' She went towards the house on hurried footsteps, now and then furtively glancing towards Packhorse Bridge and the direction from which she knew he would come. When she neither saw nor heard any evidence of his approach, her frantic heart became quieter. 'Oh Scarlet . . . Scarlet Pengally,' she muttered, raising her eyes to the darkening sky. 'Whatever will become of you, child?' Hannah's fear was never for herself. It was for Scarlet, the girl who was almost a woman, rebellious, unpredictable, often cruel in her treatment of others; yet at the same time Scarlet was

71

gentle and passionately forgiving, generous and tolerant. And who could blame the girl if she *was* sometimes strange and secretive, Hannah thought, for she had never been allowed a normal childhood, never been taught how to think like a child. Hannah shivered as she thought on Scarlet's starved upbringing, and she was ashamed of the part she had played in it, even though it had been a passive part. She was not unaware of how Scarlet crept from her bedroom in the depth of night, to sneak away onto the moors, yet her fear had kept her silent. The child would not be guided by her mother, nor would she be willingly imprisoned by her father. Yet, she *was* a prisoner in many ways, ways that even Scarlet was still unaware of. And, even more dangerous, she was enslaved by her own beauty. 'Lord help us all!' Hannah murmured as she disappeared into the kitchen.

When Vincent Pengally returned home, the darkness was thickening, and the house already lit from within. Some time after their arrival, when the work was done, the boy and the man parted company: one to his straw bed in the barn, and the other to his house.

High on the hill overshadowing Greystone House, the lone figure moved at last. In the dark, the eyes glinted with a kind of madness as they swept the valley below. When, at that moment, they alighted on the face of Vincent Pengally, his mean features illuminated by the halo of light which shone from the kitchen window, the eyes smiled, a satisfied and sinister smile. The shrouded figure nodded its head, gave a low laugh, and turned away into the darkness. But it would be back. To punish and murder. That was its purpose.

CHAPTER SEVEN

'I'm telling you, wife, it ain't healthy . . . the way he watches that young 'un, gloats over her and loathes to let her out of his sight. There's bad thoughts in that twisted mind of his . . . and dangerous intent in his black heart.' John Blackwood's homely face reflected his deep concern, as he kept a vigil by the window of his darkened bedroom, his anxious gaze roving the distant and lighted upstairs window of Greystone House. There the unmistakable and stooped figure of its owner was silhouetted by the soft yellow glow from the lamp he carried; his eyes were cast downwards and on his unpleasant face was a look of rapture. Just once he reached out as though to touch something, but then, in a moment and with his expression changed to one of horror, he recoiled, straightening his back with resolve and at once stealing from the room.

Vincent Pengally's departure did nothing to allay the persistent suspicions in John's troubled mind, and still he kept his eyes on the house of his master. Carefully he followed the light as it moved from what he knew was Scarlet's room, then across the landing and into the room directly above the sitting room. That was the main bedroom, where slept the blacksmith and his wife. On different occasions, when there had been need of furniture-shifting or maintenance tasks, and, on a day back in the summer when a raven had somehow got itself lodged in the chimney-breast of the Pengally's bedroom, John was called on to give assistance. He recalled now how excited Scarlet had been at seeing the raven finally released from the window. When it spread out its huge black wings to lift its great body from his hands, John had been startled by the manner in which Scarlet had screamed out. It was a strange, unearthly sound, he'd thought; but then she was only a girl and was obviously terrified by the sight of that huge and magnificent bird, so close that she was able to stroke its wings. And he had to admit that when the raven began flapping those monstrous wings, gripping its sharp claws so firmly into his hands that they bled, the experience was enough to unnerve even *him*.

'The man's deranged, Ada,' he murmured, his gaze still intent on the light, which was now stilled. 'I'm afeared there's murder on his mind . . . or something worse, God help us!' He half-turned from the window, narrowing his anxious blue eyes as they searched out his wife in the darkness.

'Aw, give over with your wild imagination, John Blackwood . . . and come away from that window before he sees you. He's a strange 'un, I'll grant you that, but . . . "murder" . . . or "worse"? By! You do let your fancies run away with you, don't you, eh?' Ada Blackwood gazed fondly into the cradle at baby Trent. Satisfied that their son was sleeping, she shook her head and chuckled, her round brown eyes instantly enveloped in the folds of flesh which deepened with her jolly smile. Tutting loudly at her husband's antics, she took great pains to tie a large and extravagant bow at the neck of her white cotton nightgown, then, cramming a loose cap over her light brown curls, she meticulously arranged the frilled edge to form a pretty frame for her chubby face. 'There!' she exclaimed, somewhat short of breath from the effort of making herself presentable. 'I do believe I'm quite handsome, if I say so myself.' She made a great fuss of turning back the bedclothes and carefully arranging herself between the sheets. 'Come and see what a pretty wife you've got yourself,' she teased.

When her husband turned from the window again, he saw that she had lit the candle on the bedside cupboard and, in its gentle flickering light, he saw the merry twinkle in her eyes. It made him smile. 'Ada Blackwood!' he chided, coming forward towards the bed and beginning to undress. 'What a shameless hussy you are.' He climbed into bed and took her hand in his. 'I'm sorry,' he told her, the smile gone from his face, 'I'm in no mind for anything but sleep tonight.'

For a moment, the room was enveloped in an awkward silence, before his wife spoke. 'No matter,' she said in a cheery voice, squeezing his fingers affectionately before turning away. 'If you're not of a mind, then that's that.' It was not a thing to bother her. In a few moments, the room was echoing to her gentle rhythmic snores, and before long her husband was also in a deep slumber.

Across the river, over Packhorse Bridge, the inhabitants of Greystone House were not so easily given up to slumber. Vincent Pengally had come from Scarlet's bedroom into his own, and he was possessed of a great need. There was a fire burning in him, a compulsion to impregnate his wife, and to perpetuate his own species before it was too late. Hannah was roughly awakened. It had been so long since he had touched her in that way, so very long, and now there was no passion left in her. She loved him still, and always would, but when she felt him crushing against her, savage and hungry, could feel no response, and it saddened her. He seemed not to notice her reticence and, being a man used to pitting his strength against great beasts brought to his forge, he had lost the art of tenderness and forgotten how to persuade. His lovemaking was fierce and predatory, his moans and cries of ecstasy loud and uncontrolled.

To Scarlet, the primitive and agonised cries that emanated from her parents' room were distasteful and unsettling. She was under no illusion as to their meaning and, when she could not bear them a moment longer, she crept from her bed, threw a cape over her nightshift, and stole from the house on bare feet.

Away from the confines of the house, Scarlet ventured onto the moors, moving with swift sure footsteps as she tracked the river on its route. Excited by a sense of freedom, she began to run and to sing softly, so softly that no creature was disturbed by it, and the gentle lilt of her melodic voice mingled with the light breeze which stroked smooth as velvet against her skin. The night was strangely warm, and the moors unusually quiet. Low in the sky, the moon sent out an eerie glow, and the tremulous shadows crept over the ground, making ghostly writhing shapes that danced and teased beneath Scarlet's floating footsteps.

Coming to the wide meandering bend at the deepest part of the river, Scarlet paused, breathless and exhilarated, her dark eyes alight with wonder. Seating herself on a boulder at the water's edge, she gazed upwards into the rising brilliance of the moon. There was magic in the air, she thought, and as always she was deeply moved by the dark mystery of her surroundings. The dry sweet smell of the wild heathland embraced her, drawing her into itself until she felt her heart beating with it and, mesmerised by the flowing chattering waters, she lay back into the carpet of heather, eyes closed, her tempestuous spirit at peace. Soon she was enveloped in the slumber which had evaded her back at the house.

When Scarlet awoke, it was with a fright. Something had disturbed her, some noise or other, though she could not instantly fathom out what the noise was, or where it had come from. Mentally shaking off the sleep which still clung to her senses, she got to her knees and quickly scanned the area. There was nothing to be seen, no noise to be heard other than the familiar murmur of the moors at night. But then, somewhere not too far from where Scarlet knelt, a creature was disturbed enough to scamper away to safety, its cry of alarm heralding a flurry of movement which rippled like a wave across the high ground. At once Scarlet was made more wary. Normally the creatures were not so quick to panic.

For what seemed like ages to her, Scarlet remained perfectly still, moving only her head as she continued to scour her eyes over the immediate area. After a while she felt assured that whatever had been prowling, if anything at all, had passed on its way. A glance at the sky told her that she had slept longer than was intended, and that soon the dawn would begin rising. Already the sky was streaked with daggers of gold, and far off in the treetops the morning birds were waking with a song. Yet Scarlet was in no hurry, for the moors were still cloaked in darkness and there was time enough before she need return home. As she turned to leisurely retrace her steps, Scarlet's attention was caught by a movement some short way off in the river, a fleeting slicing movement that disturbed the river's general flow, and threw the moon's watery reflection into shattered fragments. Someone was swimming there.

As Scarlet drew stealthily nearer, she was able to make out the dark head cutting through the water and, on seeing who it was, her heart leapt inside her. 'Silas!' she murmured, her voice lifted with joy. 'It's Silas!' Her first instinct was to rush forward and make her presence known to him, but then some deeper instinct warned her against it, telling her that such a bold move would only alienate him from her and cause him to flee with the same panic as had gripped the wild moorland creatures. She dared not risk that, yet she was desperate for his company, silent though it was. With Silas there was little need for talk, because so much more passed between them and, in spite of the fact that he would have her believe otherwise,

Scarlet knew that he craved for her just as fiercely as she craved for him. She could feel it whenever he laid his gaze on her; his need of her trembled in those sultry violet eyes and in his brooding, hostile glance. He was tied to her, just as she was tied to him. He excited her so much that, when he looked at her in that special way, she seemed to lose all control and the blossoming woman in her was awakened with a vengeance. He was forbidden to her, and that only made her want him all the more. He rejected her, but every nerve in her body told her he would die for her, and if she woke up one morning to be told that he was gone, she would search to the ends of the earth for him, even if it took her a lifetime! He was *hers* . . . hers alone. How could she *ever* let him go? The idea was purgatory to her. Not to have him near, not to plague or torment him, not to love him or to have him love her, vexed her spirit beyond endurance. Only Silas made life bearable. Only he could reach so deep inside her that, often, she was afraid. No one else could make her feel afraid in that way; no one else ever would.

From a safe distance, she watched as he swam lazily up and down the river, his lithe and muscular body twisting and turning against the current, sometimes floating, sometimes diving out of sight for so long that she was terrified he would drown. But, just when she was on the point of throwing herself in after him, his dark head would appear, and Scarlet was made to breathe a sigh of relief.

When, after a while, he climbed out, naked, shining wet and magnificent, Scarlet thought she would never again see anything as beautiful. Biding her time, and savouring the knowledge that, while she could see him, he had no way of suspecting her presence, Scarlet watched as he carelessly dabbed his shirt to his body, soaking up the surplus water from his skin, and afterwards pulling on his trousers and shaking his head until the black shining hair hung thick and limp to his shoulders. When he began pulling the damp shirt over his head, Scarlet made her move. Swiftly and silent as the night, she moved over the uneven ground to within arm's reach of him, and still he did not detect her there. When, in a moment, she slithered her arms about his bare waist, Silas instinctively drew back, making a low cry and whipping the cumbersome shirt from his shoulders, he tossed it to the ground. His instincts told him that the arms which encircled him were not hostile, though dangerously possessive all the same. In the half-light, his strong violet eyes burned down into Scarlet's triumphant gaze, and there came into his tremulous heart a feeling which was both rage and want, and amidst it all was the deep awareness of his own near-nakedness, so close to her that his heart would not be stilled. His hands had dropped gently to her shoulders and, even while the touch of her sensitive fingers sent wave after wave of sinuous delight through his entire being, he fought against it, fought with all his might, but still he was drowning in the nearness of her.

'Kiss me.' Her soft invitation sent his senses reeling. 'Kiss me, Silas . . . love me.' He could feel her warm moist mouth searching out his bare nipple and, suddenly, it was more than he could bear. His hands moved to her hair, stroking and caressing her dark head which was bent to his chest, her probing tongue teasing and torturing him and raising such passion in him that all reason fled. He shivered and murmured her name. 'Scarlet . . . you devil!'

'Take me now, Silas . . . *now*, this night, for the first time.' She had heard him murmur her name, and it had thrilled her. She had him at last, caught for ever in the palm of her hand. 'Say my name again. Tell me you love me, Silas,' she whispered. But he said no more. Instead he bent his body towards her, his hungry gaze mingled with hers. He was lost, he knew it, but all care and caution was gone. When his mouth came to hers in a kiss that thrilled her to the core, Scarlet clung to him, entwining her eager arms around his neck and pulling him into her, until his pressing weight brought them tenderly to the ground. Her heart was filled with painful desire, as she lovingly opened herself to receive him. *'Love me.'* The murmur became a demand, and there was a savagery in her voice that excited him. When she began tearing at her clothes, there rose in him a fever that swallowed him whole.

Lost in the exquisite pleasure of each other, neither Scarlet nor Silas heard the stranger approach. Suddenly there was danger in the air. Silas was the first to sense it, but it was too late. Frantically he struggled to beat off the dark that launched itself at him, ripping his flesh and gouging his eyes. He could hear Scarlet screaming and his fear was for her. Like a madman, Silas fought against the pain inflicted on him, his mind assailed by notions that he was not fending off a man, but a demon! A demon without a face, a substance with no recognisable shape, but possessed of monstrous strength and an insane desire to kill. When Silas felt himself being lifted from the ground, he was helpless. When his scarred and bleeding body smashed against the boulders, and the blackness swam into his senses, his last conscious thought was for Scarlet.

Terror-stricken, yet unsure of what had taken place in the darkness, or who had come on them with such vengeance, Scarlet froze in the ensuing silence, holding her breath and praying that Silas was safe. Suddenly, the silence was broken by the deliberate and heavy tread of footsteps, crushing the undergrowth and coming towards her at a relentless pace; yet, though all of her instincts urged her to run, she could not move. In terror she waited as the steps came ever closer. In the back of her mind rose the disturbing effigy of her father, and the murmuring suspicion that it was *he* who had tracked her down and now sought to level a harsh punishment against both her and Silas. Now, as the brute closed in on her, so near that she could hear the quiet rhythm of its breathing, Scarlet thought her heart would stop.

Suddenly a piercing high-pitched sound perforated the night: the unmistakable sound of a single whistle, in the manner that Scarlet had heard the hill shepherds use when they summoned their dogs. She listened. There it was again! This time, the footsteps ceased; there was a long excruciating silence, then Scarlet thought she heard a stranger noise, like a soft growl or the cry of a creature in pain. Again, the sound of that eerie whistle, and the crunch of bracken as the footsteps began to move. But this time they were not approaching Scarlet. They were moving away, quickly and more heavily, as though in anger or frustration. As they retreated, relief flooded into every corner of Scarlet's being, leaving her trembling in its wake.

When, finally, the moors were once more steeped in silence, she felt the tension ease from her body, and in a moment she was on her feet, searching for Silas and softly calling his name. 'Silas . . . where are you? Are you safe?' When there was no answer, she became frantic. He must be hurt, she reasoned, for she knew that he would not have forsaken her in the face of danger. 'Silas . . . where are you?' She *must* find him, before the light of day might expose them. Again she thought of her father. Yet there was something else, something about the events of this night that shook her belief in *him* being the intruder. For now though, she loathed to dwell on it. She must find Silas!

When, a few moments later, Scarlet stumbled on him, Silas was already struggling to his feet, his hands clasped to the split in his temple, but unable to stem the stark crimson rivulets of blood which trickled between each finger, falling onto his chest and staining his nakedness. Taking him quickly by the waist and leading him steadily to the running waters where she could bathe his wounds and let him fully recover, Scarlet asked the question which was branded on her shocked mind. 'Who was it, Silas . . . was it my father, do you think?'

Silas gave no answer, other than to glance a warning with his angry violet eyes. He was relieved that she was safe. And he also had suspected Vincent Pengally, but he was troubled by certain things he did not understand. If it *was* Scarlet's father who had attacked him, why had he not made himself known? And why had he allowed Scarlet to remain here with him? He couldn't reason it out at all, but one thing he *did* know, and that was his determination to keep a healthy distance between himself and Scarlet in future. To encourage her was too dangerous for them both. Not only because of her father, or because of any punishment they might be subjected to, but because he had tasted the raging fire in her, felt her need which was equal to his own, and because the desperate passion which consumed them both was a ferocious tidal wave which would sweep them to sure disaster. He would fight it. He *must*! He thought again on the fiend that had attacked him. Like Scarlet, he was still partly convinced that it *was* Vincent Pengally. Yet it was more probably that some wild beast had seen fit to protect its territory. Somehow, to Silas's mind, the latter was more comforting!

'It's savage, I tell you! The kindest thing would be for me to use *this* on it.' The man raised his shotgun, shaking it threatening before the herb-gatherer's anxious face. 'I'll do it, woman . . . I swear before God that if you keep protecting it, and if you refuse to see that it's no better than a wild beast . . . *I'll do for it* when you're not around to stop me!'

'No!' There was terror in the woman's face, and defiance and hatred. 'You'll have to kill *me* first.' She backed away from him, spreading her arms over the door of the outhouse in a desperate effort to protect its inhabitant.

Lowering the shotgun, Durnley Reece looked long at

the tiny beshawled woman who had been his wife these many long years. She was a good woman and had been both loyal and faithful, but now, since that accursed day which he'd rather forget and which he had often prayed to God he could strike from his miserable life, she was possessed, driven to hide their terrible secret, and to protect the devil who had found its way into their lives. He also had striven to protect it from harm, from itself and from hurting others, but it was an ordeal too great for him to bear any longer. Now, there were no more choices left. Either he destroyed it, here and now, or he must leave this place for good. Already the monster had killed all the tenderness and love he had once shared with his wife and, from that very first day when it all began, her love for him had shrivelled, been sucked away bit by bit, to satisfy the evil thing which preyed on them both, until now there was nothing left – nothing but for him to watch helpless while she doted on the devilish creature that tore them apart. Yet there was still a fondness in his heart for her, and it was this that made him try just once more. 'Listen to me . . . *please*. Tonight, on the moors . . . it nearly *killed* someone . . . d'you hear me? It got the taste of blood . . . and it nearly *killed*!'

'No! I don't believe you. You're lying. It's *you* that wants to kill. Well, you're not going to . . . not unless it's over my dead body!' She flattened her diminutive form against the outhouse door, her eyes staring up at him, and the hostility there crushing whatever hope he had.

'Get rid of it, or I'll be away. I'm warning you . . . I mean it. Let me put it out of its misery.'

'Leave, if you've a mind to. We'll be better off without you!'

'You old fool!' He dug into his jacket pocket, withdrew a bunch of keys and flung them to the ground. 'It'll kill you, you trusting blind fool . . . tear you limb from limb it will, given half a chance, don't you understand that? It doesn't *love* you . . . it doesn't even know what love is . . . it can only *hate*.'

'You're wrong! It's *you* who can only hate. *You* who's bred the fear and loathing that exists between you.' She was close to tears, her aged face withered by the burden she carried, and he knew she would not listen.

'In God's name . . . *let me put it out of its misery*. Look, I know it's hard for you to see the truth after all these years . . . to admit that what we prayed might be a miracle was nothing more than the devil's work.'

'Go away! Leave us be.'

'If you won't think of your own safety, think of others.'

'Nobody will be harmed. It's only you, you, with your lies and jealousy!'

He could see that it was all ended and that there was nothing else he could do. God forgive him, and keep her safe.

The herb-gatherer watched as her husband went on slow weary footsteps into the house. She watched him emerge, carrying his worldly goods in the sack on his back, and she was not sorry.

Quietly, and softly murmuring to the dark bent shape in the corner of the outhouse, she came to it, and when it looked up at her with innocent eyes, she gathered it into her small arms with great tenderness. 'Ssh, there . . . it's alright, he can't frighten or hurt you any more. He's gone . . . and we won't let him come back . . . *ever*.' She rocked the clinging shape back and forth while it softly whimpered. The whimpering intensified when she said, 'But, now, for a little while . . . I'll have to keep you locked up. Just in case.'

CHAPTER EIGHT

Scarlet gazed from her bedroom window over the bridge and the thatched roof of John's cottage and beyond, to where the moors lay on all sides, glistening in the remnants of a summer sun and displaying myriads of colours that took her breath away. It was September, a warm lazy day, when she would have preferred to wander off on her own; instead, she was duty-bound to go with John into Dunster, where they would set up at the market and ply their produce until late afternoon. There was no escape for her, not today or any other day, Scarlet thought bitterly.

'Stop your day-dreaming, young 'un . . . we'll be late for market, unless you get a move on!' John Blackwood stared up at her from the yard below, shaking his head and tutting loudly. 'I'm loading the last batch *now*,' he warned her, grunting as he swung the crate of cackling chickens onto the flat-wagon. 'Then I shall have to be away, with or without you.' His voice and attitude told Scarlet that John was already in a sour temper, which would only worsen if she was to make him late and lose his regular market pitch.

'I'll not be a minute,' she returned, at the same time scouring her dark eyes over every inch of the yard, hoping for a glimpse of Silas. When there was no sign of him, the eyes flashed angrily and she punched the windowsill with her clenched fist, muttering through tight lips, 'I *hate* you,

Silas, do you hear me? . . . I *hate* you!' And she had never hated him more than in the dark hours just gone, when she had crept into the barn, and he had cruelly rejected her! She had hoped that they might recapture the magic of that night on the moors when, even now, she could still 'taste' the conquest in those precious moments before he was viciously snatched from her. But, ever since, he had deliberately shut away his emotions and put murder in her heart.

Scarlet was not altogether convinced that the attacker was not her father, in spite of Silas's insistence that they had been struck by a prowling creature. Either way, Scarlet suspected they would never know, because to bring attention to the terrible incident would also focus interest on the fact that they themselves were prowling the moors at such an ungodly hour. They had decided to say nothing, judging the counter to be best forgotten, both of them thankful that Scarlet was unharmed and that Silas's wounds would quickly heal. There had been questions, though, when John had insisted with a chuckle that, 'You little sod, Silas . . . you've been fighting, ain't you? . . . or did one of the horses take umbrage and send you flying across the smithy?' He saw that the cut on Silas's temple might be painful, but not fatal, and he took an impish delight in it, teasing all the more in the face of Silas's brooding silence. Vincent Pengally, though, saw no such humour in the situation. For days he watched Silas with venomous eyes, making no comment and asking for no explanation. It was strange, though, how he kept an even closer watch on Scarlet, consequently heightening her suspicions that he *was* the culprit responsible. Time and time again in the days following the incident, Scarlet was tempted to confront him with the accusation, but, not being certain and having already been cautioned by Silas, she kept silent, cursing him all the same.

Now, Silas's wounds were healed. But not the deep rift

which he had purposely created between himself and Scarlet, and, if it was a source of unbearable anguish to *her*, she could not know how very painful it was to him. Nothing mattered other than the bitter knowledge that he had grown more aloof and unattainable. Even when they had the opportunity to steal a few moments together, he shunned her, never speaking, but the warning was there in his hostile violet eyes. 'Keep away,' they said, 'I want nothing from you.' He had hurt her badly, bruised her pride and shattered the intimacy between them, but he had not killed the passion in her, he had not destroyed her appetite for him. She *would* have him! Somehow. But first she craved to hurt him, first she would make him suffer and pine for her, until he was driven almost *crazy*! Her revenge would be merciless.

'Scarlet . . . I think you know that John is waiting?' When she swung round to face him, Vincent Pengally saw that his soft address had startled her, and the knowledge brought a wreath of pleasure to his ungainly features.

For a long agonising moment, Scarlet stared at him, her dark eyes scarred by his presence and her subconscious mind taking stock of the man who had the power to create such fear and loathing in her. Straddling the doorway, his legs apart and great muscular arms gripping the door-jambs on either side, he made a fearsome, uniquely splendid sight. His smooth dark hair fell lank and untidily about his coarse features, where the dirt of his labours was already settled, and only the grey eyes remained bright and vivid. The black serviceable shirt was open at the neck to reveal a thick mane of dark hair, and the rolled-up sleeves strained hard against the bulge of grotesque muscles. Over his dark cord trousers and the long ankle-boots he wore a stout hide apron, besmirched by years of use and stained with the blood of unwilling horses who had to be beaten into submission with the butt of a hammer against their flanks. Now, as he came forward, the sweat of his labours coating his skin like early morning dew, Scarlet involuntarily backed away.

'Don't keep John waiting, will you, Scarlet?' His voice was low and persuasive, his smile frightening to her. He came nearer, his disturbing grey eyes seeming to penetrate her mind. When he touched her, it took all of her will-power not to shiver visibly. It was like that whenever he came into her bedroom in the dark quiet hours. The same. And worse.

'I only have to dress, Father . . . and I'm ready.' Her voice was small, not belonging to her.

'Then you must dress right away, child . . . something plain, I think.' He laughed, but the laugh was without mirth. 'You mustn't draw attention to yourself. We don't want people's eyes on you, do we, eh?' He ran his roughened hand over her milk-white shoulder. She moved away from him, willing him to go, but that was not his intention. Going to Scarlet's small narrow bed, he reached out to pluck the cornflower-blue dress from the bedpost where Scarlet had draped it before washing. As the garment slithered into his long coarse fingers, she saw the twisted reflection of his face in the bulbous brass sphere at the bedhead and, not for the first time, she wished him dead.

'Please . . . will you tell John not to go without me?' She felt his eyes burning into her, and she was desperate for him to leave. She held out her arm so that he might lay her dress over it. Instead, he wrapped his hand around it, gripping so hard that his fingers seemed to cut like knives through her skin. When he began drawing her to him, she was horrified but not surprised. 'Please go, Father.' His grey eyes paralysed her. 'Let me get ready . . . or John will leave me behind.' An overpowering emotion rose up in her, a kind of hatred, or curiosity.

'I'll help you, Scarlet, then you'll be ready all the quicker.' He smiled again and fed the dress over her head, one hand still possessing her, the other looping her long black hair through the top of the dress. When, after some difficulty, the dress slid to her shoulders, Scarlet was nauseated to find his face so close to hers that she could taste his dry acrid breath. His mouth was open, reaching for her. 'That's a good girl,' he murmured.

'No!' Scarlet twisted away, unable to break the hold he had on her, and fearing that at any minute she would be choked to death by the garment which had tightened around her neck like a hangman's rope. In her blind panic, she could hear his reproachful tones, 'Don't be silly, you foolish girl!'

'Scarlet!' Hannah's voice sliced through the air, startling them both. 'John's run out of patience. You've wasted enough time, I think.' Though she addressed Scarlet, her timely intrusion had jolted her husband into reflecting on his own shameful part in Scarlet's delay. Casting a scathing glance at Scarlet, as though to blame her, he strode towards the door. He did not look at his wife, nor she at him, although after he had rudely pushed his way past, she turned her head to follow his path down the stairs and out of the door, her pretty blue eyes stricken more with sadness than with anger.

'I'm sorry, Mammy.' Scarlet was quick to sense Hannah's heaviness of heart. 'I didn't mean to keep John waiting . . . honest.' Quickly she shrugged herself into the dress, arranged her hair over it, and ran to hug the waiting woman.

'It's alright, child.' Hannah kissed the top of Scarlet's dark head. 'I know you didn't. Go on . . . hurry up now.' She fussed awhile with the neck of Scarlet's blue dress and then tapped her on the shoulder. 'Off you go, then.' As Scarlet raced down the stairway she called out, 'And don't you go being mischievous, my girl. Do as you're told . . . unless you want your father to stop you from going to the market altogether!'

'Don't worry,' Scarlet reassured her. The last thing she wanted to do was to incur her father's anger! As it was, he only suffered her going to Dunster market on account of John insisting that he needed help. Her father was always reluctant to pay wages to an outsider, especially when he could call on Scarlet's labour for nothing. Besides, he knew that John valued his own place enough to be trusted not to let Scarlet out of his sight.

Thankful to be gone from the house and away from her father's scrutiny, Scarlet ran across the yard to where John was seated up in front of the loaded wagon, tapping his feet and itching to be gone. 'By! There's nothing worse than waiting for a woman to get herself ready . . . unless it's waiting for a girl called Scarlet!' He tutted loudly in the manner he always did when he was lost for words. Shaking his head, he waited for her to scramble up beside him, becoming more irritated when, her attention drawn by the handsome striding figure of Silas leading the cob from the barn to the smithy, Scarlet allowed the hem of her dress to become tangled in the wagon wheel spokes. 'Whatever next, young 'un?' John moaned, a look of exasperation on his face. Yet he made no move to help her. The horse was fidgeting between the shafts, his own patience was exhausted and, while Scarlet's head was bent to the problem, John saw that Silas was coming to her assistance. Scarlet also saw his approach, and her dark eyes smiled as she looked up, her intimate gaze persuading him on, and her own efforts to free the offending hem abandoned in favour of more loving hands. A great surge of joy flooded her young heart as Silas came nearer, his sultry gaze bathing her lovely, arrogant features.

When he was close enough to see the meaning of her smile and the triumph there, a breath of suspicion rippled over his face, causing his eyes to darken with anger. In a minute, he had stopped, turning the cob's head in the direction of the smithy, and casting a cursory glance towards Scarlet's knowing smile. She had nearly fooled him, he thought. *Nearly*, but he was on his guard now and she would never find him so easily drawn by her cunning wiles. He knew also that Vincent Pengally was watching from the smithy window; he could not see him, but Silas's every instinct told him that his movements were being closely followed by those piercing grey eyes. Yet, for all that, he would have gone to Scarlet's assistance, he would have derived great pleasure from touching the hem of her dress, when his hand might have surreptitiously stroked the smooth skin of her leg; the recent memory of it taunted his every waking moment. He might have done all that and murmured softly in her ear of his terrible longing for her. If only he had not seen the look in her eyes! A look that rankled him and raised the feeling of fury in him; a look he had seen in those beckoning devil's eyes too often before; a look of triumph, of satisfaction and possession. He would not gratify it by bending to Scarlet's will so easily! There was something else that also disturbed him. Foremost in his thoughts was Vincent Pengally; then a dark shape with the strength of ten men and the instinct to kill; but, to kill *whom*? And why had it come upon them with such violence? Were they just unfortunate enough to be in a particular place at a particular time, or had they been quietly observed and, most disturbing of all, was it *he* whom the attacker meant to kill, or was he merely a casualty, when the *real* quarry was Scarlet? All of these matters were a source of deep anxiety to Silas, and always paramount in all of his thinking was his desperate concern for Scarlet's safety. For that he would sacrifice everything, his love for her and, if it was demanded, his very life. Time and time again he had thought to break the shackles that held him here, to flee this place and to desert the man who loathed him for what he was, a painful reminder of things long gone. But something tied them together . . . vengeance, guilt, shame? Silas was never sure of what went on in Vincent Pengally's festering mind, nor did he want to know . . . unless it threatened Scarlet's safety, as he had come to believe it did.

For that reason alone, Silas knew he could not strike out on his own because, God help them both, he loved Scarlet with terrible passion, wanted her with every fibre of his being and, even though he knew Scarlet loved him in the same way, his deeper instincts warned him of two things; firstly, that Scarlet's passions were dangerously conflicting and that the girl in her was not yet mature enough to realise the depth of her own raging emotions; she was not in control of them, but all too often they were in control of her. He knew that she could kiss him just as eagerly with venomous lips as with adoring ones. Scarlet was right for him, and she was wrong for him. He wanted her, and yet he did *not* want her. She was too devastating, too exquisite, too dangerous and captivating; she confused and infuriated him, yet above all else she was *part* of him. Their destinies were irrevocably entwined, and he must protect her. And so he would stay, for as long as she needed him. But, like now, he would not let her devour him purely for the pleasure it brought her!

He had the power to infuriate her with his unpredictable moods and, when he turned away, Scarlet's hatred for Silas boiled inside her. She silently laid every curse on his soul. Enraged and trembling, she grasped at the hem of her dress and snatched it, tattered, from the wheel where it was trapped. 'Get us away from here!' she hissed at John, who was astonished by her vehemence.

As he urged the horse and wagon away, an uncomfortable silence fell between John and his brooding passenger. John was no fool, and he was not blind. He was aware of the magnetism that existed between Silas and Scarlet. He had seen Silas turn away just now, and he was not surprised because he had also seen Vincent

Pengally skulking at the mouth of the smithy. Such a situation was potentially dangerous, and even the smallest thing could set it off, like the touch of a match against a powder keg!

'Hold on, young 'un,' he warned Scarlet, as he clicked the horse into a faster trot along West Street. 'We'd best get a move on if I'm to stake my regular pitch.' He might have said more, warned her of other things. But, as his good wife said, t'weren't none of his business. He was employed to grow cabbages and sell chickens that were past laying. He'd do well not to get involved in things that were deep enough to drown a man!

Normally, Scarlet loved the noise and confusion of the market. All along the High Street, the various stalls were set out and many traders, like John Blackwood, would unhitch the horses from between the shafts and tether them close by with a bag of hay to munch on while they themselves sold their wares directly from the flat-wagon. By eight thirty a.m., the noise and hubbub was already a crescendo and the excitement at its peak, with everyone calling out the virtues of their produce, villagers clambering to get first pick and stray animals foraging and fighting amongst themselves, and occasionally launching vicious attacks on the live fowl which were crated for sale.

'Be off with you . . . you mangy cur!' John shot out his booted foot at the persistent black-coated canine which seemed intent on creating chaos amongst his livestock. Growling low and showing him the whites of its eyes, it reluctantly slunk away to torment someone else less vigilant.

'That's the herb-gatherer's dog.' Scarlet's observation was uttered in little above a whisper, causing John to swing round and regard her in a curious manner. He was out of patience with her, for she had been no company at all, not since that business with the hem of her dress, when Silas had deliberately shunned her. She was a strange girl, he mused now, while quietly observing her noble features and proud bearing: a girl not yet thirteen years old, but far too lovely and worldly for her own good. He had often mentioned to his wife how 'That there Scarlet Pengally was *never* a child . . . she's *allus* had a way with her that speaks more *woman* than *child*!' It was true, he thought now, she had a woman's wiles and she knew well enough how to use them to her own advantage. But still, he reminded himself, she *was* only a child, although she would be a woman soon enough, and one to be reckoned with, if *he* knew anything about human nature!

'Get down from there, Scarlet,' he urged, 'and for mercy's sake stop shredding that cabbage. It won't be worth a ha'penny by the time you've finished with it!' A thought suddenly occurred to him, and it triggered a series of questions in his mind. 'What was that you said about that wretched animal?' he asked.

'It's the herb-gatherer's dog.' Scarlet went on vengefully tearing the cabbage apart. She was sitting on the cart, her legs swinging at a furious pace over the cold iron rim, and now, with her two hands she wantonly peeled the leaves from the cabbage, which was tightly wedged between her knees. She had done her duty: helping John to set out the perishable produce in an attractive layered display on the cart. Now, she was bored, still smarting from Silas's rebuff of her, and taking great pleasure in imagining the trapped cabbage to be his head. 'It *is* her dog,' she emphasised, seeing the doubtful expression on John's face. 'I've seen it running at her heels.' She viciously wrenched the heart from the cabbage and dropped it into a nearby barrel, afterwards discarding the leaves one by one, her smile deepening until the last one was gone. Wiping her hands together, she raised a satisfied, if unpleasant, expression to her intrigued companion, who inclined his head to one side, a cunning look in his mischievous blue eyes as he quietly remarked, 'I'd say that, in order to see that there dog . . . and it being so close to the herb-gatherer, well . . . a body would need to be deep in the heart of the moors . . . where they'd *no right* to be.' He feigned seriousness for a moment, then, his face crinkling into a half-smile, he asked quietly, 'What d'you think to *that*, me beauty, eh?'

For a moment they looked intently at each other, the impish John bursting with pride at his cunning, and Scarlet knowing full well that he was probing, but without malice. She suspected there was very little he did not know about her secret visits to the moors and her desperate need to escape whenever the opportunity arose. John was a pleasant fellow, but he was also deep and devious when he chose to be. He was one of those people who saw and heard things, but you were never quite sure how much he really knew. She recalled the last time she had ventured onto the moors, into Silas's arms, and the memory was so pleasurable that she was helpless to stop the warm pink blush that spread over her face and made her want to squirm beneath John's continued observance of her. But then she grew angry with him, incited by the gloating expression on his homely features. 'You want to know what I think?' She inched herself forward. '*I* think you should mind your own business, John Blackwood, and not be such a mischievous troublemaker!' She scrambled to the ground, eyeing him coldly. 'As for that dog . . . you're lucky it didn't bite you,' she warned, 'it's got a nasty streak and it doesn't take kindly to strangers.'

Thinking to agitate Scarlet out of her dark mood, John replied humorously, 'The wretched beast wouldn't *dare* bite me!' He half-smiled, seeming amused as though he had suddenly found her out in a secret. 'You appear to know a great deal about that black cur,' he teased, 'and *when* have you seen it "running at the herb-gatherer's heels", I'd like to know . . . her being a *private* sort o' creature and not partial to folks catching sight of her.'

When she glanced scathingly at him, tilting her dark head backwards and setting her lovely mouth in a thin tight line, he regretted having tormented her. Eager to make amends, he said with a quiet chuckle, 'I'm surprised at you, young 'un ... fancy calling your faithful John a "troublemaker".' He made a wounded expression. 'You've cut me to the quick, and I don't know if I can forgive you. Come on then ... give us a smile and I might just change me mind.'

Scarlet was in no mood to smile, although she was relieved when he showed no intention of pursuing the matter of the herb-gatherer and her wretched dog. Even so, her fretful mood was not eased in any way. Since her encounter with Silas in the yard that morning, her soul had been feverish for revenge. Her father was right! Silas was nothing more than an illiterate servant, not fit to lick her boots. Oh, it was true that she herself was no eager scholar, and had been denied proper school, but at least she had received enough tuition from her mammy to write her own name and tell the time. She was superior to Silas, and now she had no intention of letting him forget it! She suppressed her love for him with deliberate malevolence.

As the day wore on, and the wagon was constantly surrounded by eager customers, all wanting to purchase John Blackwood's good wholesome produce, Scarlet grew increasingly frustrated. She was tired and hot, weary of having to smile and return kindly greetings. 'How's your dear mammy?' they would ask, seemingly content enough with Scarlet's reply, 'Fine, thank you.' Then she would inwardly bristle as they wandered away, arms linked and heads bowed close, whispering amongst themselves. Scarlet was half-convinced that the furtive whispers concerned herself and her father. Yet how could they possibly know, she reminded herself. How could they even *begin* to know of the painful secret she kept locked away in the deepest part of her? That loathsome, terrible secret that was an accursed burden she must suffer for the sake of her gentle mammy. Scarlet was made to console herself with the truth that they did *not know*, and they never would. *No one* would ever know, because there was no one to save her. Only herself. And she *would*, with the first opportunity.

'Well, young 'un ... there ain't much left. I should think we can shortly be on our way.' John watched as Scarlet busied herself tidying the wagon, neatly piling the empty crates to one side. 'You're a good little worker,' he told her, reaching down and lifting the last full box of apples, which he swung up onto the wagon. 'Set this lot out prettily,' he said, 'while I put the old horse 'atween the shafts.'

Scarlet raised her head to watch his untidy figure amble away. She was not ready to return to Greystone House; nor did she want to stay here. There was a longing in her, a compulsion to walk the moors, alone with her innermost thoughts. The prospect excited her, until she remembered how confined she was. Depression settled on her.

'My, my ... you look fierce enough to fight the world!' Garrett Summers had come up on her, and he was smiling at the deep frown which marred her lovely features. When her dark eyes alighted on him, an uncomfortable pleasure warmed his blood. 'Would John let you take a stroll with me?' he asked. 'Would you like to?' His face was alight with anticipation.

Seeing him there, tall and clean, his fair hair glinting in the sunlight and his admiring hazel eyes pleading with her, Scarlet was possessed with a sense of devilment. 'Why not?' she laughed, coming to the wagon's edge and stretching out her hand.

'But what about John Blackwood?' he asked, half-turning his head to where John was already leading the horse towards the wagon. 'Won't he mind?' Reaching out, he took Scarlet by the waist and lifted her to the ground.

He was not surprised to find that she was gossamer-light.

'Don't worry about John,' she laughed, her dark eyes looking up, making his foolish heart spin like a top. 'Let's go quickly.' She slipped her hand in his, and together they began hurrying down the High Street. Scarlet could feel John's eyes on her; she heard him call out, 'You little vixen! . . . If you ain't back in the hour, I'll set off *without* you.' She laughed aloud and turned to wave at him. 'I'll be back,' she called. She wasn't worried by John's empty threat, because she knew he would not go home without her, to face her father's fury. It would take far more courage than John Blackwood possessed.

At the bottom of the High Street, Scarlet drew her companion towards the castle entrance. She had a plan in mind, but she was not inclined to reveal it. 'Let's go into the castle grounds,' she said, her face alive with excitement. When Garrett made no resistance, she went on ahead, occasionally skipping and turning to beckon. He followed, anxious not to lose sight of the entrancing creature who had bewitched him. He knew in his heart that if she beckoned him to hell, he would gladly go, as long as she was there to comfort him. Quickly they went along the winding paths that led them ever deeper into the castle grounds; across green expanses of tended lawns and through thick rampant shrubberies, and always Scarlet's slight figure was just a few steps ahead, dipping in and out of sight, her long black hair like a dark beacon leading him on.

When, after momentarily losing sight of her, he came into a small clearing surrounded by weeping boughs and tall stone walls abundant with dripping blossoms, Garrett was stilled in his tracks, rivetted with shock and delight at what was before his eyes. For there stood Scarlet, exquisite in her nakedness, her tantalising eyes calling to him and her slim white arms reaching out. In all his life he knew he would never again see anything so unearthly or glorious. His unbelieving eyes roved her body, her long slim legs and small shapely thighs, the dark area of womanhood between, and the perfect curves that shaped a form which was astonishing in all its enchanting beauty. His eyes devoured her, and there rose in him such a great yearning that he could hardly breathe. He was mesmerised, jubilant and fearful. 'Scarlet,' he murmured, seeming paralysed to the ground. On leaden steps he went forward, his gaze locked in hers, and his heart pounding.

'Take your clothes off,' she murmured, nuzzling up to him and writhing her body against his. When he hesitated, she began picking at the buttons on his shirt, unbuckling the belt around his waist, and all the while she murmured, teasing him, tearing him apart inside. 'I won't tell,' she promised. 'No one will ever know.' She smiled at his nakedness, her black eyes amused at his obvious need of her, and, when she pulled him into her, the two of them sinking into the ground, she laughed out loud.

Her laughter stopped when he possessed her, his embrace became a prison, and she turned her head aside as though the pleasure on his face was more than she could bear. He showered her with kisses, and they repulsed her.

Afterwards, when their path took them away from the castle and towards the gates that fronted West Street, Scarlet was morose, lost deep in thoughts of the young man beside her. She hated herself for the wanton behaviour which had captivated him, and she wished with all her sorry heart that she could die, here and now. But she was not finished with him. Not yet!

Skirting the open lanes, Scarlet cut across the back fields that ran all the way to the Mill, then beyond to the Packhorse Bridge and Greystone House. She felt Garrett close by, she saw his shadow over hers, and it made her shiver.

'I love you, Scarlet.' His voice bathed her ear and his

breath warmed her face. 'We did wrong, I know . . . and, if anyone should ever find out, we would be severely punished.' He touched her shoulder and she could feel his pain. 'Scarlet . . . I love you so much. I can wait until you're old enough, until we can be married. You love me too, don't you, Scarlet?' There was agony in his voice that left her cold and infuriated her. No! She did *not* love him. She could *never* love him, weakling that he was. In his arms she had prayed for so much, but had felt nothing, only disgust and contempt, and shame. Images of another rose in her fevered mind, of a dark-haired and fierce young man with violet eyes and quiet tongue: Silas, who had the power to create both gentle passion and unbridled fury in her. *Silas*, who need only crook his finger and she was his. *Silas*, who had taken her to the brink of paradise, only to cast her aside. Her heart was bursting with a desire for revenge and, if Garrett had no *other* worth, he would serve her purpose now!

'*Do* you love me, Scarlet? Will you be my wife one day?' He drew her to a halt, his anxious eyes looking down into hers. 'I must know,' he said.

Wanting to humour him until her scheme was played out, Scarlet smiled. He was talking about the future. It seemed far enough away and promises were easily forgotten with the passage of time. 'One day,' she told him with a tenderness which belied the chaos within her. 'I might be your wife.' It was enough; he was appeased. When he bent to kiss her, she suffered it graciously.

'We ought to be making our way back to the market,' he pointed out. 'Remember you promised you'd be back within the hour?'

'There's time enough yet,' she said, linking her arm with his when she realised they were almost in view of her father's smithy.

'Be careful, Scarlet.' Garrett also knew the path well, and was suddenly afraid. 'If your father sees us together . . .!' He could find no words to describe his horror of Vincent Pengally's temper.

'He *won't* see us,' Scarlet assured him, gripping his arm tighter as they drew nearer to the smithy. She was also afraid of such a prospect, but she knew her father's habits well. At this time of the day, when his back was set double from stooping to the horses' fetlocks, he would take over the forge, while Silas tapped the shoes onto the horses' hooves. Scarlet calculated that, while her father was occupied at the forge, Silas would be employed at the mouth of the smithy and, if she was very clever, only *his* eyes would see. That was how she had planned it.

Fronting the smithy was a small spinney, where a body could either hide or show itself half-hidden from view. This was Scarlet's intention now, as she persuaded her companion to 'Trust me, Garrett . . . no one will see us from here.' When, mesmerised by the look in her eyes, he took her in his embrace, Scarlet manoeuvred their position until she was certain that, were Silas to look up, he would see her and Garrett locked in each other's arms. Her thirst for revenge had not diminished with the passing of the day!

Bent to the ground, with the great shire's shank lying heavy across his legs and all his strength employed in filing down the horny hoof, Silas kept his gaze to the task at hand. When, out of necessity, he raised his head to shake the sweat from his brow, his eyes were involuntarily drawn to the slight movement some way into the spinney. Focusing his gaze, he glanced at the lovers, and smiled. But then, as he began to lower his eyes, a cold hand caught at his heart, causing him to look deeper on the couple who were partly camouflaged by the undergrowth. Suddenly the girl's face was turned towards him, smiling and triumphant. 'Scarlet!' Her name fell from his lips in a whisper; a wave of disbelief and desolation surging through his soul, until he thought all his willpower would not be enough to keep him from rushing forward and plucking her out. Jealousy burned in every corner of his being, but he was no fool. That was exactly what Scarlet wanted, and he would not give her the satisfaction of letting her see how the sight of her in Garrett's arms tormented him so! All the same, it took all of his determination to draw his gaze from hers, and to carry on with his work as though he had seen nothing. Yet such was the fire within him that his hands trembled and the sweat ran down his back like a torrent.

'You little tyrant!' John had been pushed beyond patience. 'I've a good mind to tell your father how you ran off!' He had been frantically scouring the High Street for a sign of Scarlet. 'Get yourself up on that wagon,' he told her, further infuriated by the smile she gave him. 'And *you*, young Summers!' he turned on the young man. 'You oughta know better than sauntering off with a slip of a girl.' When he saw how the young man blushed pink, he feared the worst, but deliberately thrust it from his mind. 'Get off home,' he snapped, 'and just think on . . . I'll be watching the pair of you like an eagle from now on!'

Garrett Summers's soulful eyes followed the wagon as it lumbered away down the High Street. He willed Scarlet to turn round, to wave, or to smile at him in that devastating way she had. But she did not turn round. And he was desolate.

Scarlet was troubled. In the daytime she enthusiastically launched herself into every menial task, hoping to bury the doubts and fears which constantly gnawed at her. When the day was done and every limb in her body exhausted, she would crawl into bed, praying that sleep would blanket those secret things that conspired to drive her mad. But it never did. Even in the deepest of slumbers the fearful apparitions would rise to haunt her. Sleeping or waking, there was no escape, no peace, and in her sorry heart Scarlet knew there never could be. She was driven by fiends who would not let her be.

'What is it, child?' Hannah murmured, taking the trembling girl in her arms. 'Another nightmare, was it?' She rocked the limp and terrified child against her breast, deriving comfort as much as giving it.

As though her very life depended on it, Scarlet clung to her mammy, her dark eyes big and afraid and the beadlets of sweat on her back bursting open to trickle away in meandering rivulets that fused the nightgown to her skin. 'I'm so glad you're here, Mammy,' she whispered, thankfully burying her head in those comforting arms, and she wondered how that gentle woman could have come so quickly to save her. She could not have known that Hannah had lain awake in the early hours, disturbed by her own terrifying premonitions. In the darkened room that was hers and Vincent Pengally's, where he had taken her unyielding body to him again and again, Hannah had turned her head on the pillow to stare at his sleeping face, her quiet blue eyes scarred with accusation. There were times when she had seen him as her strength, and there were others, more recent, when she saw him for what he was, a man bent only on his own pleasures. Scarlet's cry had not disturbed him, nor did his wife's furtive movements as she crept from the bed and went on stealthy footsteps towards her daughter's room.

After a while, the terror ebbed from Scarlet's senses, and only the shame remained. 'I'm sorry, Mammy,' she said, drawing herself away from the haven of Hannah's arms. 'I'll be alright now . . . I promise. Go back to your bed before Father misses you.' The thought of his formidable form and sinister face coming into her room was only another facet of Scarlet's nightmare. She lay back in the bed, her black hair fanning out against the pillow and her face stark white, save for the gyrating shadows that emitted from the candlelight and played creeping shapes upon her velvet skin.

'You're sure now, child?' Hannah stroked the magnificent tresses, taking pleasure in the touch of the locks against her fingers. 'You'll be able to sleep now, will you?' When Scarlet nodded and gently patted her hand, Hannah was satisfied. 'Goodnight, God bless,' she whispered, bending towards Scarlet with a kiss. Then she got to her feet, lifted the candle and, shielding the light with her hand, went silently from the room.

Some short time later, Hannah heard the familiar creak on the stairway, and she knew that sleep had eluded her daughter. No matter, she thought, let the child find her peace on the moors, for she can find it nowhere else. But where would she find *her* peace, she wondered; not on the bleak primitive moorlands, where every sound filled her with dread. Not here in this house either, she realised with a rush of pain, and *never* in the arms of her husband. Of late, she was convinced that something monstrous had happened, and was happening, even now, yet she feared it was too late. What could she do? Dear God in heaven, what could she do?

Outside, in the cool October morning, when the dawn wrestled the night for supremacy and the sky was marbled with fingers of crimson, Scarlet found a measure of contentment. She looked up at the sky, and she wondered whether there really was a force more magnificent and greater than any other, a power of truth and love, from which mortals such as she might receive guidance. She thought not! It had been just over a week since she had enticed Garrett into the castle grounds, where they had committed the sin that had enslaved him to her, and had filled her with such conflicting emotions that made her wonder whether she was losing her sanity. What made her do it? Time and again, she had asked herself that question. She asked it now, aloud, to the sky. 'What makes me do these things?' She waited, as though for an answer, a sign that the fault was not in her, but in the make-up of that 'powerful being' who, according to John Blackwood, was supposed to 'watch over us'.

For a while, Scarlet wandered the heathland, pausing now and then to dip her hand into the fast-flowing waters of a brook, or to listen enraptured when the dawn chorus burst forth. Presently, she made her way back to the house, before the daylight swallowed the last vestige of darkness. Hurrying by the barn, she stopped when a great temptation took hold of her. Soon Silas would be stirring, she thought, and if she was there, warm and tender beside him as he opened his eyes, surely he could not turn her away? The longer she thought of Silas, and of the way in which she had used Garrett to torment him, the more damned she felt. But then her heart was flooded with resentment at Silas's treatment of *her*. After all, she reminded herself, it was Silas who had driven her to such lengths, with his brooding silence and his deliberate rejection of her.

As she lingered by the barn door, overpowered by temptation, yet burning with anger that he could so easily spurn her, Scarlet's emotions were in a turmoil. Always, she wanted him, yearned for him in every corner of her being. Those shameful moments which she had spent with Garrett were as nothing compared to the glory of being held by Silas. In his arms their two souls became one, and all of her nightmares ceased. And yet, there was something awesome about Silas, some strangeness about him that both frightened and excited her. She felt it now, that special way he could wring her heart until she wanted to cry out. There were things about him that made her curious, that caused her to be vicious towards him. All the same, she needed him. She needed him *now*, more than ever, but she was desperately afraid that he would send her away and the terrible rift between them would grow even wider. She did not want that. She must not risk making an enemy of him. Not that. Quietly, she turned towards the house.

Silas saw the shadow move away from the barn door and he was both relieved and saddened. The tender anticipation in his face gave way to regret. If only Scarlet had found the courage to come to him, he thought tenderly, she would have found him waiting, longing for her company. No matter what pain she inflicted on him, or how deliberately cruel she had been to use Garrett against him in that way, just then, in that exquisite moment when she had lingered outside the barn and his heart had quickened, he could have forgiven her anything. But the moment had passed, and with it a weakness that would have proved too dangerous.

In the morning with the breeze rustling the treetops, the sun bright in a quiet sky, and all manner of work waiting to be done, the ogres of darkness seemed a million miles away. In spite of her disturbed night, Scarlet had risen early, washed at the pump and dressed herself in a pretty blue dress with an oversmock of white. Her long black hair fell in loose abundance about her shoulders, and her dark eyes sparkled. Coming into the kitchen, she put down the wooden bucket which was half-filled with water. 'Are you alright, Mammy?' she asked Hannah, who presently leaned on the stone sink, gazing out of the window, her thoughts seeming to carry her far off. 'Mammy . . . are you ill?' Scarlet came to Hannah's side and, sliding a loving arm round her waist, she asked again with increasing anxiety, 'Are you ill . . . ? You can go back to bed, Mammy, and *I'll* look after things. It'll be alright.' Scarlet had never seen her mammy in such a strange mood. She had served breakfast in silence, and twice when Scarlet had spoken to her earlier, she had not replied. Nor had she fussed about her husband in the way to which he was accustomed. Indeed he had watched Hannah going reluctantly about her domestic duties, and he also had addressed her but received no response. After finishing his breakfast of gammon and eggs, he had banged his fist on the table and stormed out in a fit of pique. Astonishingly, his attitude seemed not to have shaken Hannah from her peculiar mood.

'Of course I'm not ill, child,' she told Scarlet now, swinging round to lift the water bucket to the sink, into which she emptied its contents. 'Whatever gave you that idea?' She smiled, and Scarlet saw that the gesture did not reach her pretty blue eyes. 'I'll manage in here. You go and give John a hand . . . what with all the summer crops out, he'll be eager to get the ground ready again.' She saw Scarlet hesitate. 'Off you go,' she urged, and reluctantly Scarlet left to do her mammy's bidding. There *was* something wrong, she *felt* it! But for now she chose not to irritate Hannah further.

'Poorly, you say?' John straightened his back from the digging, leaned on his fork and used the back of his hand to wipe away a lingering dewdrop from the end of his nose. 'Aye . . . that wouldn't surprise me at all, young 'un . . . not at all.'

'What do you mean?' Scarlet was both concerned for her mammy and intrigued by John's comment. '*Why* wouldn't it surprise you to know Mammy was poorly?'

A look of consternation crossed John's homely features as he regarded Scarlet's frowning face. 'Hmph!' he muttered, dropping his head to his chin and seeming to examine the churned earth at his feet. He was thinking of the observation his own dear Ada had made with regard to Hannah Pengally only that morning. 'If you ask me, that husband of hers has finally sent the poor soul over the edge! What woman in her right mind would go into Pelham's stores, spend half an hour picking and choosing what she wanted . . . then, when she'd paid for 'em with hard-earned money, wander off *without* 'em? Why, even when poor Mr Pelham went rushing down West Street after her, all puffed out and near collapse, she just stared at him like he was a fool . . . so the poor man said.' Ada Blackwood had gone on to remark that it wasn't like Hannah Pengally to behave in such a strange way. And John agreed wholeheartedly. All the same, he did not relate any of this to the anxious Scarlet. Instead he told her, 'It's a well-known fact that your mammy works far too hard for her own good. We shall just have to see she don't overdo it, won't we, eh?'

'Can I leave the raking until later?' Scarlet was eager to return to the house. It was true that her mammy worked too hard, what with that big house to keep clean, and all the cooking, washing and other things. Then she was often called on to help out at market, and to give John a hand when he found himself battling against the seasons. It wasn't unknown, either, for Hannah's husband to summon her assistance when a horse needed several pairs of hands before it would be restrained. On top of all that, Scarlet had been quick to see how peaky and frail her mammy had looked of late, and there had been the odd occasion when her kindly blue eyes had seemed almost haunted.

'The raking can wait a while, I'm sure.' John smiled reassuringly, 'But don't you be wasting no time, young 'un. As soon as you're satisfied that your mammy's well enough, get yourself back here straight away!' He watched as Scarlet ran towards the house. Then, shaking his head, he resumed his digging.

John wasn't the only one to watch Scarlet's slim young form as it sped across the rugged mounds of dry earth where once had been neat rows of vegetables. From his place at the forge, Silas had seen John and Scarlet at their work. Now he paused in his labours to follow her in her urgent flight. With her two hands raising the hem of her skirt from the dirt, and her black hair swept out behind her in the breeze, she made a captivating sight; one to hold his heart still.

Mesmerised by Scarlet's wild beauty, Silas was unaware that Vincent Pengally had both observed him and was enraged by what he had seen. Suddenly his gaze was brutally torn from Scarlet, when the large coarse hand descended on his bare shoulder, wrenching him round. 'You'll never learn, will you?' The voice was low but vehement, as Silas found himself looking into vicious slitted eyes. With alarming speed, Vincent Pengally slid his hand around Silas's throat and, snatching the tongs which rested on the lip of the forge, he drew the white-hot shoe from the coals. 'Must I teach you a lesson you'll never forget?' he hissed, inching the glowing iron towards Silas's naked chest. 'Should I *brand* you . . . for the leper you are?' The smile on his face was evil. When the heat seared into Silas's flesh, he flinched, but did not cry out, even though the pain was excruciating.

The smell of burning flesh at first excited Vincent Pengally, but then he remembered a certain day and a certain oath that Silas's mother had lain on him, and for a moment his eyes showed the fear that had grown within him over the years, until it was almost an obsession. But now, with Silas at his mercy and the iron poised to strike again, only *deeper* this time, he was almost tempted to defy that power which he knew existed even beyond the grave. Suddenly the air was rent with a long and terrible scream. With wide and terrified eyes, he stepped away from his victim, dropped the tongs and stared, horrified, at the blood-red indentation low down on the boy's chest. He watched as Silas hung his head in pain, and he was lost. 'Evelyn,' he muttered, putting his fists to his temples in an effort to shut out the echo of that piercing scream. Suddenly out of the corner of his eye, he saw John running towards the house. A tremendous tide of relief ebbed through him. Of course! The screams had come from the *house*. He laughed out loud. In a minute he was gone from the smithy, leaving Silas drained of all but the strength to take himself to the trough, where he splashed the cooling water over his wound.

Inside the house, down in the cellar, John and Scarlet were frantically trying the placate the trembling Hannah, who seemed not to hear them. Her stark blue eyes stared fixedly on a certain spot on the cold stone floor, and she was mumbling over and over, 'It was here. *Here!*'

'Come away, Mammy . . . *please*.' Scarlet had been both astonished and anxious when she had returned to the house to find her mammy down in the cellar, especially since it was forbidden for anyone but her father to go down there. Scarlet herself had been allowed in the cellar only once, and that was many years ago, when her father had given in to her persistent requests to 'show me where I was born'. He had taken her down and pointed to the very spot. The dark stain was still there. And so was the evil atmosphere that had marked the event. Scarlet had sensed something in that cellar, something that created discord deep inside her. She never again asked to go down there. Soon after, the cellar door was securely locked and only Vincent Pengally kept the key. No one else ever went down there. Until now!

'Go back to your work!' Vincent Pengally's face was a study in rage as he slowly descended the flight of steps. 'Leave her to me,' he instructed the two who looked up at him with concerned faces. 'Back to your work, I say!' Without a word, John nodded his head and moved away from the bent tormented creature in Scarlet's embrace. 'You too, Scarlet. Leave her to me.'

'Come on, young 'un.' John touched Scarlet on the shoulder. 'Your father knows what to do better than us.' His nerves had been shattered by the poor soul's terrible scream, and now he wanted to escape from that dark damp place where even the air seemed to choke a body. He had no great desire to stay in such close proximity to Vincent Pengally, either! He began his way up the steps.

'Do *you* want me to stay, Mammy?' Scarlet dared to defy her father. But when she looked into Hannah's face she found no response, and was obliged to follow in John's footsteps. 'Call me if she needs me,' she told her father. He did not look at her, but nodded briskly as he wrapped his long fingers about his wife's shoulders. When he was satisfied that he and Hannah were alone, he tightened his grip on her, at the same time leaning towards her, his grey eyes like steel as he demanded softly, 'What foolish thing is this, Hannah? How did you get *in* here? . . . Did you go to my private drawer and take the key?' When she gave no answer but, trembling beneath his fingers, went on staring at the ground, he gently shook her. 'That was a bad thing to do, wasn't it, Hannah? . . . Whatever possessed you to do such a thing?' His fingers tightened even deeper into her flesh, until the pain showed in her face. '*Why* did you want to come into the cellar, Hannah?' His voice was softer now, but the eyes remained hard. 'I asked you . . . what made you want to come down here?'

Slowly she raised her head, and when her frightened blue eyes met his stony glare there was something about them that shook him rigid. 'Scarlet was born here,' she murmured. When he nodded, she went on in a tremulous voice, 'What else, Vincent?'

'What do you mean?'

'*What else?* . . . Did something *else* happen here, in this cellar?' All these years, there had been something murmuring deep within her. *Something*. But she didn't know . . . could never be certain. Always, when it rose to disturb her peace of mind, she had learned to suppress it. But *now*, because of what was happening, it wouldn't go away. It was like it might happen all over again, and the thought was too unbearable.

'What a foolish woman you are.' He laughed, a little nervously. 'You *remember* what happened here. I came home to find that you had fallen down the steps . . . broken your leg. You were already close to giving birth and there was no time to get a doctor . . . no time to move you. I set your leg . . . when Scarlet was born, you were unconscious. So you see, it's not surprising that you remember so little of that part.'

'I *do* remember . . . not clearly.' Her voice was little more than a whisper.

'No, no . . . you were unconscious the whole time . . . and for a long while even after I got you upstairs.'

Hannah continued to stare at him, in her eyes a mingling of doubt and confusion. 'I can't recall . . . all of it. There were dreams . . . awful dreams. I was so afraid . . . but not for myself.' She shivered and lowered her gaze to the ground, to that dark stain. How many times had she told herself the very things that her husband now told her? She didn't know. She only knew that she was not reassured. In her fitful dreams she had seen images. 'Was there nothing else, Vincent?' she asked again, the tears flowing down her face. 'Was there . . . *no one else?*'

In that moment he was thankful that she had her gaze lowered to the ground, for if she had been looking into his eyes she might well have seen the astonishment there. 'No one else?' He disguised his fear well, as she now lifted her gaze to his. 'What are you talking about, woman?' His fear became anger that spilled over. '*Are you losing your mind?*' The intensity of his grip raised her to tiptoe. 'There was *you, me* . . . and your newborn daughter. No one else! Who else *could* there be?'

Hannah knew that he was challenging her to speak out what was on her mind, and she was greatly tempted. Yet she would not. *Could* not! He was not a man you could confide in. He did not know how to give comfort and assurance, only how to breed fear and distrust. She could *never* lay bare her soul to him, for he would only ravage it. Yet he had ravaged her once too often, and now, because her instincts told her one thing and *he* told her another, she lived in dread of the consequences. Her course was clear, and she must lose no time!

'Come . . . I'll take you to your bed, and I insist you stay there.' He did not like the chaos she had wrought in him. As he led her away he warned, 'If I find you down the cellar again . . . I'll have to punish you. You understand that, don't you, Hannah?' When she nodded, he added in a quiet voice, 'You also know that there are special places for people who lose their sanity?' She nodded again. 'You see! We *do* understand each other,' he smiled.

'The Lord above created a *monster* when He made *that* one!' John and Scarlet had emerged from the house to see Silas standing with his back to the smithy wall, stripped naked to the waist and his face so white he might have been a corpse. Drawn by both curiosity and concern, they had made their way over to him, only to find that he was close to collapse. Scarlet had been the first to notice the deep weeping burn beneath his ribs; arched it was, like the top half of a horse's shoe, and all around it the skin was split and bleeding. When she cried out, Silas found the strength to push her away, his eyes cutting at her so cruelly that she found delight in his pain. John, however, realised a new admiration for the young man who had never really belonged. 'It was *him*, wasn't it?' he asked, taking Silas's arm over his neck and gently walking with him to the barn. '*He* did this, didn't he, eh?'

All the while John attended the wound, Silas made no sound, but vehemently denied John's suspicions by shaking his head with conviction at John's every accusing word.

'You can deny it all you want, me boy,' John told him, securing the bandage tightly, 'but I'm no fool. If you're thinking to spare Scarlet with your silence, or if you're deluding yourself that Pengally might think all the better of you for keeping your mouth shut ... then you're wrong! There's *nothing* to be gained by it.' Here he chuckled, 'But you're no fool either, are you? I expect you'll find a way to pay the bugger back. Oh, and when you *do* ... happen I wouldn't like to be in *his* shoes, eh?' He looked towards the house. 'The swine has scarred you for life, I'm afeared. Still ... if you're feeling up to it, you'd best get back to your work. He'll not take kindly to you being gone when he finds his way back to the smithy.' He patted Silas affectionately on the shoulder. 'You've a heavy cross to bear, an' that's a fact.' Shaking his head in that slow characteristic way he had, he ambled out of the barn, unaware that Scarlet was hidden close by, having watched while he had so carefully tended Silas's wound, and having heard every word.

On soft silent footsteps, she came forward to where Silas was seated on the upturned bucket, lost deep in thought, his eyes cast downwards and his face set like chiselled stone. From a short distance away, she called softly, '*Did* he do this to you? ... *Was* it my father who burned your flesh, Silas?' Like John, she knew in her heart that it was. 'Won't you speak to me ... *please*?' When he made no response, she edged closer. 'Why won't you love me, Silas?' Her voice was laden with remorse. 'I know he's hurt you ... and *I've* hurt you. Oh, but I don't mean to, Silas. I don't mean to.' She was standing over him now, but still he made no move, not even when her fingers lovingly touched the top of his head, sending a sensation of pleasure through him. '*Who are you?*' she murmured, 'and why does he hate you so much?' Silas stirred. 'Why does he say such terrible things about you?' She recalled how her father insisted that Silas was worthless. Even before she was old enough to fully understand, it was impressed on her how 'the boy's no good ... so much rubbish. Use him as such. He's here to fetch and carry, and to earn his keep. No more!' There was always so much vehemence in her father's voice when he spoke of Silas. She had been made curious by it, and a little afraid. After all, why would he say these things? And, most intimidating of all had been her father's favourite way of keeping her from the boy. 'He's savage. He *eats* little innocents like you!' When she was very small, these words had conjured up awesome images of Silas greedily tearing her apart. Over the years her fears had become fascination, and then a passion which had consumed her. 'Why don't you love me, Silas?' she asked softly, 'I love *you*.' She folded to her knees and looked up into his face. 'If he hurts you again . . . I'll kill him.'

Slowly he moved his head and looked into her eyes, and the dark beauty there touched his tortured soul. He felt the simple truth of her words and his heart was torn. He reached out to stroke her face, gently wiping away the tears. A fierce and overwhelming surge of pride took hold of him, and such need of her swamped his reason. He wanted her, here and now! Nothing else mattered. Wrapping his arms about her slim form, he drew her close, touching his lips against her eyes, her temples, her open eager mouth. In a minute they were caught fast in a daring embrace, trembling with anticipation of each other; she, helpless in her love for him, and he a prisoner of his soaring emotions. Suddenly, in that delightful moment, Scarlet was not the arrogant and vindictive temptress who had so long tormented him; instead, he found in his arms a soft and gentle creature, as vulnerable as he himself was, and whose young heart was used just as cruelly.

In the dark shadows of the barn, it was as though nothing existed beyond. But there were those who could see into the darkness, those who watched, and who cared enough to save the young ones from themselves. Such a one was John. He had searched for Scarlet, and had guessed how she might have been drawn towards Silas. Now, seeing Vincent Pengally striding from the house, his one thought was to prevent a tragedy.

Silas saw John's shadow fall across the doorway. It was enough. Tearing himself away from loving hands that would keep him there, he went swiftly from the barn and back to his place of work, his back bent to his labours when Vincent Pengally arrived to receive their first customer of the day, a passing rider whose mount had thrown a shoe. Only once did he glance at the bandage swathed about Silas's chest; a curious glance which, to Silas's astonishment, appeared to hold a sense of fear.

Resisting John's attempts to persuade her from the barn, Scarlet begged him to leave her be. 'You should be at your work!' he chided, 'not looking to rile your father into shutting you up in that there attic amongst the rats.'

'Please, John,' she pleaded with dark forlorn eyes, 'I'll be along shortly . . . when I've made sure Mammy's alright.' She was hunched on a bale of straw, the tear-smudged face raised towards him, tugging his heart-strings.

'Lord above, young 'un . . . where will it all end, eh?' He had never seen the girl so unhappy. 'When you're ready, then,' he said, wagging his unkempt brown head from side to side. 'When you're ready.' In a few strides he was gone, leaving Scarlet quietly sobbing in the gloom. John was right to wonder, she thought, right to ask 'where will it all end?'

Hannah would not be comforted. 'Did you see that gypsy here . . . at the door of Greystone House?' Her blue eyes were strange as she stared at Scarlet and waited for her answer.

'Gypsy?' Scarlet cast her mind back. 'A little shrivelled creature, was she, Mammy? . . . in a long grey shawl and carrying a wicker-basket overflowing with pretty lace and the like?' She recalled such a woman approaching the house while she and John were tending the apple trees some days ago, but hawkers were always a nuisance and she had paid this one no mind.

'A fortune-teller she was . . . a soothsayer, who told me things.' Hannah's face crumpled into an expression of secrecy.

'Told you things? . . . What *kind* of things?' Scarlet had been distressed to find her mammy confined to bed. Now, seeing the wild look on her face, she was deeply disturbed.

'Things . . . about secrets . . . and long ago.' She shivered and shrank into the bed. 'But you mustn't tell your father! Promise me, child!'

'Of course, Mammy . . . I won't tell *anyone*.' Suddenly Scarlet was afraid. 'But you shouldn't take any notice of fortune-tellers,' she said. 'They can't see into the future . . . or the past . . . any more than we can.'

'Oh, but you're wrong! . . . You're *wrong*, child. She only told me things that have already played on my mind. And she *knew*, I could tell. She was a kindly soul, with a gentle way and soft eyes that couldn't lie. Oh, she *knew* all right. That's why I had to go down in the cellar . . . to see for myself. I can't trust him any more, you see . . . I dare not!' Her voice dropped to a whisper as she cast a nervous glance towards the doorway. 'I can *never* trust him again.'

'*Who* can't you trust?' Scarlet feared for her mammy's well-being.

'*Him*, of course, child! . . . your father. He's not to be trusted, don't you see?'

'Tell me exactly what the gypsy told you, Mammy,' Scarlet urged.

'Oh no! . . . No, I mustn't do that, or I'll be cursed. I know what she told me. *I know*, and that's enough!' Beyond that, Hannah would not be drawn, and Scarlet thought it best to let her sleep. She looked so very tired.

★ ★ ★

'Your mother's a fool.'

'But she's *ill*.' Scarlet collected the dishes from the table, never once meeting her father's stony glare as he followed her every move. Throughout the evening meal he had fixed his unnerving grey eyes on her, destroying both her appetite for the meat pie prepared by her mother the previous day, and her dignity. When John had come for the tray which would be left outside the barn for Silas, Scarlet had dished up an extra large slice of her mother's succulent pie. In a rage, her father had ripped it apart with his bare hands, throwing one half into the slop-bucket. Later, when she made up a tray for her mother, he refused to take it, saying, 'If she can't come down to the table . . . let her bloody well starve!' When Scarlet climbed the stairs to take her mother's meal, she found her sleeping soundly, and thought better of disturbing her. She would keep the tray for later.

'She's a fool, I tell you!' Vincent Pengally thrust back his chair, sprang to his feet, and thumped his fist on the table. 'Feigning sickness, when we need every pair of hands we've got for the running of this place. If she will insist on it . . . then see that you make her a bed in another room. I've no stomach for lying alongside a weakling!' Soon after, he descended into a mood of hostile silence, when he continued to keep his eyes fixed on Scarlet as she went about the business of wiping down the big old table, then washing the dishes and afterwards stacking them into the tall pine dresser. She took great pleasure in arranging everything exactly as her mammy would have left it.

Scarlet was thankful when, after an awkward span of silence, she heard the kitchen door slammed. Emerging from the pantry-cupboard where she had been replacing the condiments, she saw that her father had indeed gone from the room. The reason for his departure, or his destination, mattered not to her; all that mattered was the welcome fact that he was gone, and that the room was a brighter place because of it. Pleasant thoughts filled her mind, thoughts of solitude and freedom, thoughts of Silas and of the glory he created in her. For a brief moment, she was tempted to go to him, but then she thought of her father skulking out there in the darkness; she thought of that special time today when she had felt the strength of Silas's love, when their two hearts had touched, only to be split asunder yet again, by the fear of one who was more devil than man.

Inevitably, Scarlet's thoughts were led to what her mammy had said earlier. 'I can't trust him, you see . . . I *dare* not!' And, not for the first time, she wondered at the love which her mammy had kept for her man all these years, and which only now was beginning to waver. Sighing, she made a jug of steaming hot milk, and placed it on the wooden tray beside a piece of cold pie and the brown earthenware cup that was her mammy's. Taking the tray in her hands, she went towards the door, turning there to satisfy herself that all was well.

Scarlet found Hannah wide awake and listening for every sound outside her room. On seeing that it was Scarlet who entered, she visibly relaxed, the smile on her pretty face being almost as Scarlet remembered it. *Almost*, but not quite!

'Come in quickly, child. Close the door.' Her anxious gaze reached beyond Scarlet. 'Where is . . . he?' she whispered.

Scarlet knew well enough whom her mammy meant. 'It's all right. There's only me in the house . . . and you,' she told her gently, placing the tray on the chest of drawers. 'I've brought you a piece of your own tasty meat pie, and some hot milk.'

'Oh, I can't *eat*, child!' Hannah protested, making a dismissive gesture towards the tray. 'There's more important things on my mind than *food*.' She was greatly agitated.

'You *must* eat . . . or you'll *never* feel well again.'

'Come here, child.' Hannah held out her thin strong arms. When Scarlet was held tight to her breast, she said softly, 'Don't be afraid . . . I won't let him hurt you. Not like all those years ago. I didn't know . . . never sure. But how can I have imagined it?' Her voice tailed off and she began crying. 'It's so hard to remember . . . like it's all a nightmare,' she sobbed.

Concerned, Scarlet tried to pull away, but she was held fast. 'That boy!' Hannah's voice became excited. 'The one he calls Silas. There's something about him. Where does he belong, child? . . . not here! I know he doesn't belong here! Don't trust him. Don't trust *either* of them!' She fell back into the pillow, drained of energy, her blue eyes glazed and unseeing.

Scarlet had never seen her mammy like this before, and it greatly worried her, 'Ssh, Mammy . . . you mustn't upset yourself.' She poured out a small measure of the warm milk and touched it to Hannah's lips. 'If you won't *eat* . . . at least sip this for me.' Coaxing her mammy to drink was a slow and painful process, leaving them both exhausted. Scarlet dreaded her next task, but it had to be done. 'Come on,' she slid her arm around Hannah's tiny waist, easing her from the bed. 'You're to go to the spare room, but . . . you'll sleep better there.' She had expected a degree of resistance, but was both relieved and surprised when Hannah got eagerly from the bed. 'I'm done with the devil!' she remarked with a laugh. 'The gypsy was right, I'm certain of it.'

'Now you're sure the bedding doesn't strike cold?' Scarlet had filled the stone bottle with hot water and was moving it about in the bed. 'Are your feet warm enough?' She was anxious that her mammy shouldn't get a chill on top of everything else.

'Stop fussing, child.' For a minute, Hannah seemed like her old self, and Scarlet laughed. 'Oh, it's *me* that's fussing now, is it?' She bent to kiss the familiar face, saying fondly, 'Sleep well, Mammy.' She was convinced that when the morning came, Hannah would be well.

'Yes, I am tired.' Hannah slid beneath the eiderdown, smiling serenely and closing her eyes. 'You sleep well too, child,' she murmured drowsily.

As Scarlet went softly from the small darkened room, Hannah's eyes sprang open, furtively watching until the halo of candlelight was gone, and the door closed. At once she quickened into life. With deft movements she got from the bed and drew back the curtains; the moon was high, sending out a brilliance that crept into the little room and lit up its dark corners with an eerie glow. Going to the upright chair over which Scarlet had laid Hannah's day clothes, the little woman quickly dressed. Afterwards, fancying she heard a noise, she scurried back into the rickety brass bed, momentarily alarmed when it gave out a creaking noise. They mustn't stop her now, she thought, not now, when she was so close to putting things right.

As the silence thickened and even the house itself seemed to slumber, Hannah ventured from her room, softly closing the door behind her and going on tiptoe down the stairway. With every step her heart was in her mouth, but she was not deterred. Spurred on by the gypsy's warning, and fearful of the thing already growing inside her, she left the house and went into the heart of the moors; she had a vague idea where the herb-gatherer's cottage was situated.

If Hannah's dormant fears were dangerously aroused by the gypsy's words, then the terror she felt now was tenfold. Even in daylight, when the sun played on the treetops and emphasised the splendid colours of the many heathers, when every nook and cranny was illuminated, her fear of the moors never diminished. Now, in the darkest hour, when shadows leaped across her path and the night creatures ventured out to stare with glittering beady eyes, Hannah trembled with terror. Yet still she went on, fleet of foot and half-afraid that she might get lost; she followed the brook and was strangely calmed by its tinkling song as it bubbled and frothed on its endless journey.

In her mind's eye she planned the route she had been preparing ever since the gypsy's visit, and perhaps even before. It had been difficult ferreting out information regarding the herb-gatherer. She was a strange woman. Though not entirely a recluse, because she had a husband, over the years they had become estranged, each living in isolation from the other, going their separate ways and sharing only the roof over their heads. The old herb-gatherer was a solitary figure who shunned all social contact. It had been John Blackwood who had innocently revealed where her cottage was reputed to be, and Hannah had gleaned snippets of details from various other folk. Nobody knew *exactly* where the herb-gatherer's cottage was, but Hannah had deduced enough for her to venture along a particular path: a path which would take her to where the brook veered away to the right; afterwards she would follow north until she came to the spinney, then she would skirt the spinney until she came to a clearing. Beyond that, some way down the valley, she should find a remote cottage, flanked on one side by a great towering oak tree, and on the other by a long low outhouse. Hannah prayed she would not be lost and swallowed up by the moors.

Whether by instinct or desperation, or both, Hannah came to the spinney, formed by a small group of majestic poplars that rose up from the open flatland, silhouetted by the light of the moon, and their formidable ranks seeming impregnable to the human eye. Hannah gave thanks that she was not obliged to enter their dark interior. Staying faithfully to the edge of the spinney she went on more urgent footsteps to find the clearing which she thought must be only a short way ahead.

After a while, when all she could see before her were trees and tangled impassable shrubbery, Hannah despaired. In her panic, she began to run, her ankles soon ripped and bleeding from the many rambling thorns which clawed at her from all directions, and her hair tugged into wild disarray by the overhanging branches. As she ran in blind panic, her terror mounted, until she was reduced to tears. Her cries rose into a scream and, all presence of mind beginning to flee, she was convinced of two things: that she would die out here in these God-forsaken moors, and that it was her husband, Vincent Pengally, who had set loose the witchcraft that pursued her now. Her mind was besieged by brutish images, all reason torn asunder, and all hope gone; her screams became hysterical as she stumbled deep into the spinney.

Some time later and having been urged from her cottage by those awful screams, the herb-gatherer came to the spot where Hannah lay, white as death in the moonlight. When the black dog began sniffing Hannah's seemingly lifeless body, the herb-gatherer shooed it away. 'Lift her,' she told her silent companion, 'take her to the cottage.' The dark shape bent over Hannah, blocking out the light of the moon, then sliding its grotesque limbs beneath her slight form, it lifted her with surprising tenderness, its burden jerking awkwardly, when Hannah's arm raised something from the ground. As it fell away, neither the herb-gatherer nor her companion noticed that it was a garment, a long grey shawl, caught on the strands of a wicker basket which contained pretty lace and the like.

In silent procession, the strange party wound its way down the valley, the black dog bounding ahead and the herb-gatherer softly instructing her companion to 'take care', until at last they came to the cottage.

Though sparsely furnished with basic articles of sound old oak and having only a rush mat on the stone-paved floor, the parlour was warm and cosy. The two lamps which were suspended from the ceiling beams bathed the whole in a kind gentle light, and the cheery fire gave out a rosy warmth. The herb-gatherer was never one to retire to an early bed, knowing from long experience that some of the most beneficial herbs only flourished when bathed in moonglow.

Presently, when the small limp form was laid out on the oak table and, in the reviving warmth, was beginning to stir, the herb-gatherer peered deeply into Hannah's face. *'It's the Pengally woman!'* She was astonished. 'What in God's name is she doing . . . wandering the moors at all hours?' She turned to the dark shape which was hiding in the shadows. 'The *Pengally* woman,' she murmured, a deep frown creasing her brow and her head shaking slowly from side to side. 'What's she doing in the spinney . . . so far from home?'

The dark shape also shook its head, but vigorously, as though irritated. It came forward, hesitantly, and with a strange sorrowful expression on its twisted features. It reached out as though to touch Hannah's face, but then retreated a little, its soulful eyes gazing on Hannah's still features and making small unintelligible noises in the back of its throat, noises that were strange, even to the herb-gatherer. 'What is it?' she asked, disturbed by its obvious distress. The noise was like that of a child crying, and it startled her.

Hannah's eyes flicked open and saw everything, yet they were unseeing, glazed with pain and confusion. Slowly they closed again, and the herb-gatherer continued to watch her loved one as it reached out to take Hannah's hand in its own. She was made both jealous and alarmed at the great tenderness there. 'Away!' she snapped, 'to your bed.' She pointed to the door, and was shocked when her instruction was not swiftly heeded. 'I said . . . away to your bed!' This time, she went to the door and opened it, waiting until the bent figure reluctantly sidled past her. Quickly following, she trailed it to the outhouse, where it turned once with pleading and uniquely beautiful eyes. When it saw that she was adamant, a look of hatred darkened its features. 'No, no,' she protested gently, her heart flooded with compassion, 'it's for your own good.' Her smile was deep with love as she reached out to stroke its temple and, when her smile was returned, albeit hesitantly, her relief was obvious. When she turned the key in the lock and called out softly, 'God bless,' there was no acknowledgement. There never was.

On her return to the parlour, she found Hannah struggling to a sitting position, her blue eyes more alert as she cast a nervous gaze around the room. 'It's alright,' she was told, when it seemed she might panic. 'You're in the herb-gatherer's cottage . . . you'll come to no harm here.' Quickly now, she was at Hannah's side, to help her down from the table. 'Take your time,' she coaxed kindly.

'I'm sorry if I woke your child.' Hannah's scared eyes searched for the cradle.

'You're imagining things.' The herb-gatherer had stiffened at Hannah's remark. 'There's no child here.'

Hannah looked at the woman's face. She saw how the passage of time was written there; she saw the sad aged eyes, and she was puzzled. Of course. It was not the herb-gatherer's infant she had heard. *It was her own.* That was why she was here. 'Forgive me,' she murmured.

'Pay no mind.' The herb-gatherer eased Hannah into the rocking-chair by the fire. 'You're the Pengally woman, aren't you?' When the revelation appeared to startle Hannah, she quickly reassured her. 'Don't worry . . . I know how to mind my own business. But . . . how did you come to be in the spinney?' She was greatly intrigued. 'What frightened you? . . . we heard the screams.'

'*We?*' Hannah's voice was marbled with fear, as she jerked her head towards the door.

Thinking quickly and cursing herself for her foolishness, the herb-gatherer bent to pat the dog who was stretched out by the hearth. 'Me and my old faithful,' she chuckled. 'This one's got ears as sharp as a rabbit's. There's nobody else, only me and him. My husband's away . . . don't know when he'll see fit to find his way back here again.'

Presently, after Hannah was rested and the old herb-gatherer had brewed a fresh pot of tea, it was time for questions. 'You still haven't told me what you were doing in the spinney.'

'I was looking for you . . . searching for your cottage. I knew it wasn't far away . . . but I strayed from the path.' The memory made Hannah inwardly shiver.

'Looking for me? . . . Why would you be looking for *me*? And at such an ungodly hour?' The old woman thought her visitor was a little deranged, but she understood how a body might seem so, if the mind was deeply troubled. 'I don't know you . . . only by sight and reputation,' she explained. 'You have a heavy burden as the woman at Greystone House.' She made no mention of the fact that she knew of Vincent Pengally's unsavoury reputation, but he was the burden that she spoke of!

'I carry a greater burden than you'll ever know.' Hannah's voice dropped to a whisper, and her eyes betrayed a tortured soul. '*You must help me.*'

'Help you?' The herb-gatherer leaned forward in her chair, her curious gaze searching Hannah's anxious face. 'I can think of no way in which *I* can help you.'

Hannah became greatly agitated, gripping her cup with such frenzy that it was taken from her, for fear of it snapping asunder. 'Yes! . . . yes, you *can* help me, the gypsy said. I must find a way to destroy him . . . before he sends me to Hell. She said he was a devil, and he is.'

The herb-gatherer's instincts served her well. 'Your husband . . . this "gypsy" told you that he was the devil?' She smiled, but not unkindly. 'You must pay no mind to gypsy-talk. Your husband is only a man.' She nearly said 'like any other', but she bit her tongue.

'You don't know what *I* know.' Hannah closed her eyes, hoping to shut out the vision of that darkened cellar so long ago, but the vision only grew stronger. She pressed her two hands over her ears to shut out the haunting sound of a newborn's cries. Not one newborn, but *two*! Something evil had happened on that day, some terrible monstrous thing that she would never know, but which would haunt her to her grave. She lived in dread that it might happen again, but she must not let it. *She must not let it!* Her fingers savagely plucked at her stomach, as though seeking to draw out that which plagued her.

All manner of questions had risen in the herb-gatherer's mind, as to how this poor soul had come to seek help at *her* door. Now, seeing how she tore at herself, everything became clear. 'Are you with child?' she asked softly, reaching out to still the frantic hands.

'No!' Hannah gripped the gnarled fingers, clasping them between the palms of her hands and holding them in a posture of prayer. 'No, not with "child" . . . it's *his*. It's no child. I must be rid of it, do you understand? A terrible thing was done . . . oh, he denies it all, but *I know*. In my heart, I know!' Her words tumbled one over the other and her blue eyes swelled with terror. They stared beyond all earthly things, seeing only the past, and the monsters which her agonised mind had created. To the watching woman, it was like a madness unfolding before her. 'You will help me, won't you?' Hannah pleaded, in a whisper. 'You *must* . . . for I can't bear the thought of it growing inside me!' She began trembling, and the herb-gatherer felt her terrible fear. '*Please.*' The word was a desperate plea and, though she could not fully understand, the old woman realised that should she *refuse* help, the consequences would be disastrous.

'Calm yourself,' she told Hannah, her voice soft and

kindly. 'I can see I have no choice but to help you.' She saw the tide of relief sweep Hannah's face, and she was glad. 'There are things I need to know . . . how far has it gone? Are you strong?' she went on, delving until she was reassured. 'I'll make ready,' she said at length. 'You just relax . . . drink your tea and stay calm. It will soon be over.'

When the square pine table was well-scrubbed and laid with a strong cotton sheet, and two wooden buckets placed beneath, one filled with hot water and one with cold, the old woman banked up the fire and instructed Hannah to 'take off your clothes and wrap yourself in this'. She passed over a coarse brown blanket. 'When you've done that . . . climb onto the table.' Nervously, Hannah did as she was told, her eyes anxiously guarding the dog at the hearth. 'He won't harm you,' the old woman chuckled, bending to pat its lazy black head.

Stretched out on the table, with the blanket loosely covering her nakedness, Hannah watched while the old woman brought certain items from the dresser; these she laid beside Hannah, who deliberately kept her eyes averted. 'You won't hurt me?' she asked tremulously, 'Please don't hurt me.'

'No. I won't hurt you.'

'And you mustn't tell. You must *never* tell.'

'No, I won't tell.' The old woman stroked the hair from Hannah's brow. Then she crossed to the dresser once more, taking out a small jar, a cup, a chunk of green soap and a towel; these she returned to the table. 'I want you to drink this,' she told Hannah, 'it will give you strength.' Picking up the cup, she bent to scoop a small quantity of water into it, afterwards mixing it with a few pinches of dark aromatic herbs contained in the jar. She tipped the cup to Hannah's lips, nodding her head when she saw that Hannah was becoming drowsy. The potion was strong, and always effective. After a while the old woman raised the blanket from Hannah's lower limbs, and went quietly to work.

An hour had passed. And still Hannah had not regained her senses. The old woman spoke softly to her. 'It's all right . . . all over now.' She was exhausted, beads of sweat staining her temples and her thin arms like lead weights hung from her narrow shoulders. The blood-splashes on her apron had dried black in the heat from the fire, and her mind was haunted by the deed she had done. The Pengally woman was right: the 'thing' growing inside her was no child . . . merely an unrecognisable blob of blood and tissue. The old woman had consoled herself with the discovery that whatever it was she took from the Pengally woman, it was without life, perhaps murdered by the fear and hatred alive in its unwilling host.

At long last Hannah was roused and made to sip yet another hot revitalising potion. 'It's bitter.' Hannah pulled away, shaking her head.

'Drink it,' she was told. 'Every last drop.' When the cup was reluctantly drained, the old woman instructed Hannah to 'lie still awhile. You must regain your strength. It's all over. Don't worry.'

'Is it . . . gone?' Hannah lowered her eyes, still afraid.

'Yes, it's gone. The deed is done and . . . it's a strange thing, but if you hadn't come to me your own life might later have been in danger.' She looked into Hannah's eyes with chilling directness. 'It was dead inside you. I think you had *already* killed it.' Her words brought a smile to Hannah's face, and the old woman was convinced that the madness was still there.

'You stay. Keep watch.' The old woman raised her lamp and peered into the dark corner where the shape was hidden. When it began clambering to its feet, she shook her head and retreated. 'No! . . . the dog will accompany us. You stay here.' She was still irritated by the strange display it had made earlier over the Pengally woman. Without another word she departed, securing the door behind her. As she passed the disturbed earth, which was now a small grave, the old woman paused. It had not been a pleasant task and she had been glad of the darkness when it was done. She was comforted by the belief that no one had seen her bury that pitiful unformed substance. But she was wrong. There had been one who watched from a grime-laden window close by. And that same one watched her now, with wounded eyes that held an extraordinary beauty. There was a deal of devotion in those haunted eyes, and loathing.

'Are you sure you can find your way from here?' The old woman saw how frail and deathly-white Hannah was, and how the slow tortuous trek across the moors had drained her strength. She would have preferred her to stay at the cottage, but the suggestion had been received with great alarm.

'I'll be all right,' Hannah assured her. 'You go quickly. We must not be seen.' The thought set her trembling.

'Straight to your bed, then,' urged the old woman as Hannah stumbled away. 'Don't be too eager to take up your labours.' She watched until Hannah was swallowed by the darkness, then she softly called the dog and began her own way home.

Crossing the open ground was a trial for Hannah. In the guilt that had taken hold of her, she was convinced that she must be seen, and pounced on! It was with great relief that she safely reached the vestibule of Greystone House, and she was filled with every hope that her journey this night would remain a secret. Strange, she thought, all of her fears had not gone from her with the awful burden she had carried. For some reason she could not understand, her soul was still not at peace.

At the door Hannah turned, her anxious eyes scouring

the night. She looked at the tall trees, standing serenely against a wakening sky, and she felt threatened. Her gaze roved over the primitive landscape which stretched away as far as the eye could see, and its vastness terrified her. In the soft breeze that swayed the branches overhead, she imagined a voice, low and persuasive, calling her name, 'Hannah,' it seemed to cry, 'Hannah Pengally'. Suddenly, where the heathland gently rose, she saw a figure, cloaked in darkness. It came slowly forward, seeming to float over the ground, its cloak rippled in the breeze and the hood which covered its face appeared hollow, empty. 'Hannah,' the voice disturbed the night and turned Hannah's heart over. Pressing against the door, she watched helplessly as it came ever closer. She opened her mouth to scream, but instead she made a strange laughing sound. 'Oh, Hannah,' the voice floated into her head, into her very being. 'Ridding yourself of his seed won't save you from the devil!' The sinister warning was torture to Hannah's fevered mind, triggering those terrible things within her that she could no longer control. Now the screams came, long and terrified, unearthly sounds that cut the night air and struck terror into the hearts of all who heard them.

It was Scarlet who came to Hannah first; Scarlet who held her fast and soothed her like she might soothe a child. Hannah would let no one else near her. As Scarlet helped her sobbing mammy into her bed, and saw those wild tragic eyes, she was held in the grip of real fear, and the awful realisation that her mammy's fragile mind had snapped.

From a distance, the hooded figure waited until Hannah was taken away. Now it began to silently track the herb-gatherer as she returned on sure and hasty footsteps to the haven of her cottage. Remorseful of the surly manner in which she had spoken to the one she loved most of all in the world, the woman was desperate to make amends. When, after a while, she saw the lighted window of the cottage, she hurried forward towards the outhouse, her steps echoing across the yard and telling of her approach. Inside the dark interior of its prison, the shape stirred, still immersed in the black mood which had settled over it. Inwardly seething, it waited until the key was thrust home and the door flung open to let in a rush of cold night air, but still it made no move.

'Angry with me, are you?' The old woman bent at the door, reaching down to take hold of the lamp. Using a match from her pocket, she lit the lamp and held it before her. 'Aw, don't sulk with me, darling,' she pleaded, coming into the darkness in a halo of light, 'I didn't mean to be so spiteful.' Still it made no response. When she stooped to finely stroke the bowed head, it moved beneath her fingers, raising its face towards her and fixing her with large and curiously hypnotic eyes. The strange sound emitting from the open mouth betrayed its frustration. 'There, there . . . I promise I won't punish you again when you've done nothing wrong,' she murmured. When its long crooked fingers entwined in hers she gently laughed, 'Oh, you've forgiven this foolish old woman, have you?' There was relief in her voice, and love, and possessiveness. 'Come on then,' she coaxed, 'you can sleep in Mammy's cottage tonight . . . a special treat.' She closed her fist tighter about its fingers and, even though it did not resist, the old woman sensed that she was not entirely forgiven. The thought saddened her.

Inside the cottage, the old woman brought a blanket from her bed and spread it in a corner of the parlour. 'You'll be cosy enough there,' she said kindly, beckoning the cumbersome shape away from the door. She waited until it seemed that her reluctant charge was made comfortable for the night. She was not unaware of the sad bleak eyes that followed her every move, and she knew the unhappiness she had caused. 'I do love you,' she promised, tucking the blanket round the grotesque limbs, 'Mammy loves you more than anything or anyone in life, but . . . I have to be careful all the time. You see, my poor one . . . there *are* those who would harm you. And we must not let that happen!' She bent to kiss the dark head. 'Sleep well, child. Tomorrow we'll find a fat rabbit for the pot.'

In her deepest slumbers the old woman had dreamed that she was forgiven. She imagined herself to be held fast in a loving embrace and all was well once more. When she awoke, to find that it was no dream and that the tormented child she had long adored was seated on her bed, holding her lovingly in its poor twisted limbs, her old heart was flooded with love. 'Couldn't go to sleep without a proper cuddle for your old mammy, eh?' she said, relaxing into the embrace and wrapping her thin arms round the bulky distorted form. She had left the lamp burning in the parlour and now, with the adjoining door open, the soft light fell on the face above her. She was shocked to see that, though its embrace was tender, the face was devoid of expression. There was no love, no hate, only a kind of muted acceptance.

Slowly, the dark wondering gaze moved about the room, as though searching for something, before finally coming to rest on the old woman's upturned face. For a moment it seemed content to have found something familiar, and the semblance of a smile shadowed its deformed features, the mouth opening to show a perfect curve of white even teeth. 'That's right, darling. Everything's fine now . . . just fine.' The old woman gazed up at the large loose features and could see only beauty there. 'Go back to bed now,' she urged. 'We both need our sleep.' The smile she gave was a mother's smile, betraying the love which had grown stronger with the passing years. Suddenly, as she gazed fondly on this unfortunate creature she so idolised, the returning smile it had bestowed on her slid away. She moved to free herself from the arms which were locked about her small form, but she was caught in a tighter embrace. Tighter and tighter, like a steel band cutting her in half. She began to struggle. 'No! You're hurting me.' Her voice was squeezed in her throat, emerging in short painful gasps. Her arms flailed the air, fighting and struggling, but they were puny and ineffective against the brutal innocent strength that held her captive. Horror stormed her mind, reason fled in place of panic and she could cry no more. Her bulbous eyes swivelled upwards, mesmerised by the dark merciless gaze that burned down on her. Excruciating pain rampaged through her body, as her ribs cracked and pierced her lungs. And still, she gazed up with hope. When her heart burst, there was a fleeting second of stark realisation before the enveloping tide, which was her own life's blood, rushed through her. And she was no more.

Inside the cottage, the awful silence was impenetrable. Outside, in the blackness, the figure moved stealthily towards the cottage door, its approaching footsteps surprisingly light and hardly disturbing the night. The silence was broken only by the splintering sound of tearing wood as the door was forced open. The parlour was warm and cosy, just as the old woman had prepared it. The blanket was crumpled in the corner and the black dog stretched out on the straw mat before the hearth, its hind legs stiff and straight, the front paws resting on the brass fender, and its body warmed by the heat from the log fire. As the figure drew nearer, the dog made no greeting nor sounded any warning, its tongue lolled over its jowl and the startled dead eyes seemed to move in the flickering fire-light, appearing to follow the hooded figure as it moved towards the half-open bedroom door, sweeping the lighted lamp into its hand as it passed the dresser. At the door, it drew back the hood from its face, surveying the bedroom and delighting in the carnage there. The old woman was still locked in a frenzied embrace, no longer recognisable but crushed and bathed in the blood that had oozed from her every pore. The one who had so cruelly taken her life stroked and pawed at her face, its whimpering pitiful to hear when she could not smile or reassure him in the way he had come to know.

The voice was soft and sinister, accusing. 'What you've done is a bad thing. *A terrible, bad thing.* You could be locked away behind bars . . . hung by the neck, kicking and screaming until the life is choked from you.' The stranger came nearer, the light from the lamp sending an eerie arc around the room, and the voice falling to an awesome whisper. 'What you've done to her . . . that will happen to *you.*'

The whimpering became a kind of muted screaming, and when those hauntingly beautiful eyes looked up for salvation, they saw only a face that was hard, a stranger's face, a face to be afraid of.

'I don't want you to *cry.*' The voice gave an order. The crying stopped. 'I want you to *listen* . . . very carefully. I really should *tell* them what you've done . . . let them take you away and kill you.' In the deliberate pause the chilling words echoed in the air. 'But I won't do that . . . not if you do *exactly* as I say. You see, there are plans to be laid . . . wrongs to be put right. And you can help me.' The stranger gazed at the pathetic creature crouched there and, for a fleeting moment, the gaze became a fixed study in madness. 'Pengally!' The soft word issued in a hiss of loathing. 'Pengally!' A wave of rage darkened the stranger's face.

Presently, when the stranger was composed enough to ask in a quiet voice, 'You *will* help me, won't you?' the dark lolling head nodded furtively, its staring eyes bright with terror. 'Good! Then you will be safe . . . *for as long as you're useful.*' The mocking laugh filled the room, unnerving the only one to hear it, and making the wretched soul cling more desperately to the old woman's broken remains.

PART THREE

1920

DARK STRANGER

Most gentle are the souls who seek rest;
Most evil are those who crave revenge.

J.C.

CHAPTER NINE

'The girl's been made to manage long enough . . . she's at breaking point.' John Blackwood had seen it happening, ever since poor Hannah Pengally had collapsed in mind and body some two years back. Now he was not prepared to hold his tongue any longer. It was *he* who had carried Scarlet in from the fields a week ago when she had crumpled, exhausted, to the ground; *he* who had toiled alongside her on a freezing January morning a month since, when the frozen Brussels sprouts they were picking stuck to her small hands and peeled away the skin from her fingertips. Only he knew how her strength was drained, for she confided in no one. He had seen it with his own eyes, yet she never once complained. Scarlet was strong and wilful, and even though she might be brought to her knees by the weight on her shoulders, her *spirit* would never be broken. John knew that, and he was filled with admiration. He chose to ignore his wife's warning to 'let well alone, or you'll lose your *own* place at Greystone House'.

'I don't need *you* to tell me my business, Blackwood.' Vincent Pengally was in a particularly surly mood this morning and did not take kindly to the likes of John Blackwood poking his nose in matters that didn't concern him. 'Get about your work!' he snarled, beginning to stride away.

'Hear me out, Mr Pengally. You'll have her sick on your hands if you're not careful.' John hurried after him, stepping back a pace when, suddenly, the other man stopped and rounded on him. Quickly, he spilled out what was on his mind. 'I know it ain't my place to tell you, but if you can't see what's right under your nose, I'm obliged to speak out, come what may.' He was surprised at his own boldness, but he stood his ground all the same, rubbing his hands together and stamping his booted feet on the ground, to send the blood more furiously round his shivering body.

'Get on with it, man.' Pengally's breath turned to clouds in the bitter February air.

'It's too much for a young 'un . . . taking over her mammy's duties this long while . . . working on the land till all hours, and caring for poor Mrs Pengally into the bargain.'

'The girl's fifteen in a few weeks. She has no more of a workload than any of us . . . she's of strong Pengally stock and up to her tasks.'

'But she's only a *girl*, don't you see?' The homely fellow was exasperated by Pengally's attitude. 'You're asking her to take on all of her mammy's duties, besides her own . . . and to do a man's job in the process.'

'What are you suggesting? Are you asking *me* to pay a labourer's wages to work alongside you?' Vincent Pengally's face was as black as thunder. 'If the work's become too much for you, you've only to say, Blackwood . . . shouldn't be too difficult to replace you.' He knew that was not true. John was a first-class worker and a reliable employee, and though he wouldn't admit it Pengally knew also that what John Blackwood said was the truth. He had seen for himself how Scarlet was beginning to buckle beneath the heavy burden which had fallen on her back.

'There is a better solution,' John suggested, 'and it

wouldn't cost as much as a labourer's wages.'

'Go on.' His patience was coming to an end.

'Another woman . . . to help in the house, and with your good wife.' John saw the thoughtful look on the other man's face and he was encouraged. 'Domestics can be got for a few shillings. A good 'un can take a load off your daughter's shoulders . . . it'll cost you next to nothing.'

Vincent Pengally stroked his chin, then began hurrying away towards the smithy. 'I'll give it a try,' he called back. 'Have a word with Mrs Blackwood . . . I won't pay silly wages, mind!'

'No sir!' John ran after him. 'Ada has her own work cut out . . . what with baby Trent an' all. It'll have to be somebody else, I'm afeared.'

'Then get your wife to *find* "somebody else"! She can manage that, can't she?' Pengally snapped, casting a scathing glance at the man running alongside him.

'Oh, aye! She'll manage *that*, right enough.' John stopped, letting the other man go and drawing his breath with difficulty after trying to match those long angry strides. Still, he was glad he had persevered, and he was sure that his Ada *would* find somebody suitable. She knew a great many folk in the village of Dunster and, if there was even the slightest chance of someone being found to work at Greystone House, his Ada would ferret them out. He returned to his work with a lighter heart.

It had taken John Blackwood a long time to work up enough courage to tackle the blacksmith like that, risking losing his job and all . . . but, thankfully, it hadn't come to that. And, after all, he felt he owed Scarlet so much more. What an impatient and surly fellow that Pengally was though! John leaned on his fork and glanced towards the smithy. 'Most miserable peculiar bugger I've ever come across!' he muttered, shaking his head at the way a man like that could make enemies. He recalled some of the strange and disturbing incidents that had taken place at Greystone House over the past two years, ever since Hannah's illness. All of the chickens slaughtered; the kitchen teeming with rats when Vincent Pengally came down one morning; the forge already burning white-hot when Silas opened the smithy, and on the smithy door the drawing of a life-size body swinging from a noose.

The constable had blamed it on visiting ruffians, and Greystone House was kept under close watch for a while. Recently, things appeared to be back to normal, and the disturbances had ceased. All the same, the strange happenings had put the fear of God into John. These dark nights, he was thankful to hurry home to his little cottage, and to the loving arms of his wife and child. He shuddered inwardly as he remembered that it wasn't only fear of the unknown that drove him quickly home every night. It was fear of the *ungodly*. On the night she was taken ill, Hannah had made some wild and terrifying claims of a 'dark figure' floating towards her and 'whispering'. It was all dismissed as being the wanderings of her poor mind. But once, just once, in the winter of last year, John had worked late crating up vegetables in the shed. It was when he was stumbling home across the moonlight familiar path that he saw it – a dark lone figure outlined against the moon and walking the ridge above the house. It was only a fleeting glance; then it was gone. It was enough! John made no mention of it to anyone because he was convinced that his sanity would be questioned, just as Hannah's had been. For weeks following, his eyes had often turned to anxiously scour the ridge, but he had seen nothing since to cause him alarm. Now he'd come to wonder whether he really had seen a ghost, or only a figment of his imagination, excited by Hannah's ramblings. He began to doubt that he had seen anything at all. All the same, these days he made sure that he walked the path home in broad daylight. Just in case!

★ ★ ★

'You don't look well, child.' Hannah's weak blue eyes roved over Scarlet's lovely face. She was instinctively alarmed by the weariness there. The luxurious dark eyes were subdued and tainted by the deep shadows beneath, and the high cheekbones were drained of colour, making them seem painfully prominent. 'Not well . . . not well,' she repeated in an odd parrot-fashion, at the same time falling back into the pillow, where she began to feverishly plait the bedraggled strands of her fair hair.

'Oh, Mammy! *Must* you do that?' Scarlet took Hannah's frail hands in her own. 'You'll only tangle it and make the brushing harder.' Getting Hannah to sit still while she brushed her hair was difficult enough. Sighing, Scarlet reached down to collect the wooden tray from Hannah's lap. 'At least you've managed to eat all your porridge this morning,' she remarked, 'Let me get you washed and tidied . . . then I'll leave you to rest awhile.' She took the tray to the dark oak dresser, where she exchanged it for a bowl of warm water. 'I'll not take long,' she reassured the watching woman. 'There's so much work to be done, I don't know where to begin!'

'Leave me be. Go away . . . and lock the door so no one can get in.' Hannah fought against Scarlet's gentle handling of her.

Undeterred, Scarlet rubbed the bar of soap against the wet flannel, working up a lather and washing it firmly over her mother's frail, parchment-coloured skin. 'It's no good you carrying on like this every time I wash you, Mammy,' Scarlet protested. 'It has to be done, so you might as well let me get on with it . . . and stop your fussing.'

When it was over, and Hannah's wispy hair was brushed into a soft cloud about her face, Scarlet was thankful to see her close her eyes and drift into a gentle sleep, her delicate hands lying demurely on the covers across her breast.

In that moment, Scarlet felt her weariness engulf her. She was so very tired. Life was hard, and she couldn't see it getting any better. She had hoped for so long that her mammy would fully recover, but now she despaired of that darling woman's fragile state of mind. There were times when she seemed lucid and Scarlet's hopes were raised, then spitefully dashed as her mammy slid away into that dark private world of her own, where no one else could follow.

Scarlet glanced around the tiny room, at the pretty chintz curtains which she herself had hung in her efforts to brighten up the place. She looked at the peg-rug mat that she had brought from her own room, and at how the dark dresser and wardrobe sparkled from the beeswax she had painstakingly polished in. In the months when they were available, flowers were brought in and placed where Hannah could see them; they brought a splash of colour and the scent of perfume with them, and still Scarlet saw the room only as her mammy's prison. *Hers also!* These past two years life had seemed to stand still, quietly draining Scarlet's spirit, until now each day was no more challenging than the one before. Something in Scarlet seemed to have died. Something precious, and irretrievable.

'Oh, Mammy . . . if only I could talk to you, and have you hold me like you used to,' Scarlet murmured, bending down to kiss that small ethereal face. But she knew that such pleasures were gone, never to return. She felt bitter and cheated, and desperately sad. Once she had nurtured hopes of escape, but now it seemed an impossible and empty dream. Scarlet had even come to chide herself for such selfish thoughts. Her mammy needed her. How could she even *think* of deserting her? She could *not*. But knowing that only made her heart ache all the more. In a few weeks she would be fifteen years old. She thought she might as well be *fifty*, for all the difference it would make!

Later, when Hannah was peacefully sleeping and the house was made clean and tidy, Scarlet put on her outdoor boots, together with the thick fisherman's pullover that came down to her knees. She was glad of the work that seemed never-ending, for it kept her from thinking too deeply.

As she closed the door behind her, Scarlet's haunting dark eyes were drawn towards the smithy. She imagined how Silas would be labouring over the forge, stripped to the waist, with his bare flesh glistening in the fierce fire's glow. In her mind's eye she could see his dark head bent at his work, and those scathing violet eyes, so devastating in their beauty that even the *thought* of them gazing at her made her heart turn somersaults. If only things could have been different, she thought, Silas might have been her salvation.

Instead they were both more damned than ever. Oh, how she loved him, wanted him every waking moment. But he was not for her, she knew that now. Her father was not the only barrier between them. It went far deeper than that. The pain of their impossible love was rooted in a time she would never understand. Neither could she understand her instinctive *horror* of Silas. It was just there; instilled in her from the very beginning and she could not rid herself of it. Always there had been this terrible conflict inside her, the horror which fascinated, and the adulation which had become a fierce overwhelming passion. 'Oh, Silas . . . Silas!' she murmured now, a great sadness in her heart. For some inexplicable reason, Scarlet was convinced that she and Silas were destined never to be truly together. At long last she had come to see the harsh truth of it, but she could never easily accept it, and she would never forgive the cruel fate that had decreed it. And now that Silas was a man in his own right, Scarlet had grown increasingly afraid that soon he would be gone from Greystone House and the iron hand of her father, to make a life for himself in a more peaceful and loving haven; a life *without her*. How the thought snaked at her and tormented her almost beyond endurance! How she loathed Silas for it!

'Well now, there's a solemn little face!' John Blackwood had seen Scarlet emerge from the house, and he was glad of it. The ground was set so hard beneath the frost that it was taking twice as long to cut through it with his fork. There was the trenching waiting to be done in preparation for the vegetables, and none of the hoeing had been started at all; the work was piling up and his one pair of hands was not enough to keep pace with it all. On top of that, he and Ada had suffered a sleepless night on account of baby Trent acquiring another tooth. 'Mammy's alright, is she?' He felt out of patience, but put on a cheery smile all the same, for Scarlet's benefit.

'She's fine, thank you, John.' Scarlet went into the wooden shed that was John's pride and joy. 'She actually ate her breakfast this morning. I've left her peacefully sleeping.' In spite of the despair she felt, Scarlet's ready smile radiated brilliance. 'Right then . . . I'm ready for work,' she said, pulling on the thick suede gloves. John always insisted that she wore them. 'There ain't no reason in this wide world why we should *both* be covered in unsightly corns,' he had told her.

'Happen you'll just make a gentle start with the hoeing,' he suggested, 'but first, I've some'at to tell you.' He lumbered across the uneven ground until he was close enough to talk to Scarlet in more intimate tones. 'Now, I ain't *supposed* to tell you this.' He looked furtively towards the smithy, and seeing only Silas at the entrance there, he went on, 'I tackled your father about getting somebody in to help you round that great rattling house . . . y'know, to take some o' the work off your shoulders.'

'Oh, John!' Scarlet was horrified. 'You shouldn't have

done *that*. It's a wonder he didn't give you your marching orders on the spot!'

'Aye, but he *didn't*! Because I made him see that if you weren't given no help, then he'd have both his wife *and* his daughter sick abed.' John gave a crafty little chuckle. 'That frightened him, I can tell you. He'd *have* to get somebody in then, wouldn't he, eh? And he knows it. Anyroad, my Ada's found a young woman, a tidy hard-working soul . . . been working as a kitchen-help at the Luttrell Arms. According to my Ada, the girlie's worth her weight in gold. She's strong as an ox, too, by all accounts.'

'Is she local?' Scarlet was both relieved and intrigued.

'Been here close on two years. She comes from Taunton way.'

'What's her name?'

'Williams.' John thought hard, the frustration showing on his homely face. 'Aye! That's it . . . *Williams*. Shelagh Williams.'

'Has my father agreed to take her on?'

'Not yet. He ain't seeing her 'till Friday week.' And an alarming thought suddenly struck him, and he was anxious. 'Here! . . . don't you go mentioning this to your father, my girl! I were told to say nowt about it. If it comes about, I expect *he* wants to be the one to tell you, but I think you should know that help might be on its way. An' if he don't take this one on, then you just keep at him 'till he finds somebody suited. For my money, this Williams woman is just what you need . . . my Ada says so, and she's a good judge, I'll have you know.' He wore a look that challenged anybody to say differently.

'Let's wait and see.' Scarlet was used to disappointments and she wouldn't let her hopes be built up only to come crashing down. 'You know how difficult my father is. I can't really see him taking on any *stranger* to come into the house.'

'He'd better!' John remarked, stabbing his fork into the

unyielding earth, ''cause if he *don't*, it'll be like I said . . . he'll have you sick, and then he'll be in a worse position!' He yanked the fork from the sods and strode back to his work.

Scarlet remained still for a while, gazing at the empty enclosure where the beheaded chickens had been found; it was strange not to hear them cackling, and the proud manner in which they had strutted about had always amused her. She wondered at the vicious way in which their lives had been ended. John had found them, and though she was made to stay indoors while everything was cleared away, she had later heard John describing to a fellow trader the bloody chaos that had awaited him that morning. 'It were a senseless massacre!' he said. 'In all my born days I ain't never seen nothing like it! Every last one of 'em . . . ripped from craw to end. An' it weren't no *animal* that did it, I can tell you that! Naw, I don't know of no four-legged creature that would tear off the heads o' twenty-four chickens . . . an' set 'em atop o' the fencing posts like grisly gargoyles. Oh, I don't mind telling you . . . it gave me a terrible fright . . . turned my blood to water, it did, and I've not had a peaceful night since!' Neither had Scarlet.

'John.' Scarlet came to his side.

'Aye?'

'Who do *you* think killed the chickens?'

He shivered. 'Lord only knows,' he said, shaking his head, 'or the *divil*.'

'Was it the same "divil" who did all the other things?'

'No question in *my* mind.' He glanced at the enclosure. 'Let's just hope they never come back. One thing's for sure . . . I ain't going into Taunton for a new wagonload of fowl . . . not 'till I'm sure!' He shivered again, this time out loud. 'I never want to find such wanton butchery like that again!' Just for a minute his mind's eye saw every gory detail and, in the background, before he thrust it all away, the shadowy image of a figure in a long dark cloak. 'Fetch me that wheelbarrow from beside the shed afore you set to with the hoeing.'

In the mouth of the smithy Silas leaned his weight against the great shire, determined that, in spite of its resistance, he *would* master the beast.

'She's a stubborn old mare,' remarked its owner, a jolly whiskered fellow as round as the barrels he carted on his wagon. 'The bugger won't let anybody near her hooves if she can help it . . . allus has been a cantankerous old sod!' he chuckled as the shire threw a tantrum that almost trampled Silas underfoot. 'Go on, lad,' the portly fellow urged, 'if anybody can master her, *you* can!' He was obviously enjoying the entire proceedings with pride, grinning broadly when Silas grabbed the shire's feathers in his fists and thrust the hoof between his knees, where he wedged it tight once more. 'She'll not be still, I tell you, young man . . . she's an obstinate old bag.'

Vincent Pengally had also been watching and now, when he came forward, the whiskered fellow saw what he carried and was appalled. 'No . . . I'll not let you put a twitch on her,' he protested, staring at the small noose in the blacksmith's hands. It was a hateful device that pinched a horse's upper lip and caused it to be subdued by terror.

Silas also saw the blacksmith's intention, and he fiercely shook his head, gesturing with his hand that the shire was calming down. He could manage.

'Want to do it the *hard* way, do you?' The question was a sneer, but Pengally was halted, not by the dark hostility in Silas's eyes, but because the whiskered fellow ran a wagon and *four*. His customer was valued, and out of the four, only this particular mare was troublesome. Quietly seething, he nodded his head and returned to the forge.

In that moment, Silas raised his eyes as Scarlet returned

to the shed for the wheelbarrow. The pleasure he felt in just *seeing* her betrayed itself in his quiet gaze. Pengally saw it and was infuriated.

Finally, when the mare was shod and the whiskered fellow had led her away down the path and out of sight, Silas found himself confronted by Vincent Pengally, his face dark with rage. 'I ought to skin you alive,' he hissed, 'and so help me, *I will* . . . if you ever again challenge me in my own smithy.' Silas was not intimidated. He felt only contempt for this man. 'D'you hear what I'm saying? Don't try it again, or you'll feel the weight of leather on your back!' Silas continued to boldly return the hostile stare, although it mellowed when the other man continued. 'And *Scarlet* . . . don't think I didn't see the cow-eyes you were making at her!' He thrust his face forward, his voice dropping to a whisper and only then, at what he said next, was there real fear in Silas's young heart. 'I can't stop you from *looking*, you bastard . . . unless I gouge out your eyes. But, if you have dreams of *touching* her, you'd best put them out of your head. I'm warning you because . . . before I'd see you lay a finger on her, I'd rather she were dead.' In his terrible rage he began trembling, his vivid grey eyes swimming with tears. 'Make no mistake about it,' he said gutturally, '*I would take her life without a second thought!*'

Silas was surprised to find himself shaken to the core, even though he knew he should not be so shocked at whatever threats this man made. *He was unstable*; made even more so by the weird happenings of late, directed towards Greystone House and claimed by Pengally to stem from witchcraft. At first he had sworn that it was *Silas* plotting against him, but then the drawing of a hanging body had appeared on the smithy door on the very night when Pengally had stood watch over Silas with a primed shotgun. From then on, and for many weeks after, he had been like a man possessed, inconsolable, and going in fear for his life. Only after a prolonged period when no further incidents occurred did he become calm enough to carry on his work as before. But the whole series of bizarre events had desperately unnerved him.

Silas was in no doubt that the words uttered by the blacksmith just now were no idle threat, but a sincere intent. Because of the magnetism that existed between himself and Scarlet, there must inevitably come a time when her life was in great danger. He had been deeply aware of it for some long time, and he saw that the awful responsibility was *his*. And, even though it would be a painful thing, he had vowed to make the ultimate sacrifice, for Scarlet's sake. It was almost time. Particularly since John had confided in him the possibility of a companion and help for Scarlet.

'Come in! Stand over here where I can see you in the light.' Vincent Pengally turned a sour face towards the young woman who was lingering in the doorway of the parlour, her brown eyes seeming nervous under his bold glowering stare. She was a slim figure of medium height, demurely dressed in a brown fitted tweed coat, with a cream cloche hat squashed over her short brown hair. Round her neck was a long broad scarf in a vivid green and yellow chequered pattern. She was neither pretty nor plain, but having the sort of face that rarely attracted a second glance. When she hesitated, Pengally's voice boomed out across the parlour, causing her to jerk forward. 'Move yourself . . . I haven't got all evening.' He indicated the chair which was situated opposite, at the other side of the black-leaded fire-range. When she was seated on the edge, seeming uncomfortable and ill at ease, he let his scrutinous grey eyes rove over her stiff upright form, regarding with satisfaction her sober and neat appearance. 'Be so good as to remove your hat,' he told her in a surly voice.

'Pardon me, Mr Pengally.' She snatched the hat from her head and placed it most carefully on her knee, clutching the brim so anxiously that its shape was altogether changed.

'You don't look very old to me, girl!'

'I'm not a "girl", sir. I'm a grown woman.' Her brown eyes observed him intently, 'I have experience . . . and I'm not afraid of hard work.'

'What kind of experience?' He was shocked to find that her staring brown eyes disturbed him. To hell with this damned business, he thought, and damnation to Hannah for putting him through it!

'I went to work in an asylum when I was only fourteen. There were twelve old people in the institution. I cared for them all at different times. Besides the nursing, I was obliged to carry out various other domestic duties. The work was hard and unrewarding, but I did it well.'

'Hmh!' He regarded her in a hostile manner, 'You do have references, do you?'

'When my father died, I left the area and haven't been back since. It isn't possible to obtain further references for that particular period in my life . . . not now. The institution closed down some time back.' She saw that he intended to speak, and was fearful that she would be dismissed. 'However, I have been employed at the Luttrell Arms for almost two years . . . as general domestic assistance. I have here a formal reference regarding my good qualities and amiable manner whilst in their employ . . . and a note from my first employer.' She reached into her deep leather bag and withdrew a long brown envelope which she handed to him. 'You'll be pleased to know that I can read and write, and have a small knowledge of the piano.'

'Huh!' He gave an insulting laugh, 'You'll find little use for "piano knowledge" here at Greystone House . . . indeed, I would positively frown on it!' Opening the envelope, he perused the contents with remarkable swiftness, his impatience with the whole proceedings clearly evident as he thrust the documents into her hand. 'Read and write, you say?' She nodded. 'Hmh . . . well, the Luttrell Arms manager speaks highly of you and your work there. "An exemplary and outstanding employee" is how he describes you.' She nodded again, a satisfied smile playing at the corners of her small thin-lipped mouth. 'Why do you want to leave?'

'I hadn't thought of leaving, sir . . . until Mrs Blackwood made mention of it, when I happened on her in Pelham's shop the other week. Oh, I like the domestic work well enough, and I dare say it's likely I would have stayed on at the Luttrell Arms for a while, but you see, sir . . . I do miss the *caring*, the satisfaction of looking after people who genuinely need help. It's so rewarding, and there's nothing like that at the Luttrell Arms. So I do believe that now Mrs Blackwood has got me thinking about it again, I'll find myself a position of that kind . . . whether it's here at Greystone House, or some other place.'

'How much are you paid at your present employ?'

'Two pounds a week, and board.'

'Hmh! That seems over-generous to me, Miss Williams. *I* don't intend to be so foolish with hard earned money.'

'Of course, sir.'

'The position here will pay *one* pound each week . . . with a room, warmth and food. The duties will be shared with my daughter, Scarlet. Presently, she helps on the land, runs the house and cares for Mrs Pengally, and the girl is not yet fifteen.'

'I understand, sir.'

'*I* have my hands full with the smithy and overseeing the accounts. I'm a hard-working man, Miss Williams. I need an orderly house and food on the table when my labours are done. The last thing I want is to have *two* sick women on my hands.' He regarded the young woman closely. 'Scarlet is good on the land; she would continue her duties there . . . and would equally share the domestic tasks about the house. As for her ailing mother . . . I would prefer that particular burden to be eased from her altogether.' He stiffened his back and brought his piercing grey eyes to bear on her, seeming pleased when she appeared to flinch beneath his stony glare. 'So you see, Miss Williams, the work here will be hard, and the pay not so attractive. No doubt your enthusiasm has been squashed?'

'On the contrary, Mr Pengally.' She appeared to bristle, her gaze returned with confidence. 'I would be *pleased* to care for your sick wife; it's what I do best. And though the wages won't be as rewarding . . . I shall have the pleasure of your daughter's company, a deal more freedom, and the opportunity of living in a *house*, instead of business premises.' She saw the slow arrogant smile spread over his features, and her fingers tightened so fiercely on the brim of her hat that it tore.

'Are you saying that you agree to the terms?'

'I am.'

'Good!' He was both pleased and surprised, his grey eyes once more closely regarding her, a thoughtful look on his coarse features. It was a while before he went on. 'Then you may report Monday week, if that is suitable?'

'It is, sir.' The relief flooded her round face. 'May I see Mrs Pengally?'

'I suppose you might as well know what you're taking on . . . Scarlet will show you the way.' He got to his feet, gesturing for her to do the same. 'One other thing you need to know, Williams,' he said, ignoring the way she frowned on hearing him refer to her as 'Williams'.

'Yes, sir?'

'My daughter . . . Scarlet. I forbid you to behave in an irresponsible manner in her presence.'

'I don't understand.'

'Scarlet is a quiet girl. She's been brought up to find pleasure in her *own* company. She's not allowed to waste

her energy on foolish pastimes . . . no going into town,
fancy clothes, barn dances and such like. She attends the
market with my hired help, John Blackwood, and has
never found the need to mix with empty-headed young
people. Everything Scarlet needs is *here* . . . at Greystone
House. She has no need of the outside world. Do I make
myself clear?'

'Perfectly clear.' There was astonishment in her face,
and a look of doubt, or possibly disgust.

'Another thing. I have been forced, by certain past
circumstances, to take into my employ a most devious
young man by the name of Silas. Scarlet is particularly
forbidden to have anything to do with him. Part of your
duty will be to ensure that these two are kept well apart!'
He waited for her reaction, and when she merely nodded,
he went on. 'He won't give you any trouble . . . although
don't be fooled when he pretends to be dumb. He can
speak as well as you or me, only he prefers to remain
surly. He has an area in the barn, where he sleeps . . .
Under no circumstances is he ever to be allowed in the house. He
has a tray set outside the barn in the morning, and
another when his labours are done . . . if the smithy keeps
us busy until well into the evening, you'll be so good as to
fetch us a plate of sandwiches. *You* must bring them,
Williams . . . do *not* send Scarlet. The smithy is out of
bounds to her.' He led the way across the room. 'Is all of
that clear enough?'

'I shall do exactly as you say.'

'Good!' He flung open the parlour door and went into
the hall. 'Scarlet!' He directed his voice towards the
kitchen, where he suspected Scarlet to have been waiting.
'Leave what you're doing, and come here.'

Since showing the young woman into the parlour,
Scarlet had made every effort to busy herself in the
kitchen, having started several different tasks in her frustration, and leaving each one unfinished. Twice she had

heated the iron for the purpose of pressing her father's long-tailed shirts, and each time she had withdrawn the iron to the hearth where it had grown lukewarm. Several times she had set the wooden tray with her mammy's best rose china teacups, only to return them to the wall-cabinet on recalling her father's express instructions, 'I don't want you pampering to this woman when she arrives . . . no foolish notions of bringing in a tray. You stay well out of the way until you're sent for.'

Scarlet was greatly excited at the prospect of Shelagh Williams coming to live at Greystone House; how wonderful it would be, she thought, to have someone she might learn to confide in and who could be a friend to her. Every few minutes Scarlet was compelled to tiptoe down the long gloomy corridor from the kitchen to the parlour, where she would lean with her ear to the door and her fingers crossed, in the fervent hope that her father would see fit to employ the young woman. She was horrified at his tone of voice and the hostile manner in which he addressed Miss Williams, although she admired the young woman's quiet firm response, and she knew that hew father also would be favourably impressed. She hoped so; oh, she did hope so!

'Oh, there you are.' Vincent Pengally was relieved when he saw that Scarlet had seemed to be waiting for his call. He watched until she had come within the glow of the hall lamp before impatiently instructing her, 'Miss Williams has accepted the terms of employ and will move into Greystone House within the next week.' He paused at Scarlet's delighted expression, and was made to wonder whether he had come to a decision he might later regret. He felt uneasy about the whole matter, but saw it as the lesser of two evils; certainly he dared not risk the possibility of Scarlet buckling beneath the strain which Hannah's regrettable malaise had inflicted on her. Impudent though John Blackwood had been, his warning had only told

Pengally what he already knew. He had no choice!

'I'm so pleased.' Scarlet could not hide her enthusiasm, her glowing smile astonishing the young woman as she was made to realise how extraordinarily beautiful Scarlet was. She thought of her own commonplace appearance and, for the briefest moment, her returning smile was constrained by feelings of envy. 'Thank you,' she said, desperately trying to suppress those uncharitable thoughts that would well defeat her purpose here.

'Don't be so quick to assume it's *all* settled,' interrupted Pengally, who was irritated by the amiable exchanges. 'She's yet to meet your mother. Take her up there now.' His smile resembled a grimace as he added in a cutting voice, 'Once she's seen what she's taking on . . . she'll likely change her mind!' He turned from them and returned to the parlour, closing the door behind him and his quiet laughter echoing in the air.

'My father finds illness offensive.' Scarlet's loathing for her father bubbled inside her as she mounted the stairs, occasionally glancing behind her to ensure that the young woman was following.

'Does he give you no help with your mother?'

'None.' Scarlet paused at the top of the stairs as she waited for her companion to arrive. The question had revived painful and bitter thoughts. 'My mother prefers it that way,' she said, reaching out to the stairpost where she turned up the lamp there, 'and so do I.'

In the soft light Shelagh Williams detected the hostility on Scarlet's face at the mention of her father, and it only strengthened her resolve to stay. 'I see,' she said quietly, and no more was said until they reached Hannah's room.

Propped up against the pillow, with her anxious blue eyes trained on the door and her hands feverishly twisting the sheet into tight spirals, Hannah looked a haunted and pathetic figure. 'Is this the young woman you told me about, Scarlet?' she asked. There was a surprising degree of confidence in her voice.

Thrilled that her mammy had even *remembered* the conversation they had earlier enjoyed, Scarlet enfolded her in a warm embrace. 'This is Shelagh Williams,' she said, beckoning for her to come forward.

'Hello, Mrs Pengally.' Shelagh stretched out her hand as Scarlet moved aside. For a moment it seemed as though Hannah might grasp it, but then she cringed into the bed, her eyes wary as they looked into the young woman's smiling face.

'Shelagh will be such a help to us, Mammy.' Scarlet sat on the edge of the bed, her dark eyes pleading, 'and it *will* be wonderful, won't it . . . for me to have someone I can talk to . . . someone nearer my own age? And there's so much work to be done, another pair of hands will be a blessing.'

Hannah looked into her daughter's face and was moved by the loneliness there. She had so much wanted to escape from the bed which had become her prison, she had prayed for the strength that would enable her to carry out her duties, and in her most sensible moments she shamed at how the illness which had brought her down had also blighted Scarlet's already deprived existence. But her prayers had not been answered. It was as though the devil held her down, sucking the strength from her, besieging her troubled mind and darkening her thoughts with the awful belief that, if she was ever to leave the sanctuary of this room, she would be lost for ever. 'Are you coming to look after me?' she asked the kindly faced stranger.

'If you'll let me.'

'You won't make me leave this room?'

'Not unless you want to.'

'I'll never want that. I'm safe here.' Hannah returned her gaze to Scarlet. 'I'm a trial to you, aren't I, child?'

Taking her mammy's fingers into her own, Scarlet

touched them to her lips. 'Don't ever say that,' she
murmured, a little sadly. 'You won't always be ill. Soon
you'll begin to get better . . . and you'll want to do the
things you have always done.'

'Do you really think so?' Hannah was trembling.

'Of course I do, Mammy . . . and you must believe it
too.'

'Promise me something, Scarlet?'

'What is it?'

'You won't leave me, will you? . . . You won't *ever* leave
me?'

'You know I won't, Mammy.' Scarlet kissed Hannah's
brow, then she rose to her feet. 'You've got *two* people to
care for you now . . . and we won't ever be far away.'

'Let me rest now, child.' Hannah was weakened by her
self-imposed confinement.

When Scarlet enquired whether there was anything else
she wanted, Hannah shook her head. But then she said a
strange thing, and it was to Shelagh Williams. 'No one *sent*
you, did they . . . to punish us?' When, obviously taken
aback, the young woman passionately objected to such an
unseemly suggestion, Hannah looked deep and long into
her small brown eyes, saying presently, 'That's alright
then . . . but someone *will* come, one day. That's why I
have to hide.'

Scarlet lingered, eager to put her mammy's mind at rest.
'No one's coming to punish you,' she told her firmly. 'You
have done *nothing* to be punished for.' Hannah shook her
head, smiled, and lay back in the pillow, closing her eyes
and softly singing to herself.

At the door, Scarlet turned. 'I'll be up later with your
milk,' she said softly. She was surprised when the singing
stopped and the blue eyes opened wide. 'Yes, Mammy?'
she asked, hoping that Hannah was about to request that
she be given a helping of food with her milk.

'That boy . . . the one in the barn.'

159

'You mean Silas?'

'Don't be fooled by him. He *knows*! He was there . . . I'm sure of it. He's evil. Be warned.'

'All right, Mammy. Don't worry.' Scarlet's voice was soothing, but it always disturbed her when her mammy spoke about Silas in that way.

When she bade Shelagh Williams goodnight, Scarlet was not surprised when that young woman made reference to Silas, asking, 'Who is he . . . where does he come from?' Even if she had wanted to, Scarlet could not have answered, because she herself had long yearned to know the truth of Silas. After all these years, she had learned nothing; only that she loved him. 'He's just someone who works in my father's smithy,' she replied.

Shelagh Williams made no comment, merely nodding her head and seeming to be satisfied. But when the door was closed and she stood in the darkness alone, her curiosity was already aroused. Why had Vincent Pengally been so adamant that part of her job would include keeping Scarlet and Silas apart? What had so frightened that poor demented woman upstairs that she had imagined someone would be sent to 'punish' her . . . and why had she also warned Scarlet to stay away from Silas, whom she called 'evil'?

She hurried from Greystone House, finding her path lit by the soft light from John Blackwood's window. She secretly thanked his wife for leading her to the position with the Pengallys. What she had heard there tonight was strange and unsettling. But it had not deterred her, for she was not easily frightened. If anything, she was intrigued, and more determined than ever that her place at Greystone House would prove to be all that she had hoped.

'He's planning to leave. If you love him, Scarlet, then you mustn't let him go.' Shelagh had been at Greystone House for a month now, and she had seen for herself how hopelessly in love the two young ones were. She knew no more about Silas now than she had done on first arriving, but it irked her to see how cruelly they were kept apart.

'Don't torment me, Shelagh,' Scarlet implored, turning her face into the pillow. 'If he wants to go, what can *I* do to stop him?' Silas had deliberately avoided her of late. Even when she had craved that secret smile which always gave her hope, he had kept his gaze averted. Twice recently she had crept into the barn, hoping that he might take her into his arms the way he used to before her mammy was taken so ill. But he was never there. She had even wandered the moors, searching for him, in vain. Day and night she was tormented until now, she had begun to shut out all thought of him. Her mammy was right. He *was* evil!

'*Go with him,*' Shelagh urged her now, 'He *will* leave . . . and soon. I've seen the way he's gathering together all the things that are precious to him . . . that small knife with the bone handle, those carvings of wood creatures and the leather boots that John Blackwood gave him . . . all tied up in a neat bundle.'

'*Then let him go!*' Scarlet sat up in the bed, her unhappy eyes raised to the young woman who had lately become a treasured friend. 'We can only ever bring heartache to each other . . . it's *always* been that way.' She bowed her head into her hands and began quietly sobbing. In her heart of hearts she had known that Silas would soon be gone from Greystone House.

'Then you'll do *nothing* to stop him from leaving?'

'Oh, Shelagh,' Scarlet looked up and her face was desolate, 'if I thought I could stop him, I'd move heaven and earth . . . if I thought there could ever be a future for us, there's nothing in the world I wouldn't do. But Silas and I . . . we were never meant to be.' All the bitterness came flooding back. 'Let him go,' she said in a hard voice, 'it's probably for the best.' She dropped her gaze, thinking of Silas, and loving him.

'As you say, it's probably for the best. But if it were *me* . . . and if *I* loved someone, I wouldn't let him go so easily.' Shelagh stood a while longer by the bed. In a moment she was gone and the room was plunged into darkness.

Throwing back the bedclothes and shivering from the rush of cold air, Scarlet left the relative warmth of her bed and went to the window. Here her forlorn gaze was drawn to the barn. All was in darkness and Scarlet wondered whether Silas lay sleeping inside, or whether he had gone into the night, as on so many other occasions. It was almost as if he was tasting little freedoms before venturing out into the wide unknown beyond.

Scarlet's heart was heavy as she thought on the uneasy closeness that was always between her and Silas. Nothing had really changed to make life easier for either of them. Silas was ruled by a hard taskmaster, and she was at the mercy of fate. A cruel fate, that had taken away so much of her innocence and had denied her any normal relationships. She had grown up in a web of deceit and suspicion, and even the comfort she had derived from Silas's company was tainted with real fear. Life was strange, she thought, looking back over the years; strange and terrifying. Yet what was normal? Perhaps John Blackwood and his little family . . . was *that* normal? So many times she had heard John muttering about how 'Pengally's a curious fellow . . . it ain't normal the way he makes you live.' So what *was* normal, and what was unnatural? Certainly Scarlet knew very little of life outside of Greystone House. There were no friends of her own age with whom she could compare herself: the young ones in the village always kept their distance and Scarlet suspected they had grown afraid of her. John said they didn't mean to hurt her, 'it's just that folks are allus suspicious of them they

don't know . . . them that seem to be . . . different.'
Garrett Summers had been a friend. But his father had
sent him away to a business college some two years ago.
On the eve of his departure he had waylaid Scarlet on the
moors, and reminded her of her promise that one day she
would be his wife. 'That's a promise you'll have to keep,'
he had told her, 'when you're of age.' Scarlet had mixed
feelings about him going, because, although she found
him tiresome in comparison with Silas, and she soon
wearied of his uninteresting company, he was a familiar
figure in whom she could confide at least a measure of her
troubles, and he was besotted with her. She was vain
enough to revel in such adulation. It crossed her mind
that, soon, Garrett would be returning home to the
business of overseeing his ageing father's affairs. It was a
passing thought to which Scarlet paid little attention.

What played on Scarlet's mind most at that moment
was the warning Shelagh had made, and it only echoed
the fear in Scarlet's heart; she did not doubt for a moment
that Silas *was* preparing to leave. 'Go with him,' Shelagh
had said, but such a thing was impossible. Silas was a man
now, and he was free as the wind, to go wherever his
fancies took him, while *she* would be a prisoner here for as
long as her mammy needed her; that much she had
promised. Scarlet asked herself whether she would go
with Silas, even if she were able. The very thought filled
her with great excitement, yet it was a prospect that
secretly horrified her. The dark fearsome images created in
her young vulnerable mind by the beast who was her
father were too deep, too real. Even her mammy was in
dread of Silas, and though Scarlet told herself over and
over that it was the illness talking, her own ingrained fear
was always reawakened when her mammy spoke of 'that
boy . . . he's *evil*!' All the same, Scarlet could not imagine
Greystone House without Silas around. The thought was
too painful.

For a long time Scarlet stayed by the window, her dark sorry gaze intent on the barn, and a terrible conflict going on inside her. Then, so strong was the desire to go to him one more time, that she could fight it no longer. Quickly she wrapped a shawl about herself and went on silent footsteps down the stairs, out of the door and across the yard to the barn. The night air was chilly and penetrating.

At the barn door Scarlet paused. Did she *really* want to go on? . . . To find his bed of straw was cold and he was long gone? Or, if he was sleeping there, would he awaken only to send her away? What should she do? Oh, if only she could know how he truly felt towards her! She was painfully undecided. But now that she had ventured so far there was no choice, only to go in and pray that he would treat her kindly.

Coming softly into the barn, Scarlet could never remember a time when she was so unsure of herself, so afraid that she might be rejected. Her heart beat so furiously that she imagined its echo all around her. Slowly she felt her way forward, the pitch blackness relieved only by the shafts of moonlight filtering in through the dust-laden windows. With outstretched hands she touched those familiar things that marked her way . . . the railing in the horses' stable, the harness hung close by, and the studded wall that told her how close she was to the place where Silas had lain his dark head these long years: as an outcast infant, then a boy, and now a man.

The smell and unique atmosphere of the barn assailed her senses: that dry warm smell of horse and the sweet sting of leather, the sharp crackle of straw underfoot and that special cosiness that only the four walls of a wooden barn could create. Little by little she inched towards the spot which she knew Silas had made his own. In the semi-darkness, Scarlet peered downwards. *He was there!* Silas was sleeping there! Her tremulous heart skipped a beat, then a sudden urge to run away took hold of her.

She turned, but was quickly halted and then astonished by the softness of his voice. 'Scarlet.' It breathed into her heart and soothed away her fears Oh, how many times had she prayed that he would break the silence she had so deeply resented? The tears sprang to her eyes as, turning again, she gazed down at that shadowy face that was imprinted on her heart. 'You called my name,' she murmured, with a soft nervous laugh. 'You called me back.' She thought she had never heard a voice so lovely.

He reached up and, falling to her knees, she tenderly moulded herself into his arms. 'You're not angry?' she asked, a great happiness spreading through her when his answer was a kiss. She felt the shawl being plucked from her back; her nightgown was slid gently away, and she was naked beside him. The touch of his hand against her skin was like gossamer. 'I love you so,' she murmured against his mouth, shivering with unbearable delight when his fingers played with her breasts and teased her nipples. There was a fire inside her, devouring everything that was gentle. 'Take me, Silas,' she urged, beginning to claw at his nakedness.

'Ssh.' His quiet murmur sought to soothe her. She felt him harden against her and her passion was all-consuming. His warm firm nakedness excited her. She wanted him, *needed* him as she had never craved anything before. When he straddled her, his mouth clinging to hers and his whole magnificent body covering her, she cried out to possess him, arching herself into him and gripping his skin with such fierceness that he began moaning. When he entered her, it was as though her very heart had burst with ecstasy. They were one. At last! At last, he was hers. Oh, how naturally they moved together, how desperate was their need of each other. The tender gentle rhythm became frenzied, the exquisite pain he created in her made her gasp, but she felt herself fulfilled at long last. Something beautiful was happening and she wanted it never to end. 'Oh, Silas . . . I love you so!' He was in her arms, in her body and soul, and nothing else mattered in the whole world.

Time and again they spent their fevered passion until, exhausted and gratified, they lay in each other's arms, in awe of what they had done and a little afraid because of it. In his strong warm arms, Scarlet was bathed in happiness. There was no wrong in their taking of each other, nothing shameful: it was always meant to be. She felt that instinctively, and she told him so. 'You *do* love me, don't you?' Suddenly she was afraid. For a long time he gave no answer, and she prayed that he would not put up that awful barrier of silence between them again. Not now. Not when everything had changed. At length he spoke, hesitant and vibrant, like music to her ears.

'You must know I love you,' he said. But then he raised himself to look into her face, and what she saw in those incredible violet eyes caused her heart to miss a beat. 'I have to go. Trust me, Scarlet, but I have to leave this place . . . I have to find an identity, to find *myself*. I *must*, if I'm ever to know peace of mind. I'll come back for you, I promise.'

Every word was like a knife through Scarlet's heart. 'No!' She threw her arms round his neck and clung to him. 'You can't leave . . . not now.' He shook his head and lowered his gaze. Scornfully she recoiled from him, raking her clothes together and fighting them on. '*Then damn you!*' The words spat out. 'Damn your black heart. Go then! . . . But remember this. If you go, don't ever come back. D'you hear?' The tears ran unheeded down her face.

Suddenly he was on his feet, grabbing her to him, fighting her resistance. 'Don't you see . . . things have to change for us? The time isn't right for you and me, Scarlet. But it *will* be, one day. On that day, I'll come for you. *Nothing* will keep me away, I swear!' His voice was low and controlled, designed to placate her.

Pulling away, Scarlet fell back against the studded wall, her coal-black eyes made magnificent by the incoming moonlight. 'Go to Hell!' she hissed, spitting on the ground with contempt. 'You're no different, are you? . . . No different from *any* of them.' Suddenly her eyes were wicked. 'Oh, but maybe you are different after all.' The urge to torment him rose in her like a devil. 'All my life I've been warned against you . . . even my *mammy's* afraid of you. *Are you evil, Silas?*' She was beyond reason now but, even in her insane desire to hurt him, she was hurting herself more. 'Were you in the cellar, Silas? . . . what was it you did that so terrified my mammy?' Horrified, she saw that she had gone too far. She saw his face darken and all the old nightmares took hold of her. When he stepped forward to take her by the wrists, she was shocked to find that she was quivering with fright.

'*Your mammy's right.*' Scarlet's accusations had only fuelled the very reasons why he must flee from Greystone House. He *also* had nightmares to erase and fiendish images to lay to rest. 'She has every right to be afraid.' His violet eyes were brilliant as stones, yet scarred with pain. '*I am evil!*' he snarled, bearing down on her. Suddenly he looked into Scarlet's wide frightened eyes and he sensed her deeper horror of him. It cut him to the core. 'Get out,' he moaned, roughly thrusting her aside. 'Get out of my sight!'

Blinded by her tears, Scarlet ran from the barn. Besieged by terrible feelings of confusion, shame and horror, she wanted only to escape. In the comparative safety of her room, Scarlet knelt by the window, watching and waiting. After a while, she saw him leave, disappearing into the night like a shadow. With a cold heart she climbed into bed and gave herself up to the monsters that had long haunted her sleep. She felt cheated and lonely. But, for some strange reason she could not fully understand, she felt something else, something she had not experienced in a long long time. She felt *safe*!

From deep in the shadows, there was another who had watched Silas disappear into the night. The eyes that followed his departure were cruel and quietly smiling. The voice that softly permeated the night air was uniquely sinister. 'May the devil prevent you from ever returning,' it whispered, 'for only *you* might have stopped me. Now, there is no one to stand in my way!'

The dawn was beginning to struggle through a greyish sky when Silas came upon the cottage. The events of the night had sent him fleeing from Greystone House with desperate urgency. He had stumbled away, his heart and mind bursting with thoughts of Scarlet but, however much he adored her, he could not stay. The past would not let him stay, and it was the past that dictated his future with Scarlet. There was too much unresolved, too many questions, too much fear. He had to put a distance between himself and all of that. Or go slowly mad!

In his blind haste, Silas had missed his footing at the top of a dangerously steep incline. In the darkness he had tumbled some short way down the stony slope, slipping and sliding until his fall was broken by a gorse bush whose wickedly sharp thorns had ripped and clawed at his leg. Now, bleeding and exhausted, he hobbled towards the cottage, his eyes peeled for a water trough or a pump where he might wash off the dirt and blood that was caked to the ugly gash below his knee. The awful experience had left him bruised and aching in every bone.

He could find no pump or trough. But situated by the outhouse door was a partly filled rain butt. There was no sign of life in the immediate vicinity of the cottage, and Silas assumed that whoever lived there was still slumbering. He washed his leg as best he could, then after some deliberation Silas decided to make himself comfortable in a corner of the outhouse, where the sharpening breeze wouldn't chill his bones, and where he might avail himself of a few hours sleep before resuming his long journey to Barnstaple. He suspected there was a route many miles over the moors, going through the tiny isolated hamlets and trekking across hostile land with which he was not immediately familiar, but he had chosen to follow an established route, by way of Lynmouth. Once in Barnstaple, he would seek out work of the kind he knew . . . blacksmith's work. But his ambition was to eventually acquire his own smithy, when he would be free at last, independent of anyone, and in a position to return for Scarlet. It never crossed his mind that she might refuse him, because he himself could never envisage a life without her by his side. For now, though, he had to prove himself; he had to *find* himself. He thought he had never done a harder thing than to thrust Scarlet away, even while the memory of her in his arms still warmed his heart. But it would all come right one day, he knew it must. He prayed it would, for there was no other reason to live.

Opening the outhouse door, he peered inside. It was dark. A strange sweet smell clogged his nostrils. But it was dry here, and out of the wind; he would settle down for a while, rest until daylight. Then he would be on his way. The thought cheered him as he ventured inside, closing the door behind him. *That smell!* Dry, rancid, offensive smell. It turned his stomach. But, no matter, he had lived in a barn these many years, shared his abode with horses and other creatures that found shelter alongside him. They all carried their own smells. He had grown used to them. But this smell was somehow different. It was sickening to his senses, and stuck in his throat like a bad taste.

Silas felt his way along the wall to the farthest corner, away from the door and window where the increasing cold wind might force a way in. Putting down the small bundle of belongings, which had been safely tied to his belt, he made a pillow of it and, after comfortably positioning his torn leg, he curled up against the wall, and fell into a light uneasy sleep.

It was the scream that woke Silas. The muffled scream that was his own, and the pain that seared through him with a vengeance. With a start, he sat bolt upright, staring about with wild frightened eyes and an inexplicable sensation of terror causing him to tremble violently. The beads of sweat on his back broke out to trickle furiously down his spine and, for what seemed the longest moment of his life, he was held in a grip of terror that paralysed him. It was still dark, but the dawn light was already invading the sky and probing its way through the tiny window. Inside the outhouse little pockets of light began to spread, illuminating the gloomy interior. Suddenly the penetrating pain that had woken him caused him to cry out loud. His hand went involuntarily to grasp the wound on his leg; instead his fingers closed round a scurrying shape, warm and alive, staring at him with glittering beady eyes, its long sharp teeth bared and stained with blood. *His* blood! With a cry of terror, Silas scrambled to his feet, his one frantic thought was to flee. In his blind panic, he fell headlong onto what he at first thought was an old grey blanket, but beneath his weight it was split asunder, its thousand brilliant eyes all turned in his direction. *Rats!* Countless numbers of them, and all crazed by the smell of blood! Quickly the rats were on him, swarming over him and pressing him down. Down, down, he stretched out his arms and then he saw the bones! *Human bones*, stripped of their flesh by razor-sharp teeth and relentless ripping claws. All of Silas's senses were assailed by the horror of what was before his eyes: the two skulls stared at him, the smaller one picked clean until it shone, the other ungainly, strangely deformed, still ragged with blood and sinew, and its one remaining incredibly beautiful eye looking right through him, pleading, damning! He heard the unearthly scream. *Was that really him?* He felt the sharp incisors cut into his neck. He cried out, violently shivering as he scrambled to his feet, shaking them off, hitting out like a demented thing. He was both horrified and astonished at the tenacious way in which they clung to him. At last he was free, and then he ran, his mind reeling with shock, oblivious to everything but that he must escape, *escape, escape*! But he could not escape those skulls and that uniquely beautiful eye that seemed so alive. *And familiar!* He had seen such eyes before, *but where?*

A new and even more terrible sense of horror took hold of Silas. He was a small boy in a darkened cellar. The eye stared in his mind; *it was in the cellar with him*. No! He must not go on torturing himself. It was all too real. *Too damning!*

Behind him, he could hear a door being whipped back and forth by the howling wind. But he did not look back. He dared not.

'We're warning everyone in the area.' Constable Stewart was a portly fellow with a perfect set of teeth and a black moustache that drooped to his jowls. He had a habit of constantly fidgeting with the chin-strap of his helmet, as though he was fending off a horrible choking death. 'It's a terrible thing, Mr Pengally.' He addressed himself to the master of the house but, seeing as his errand to Greystone House had necessitated calling together all who lived and worked here, he shifted his stern expression from one to the other. 'Rest assured we'll leave no stone unturned in pursuit of whoever's responsible. Meanwhile . . . I suggest you all keep your wits about you, should any strangers happen this way. Everyone in the village will be alerted . . . I don't like to say this, sir . . . but, with you and your family living so close to the edge of the moors, you need to be extra vigilant. Lock all doors and windows securely at night.'

'I don't think I need *you* to tell me how to keep my house safe from intruders,' Vincent Pengally remarked in a surly tone. 'You've done your duty. Now, if you don't mind, I've a smithy to run.' He came from the fireplace where he had been standing, legs astride and obviously resentful of the constable's errand. 'Instead of wandering about from house to house, I should have thought you'd be better employed combing the moors. If *I'd* murdered somebody, that's where I'd make for. While you're standing here talking to us, your quarry's long gone!' He snorted and laughed, shaking his head as he brushed by. At the door, he turned. 'No doubt you'll be on your way any minute now?' When the constable remarked that he was just about to leave, the blacksmith briskly departed. Outside, though, he paused and leaned up against the wall, his colour drained and his breathing erratic. His nerves were frayed. The constable's visit had further unnerved him, more than he would ever admit. 'Murdered they were,' he had said, 'we don't know for sure how it was done . . . being as there was little left to examine after the rats were finished with them. But one of the skeletons was crushed to a pulp . . . very strange.' He hadn't wanted to hear any more, especially when the constable had pointed out, 'it's not likely the murders are connected in any way to the disturbing incidents that took place here some time ago. But it is something we need to bear in mind.' Fearful that he might be seen at any minute, the blacksmith hurried to his forge, but the constable's words wouldn't leave him. They haunted him . . . just as Evelyn's warning had haunted him since the day she died: 'If you harm him, I swear I'll come back.' 'I fed him, and gave him a place to sleep,' he muttered, the sweat running down his back and his every limb trembling. 'He went of his own accord. I can't hurt him now . . . so leave me be!'

'So, you'll remember what I said?' Constable Stewart prepared to leave. 'Oh, by the way, Miss Williams, thank you kindly for the tea and biscuits . . . much appreciated.'

'You're very welcome,' Shelagh Williams smiled warmly, collecting up the soiled crockery, 'and I do hope you catch whoever did such a dreadful thing.' She shivered, and the tea cup rattled in her hand. Giving a little cry, she hurried away into the kitchen, where she proceeded to wash the constable's tea cup vigorously.

'Oh, don't you worry,' the constable addressed himself now to John and Scarlet, 'it won't be easy, I dare say, but we'll no doubt track him down.'

'And you've no idea at all what happened?' John was afraid for his wife and baby Trent.

'Well now, I'm not at liberty to say too much, you understand . . . but, well . . . we do have our suspicions, of course. There's the fact that one of them . . . we assume the old woman known as the herb-gatherer . . . had most of her bones broken.' He shook his head, 'Terrible . . . terrible! We haven't established the identity of the other, a young lad . . . horribly crippled it seems. A relative, perhaps. When we contact the old woman's estranged husband, he'll no doubt be able to throw some light on that. Another thing . . . we discovered the old woman's collection of plants and herbs . . . potions, that sort of thing. Curious thing, though. The jars were all neatly labelled on a shelf in the pantry, all mostly full . . . with the exception of two that had been ransacked. Both of these jars had been emptied and flung aside. They were marked "poison".' He looked from Scarlet to John and back again to Scarlet's white face. Touching his fingertips against the brim of his helmet, he told her in a kindly voice. 'Sorry to have been the bearer of such unwelcome news, but *do* remember, miss . . . secure the doors and windows at night, and don't wander outside in the dark.' He bade them good-day, hurrying away and cursing himself for blurting out privileged information. But then again, he reminded himself, the old tinker who found the bodies knew about the missing poison, because in fact he was right there when the matter was pointed out. The constable smiled to himself. That poor tinker, now *there* was an unfortunate soul if ever he saw one. What a terrible fright the old man had experienced. And all he had in the world was a little tied-up bundle, containing a bone-handled knife and a few surprisingly attractive carvings.

CHAPTER TEN

'What's ailing you, young 'un . . . has the cat got your tongue?' John Blackwood dug his fork into the decaying vegetable matter which he then pitched up onto the wooden handbarrow. His words were jovial, but laced with real concern for Scarlet. 'I thought you'd be over the moon . . . now that you've got that nice Miss Williams to share the workload.' He paused in his labours. 'She seems a pleasant enough soul . . . and from what you tell me your mammy's taken a real liking to her.' He pressed his own hands on the small of his back and stretched with a groan. He was not fond of hot weather, and this month of June, in the year of our Lord 1920, was one of the hottest he could remember.

Scarlet was also glad of a short rest, and not only because of the sun blazing down on them. There was another, more disturbing reason, but her ready smile betrayed nothing of the trauma in her mind. 'Shelagh coming to Greystone House was the best thing that's ever happened,' she said, momentarily glancing towards the smithy, 'but how she puts up with my father's black moods I'll never know. It has been wonderful . . . the way Mammy has come to trust and like her. She's so good for me, too. I can never thank you and Mrs Blackwood enough . . . if it hadn't been for your persuasion, Shelagh would never have been taken on.'

'Then what's ailing you?' he insisted. But then a thought struck him and he called himself all kinds of a fool. Using his fork as a crutch to lean on, he drew closer to Scarlet, and in softer voice he asked, 'It's Silas, ain't it? . . . you're missing him real bad?' He had thought it unusual that Scarlet had not once mentioned his name these past three months, though he suspected the young man was never far from her secret thoughts. Vincent Pengally had made it clear to them all that Silas's name was never again to be uttered, but John thought it strange that Scarlet had not confided in him, in spite of her father. 'Happen he'll turn up again one of these days.'

'It does seem peculiar not to have him around,' she confessed, 'but perhaps it's all for the best. I don't think of him much,' she lied, 'and I don't care if he never comes back.' Contrary to what she had told John, Scarlet thought of Silas often, and there were times when she loved him more fiercely than ever. But she could not rid herself of the horror she felt whenever he invaded her most secret thoughts. Somewhere, deep inside her, she truly believed that he was every bit as evil and harmful as her father had always insisted. Even now, long after Silas had left Greystone House, her poor mammy would constantly ask after 'that boy in the barn', and she would work herself up into such a sorry state that only Scarlet could soothe her fears.

But there was no one to soothe Scarlet's own fears. In the week following Silas's departure, she had confided in the kindly Shelagh, but that dear soul could offer no real comfort; in fact, the comment she *did* make only seemed to heighten Scarlet's inherent suspicions, for what she said was, 'Nobody knows who he is, or where he came from, and why did he choose to remain silent all those years? That alone is strange. I only know of Silas what little you've told me, but I think you should be guided by your father who loves you . . . and by your mammy's instincts. After all, Scarlet, it seems to me that the young man was never like other young men; though of course I can only judge by what you and John Blackwood have confided in me. I do know this though . . . your mammy is driven beyond endurance by the very *mention* of him!'

Scarlet had heeded Shelagh's considered warning, and it only echoed what she herself was convinced of. Yet she still needed him. *Especially now.* Overriding her need though, was an instinctive abhorrence of him. He *was* strange, just as her father, and now Shelagh, had pointed out. But that very fact still drew her to him. He was proud and beautiful, passionate and magnificent. She recalled the night when they had made such glorious love that even in a lifetime she would not forget. The memory stayed precious in her heart, as did her everlasting love for him. Her fear of him could not penetrate that love, but now she was glad he was gone from Greystone House, and she prayed he would never return. He had gone, but she had been left something precious. Something Silas must never be allowed to take from her. Something she need *never* be afraid of in the way she had grown afraid of others. A warm feeling spread through her. The deeper consequences of her night of love with Silas were yet to come, she knew that; she also knew that when he was made aware of the facts, her father would bring the wrath of Hell down on her. But this time she would stand up to him. This time she would not be fighting just for herself. She was afraid, there was no denying it: afraid and unsure of what the future held in store. But she was made even more desperate by the nagging fear that, on a day in the future, Silas might well return to claim what was his. She was reminded of his strange and unpredictable ways and the sadistic manner in which he had taken her to him, and then so callously walked away. Was it so surprising that she had deliberately hardened her heart towards him? She recalled the words her father had drummed into her over and over, until she knew they must be true. 'He's evil . . .

he eats little innocents like you!' How then could she let him destroy that wonderful new creation that even now was growing inside her. A sensation of revulsion rippled through her: supposing the child was not fathered by Silas, but . . . NO! Scarlet put up her two hands and pressed them hard against her temples. The thought was so horrific she wanted to tear it out and shred it to pieces! It wasn't true, it couldn't possibly be. Her prayers had been answered even before that night with Silas. All that was over when her mammy had fallen ill. The baby was hers! It belonged to no one else. Earth would have to shift in its heaven before she would let any man take it from her!

Plunging the white-hot iron into the cooling waters of the trough, Vincent Pengally glanced to where John and Scarlet appeared to be deep in conversation. At once incensed by the fact that they could find time to stand about, while he on the other hand was obliged to work harder than the horses he shod, it was his intention to confront them; in particular John Blackwood, who was paid for his labours in money earned by a blacksmith's sweat! It never occurred to him that adverse seasons and unyielding land could also demand a man's back to be broken.

'Good-day, Mr Pengally.' The sound of approaching hooves had caused the blacksmith to look up. His mood was not made more pleasant by the appearance of Garrett Summers, a man who, in Vincent Pengally's ill-considered opinion, had no real experience of hard work. He acknowledged the polite and amiable greeting with a grudging nod. He had little time for such useless gentry. Many of his own ancestors were afflicted with the same malingering disease. There was an envy in him, a bitterness, and an awareness that he was no longer a young virile man. The years had crept up on him. Time was seeking revenge, and it was a souring experience.

'She's thrown a shoe . . . must have happened when we

jumped the ditch; I walked her here. She's a good mare . . . won't give you any trouble.' He coaxed the big bay mare into the smithy.

'Bloody right she won't,' snapped the blacksmith, bending to run his fingers along her fetlock. Raising her hoof, he took one glance. 'Hold her head,' he instructed. After that he did not speak another word, but proceeded to attend to the mare's hoof with the speed and skill that had earned him his enviable reputation as the finest blacksmith for many miles.

Watching him work, Garrett Summers was greatly impressed by the dexterity and single-mindedness of this middle-aged man, whose broad shoulders were beginning to stoop permanently after years of back-bending. He had no liking for Scarlet's ill-mannered father, but he admired the man's devotion to the crippling labours demanded of him. 'Where's Silas?' he asked now, looking about, and hoping he might also catch a glimpse of the lovely Scarlet. Neither the blacksmith's daughter nor his apprentice were anywhere to be seen. Embarrassed by the blacksmith's silence, Garrett attempted to draw him into a conversation regarding current events. 'I'm relieved to be back from business college,' he ventured, somewhat nervously. 'I would have learned more at my father's side.' His voice betrayed a degree of bitterness. 'In my opinion, it's experience that counts . . . I did argue that very point with my father, but he would insist on my going away.' He looked down to where the blacksmith was filing the horny hoof. When he saw that his words had fallen on deaf ears, he stretched his neck again to search out any sign of Scarlet. God, he had missed her, and what trouble he had gone to, so that he might bring about a meeting between them; it was a tricky business prising off the mare's shoe in such a way that it seemed to have been accidentally thrown. The silence was unbearable, broken only by the harsh rasping of the file. 'I have it in mind to pay a visit to London again, in the next few days. King George V is opening the Imperial War Museum at Crystal Palace today.' Anything to do with war fascinated him; he had bitterly regretted that his wound had prevented him from taking a full part in the recent world war. Still, the wound was fully healed now, and the limp only slight, though he was warned that it would always be with him. He grew irritated. Where was Scarlet?

'You look lovely child.' Hannah cast her pale blue eyes over Scarlet's trim and shapely figure. 'It's a pretty dress; Shelagh's very clever.' The smile faded from her frail features as she began impatiently flicking her hand towards the door. 'Now go away, the both of you. Leave me along.' She scowled, deliberately turning her head in the direction of the window and pretending to be drawn by something interesting there.

'Alright, Mammy,' Scarlet despaired of her mammy ever fully recovering. 'I'm sorry if we've tired you out.' She was both saddened and rankled by the little woman's seeming inability to resume her proper place in this house. Together she and the equally disappointed Shelagh made their way downstairs.

In the kitchen Scarlet made a pot of tea and Shelagh cut two small portions from the fruit cake which she had earlier retrieved from the oven range. 'Don't be upset,' she told Scarlet as the two of them sat down at the big old table. 'I think we'll just have to settle for the fact that Hannah has a long way to go before she's well again.' She smiled at Scarlet with quiet brown eyes. 'Stand up . . . let me have another look at you in your new dress.'

Scarlet felt very special in the dress that Shelagh had made for her. It was calf-length and in a drop-waisted style that, according to Shelagh, was 'all the rage'. Its colour was the most flattering shade of lemon, with strips of black figured into the scalloped neck and hem. Shelagh had even persuaded Vincent Pengally that his daughter needed new footwear. The shoes were black patent leather, with little heels and dainty straps that fastened with round glass buttons, and now, as Scarlet twirled in front of Shelagh, she was more grateful than ever for the young woman's friendship. 'It *is* a lovely dress, Shelagh,' she laughed breathlessly. 'Thank you.'

As always, Shelagh was greatly moved by Scarlet's exquisite loveliness, that fine shapely figure, that seemed even more attractive of late; those dark hypnotic eyes and long rich hair that shone blue like a raven's wing. 'The dress doesn't do you justice,' she said, afterwards seeming strangely quietened by Scarlet's beauty.

'It's the prettiest dress I've ever had!' Returning to the table, Scarlet leaned towards Shelagh's brown head and kissed it tenderly. 'Mammy's right. You *are* clever,' she laughed, 'and you bake the best fruit cake in Dunster!'

'Go on with you. You're not such a bad cook yourself, Scarlet Pengally! And I dare say you could sew up a better dress than that one . . . if you put your mind to it.'

Scarlet loved the gentle rivalry that had developed between her and Shelagh. Suddenly she had the strongest urge to confide in her, to tell the secret that kept her awake at nights. She even began, 'Shelagh.'

'Yes?'

'Nothing . . . it's alright.' Scarlet was shocked at how close she had come to revealing what she had deliberately kept to herself these past weeks. Now some deeper instinct warned her to keep the secret for as long as possible. In that moment she felt so alone: afraid of the day when her father would discover that she was with child; and saddened because she was unable to seek solace from her mammy. Scarlet suspected that when the time came for the truth of her predicament to out, Shelagh would be the first to know. Even that thought gave her small comfort. 'I'd better go and change.' She left the food untouched.

'John will wonder what's taking so long, and there's still a great deal of work to be done before we can call it a day.' Suddenly, her small bubble of happiness had cruelly burst. She felt dejected.

Some short time later, Scarlet emerged from the house, her attractive figure once more clothed in the brown unseemly smock and on her dainty feet the familiar sturdy high-laced boots. Her long black hair was tied into the nape of her neck and her dark eyes had lost their sparkle. Seeing her approach, John appeared relieved, beckoning her on and chiding her with a stern look. Scarlet quickened her steps, unaware that Shelagh watched her from the window, and completely oblivious to the fact that Garrett's yearning eyes followed her every step.

But, if Scarlet was unaware of Garrett Summer's attention, Shelagh was not. She saw how he followed Scarlet with adoring eyes, and a plan stirred within her.

'Stop that nonsense!' Pengally banged his fist on the table and fixed Shelagh with hard grey eyes. 'I don't hold with no chanting in this house!' He had the look of a man demented.

'I was thanking the Good Lord for what we have on the table,' Shelagh told him, her gaze unfaltering.

'Thank *me*, then! . . . because whatever's on the table in this house was put there by *me*!'

Scarlet deliberately defused the situation by taking up her plate and scooping onto it a small helping of the crispy roast potatoes. When, in surly manner, her father instructed her, 'Kindly wait until *my* plate is filled,' she breathed a sigh of relief. Not for the first time she wondered why it was that Shelagh constantly flouted her father's rigid rules and purposely set out to antagonise him. The evening meal continued in an awkward silence.

When there came a loud insistent knocking on the back door, Scarlet hurriedly excused herself from the table, grateful for an opportunity to escape. Sitting down to a meal with her father was never a pleasant affair, and this evening it was especially uncomfortable. Scarlet wondered whether it was because of the secret she kept, a sordid and mortifying secret, the consequences of which she dared not dwell on for too long.

'Evening, Miss Pengally.' It was the village butcher, a tall slim fellow with a long angular face and earth-coloured eyes which, Scarlet thought, possessed the unnerving ability to see right through her. She inwardly squirmed beneath his slow attractive smile as he stretched out to hand her the tiny bundle. 'You'll find it all there, just as Miss Williams ordered it . . . neck-end, pigs' liver and two plump hearts. All fresh killed.' He drew another smaller bundle from the wicker-basket on his bicycle. 'Miss Williams especially asked for this to be kept separate.'

'What is it?' The bundle felt warm and pliable in her hand.

'Mr Pengally's favourite. Veal. I understand neither you nor Miss Williams have a liking for it?' He smiled handsomely. 'It makes cooking the very devil, when one person has a fancy for a particular thing.'

Not caring for his manner, Scarlet retreated. 'Thank you,' she said politely, quickly closing the door before he might continue the conversation. She did not like that man! According to John, the butcher was a relative stranger to Dunster, having bought up the butcher shop and adjoining slaughterhouse some eighteen months ago. Apparently he was well liked in the village but, for some inexplicable reason, he made Scarlet cringe. Since Hannah's illness he had kindly offered to deliver the meat order to Greystone House and Shelagh had not seen fit to alter the arrangement, which had proved to be most satisfactory. Scarlet had been inside his shop on only one occasion. It had been on a market-day, when John sent her for some of the herb sausages that his Ada was so fond of, and which the new butcher made to perfection. It had been a dreadful experience for Scarlet, and one she was not likely to forget in a hurry. On entering the shop, she had found it empty, so she called out. The butcher appeared from a side room, carelessly leaving the door open while he attended to Scarlet. She was able to see right into the slaughterhouse, where hung many bloody carcasses in various stages of mutilation. The sight of that, coupled with his obvious delight in severing the meat apart at his counter, had sickened Scarlet to such an extent that she could never go inside that shop again. Nor could she look at the butcher, without seeing the awful devastation caused by him. Later she had related all of this to John, who had laughed heartily at 'such girlish nonsense', telling her that butchery was no different to what *they* did to the cabbages they tore from the ground. 'It's all to the same ends, my girl!' he'd chided, 'and don't you forget that.'

At the end of the meal, Scarlet was glad when her father retired to the parlour. As usual, he had picked his plate clean. Her own meal was virtually untouched.

'What's the use of my preparing a good wholesome meal, if you're not going to eat it?' Shelagh wanted to know. 'You've hardly touched it.'

'I know, and I'm sorry.' Scarlet's insides hadn't stopped churning throughout the meal, and she had feared that at any minute she might have to make a hurried exit. She might have blamed the butcher, but she couldn't blame him for yesterday, and twice last week, when she was plagued by the same awful sensation of nausea. She could feel Shelagh curiously observing her, and at once she was on her guard. 'I'll start washing up,' she offered, beginning to gather the dishes in a pile. She dared not look at Shelagh, for fear her secret would betray itself.

'Come and sit here, Scarlet.' Shelagh sat upright in her chair and patted the table-top. 'While your father's quietly engaged in the parlour, I'd like to talk to you.' There was a concerned look in her small brown eyes.

'Talk about what?' Scarlet wanted to know as she put away the dishcloth and came to sit opposite Shelagh. Strangely enough, Scarlet had seen Shelagh regarding her in a curious manner once or twice these past weeks, causing her to wonder whether her condition had at last begun to show itself. She hoped not. 'Is it trouble with Mammy?' she asked, eager to divert attention from herself.

'No ... no trouble with Hannah,' Shelagh smiled, 'unless it's that, at times, she can be more of a handful than I ever imagined.' Her expression quickly changed to one of intimacy. 'It's you, Scarlet. I'm concerned about *you*. Oh, look ... I know I'm not too many years older than you, but I care for you, you know that. I've come to look on you more as a sister than the daughter of my employer.'

'I know that, Shelagh, and you're a good friend.' Scarlet had grown increasingly apprehensive on hearing Shelagh's words. 'But, why would you be concerned about me?' She waited for the answer, knowing what it would be.

'I'm not prying, Scarlet, believe me. It's just that ... I've heard you being ill in the mornings, when your father's gone to the smithy. Some days you can hardly *bear* to look at a plate of food, and you look so tired and thin of late.' She reached out to touch Scarlet's hand. 'Circumstances thrust me out into the wide world when I was only fourteen.' Her eyes became quiet, and painfully sad. 'I've seen so much, Scarlet ... *too* much, and I've learned how to tell the signs.' She waited until Scarlet's dark eyes were looking into her own, before going on in a gentler tone. 'Are you expecting a child?'

Scarlet had anticipated the question, yet when it came it was with a cruel bluntness that shocked her. Her first reaction was one of indignation. How dare Shelagh ask her such a thing? What right had she to pry, and yes . . . she *was* prying! For a moment she gave no answer. Instead, she lowered her troubled gaze, all manner of things agitating in her mind. She supposed Shelagh was speaking out of concern for her, and she knew that she ought to be grateful, yet she was angry. Foolishly, she had hoped to conceal the truth for many weeks yet because, once it became known, the consequences would be una-voidable. Certainly her father must not know; not until it was inevitable, and for some inexplicable reason Scarlet's instincts told her that her mother must *never* know; at least, not until she was fully in her right mind. A great loneliness settled on Scarlet, as she thought on the secret which had plagued her even more of late. It was true that she craved someone to talk to, someone who might share her anxiety and lessen the burden; it was also true that Shelagh had a certain understanding in her character, that tempted Scarlet to confide in her. Besides, she reminded herself, Shelagh was waiting; she could sense those deter-mined brown eyes on her. Now she looked up to study those same inquisitive eyes, before she spoke. 'My parents must not know . . . not until they have to.' It was said, and Scarlet was surprised to feel as though a great weight had slipped from her shoulders.

'Oh, Scarlet!' The small eyes grew wide and bright. 'I'll help you all I can, you know that. And of course we must keep it from your parents at all costs.' Her voice dropped to a fearful whisper, 'Especially from your father, or there's no telling what he might do!' She had seen for herself how unnaturally Vincent Pengally doted on Scarlet. One thing puzzled her, though, and she was urged to ask, 'Whose is it, Scarlet?' She was well aware that Scarlet had little contact with the young men from the village. That left only Silas, who had been gone for some time now; John Blackwood, and that was unthink-able, and Garrett Summers. He seemed the likeliest one.

'Is it Garrett's?' she asked at length.

'Garrett Summers?' Scarlet was astonished. 'Why should you think that?'

'I'm sorry, Scarlet.' Shelagh was suitably remorseful. 'It's really none of my business but, like I said . . . I'll help you all I can.' She couldn't help adding, 'If it *is* Garrett Summers's child, then I'm sure he'll do the right thing by you. His father's a wealthy man, and Garrett stands to inherit it all some day.'

'I don't want to talk about it, Shelagh.' Scarlet thought it strange that Shelagh had jumped to that particular conclusion. But then she reminded herself that Shelagh knew very little of Silas, or of their dangerous feelings for each other, because he had left Greystone House almost as soon as Shelagh had arrived. Perhaps it was just as well.

'Tell me only as much as you want to.' Shelagh collected the candleholder from the mantelpiece and, after lighting the candlewick, she took it up, coming to where Scarlet was still seated at the table, head bowed and deep in thought. 'Your secret is safe with me, Scarlet,' she said. 'Trust me.'

'Thank you, Shelagh. You really are a good friend.' Scarlet looked up with a warm smile. 'Later . . . I might want to talk.'

'Whenever you're ready, I'll be a willing listener.' Shelagh took the candle and quietly departed the room, leaving Scarlet more relieved, yet still deeply anxious as to the outcome of it all.

Scarlet would have been even more anxious if she had known that every word of her conversation with Shelagh had been overheard.

When Shelagh had gone before her to make Hannah comfortable for the night, Scarlet stood at the parlour door, gazing at her father, who was sleeping in the chair. The flickering light from the lamp on the mantelpiece played on his face, accentuating the ungainly features and creating such an eerie effect that, for an unnerving moment, Scarlet imagined him to be looking straight at her. Even in his sleep, he had the uncanny power to make her uneasy. In spite of the fact that he was now middle-aged and the passage of time had taken its toll, he remained a formidable force, physically powerful and mentally hostile; although of late, following the series of unpleasant and bizarre events, he had become increasingly nervous and strangely secretive, throwing himself into his work with such savagery that might cripple a lesser man; he had resisted employing another in place of Silas, and so his work was especially demanding. Before turning into the corridor, Scarlet wondered how he would react when he discovered that she was with child. The prospect filled her with dread.

Upstairs in Hannah's room, Scarlet found Shelagh softly singing as she busied herself in tidying away the paraphernalia that seemed always to accumulate during a normal day. Hannah lay, drowsily watching.

'Not asleep yet?' Coming to the bed. Scarlet kissed her mammy and afterwards sat on the nearby chair, gently stroking Hannah's brow.

'I *am* tired,' Hannah murmured, closing her eyes, 'but I mustn't go to sleep.' Her pale blue eyes opened in alarm. 'If I *do* go to sleep, you won't let anyone else come into my room, will you?'

'Of course not.' Scarlet's smile was reassuring. 'No one will come into your room, Mammy . . . believe me.' These past weeks she imagined the darling woman to be shrinking before her eyes. 'You're not to worry about such things. Shelagh and I will keep you safe.' Still the blue eyes gazed at her, almost unseeing.

'Come on now, Hannah.' Shelagh came to the bed and tucked the eiderdown tighter across Hannah's narrow shoulders. 'You know perfectly well that you'll come to no harm. Not while we're both here to keep an eye on you. So you can go to sleep with an easy mind.' When she saw Hannah's tired eyelids droop, she blew out the candle, collected the lamp and touched Scarlet on the shoulder. 'We'd best leave her now,' she whispered, 'she'll be alright, don't fret.'

Glancing at the small still figure in the bed, Scarlet was satisfied that if they went now, they would not be missed. She followed Shelagh, going on tiptoe across the room. As they drew level with the window, Shelagh gasped aloud and drew back as though shocked. Half-turning her head, she stared at Scarlet with round frightened eyes. *'There's someone out there!'* she said in a loud whisper, the lamp trembling in her hand.

Quickly, Scarlet came to the window and peered out into the night. It was pitch black, but the moon was high, casting a yellowish glow over the bleak moorland below. Scarlet raked her eyes over the primitive landscape, from the high ridge to the yard below; she could see nothing untoward and she told Shelagh so.

'There *was* something . . . *someone*!' Shelagh assured her, with a shaking voice. 'A dark figure . . . walking the ridge, *and looking in this direction*!' In her fright, all thought of Hannah must have fled her mind. It was only when there came a cry from behind her that Scarlet realised how Hannah must have listened to it all. *'Who's out there?'* she demanded to know, coming quickly to Scarlet and clinging to her, her every limb quivering with terror. 'Is it the same one who taunted me? Has he come for me? . . . Has he?'

'Don't talk nonsense, Mammy . . . there's no one out there. Isn't that so, Shelagh?' She looked on the white-faced young woman for reassurance.

'Dear me! What a perfect idiot I am, Hannah!' Shelagh remarked, forcing a laugh and pointing out of the window to the ridge above the house. 'See there,' she said, taking Hannah by the arm and gently drawing her out. 'D'you see . . . along the ridge, to the right . . . that clump of trees?' She pointed again and lifted the lamp towards the window. 'The breeze is getting up to a fearsome strength . . . it was the *tree* I saw . . . and its branches blowing in the wind.'

'There you are, Mammy,' Scarlet *herself* was relieved. 'It was nothing sinister, was it? . . . Nothing to be worried about.' She folded her two arms about Hannah's frail shoulders and began leading her towards the bed, being more insistent when she sensed Hannah's resistance.

'As Shelagh told you, Mammy . . . it was only the wind blowing the trees,' she told her firmly.

'You wouldn't lie to me, child . . . would you?' Hannah climbed into bed and, on Scarlet's direction, she slid down beneath the covers, her wide blue eyes staring up. 'If you lied to me . . . that would be a terrible thing,' she warned.

Shocked by the sternness in her mammy's voice, Scarlet told her firmly, 'I would never lie to you . . . I never have!'

She indicated for Shelagh to leave. After a while, all was quiet, and soon Hannah's rhythmic breathing told Scarlet that she also could leave. Her mammy seemed to be resting easily. She would have departed the room, then and there, but for her father's heavy footsteps mounting the stairs. Quietly she waited until she thought he too would be asleep.

When she felt it was safe to do so, Scarlet came out onto the landing and went quickly to her own room a short distance away. There she undressed and strip-washed in the cold water from the jug. Normally she would have taken the bowl downstairs and emptied it, but tonight she felt exhausted. Drawing on her cotton nightgown, she climbed into bed, and was soon in that dreamy comfortable state between being awake and sleeping; and she could not get Shelagh's words out of her mind. 'If it *is* Garrett Summers' child, then I'm sure he'll do the right thing by you. His father's a wealthy man, and Garrett stands to inherit it all some day.' Scarlet wondered at the deviousness of her own thoughts. All of what Shelagh had said was true. And, if it proved to be necessary, Garrett might well provide a useful means of escape!

Yet, even while the possibility presented itself, Scarlet was drawn into other, more tormenting thoughts, thoughts of Silas. What had become of him, she wondered. Was he many miles away, perhaps in some other girl's eager arms? Had he forgotten her, as she intended to forget him? Or did he mean what he said when he had vowed to come back for her? The prospect gave her no pleasure. 'Stay away,' she murmured. 'You stay away from me!' She deliberately thrust all thought of him from her mind. But the pain was still there, in her heart. Soon, weariness overwhelmed her, and she drifted into a deep fretful sleep.

Hannah could *not* sleep. Something had disturbed her and now it was playing on her imagination, being made to grow out of all proportion by her own terrible fears. Time and again she screwed her eyes up tight and willed them not to open, not to look towards the window. But they would not stay closed. They would not be drawn from the window, and her fears would not be stilled. She knew that, in spite of her denial, Scarlet had lied to her! In her poor twisted mind, Hannah was convinced that something terrible was about to happen. 'Scarlet.' Her voice was little more than a whisper, a desperate cry for help, but she knew that help would not come; *Scarlet* had lied to her! Who *would* help her, then? Hannah could think of only one soul who would come to her aid . . . just as she had done once before. The herb-gatherer! Yes. She must get to her. Before the others came, and it would be too late.

In the darkness, Hannah stumbled. 'Ssh!' She remained perfectly still, listening. They must not hear, or they would stop her. *They must not stop her!* Encouraged by the ensuing silence she went on, pausing at the window and looking out, just as she had done earlier when Shelagh frightened her. But it was only the branches of a tree blowing in the wind, wasn't that so? See! There it was again, on the high ridge. Hannah peered deep into the darkness, her attention drawn to the ridge and the clump of trees. Yes, there it was. It *was* the wind, moving the branches and making them look so real it was fascinating. There was something strangely hypnotic about the way in which the branches swayed and beckoned. Hannah was mesmerised. But quick! She must escape this house, before it was too late. They were all her enemies. Even Scarlet!

Outside, the wind gently howled and the moon grew dim as Hannah climbed towards the high ridge and the one who waited there. She was not afraid, because the voice was kind, soothing. 'Hannah,' it whispered, 'don't be afraid. I've come to help you . . . I'm your friend.' And she believed it with all her heart. It was the herb-gatherer, come to take her to safety, she thought.

Blindly, as though in a dream, Hannah followed the voice, over the ridge, along by the spinney, and down towards the fast-flowing river. The wind tore at her hair and pierced her nightgown with bitter fingers; the moon slipped away behind the grey clouds, and all around was steeped in darkness. Hannah stumbled on, her bare feet cut and bleeding. She must not be left behind. The thought made her frantic. On and on she went, watching and following. Now she was led to the river's edge. The voice murmured in her ear, 'Now you'll be safe, Hannah.' The hand on her shoulder was gentle, loving. A sensation of falling. Then the cool lapping water, smooth as silk against her skin, enfolding, embracing. At long last she was safe.

CHAPTER ELEVEN

'But *why* won't you go to her grave?' Shelagh demanded. She followed Scarlet into the shed, where she and John were busy crating apples. 'It's been three months now, and *still* you won't pay your respects.'

'She knew how much I loved her . . . *needed* her, yet she took her own life!' Scarlet rubbed the apples with such vigour that the skin ruptured. 'She deserves no respect.'

Shelagh gave a small cry of frustration, before appealing to John. '*You* talk to her. *I* can't make her see sense!'

John looked at Scarlet. He saw how distressed she was, and how vicious her temper was becoming, and he knew when to leave well alone. Returning his anxious gaze to Shelagh, he softly mouthed the words, 'Best leave her be.'

Sighing deeply, Shelagh understood his meaning and, collecting up her wicker basket, she resumed her journey into the village, 'I shan't be long,' she called out behind her, 'I've a deal of shopping to do. And I mean to see a friend. You think on what I've said, Scarlet!' Her voice fell away. 'She's only hurting herself . . . nobody else,' Shelagh could be heard muttering as she picked her way along the rows of newly set greens. 'I've tried . . . nobody can say I didn't try to warn her.'

'Going to see that pot-girl from the Luttrell Arms,' observed John indignantly. 'Huh! Some friend *that* one is . . . if you ask me, she's a brassy, conniving sort!' He glanced at Scarlet. 'Don't be so savage with them apples, my girl,' John warned Scarlet, 'you'll have 'em splitting apart in your hands.' When Scarlet made no response, he changed the subject. 'Shelagh's settled in a treat at Greystone House, don't you think? And she copes very well with your father.' He straightened up from the workbench, tipped his neb cap back on his head and groaned, 'By! These day me bones seem to creak more than they used to, but we none of us get any younger, do we?' He glanced at Scarlet, thinking how she'd filled out lately, and attributing it to Shelagh's wholesome cooking. But her face was unusually pale, especially considering that today was one of the hottest they'd had during the whole of September, and she tired quickly; that was not like her. His heart went out to her. Poor girl, he thought. Deserted by Silas, and now by her mammy. Ah, but then Silas would likely be back one of these fine days, seeing as how he worshipped the ground Scarlet walked on. As for Hannah, well, she was past the helping and was likely better off where she was, poor demented soul. He wouldn't forget that night when Scarlet raised the alarm and the whole village turned out, tramping the moors till daylight. It were *him* as found the wretched creature, some way down the river and caught fast between the tentacles of an overhanging tree. She was lying beneath the surface in a shallower area, with her long white nightgown billowing above her like a mantle. He recalled the look on her face when they brought her onto the bank! Strange it was, almost as if she was smiling. It put the fear of God in him, and that was a fact. As for Vincent Pengally, he had gone to pieces . . . locking himself in the smithy till all hours, and falling into a black, silent mood when he wouldn't talk to a single soul for days on end. Funnily enough, he even recoiled from Scarlet, and it was *Shelagh* who finally coaxed him into a better frame of mind. She positively spoiled him, going to the trouble of enticing him to eat by cooking his favourite dish of veal, while she and Scarlet were made satisfied with a lesser dish, which wasn't quite so costly. It seemed almost as though Shelagh had naturally slipped into Hannah's shoes. She was a real godsend.

'Don't be so hard on yourself, Scarlet,' he said now, hoping to lighten her mood. 'You've nothing to reproach yourself for, you know . . . your mammy did what she did because she was a very sick, misguided woman. Oh, look, Scarlet . . . can't you find it in your heart to forgive her?'

'No!' Scarlet rounded on him with such vehemence that he was visibly shaken, 'and I'll thank you not to talk about it. You and Shelagh both.'

'We're only thinking of *you*. I don't like to see you punishing yourself. And you know how fond Shelagh is of you.' He might have said more, but the forbidding look on her face dissuaded him. 'Alright . . . I know when to keep my mouth shut.'

For the remainder of the day they worked in silence, with Scarlet deep in thoughts of her mammy and of the child who would not be still inside her. She knew that the moment was not far away when her father would begin to realise, now that he was coming to terms with the awful way in which Hannah's life had ended. She would *never* come to terms with it!

In the village Garrett Summers had stopped Shelagh to ask after Scarlet's well-being. 'I've been to the smithy under every excuse I could devise and *still* I haven't been able to exchange a single word with her.' He looked at her with pleading eyes. 'I was away for a while, and I'm desperately afraid she's forgotten me. How is she, Miss Williams?' He walked beside her. 'I was shocked to hear about Mrs Pengally . . . a terrible thing. Scarlet must have been devastated.'

'She was, and still is, I'm afraid. But Scarlet is strong-hearted. She'll be alright.'

They came to the corner of Church Street, where they paused to discuss quietly other matters concerning Scarlet's well-being. They talked of the manner in which Silas had gone from Greystone House – 'like a thief in the night' explained Shelagh, adding that she was of the same opinion as Scarlet's parents 'where that one was concerned'. All the while they talked, Shelagh toyed with the idea of acquainting Garrett with Scarlet's condition. Yet she was not altogether certain whether that would be a useful thing to do. Uppermost in her mind was the intention of bringing the two of them together; she saw Garrett as a means by which Scarlet could evade the wrath of her father, when he found out the truth. She suspected that Vincent Pengally was a man who would show no mercy.

'Will you tell Scarlet how very much I've missed her . . . how much I need to see her and talk with her?' Scarlet had remained an obsession with him. During his absence from Dunster, and ever since his return, he had tried to put her out of his mind, but he could not. He adored her now, more than ever. 'Her father keeps her so isolated. Once upon a time she would escape to the moors in the dead of night . . . or on the day when Mr Pengally does his rounds. Recently I've wandered the moors . . . looking to find her there, but I never have.' There was desperation in his voice.

'These days Scarlet rarely leaves the house,' Shelagh remarked cautiously. 'Losing her mammy in that way was a terrible shock. Scarlet has become very withdrawn and quiet in herself.' She was aware also that Scarlet had suffered badly because of her passion for Silas, and because of the way he had deserted her. There had been times when she sensed that there was something about Silas and Scarlet that went far deeper than mere passion or love; some inexplicable thing that had drawn them together with the same relentless power that had eventually wrenched them apart.

'Can you help me, Miss Williams? I'm told you're very close to Scarlet.' In his eagerness he was bold enough to place a hand on Shelagh's arm. She was not surprised to feel it trembling.

'I'll do what I can . . . I promise.'

'Then I must be patient.' He thanked her profusely and proceeded towards Castle Hill, where he had a matter of his father's business to conclude.

Shelagh stood a moment longer, watching him go and thinking that that amiable young man might yet be the solution to Scarlet's dilemma. And consequently, *to her own*, for she had secretly set her sights on Greystone House. And Vincent Pengally with it!

'I've told you before!' Vincent Pengally flung down his knife and fork, a look of thunder darkening his face as he glared at Scarlet across the table. 'I don't like my veal done to a crisp. It sticks in my craw . . . turns my stomach. Have we money to waste by ruining good food?'

Scarlet gave no answer. These days she had more important things on her mind than the manner in which her father's food was cooked. She calmly returned his stony glare, although, as always, the viciousness of his attack had set her trembling. With as much dignity as she could muster, Scarlet replaced her own knife and fork. Her small appetite had gone.

'It wasn't Scarlet's fault,' Shelagh quietly intervened, 'it was mine. I was the one who cooked your supper.' She rose from her seat and calmly collected his plate. 'I'll bring you some of the steak pie that *we're* having.' Her smile was coaxing and strangely unsettling to him.

'My appetite's ruined,' he snapped ungratefully, getting to his feet and thrusting back the chair. He returned his accusing grey eyes to Scarlet, instructing her sourly, 'Bring me a pot of tea. I'll be in the parlour.' He was quickly gone from the kitchen, and the stamp of his feet along the corridor seemed to shake the whole house.

'You know . . . he's right about that veal,' Shelagh told Scarlet, 'it isn't so much the cooking as the *texture* of it. I'll have to speak to that odious butcher. *He* gives me the shivers as well! If only your father wouldn't insist on his ration, I'd stop ordering the wretched stuff.' She shivered and made an unpleasant face. 'I'm like you, Scarlet . . . I never could abide veal, it has a peculiar taste.'

Scarlet would not be drawn. How could she, when her own problems seemed mountainous compared to such unimportant issues? These past few weeks, in fact ever since John had found . . . no! . . . she could not bring herself to think on it. Yet, since then, there had crept into her mind an idea of running away. But where could she go in her condition? What would she do for money and how would she live? Of course, she could always search for Silas; after all, it was his child she carried. *Search for Silas!* Hour after hour she had churned it over in her mind. And each time when she found herself weakening, that same well of horror would open up to engulf her. Now she was certain of only one thing. She must *never* go to Silas. She had no way of knowing what kind of monster he might be.

Carrying the tray along the lamplit corridor towards the parlour, Scarlet hoped her father would be asleep. Lately she had felt his probing eyes on her, and she had lived in terror of him seeing what she had tried so hard to conceal. She was grateful that the bulge beneath her loose-fitting dress was not too prominent, thanks to her diminished appetite and the practised habit of binding herself with a broad cotton band each morning. The discomfort was a small price to pay for the extra time it would allow her before she must inevitably speak out. For a long time, her natural rebellious spirit had been smothered by the loss of the two people she had greatly loved, and always there was her father's overwhelming presence seeming to beat her down and push her deeper into the blackness. Now, as the child grew inside her, becoming stronger and its little soul permeating every corner of her being, she also was growing stronger again. That wild wilful spirit was returning. It would help her to survive.

Balancing the tea tray on one arm, Scarlet pushed open the parlour door. One swift glance towards the black high-backed chair told her that her father was quietly dozing. She inwardly sighed with relief. A sense of urgency took hold of her. She had to be in and out of this room as fast as was humanly possible. She hated the atmosphere that his presence created, and she bitterly resented the crippling fear which he set loose in her.

Going to the small circular table which stood beside the chair, Scarlet put down the tray, careful not to rattle the cup against the teapot, or to betray her presence there. Softly! And he was not disturbed! Suddenly the candle which was situated on the mantelpiece began to cough and splutter, its dying light casting erratic shadows on every surface. As there was already a lamp burning on the lace-covered table, Scarlet thought it best to snuff out the candle's remains quickly, before it should irritate her father and restore his venomous mood.

With bated breath, Scarlet went on tiptoe to the fireplace. There she reached up high to pinch the fluttering flame with her finger and thumb. In that instant, before she could extinguish the flame, the atmosphere in the room was suddenly charged. A creeping sensation quivered down her spine and, for a moment, she was afraid to look round. Her every nerve was on edge and her instincts warned her that those penetrating grey eyes were feasting on her, like they had done so often before. She inwardly shivered, forcing herself to turn her head and look. The grey eyes were dangerously intent on her!

The swish of Scarlet's skirt as she moved towards the fireplace had alerted Vincent Pengally to her presence.

Cunningly, he had made no outward sign that would betray the fact that he was wide awake, other than to open his eyes and covet Scarlet's every move. He had seen her reach up towards the candleflame, and he was excited by her wild, dark beauty. His rapacious gaze travelled her entire body, from the rich abundant hair that cascaded so wantonly over her shoulders, to the curve of her hips and the long slim legs with their exquisitely rounded calves and perfect, dainty ankles. It had not missed his attention that, lately, Scarlet's delightfully girlish figure had begun to mature, to become even more beautiful. He languished deeper in the chair, only his eyes alive as they greedily roved her body. He wanted her more than ever, and though the shame of it caused his face to burn, the need in him burned more fiercely. His imagination unclothed her, saw her as he had seen her countless times before. He could feel the warmth of her nakedness against his, and feel the strands of her vivacious hair between his fingers. His mouth watered at the thought of her warm moist lips mingling with his. Longingly, he continued to ogle, to imagine, to see the round smooth nakedness that he could take to himself whenever the need grew too powerful for him to deny it. Yet, even as he gazed on her, something was disturbing him, he did not know what. Something about *Scarlet* was disturbing him. Something new and repulsive. His gaze stiffened and he became agitated. She had sensed him looking at her, and now she had turned. There was fear in her spacious dark eyes. Realisation dawned. In an instant he was on her, and she was screaming, beating him back.

'*Whose is it, you little whore?*' He was like a crazed thing as he crushed her small shoulders in his fists, shaking her until she was a rag doll in his grip. 'Whose is it? You tell me . . . or I'll flay you to within an inch of your life!'

Suddenly, the door burst open. It was Shelagh. 'Let go of her!' she yelled, grabbing him by the arm, making every effort to pull him away. When the blow came she was not expecting it. The clenched fist caught her on the temple, sending her reeling back into the wall where she fell. Too dazed to get to her feet, she did not see how Vincent Pengally roughly propelled Scarlet up towards the attic. 'I'll ask you again. Tell me his name!' He was not shouting as before, but his voice fiercely trembled.

Scarlet looked away. His eyes were almost black and his pent-up fury was terrifying to her. She felt his fingers digging into her flesh, and she was mortally afraid. Yet she would not give him the name of the one who had fathered her child. Instead she remembered how it had always been and she fought him with all the strength left in her. '*It wasn't you!*' she taunted. 'That's all you need to know!'

'You slut . . . dirty slut!' He flung open the attic door and thrust her inside. 'You'll tell me who the bastard is . . . or stay here and rot!' Her bold black eyes defied him, infuriated him beyond all reason. The door was slammed; she heard the lock spring. And she was along.

Scarlet woke with a muffled gasp. Someone was trying the attic door! She trembled in the sticky clinging heat, hugging herself and waiting for the inevitable. He had returned. She waited for his eerie voice. '*His name,*' it would ask, '*tell me his name.*' And, as before, she would remain silent, praying that he would go away.

Scarlet had no idea how long she had been in the attic. She only knew that her throat was raw and parched as the dry earth, and her bones were stiff with cramp. The heat was stifling. Scarlet wondered whether she might die, here in this attic that she knew so well. Here, where the tiny window, which had once given her light, was now boarded over. As a child she had often imagined that one day these four walls would make her a splendid coffin. Now he was here to finish it. She waited. What was he up to? Why was he at the door, if not to demand that she must give up the name or starve to death?

'Scarlet!' The urgent whisper was a shock. Slowly, agonisingly slowly, Scarlet inched her aching body along the floorboards. At long last her energy was spent. In the pitch blackness she was directed by her instincts, and by the long, ingrained memories which had mapped out every inch of her prison. It surprised her to find that time never dimmed the painful engravings in her mind. The attic was a part of her. It must stay with her for ever, draining her life until it possessed her completely. One day, if not now, *there would be death in this attic*. She felt that it was destined to be. And she was not afraid.

'Scarlet!' The whisper was distorted, urgent and shaped by fear. 'Are you alright? . . . answer me.'

Scarlet recognised the voice. It was Shelagh! She put her hand flat against the door. 'Oh, Shelagh.' Tears of relief trickled down her face. 'I'm afraid for my baby,' she said, the words issuing painfully between cracked and swollen lips, 'my baby . . . please.'

'You've been locked up for three days! Tell him what he wants to know . . . *you must tell him*!'

'I'll *never* tell him. Never!' Scarlet had not expected Shelagh to understand the unique and destructive relationship that had evolved between her and her father, a terrible and inescapable bond that was corrupt and evil beyond imagination. The issue was not about her telling him a name, but of her refusing to submit. She would not gratify him, never again, *in any way*!

'You must tell him, Scarlet, you must!' Shelagh still insisted, and Scarlet forgave her because she was a stranger to Greystone House. She could not know.

'Very well. I have a plan . . . trust me.' There was a pause, then, 'Put your hand to the bottom of the door. Quickly . . . he's climbing the stairs!' Scarlet did as she was told. Her fingers touched something cold. 'It's the best I can do . . . he watches me constantly. He's even closed the smithy so as not to be drawn from the house. You'll be alright, I promise. I have a plan to get you out.' Suddenly Scarlet also could hear her father approaching, nearer and nearer, climbing the steps in that heavy methodical manner that could strike fear into her deepest heart. 'Quickly, Scarlet!' The voice was frantic. 'Drink . . . and push the saucer back under to me. Hurry . . . hurry!'

With painstaking slowness, and being loathe to spill a single drop of the precious liquid, Scarlet lapped the water from the saucer, its coolness slicing into her cracked lips like a knife, but soothing the dry fire in her throat. 'Hurry, Scarlet . . . return the saucer, or he'll know. *He will know!*' When at last the saucer was returned, Shelagh whispered, 'Trust me,' then she was gone.

The footsteps trod along the floor, coming ever nearer. Scarlet prayed they would not stop, but her prayers went unheard. The footsteps came to rest immediately outside the door. Then silence! The soft lamplight filtered in through the narrow gap beneath the door, there was a shadow, a movement. Scarlet waited. Soon he would quietly unlock the door and push it open. His formidable presence would fill the attic and he would interrogate her once more. But Scarlet was ready to defy him again and again. He would not wear her down. A hand scraped the door, and in the desperate silence Scarlet could hear his heavy rhythmic breathing. Now! Now, he would begin, '*Tell me his name.*' She waited, preparing herself. The prolonged silence was agony. Scarlet held her breath, wondering whether tonight he might end it all and take her life, or she would take his. Suddenly the shadow moved again. The footsteps echoed away and all was darkness again.

Scarlet breathed a sigh of relief and settled uncomfortably against a wall. She would sleep, and wake, erratically. With the window boarded up, there was no way of telling whether it was day or night. But thank God for Shelagh, she thought, thank God for a close ally.

'You're a liar! A bastard little liar!' Vincent Pengally was like a crazed man. With one vicious swipe of his arm he sent everything flying from the table. He crossed the room to where Shelagh stood, her back against the dresser and her round brown eyes betraying something of the fear he had created in her. Yet there were other emotions there, not least the grim determination to see Scarlet released from the attic.

'I'm no liar,' she said. 'What I've told you is the truth. *Garrett Summers is the father*. They love each other . . . let Scarlet go to him.'

'Get out!' He grasped the dresser edge with both hands, trembling uncontrollably and his violent grey eyes boring into hers. 'GET OUT!' His voice was like thunder. Quickly she went from the room, as he began destroying everything around him. His cries were madness, and the whole house seemed to quiver as he vented his rage on everything in sight.

Upstairs, Scarlet was horrified by the fearsome uproar that emanated from below. Imprisoned in that dark echoing attic, she was made to imagine all manner of terrible things. She knew instinctively that it was her father, and now, after what seemed a lifetime, when she heard his footsteps stamping up the stairs, those same instincts urged her to go to the furthest corner away from the door. She could hear Shelagh pleading with him, and his booming voice warning her, 'Stay out of it! I want to hear it from Scarlet's own mouth . . . *the truth*. Or the devil take her eyes!'

There was a movement of frantic activity at the door, then suddenly he burst into the room, pausing briefly to seek Scarlet out in the gloom, his face a terrible sight to behold and made phantom-like by the eerie glow of watery daylight that silhouetted him and made her eyes play tricks. When his manic glare alighted on her, Scarlet was stricken with fear, but she disguised it well when he came to stand over her, his glittering grey eyes boring into her face as she struggled to her feet. '*Whore!*' He spat the words out, at the same time viciously grasping a hank of her unkempt hair and raising her up towards him. When she winced at the pain he caused her, he laughed, a low sinister sound that warned Scarlet not to satisfy his sadistic nature.

'Leave her alone . . . she's no more than a child!' Shelagh had rushed into the attic behind him and was attempting to come between him and Scarlet, who was emaciated and weakened by her prolonged captivity.

Shelagh's words went unheeded as Scarlet was immediately subjected to a barrage of questions. 'Who was it? I want the truth . . . *was* it Garrett Summers who violated you? *Was it?*' With every question he spitefully twisted the hank of her hair, until it was tight against her skull and close to being uprooted.

'Let her go,' Shelagh tried in vain to release Scarlet's hair from his iron grip. 'I've already told you it was Garrett Summers.' She pleaded now with Scarlet. '*Tell him,*' she urged, 'tell him that it was Garrett, and you'll come to no harm I'm sure.'

In her pitiful condition and with her consciousness fast slipping away, Scarlet was astonished that Shelagh had pointed the finger at Garrett. Her first instinct was to vehemently deny it, but she recalled Shelagh's words. 'I have a plan,' she had promised. 'Trust me.' In that moment, Scarlet came to realise that only Shelagh stood between her and this monster. She *would* trust her. She could do no other. 'Yes!' she called out, 'Garrett Summers was my lover . . . I'm carrying his child.' There was a loud gasp as he loosened his grip on her, then the ensuing silence became unbearable. Presently he cried out and thrust her from him. The look he gave Scarlet was both scathing and malevolent. '*I loved you,*' he told her in a shocked voice, 'no man ever idolised a woman in such a way.'

To Scarlet, his confession was the worst kind of blasphemy. The dark disturbing images of his 'love' seared through her mind and turned her loathing inwards. He had wantonly scarred her innocence, using her as a woman, when she was but a child. And now, even now, his vision of her was just as warped as it had always been, and he saw nothing sinful in his own words: *no man ever idolised a woman in such a way.* His vile atrocities had shaped her life, moulded and debased it; now she felt his loathing of her as he stormed from the attic, and she was overwhelmed by the crippling confusion he always wrought in her. The tears ran down her face and the name on her lips was whispered like a prayer, 'Silas . . . oh, Silas.' Deeply disturbed, she swiftly banished all thought of both Silas and her father. In her deepest horror, those two were always side by side.

'Hold on to me.' Shelagh slid her arms around Scarlet's middle, supporting her as the two of them went gently down the stairs. 'I'm taking you out of this house,' she told Scarlet, 'to a place where you'll be safe from him . . . you *and* the child . . . a place where you can get your strength back.'

By the time they reached the kitchen, Vincent Pengally had already gone from the house. As he rode furiously out of Dunster and over the moors towards Selworthy some short distance away, he cunningly ruminated on a particular score he had to settle: a score that would not wait. His thirst for vengeance, however, *must* wait, if it was to be properly quenched; and in such a way that would not lay the blame at *his* door!

'Alright . . . alright!' Ruth Taylor had been the housekeeper at Selworthy Manor for many years; since Mrs Summers's fatal heart attack, she was now solely in charge of the manor and held in awe by the two servants who took their orders from her. She was a difficult woman, tall, slim and authoritative, with quick dark eyes, steel grey hair and a forbidding manner.

As she hurried across the vast hall, the sound of her echoing footsteps carried to the outer steps, where Vincent Pengally was now impatiently pacing up and down. Infuriated by his loud persistent thumping on the outer door, the housekeeper swung it open, demanding to know, in a rasping voice, 'What is it you want?' She regarded Vincent Pengally with contemptuous eyes, surveying his common jacket and ungainly appearance with obvious distaste.

'I want the young man of the house!' His manner was equally surly. 'Garrett Summers. Send him out, or I might have to come and *fetch* him out . . . by the scruff of his neck!'

'Young Mr Summers is not at home. And if he *was* . . . I doubt whether I would be inclined to "send him out", as you say. Certainly not to such an ill-mannered and offensive person as yourself!' She attempted to quickly shut the door, but was astonished when he thrust his booted foot between the door and its frame, 'I'm not shifting until I've seen him. There are serious things to be settled!'

'I tell you, he's not here!' She deliberately put all of her weight against the door, pushing hard until the pressure crushed the toe of his boot into a peculiar shape. Still he would not be moved, 'Get away from here, you scoundrel!' she cried in a shrill voice, 'unless you want me to send for a constable.' When he gave no answer, but continued to stare at her through the narrowed gap, his eyes wild and threatening, she became exasperated. When he began hurling obscene abuse at her, she kicked out at his foot, belying the dignity for which she was renowned.

'What's going on here?' The voice was refined, but sharply impatient. It surprised them both.

'Oh, Mr Summers!' The housekeeper swung round to address the thin-faced elderly man in the wheelchair, 'This . . . man is asking for your son. I've already informed him that young Mr Summers is not at home.' She turned to cast a withering glance at Vincent Pengally, who was glaring at them both through the now wide open door. 'He refuses to go away! Shall I send for a constable, sir . . . and have him forcibly removed?'

'It's alright.' Mr Summers put his large slender hands on the wheels of his wheelchair and propelled himself to the doorway. 'You go about your business,' he told her, 'I'll see to this gentleman.'

'Oh! So you'll *see to me*, will you?' Vincent Pengally came forward to place one hand on the arm of the wheelchair, then leaning his scowling face towards the other man he said in a low gruff voice, 'If there's anyone to be "seen to" it's your son . . . and *I'll* be the one to do it!'

'State your business.'

'I'll state my business to your son. I have none with you.'

'You'll tell me what you want with him, or you'll get off my premises!'

'I told your woman I won't shift till I've settled a score . . . and I'm telling you the same!' The half-smile on Vincent Pengally's face was devilish to see.

'Very well. You leave me no choice!' The wheelchair made a small grating sound as he inched it backwards, causing the other man to withdraw his hand in order to stop himself from falling forwards over the step. '*Send them out, Mrs Taylor.*' Mr Summers addressed himself to his diligent housekeeper who had positioned herself by the drawing room door. On his command she flung it open and out bounded two large savage looking dogs. When they saw how menacingly close was the stranger to their master, they began loudly barking, then advanced slowly, their lips curled back to show long fearsome teeth and emitting low threatening growls. Even when their master put out his arm and cautioned them in a quiet commanding voice, they were not easily restrained.

'Keep them away from me, or I'll not be responsible for the consequences!' Vincent Pengally had nothing but fear and contempt for dogs, always believing them to be noisy, unnecessary creatures who did nothing to earn their keep. He would never admit his innate fear of them, for the same reason he would never acknowledge his horror of the unknown: he saw such weakness as being the base of cowardice. And that he would never admit to!

'Again, sir . . . what's your business?' The man in the wheelchair had the dogs, one either side of him, his fingers tightly gripping their collars as the animals remained taut and threatening, a low guttural sound issuing from their trembling throats, and their vicious bright eyes trained relentlessly on the stranger.

At the sight of the two dogs Vincent Pengally's fury was tempered with caution. 'You would do well to ask your *son* what my "business" is!' he snarled, being careful to keep his distance.

'I'm asking *you*. And I must say I don't like either your manner or the tone of your voice.' The old man peered deep into the hostile grey eyes, '*I know you!* It's Pengally, isn't it . . . the blacksmith from Dunster?' Suddenly, realisation dawned. Damn and bugger it! How many times had he warned Garrett to keep clear of the blacksmith's daughter? The village gossip had long reached his ears, and he did not like the implications. Not one bit. He liked even less the consequences of his confrontation with Garrett, who foolishly confessed that he was besotted with the girl. In fact it was this unhealthy business with Scarlet Pengally that had been at the root of Garrett being sent away to a business college. Good God! The girl was far too young and utterly unsuitable for a son of *his*. Would Garrett never learn? The old man braced himself. He had an unpleasant feeling that this Pengally fellow had seen the advantages inherent in his daughter's association with the young Mr Summers, a man of position and consequence. Even a fool could deduce that Pengally was here on an errand of blackmail. 'What's on your mind, Pengally?' he demanded. 'Spit it out, man . . . let's have it done with! I take it your daughter's at the bottom of it, but I'll tell you this. If you're here to extract money, I warn you to be very careful.'

'Do you think I'd lower myself to take a penny from the likes of *you*?' came the swift, scathing reply. 'It's not money I'm after, damn you. I don't mind telling you, Summers, if your son had answered my knock on this door, he'd have had my hands round his throat, and neither you nor your dogs would have prised them away until they had choked the life out of him!'

'Are you insane?'

'Happen I am! And happen I'm not about to be satisfied on this particular occasion. But I'm a patient man when needs must . . . my time will come. *And so will your son's.* He's defiled my daughter . . . used her for his own gratification. *He's given her a bastard to carry.* I won't forgive him that, and I won't forget.' When he saw that the other man was shocked and about to intervene, he thrust himself forward, being wary enough to stay out of range of the dogs who seemed desperate to tear him apart, 'You tell your son that. And tell him *this*. I won't keep soiled goods in my house! She'll be thrown out bag and baggage. From this day on . . . *Scarlet Pengally is no daughter of mine!*' With a last lingering look of malevolence that made the old man's blood run cold, he straightened his formidable frame and turned to stride away, his booted feet stamping the ground as though even the earth offended him.

'Stay out of it, John. The two of them have made their bed, and now they must lie on it!' Ada Blackwood came down the narrow stairs from the bedroom where she had put young Trent to sleep. Hurrying across the tiny parlour, she put out her hand to stop John from following Scarlet and Garrett Summers, who were going up the path towards the trap which would carry them to Selworthy Manor and a new life for Scarlet.

'Don't be so heartless, woman.' John had been both surprised and disappointed at his wife's blatant disapproval of Scarlet's terrible predicament. She had shown little sympathy, while he himself was appalled by Vincent Pengally's callous treatment of his daughter, though he was not surprised. What *had* astonished him was Shelagh's revelation that Scarlet was expecting Garrett Summers's child. And though Ada openly condemned such 'wanton and shameless conduct', she had not hesitated to help when Shelagh sought temporary refuge for Scarlet at the cottage.

Later, when her strength was beginning to recover and Shelagh had returned to her duties at Greystone House, Scarlet had sat on the window seat, gazing out of the tiny bay window to the garden beyond, quietly refusing all offers of food or drink, inwardly punishing herself for the impossible situation she now found herself in. She wondered whether life was worth living. But then she thought of that new life surging inside her. It gave her hope for the future.

At nine-fifteen, when John answered an urgent knock on the door, it was to an agitated and greatly concerned young man. He had gone first to Greystone House, only to be warned by Shelagh that he should make all haste away from there. 'Scarlet's father is like a man demented,' she had told him. 'You'll find Scarlet at John Blackwood's cottage. Take her quickly to a safer haven.' She also revealed how it was she who had implicated him as being Scarlet's lover and had brought the wrath of Vincent Pengally down on him, 'all to save Scarlet from being further imprisoned in the attic'. She was greatly relieved when Garrett Summers had professed his love for Scarlet, together with his intention to 'marry Scarlet . . . if she'll have me, and to give the child my name and protection'. He had never forgotten how they had made glorious love, and how he might so easily have fathered a child in her. As far as he was concerned, this child that Scarlet carried was a bond, drawing them together when otherwise she might never have been his.

Earlier that evening, on his return from overseeing the shipment of cattle from the lower pastures, he had found his father beside himself with rage. When he had confronted Garrett demanding, 'What kind of damned fool are you . . . that Pengally girl made pregnant?' he was even more enraged when his son would not deny it.

At first, when Garrett explained to Scarlet how he intended taking her to Selworthy Manor, where 'we can make plans for the future', she had resisted. But when she saw how he adored her and was willing to accept the child without question, she felt ashamed. Besides which, she was weary and her spirit was desperately tired. There was no question of her returning to Greystone House or of imposing herself on John and Ada Blackwood in their little cottage. She needed time to recuperate, time to breathe. After thanking the Blackwoods she went with Garrett, though in her heart she knew there must come a day when she would regret it.

'You take care of her!' John had come out onto the doorstep as Garrett helped Scarlet into the trap. He was pleasantly surprised when Ada appeared beside him to call out, 'Mind how you go.' He knew she would not change her stern attitude concerning those two, especially Scarlet whom she had always proclaimed was 'too flighty by half!' But it pleased him to know that her heart was in the right place after all, or she would not have taken Scarlet in after Pengally had thrown her out, and she wouldn't be here beside him now, telling them to 'mind how you go'.

John turned to his wife with a warm loving smile on his

face. Then, as his gaze was drawn beyond the cottage, to the rising ground above the river, the smile froze on his face. There in the moonlight, like a haunting apparition, was a dark hooded figure, its hollow face turned towards the cottage and seeming engrossed in what was happening there.

'Come away, Ada!' John put his arm across his wife's shoulders to propel her through the door and on into the cottage. When safely inside, he thrust home the bolts on the door and quickly drew the curtains across every window, laughing nervously when Ada told him, 'I do believe you're getting frightened of the dark in your old age!'

Outside the wind played in the treetops, creating a weird moaning, melodic sound. The figure remained still and silent, watching the trap as it carried the young man and Scarlet out of sight. Then it slowly nodded its head, before moving softly away. Presently the moon was smothered by cloud, and all was engulfed in darkness.

CHAPTER TWELVE

'And when will you be sixteen?' Edward Summers stared across the table to where Scarlet was restlessly picking at the fine food on her plate.

Suddenly the idle chatter ceased and all eyes were turned in her direction. She resented the way Garrett's father relentlessly sought to belittle her. She had an urge to hurt him somehow, to surprise him and strip the arrogance from his shrewish, refined features. As always, she suppressed the urge, yet told him in a cool voice, 'But I understood that Garrett had already discussed that with you. If I agree . . . and I still haven't decided . . . the date of our wedding will coincide with my sixteenth birthday, in March . . . four months from now.' She saw his back stiffen at her impudence, and his discomfort goaded her on. 'Of course, the child will be born long before then. I know you have wished it otherwise, and, if *I'm* to be the cause of introducing the first bastard into the Summers family, then you will forgive me, I'm sure.' She bestowed a darkly angelic smile on him and was inwardly delighted when he visibly squirmed.

'Won't it be wonderful though, Edward . . . a *baby* in the house after all these years?' Nancy Thornton's distinctly American accent drew attention away from Scarlet. She was a delightful little woman, demure and pretty in an expensive silk dress fashioned in the latest design; she wore a string of pearls round her throat, and a smart mother-of-pearl comb kept her long fair hair securely pinned up into a fold at the nape of her neck. Her wide green eyes were almost childlike which, together with her small slim figure, belied her fortieth year. Yet there was a sadness in those honest pretty eyes, a long and bitter regret at never having produced a child for the husband she adored. The sadness was in her voice when she now addressed Scarlet. 'Oh, I do envy you, child,' she said with a warm smile. 'What more could a woman ask than to hold her own newborn safe in her arms?' Her voice trembled with emotion.

'Now, now . . . enough of that.' Jonathan Thornton was a large portly man with a thick shock of golden hair. He had been acutely embarrassed by the blatant animosity between his host, Edward Summers, and the girl Scarlet, who he thought was not only the loveliest creature he had ever seen, but who had something about her that made him unusually cautious. Or perhaps it was something in himself, he mused. All the same, he felt obliged to change the subject at once. He had already been an unwilling witness to the heated arguments between Edward Summers and his son, with regard to the girl's reluctance to marry.

While the ensuing discussions centred on matters such as King George's approval regarding the interment in Westminster Abbey of an unknown British soldier, and the recent bomb explosion on Wall Street in America which killed thirty people and injured hundreds, Scarlet grew increasingly uncomfortable. All day there had been a gnawing restlessness inside her that she could not rid herself of. Even when she and Garrett had walked the moors and there she had rediscovered a measure of inner peace, there was this sensation of urgency and panic that would not let her be. When they had paused to watch the creatures at play in the fallen leaves deep in the woods, she had been seized with sudden uncontrollable terror. It was as though some vindictive devil had wormed its way inside her and meant to haunt her to destruction.

Some days ago, after she and Garrett had inadvertently come to wander the ridge above Greystone House, two things had happened that had since caused her nightmares. She had stood on the high ridge, gazing down at that monstrous beautiful house, and in her deepest mind she was compelled to relive the fear and horror that stalked every nook and cranny there. Memories so vivid that they became uncannily real: fearful images flooded her mind, of a small terrified child shut away in a dark attic with only the rats for company; visions tormented her of her father's shadowy figure at her bedroom door and of Silas enacting unspeakable deeds which were forever printed on her impressionable mind. In that house was love and hatred, unbearable guilt and exquisite desires, suspicion and fear. *Always* the fear. That inexplicable fear that spread through the house, permeating the very air and invading all who lived there: herself, her mother, and even her father. It was relentless, there was no reprieve, not even now, when she thought herself to have escaped its evil.

On that day when she and Garrett had come to that certain spot, Scarlet knew beyond any doubt that she could never escape. Because, in spite of the fear and the horror wrought in her on seeing Greystone House again, there was something else that was stronger and even more terrifying. *The house was calling her!* The man who had defiled her was beckoning, and even her poor suffering mother would not let her go. Silas was there, he would always be there. And now Scarlet believed beyond all reason that Silas, like her, would forever be drawn to Greystone House. It was their destiny, it was in their blood. Too much had happened to be dissolved by time or distance. In her stricken heart, Scarlet knew that however much he might fight his awesome fate and run from it, it was inevitable that Silas would meet his end in that house. *Just as she would*. It was strange, she thought, how the awful premonition brought with it a degree of comfort; almost as though she knew how, when the end *did* come, it would bring with it an everlasting peace.

Lost in her own innermost thoughts, Scarlet had not been aware of how deeply even Garrett was affected by the awesome sight of Greystone House. When, disquieted and eager to be gone from there, she turned to address him, she was shocked by the look on his face, a look she had never seen there before. A look of mischief and, did she imagine it, a look of terrible revenge!

Now, when he gazed at her so lovingly across the table, his face so open and honest and his hazel eyes so pitifully innocent, she wondered whether on that day when her own emotions were so turbulent, she might have imagined that look on Garrett's face.

'Don't leave it too long before you visit me again.' Edward Summers was always disappointed when his old friends the Thorntons returned to America.

'We'll keep in touch, Edward, and we'll certainly be back . . . but never again in November. It's too darned cold!' Jonathan Thornton manoeuvred his wife into the motor vehicle then climbed in beside her. In a minute they were going down the long winding drive, and the ever-vigilant housekeeper was hurriedly wheeling Edward Summers back into the house, out of the damp November air.

From her bedroom window above, Scarlet had watched the proceedings with passing interest. During the week when the Thorntons had stayed at Selworthy Manor she had come to dislike the wealthy Jonathan Thornton, whom she saw as a pompous, arrogant man. She suspected that, although he obviously idolised his wife, he had an unhealthy appetite for the opposite sex. It was there, in the sly appreciative way he looked at her when he thought he was not observed. And in the quiet intimate manner in which he spoke to her out of earshot of the others. Her every instinct told Scarlet that he was a man to be avoided.

For a long time after the Thorntons had departed, Scarlet's dark eyes scoured the skyline beyond the vast meticulous tended gardens. Would Garrett never come home? How long and empty the days were when he was obliged to leave her in order to execute his father's business affairs; a demanding and profitable business that incorporated the overseeing of twelve tenanted sheep-farms and a vast herd of prime cattle spread over more than five hundred acres. There was a workforce of forty men, but even *they* must be directed and controlled. Since Edward Summers's crippling illness, that awesome responsibility had fallen on the quiet capable shoulders of his son.

Scarlet was under no illusion where Edward Summers was concerned. He was a proud man who, though he had conceded to her having a room in his house, disliked her intensely. He saw Scarlet and the child she carried as a threat to his son's future. Yet he was shrewd enough to realise that Garrett would leave Selworthy Manor rather than lose his precious Scarlet. It was a thorn in his side but, to keep his only son there where he belonged, Edward Summers was prepared to suffer the blacksmith's daughter, albeit reluctantly. Besides which, if an opportunity presented itself whereby he might split the two of them asunder, he would not hesitate to exploit it to the full. And though he was outraged by Scarlet's stubborn refusal to be rushed into marriage, he saw it also as a situation he might turn to his advantage.

Selworthy Manor was a large grand house in the old tradition, built with white stone and having numerous deep bay windows. It was both magnificent and inviting. Inside it was equally impressive, with its broad galleried stairway, vast hall and wood panelled walls. There was an air of wealth and pride about it. Throughout its entirety it was furnished in only the very best that money could buy. On a bright day the sun poured in through every window, giving the house an inspiring air of light and spaciousness. Scarlet was made to compare the manor with the dark brooding Greystone House, with its many narrow forbidding corridors and that terrible oppressive air that seemed to linger with you long after you had departed. The comparison was stark. Like night and day, she thought. But, in one disturbing way, they were alike. *Each was a prison.*

In the six weeks and more that Scarlet had been here, she had grown lonely and morose. At first Garrett had taken her along on his supervisory visits to the outlying farms, and it had relieved the awful loneliness which seemed to engulf her. But then she grew cumbersome and prone to bouts of nausea. Garrett became increasingly concerned for her and eventually insisted that she should remain behind at the house, promising, 'I won't stay away a minute longer than I have to.' So she had spent her days walking the lovely grounds and sitting in her splendid room, painstakingly embroidering the exquisite shawl he had bought for the child, and wondering whether Shelagh might soon come and see her as she had promised. There were times, in these last few days, when Scarlet had been tempted to go herself to see John and Shelagh. But each time she had been deterred by many things: the prospect of perhaps coming face to face with her father was an unnerving thought. She could never forget the wild murderous look in his eyes when he had physically ejected her from the house and warned her to keep away. *'You're no daughter of mine.'* The most disturbing thing to Scarlet was that, even in her acute pain and distress, she should have been gladdened by his words. Yet she was not. She felt an outcast and though the bond between herself and her father was one of cruelty, debauchery and terror, it was nevertheless a bond that had been forged so intimately over the years that when it was broken, she felt cut adrift, abandoned, and terrified of all that was strange to her. Only Garrett and the thought of her child stood between her and a dangerous inexplicable yearning to return to Greystone House. Nor was she happy, being forever restless and afraid. Garrett did not understand her, how could he? He was not her father; he was not Silas!

Suddenly there came over Scarlet an overwhelming desire to put distance between herself and this beautiful house that could never be home to her. She needed to feel the magic of the moors around her. Her need became a compulsion.

'No, miss . . . don't take him!' The stable boy was horrified to see Scarlet saddling up the big bay hunter. 'He's got a real vicious streak. It'll be dark soon, and the moors can be treacherous,' he appeared to blush, 'especially for someone in your condition.'

'Don't worry. I've grown up around horses,' Scarlet assured him as she swung her misshapen frame into the saddle. She winced at the jagged pain that tore through her back. 'I know the moors like the lines of my hand,' she called, kicking the horse into an easy canter.

After a while Scarlet gave her horse free rein, and though she was greatly exhilarated by the ensuing furious gallop across the open moors, she knew how foolish it was to indulge in such demanding pursuits. The niggling pain in her back and side became increasingly insistent. But for some reason Scarlet felt wickedly rebellious, compelled to strike out at those who constantly sought to imprison her wild free spirit. There was hatred in her, burning and fierce, yet mingling with the hatred was an overwhelming need for love. There were times when she felt desperately lonely, afraid and vulnerable. It was then, in her most insecure moments, when she craved for love of *any* kind.

Presently, when every bone in her body was jarred and hurting, Scarlet slowed the mount to a gentler pace and headed for a narrow path that would take her through the valley and out by the bridleway above the river. There she would rest awhile and take stock of all that had happened. Oh, it was good to be riding again, to feel the fresh wind in her face and to know that she could go alone deep into the moors, to the secret places she had found as a child. The moors were a kindred spirit, never demanding, always comforting. Here she could regain partial peace of mind, in the way she always had. Already her spirit was uplifted.

In her glorious freedom, Scarlet lost all sense of time. Soon the darkness began creeping into the bright sky, layering it with long grey shadows and plunging the moors into uneasy twilight. This was the time of day Scarlet loved best. On and on they went, the horse picking his way carefully in the growing darkness and Scarlet coaxing him on with loving words. He sensed her gentleness and was calmed. After following the winding river for what seemed an age, they came to the cliff top where the river ran away down into the dells. Beyond was the sea, stretched out like an inky canvas, the flickering daylight touching the tips of the waves with shimmering crescents of light. The sky was darker now, almost black and festooned with scintillating stars that to Scarlet seemed more beautiful than she could ever remember. The sound of the gently lapping ocean was like a lullaby to her ears. She watched as the waves began to grow agitated, spewing wild frothy mountains over the rocks below, then dissolving to gather strength before surging forward again and again with relentless force. In the turbulent waters Scarlet saw a familiar face, small and haunted, with wide china blue eyes: *her mother's eyes.* And she hated herself for not having the courage to give herself up to the same watery grave.

Deeply disturbed by tormenting memories, Scarlet urged the horse ever onwards, deeper into the moors, and on towards the spinney where she thought to rest awhile before turning back. *Turning back!* To *what*, she asked herself. She was not comforted by the answer.

When at last Scarlet brought her mount to rest on the edge of the spinney, the twilight had given way to impenetrable blackness. The niggling pain in her back had become a crippling sensation, and her insides were gripped by a strange compulsion that almost bent her double. She knew instinctively that the child was impatient to be born. In the distance some way down the valley was a cottage; there was a light burning there. Gratefully, Scarlet began her way towards it.

'Easy, boy . . . easy.' Scarlet slid from the horse's back, unable to stifle the cry when her whole body was convulsed in gripping pain. Tethering the bay nearby, she stumbled towards the cottage door, the deluge of agony raging through her with such frenzy that she felt her senses dimming. When the door was inched open and the arms reached out to embrace her, she sank gratefully into them, succumbing at last to the darkness that sucked her ever downwards.

Small brilliant lights flickered all around her. For a moment, Scarlet imagined herself to be underneath a sky dotted with stars. A strange feeling took hold of her as she raised her dark eyes upwards. She saw the thick oak beams and grey walls in between; she saw the patterned curtain across the window, and the shape of the candles in their brass holders. *Of course!* She was inside the cottage. She should feel safe and warm. But she was mortally afraid, and her every limb was trembling. The pain was stronger inside her, more rhythmic and insistent. Someone was there, in the shadows. *Thank God!* She tried to move, but was held fast. 'Who's there?' she asked, peering into the gloom, her voice marbled with fear and suffering. A tide of relief swept through her when the figure ventured forward, dark and silent, its hollow face bent towards her. 'Help me,' she pleaded, her eyes beseeching. 'The child . . . I need your help.' When there came no answer, Scarlet grew alarmed. She would have risen towards the stranger, but was horrified to find that she was pinned fast. Paramount in her anguished mind was the child struggling inside her, struggling with such frenzy that erupted in every corner of her body with unbearable agony. Her senses were slipping away. *She must hold on!* 'Who are you? . . . Why won't you help me?' she pleaded. The figure came forward, its footsteps soundless, its two arms held high. 'No! PLEASE GOD, NO!' Scarlet saw its evil intention and her terrified cry echoed against her brain as though in a nightmare. In that same nightmare she saw the glinting blade of the cleaver as it swung towards her. Fragmented visions of a blood-splattered apron leapt into her horrified mind. In the distance she heard the unearthly screams. Were they *hers* . . . those awful screams that rent the air? She struggled and fought; in vain.

'*Scarlet!* . . . Scarlet for God's sake, where are you?' Garrett's frantic voice sailed into her mind and in that split second of deliverance she glanced up. The candlelight played tricks in and out of that sinister hollow face; she imagined the eyes deep within, and the name fell involuntarily from her lips in an awesome whisper. 'Silas!' There was a quickened movement, something was swiftly drawn over her body, then the figure turned and melted into the shadows. *She was safe.* Dear God, she was safe. *For now!*

'It's *true*, I tell you!' Scarlet rounded on Garrett, her dark eyes ablaze and defiant. 'There was someone in that cottage . . . I was tied down. Don't treat me like an idiot.

For God's sake, Garrett . . . *I know what I saw!'*

At once Garrett was full of remorse. He came forward to where Scarlet was seated, his shoulders stooped and a look of dejection in his candid hazel eyes. 'Don't torment yourself,' he begged her, 'you were in so much pain and confusion . . . it's only natural that your imagination should play tricks. When we found you, you were almost out of your mind about the baby. Oh, look sweetheart . . . there was no one there but you . . . I swear it.'

'Then what about the *candles*?' Scarlet had raised the same issue so many times, and each time Garrett had patiently explained that, when he and two of his men found her, she was alone. There was no sign of anyone else.

'*You* must have lit them, before you lost consciousness.'

'I was tied down . . . did you not find a rope . . . a strap?'

'Nothing, I promise. You were not tied down. You know how we searched the cottage when you wouldn't be calmed. There was no sign of anyone having been there . . . except you. Even the dust and cobwebs were virtually undisturbed.' He sat on the bed beside her and gathered her hand into his. 'Believe me, Scarlet . . . it was all in your imagination.' He laughed, but not unkindly, 'And who would want to kill you, my darling? . . . Why?' He was at his wits' end. Scarlet seemed obsessed with the crazy belief that someone had meant to take her life that night, nearly two weeks ago. 'Answer me, Scarlet . . . *why* do you think anyone would want to kill you? The idea's not only unthinkable, but bordering on hysteria.'

Scarlet chose not to answer. Instead she went to the small wooden cradle which was bedecked in white frilly curtains and pretty ribbons. Here she spent a long precious moment gazing at the child warmly curled in the softest shawl. She bent to touch her finger against the tiny pink face, and her heart spilled over with love. If she had nothing else in the whole world, she had this little darling creature that was her own flesh and blood; hers and Silas's. *SILAS!* Was *he* the hooded stranger at the cottage? *Did he want her and the child dead?* The thought was too awful to contemplate, and yet, *and yet*! Shivering, she thrust him from her mind, resolving at the same time to keep her own counsel from now on. Garrett had begun to suspect she might be unbalanced. He would never believe her; his soul was too gentle and innocent to understand such violent thoughts. What could *he* know about the darker emotions, of horror, revenge, and a love so inter-laced with fear and hatred that by its very nature it must transcend all that was decent. *NO!* Garrett could never truly comprehend the tortured thing that was her soul. *No one could.* She would never again speak to him of her fears. Yet for the sake of her daughter, Cassie, she must be ever vigilant, always watchful for the one who would harm them both. Immersed in Scarlet's deepest trembling heart was the image of that hooded face and the eyes set back in the darkness. *SILAS!* More than ever, the name was synonymous with all that tormented her.

'Put it all behind you, my love,' Garrett pleaded now. He made no move to cross the room towards her, but remained with his back to the window, his adoring eyes drinking in the beauty that was Scarlet. He had never seen her more devastatingly lovely. In the flowing crimson robe, with her long black hair loose about her shoulders, there was something primeval and untouchable about her. But the fact did not deter him. He wanted Scarlet for his wife, more than he had ever wanted anything, and he was astonished at the lengths he was prepared to go to, in order to secure her for his own. *Nothing else mattered!* Not his father, or his father's fortune; not even his own life, because without Scarlet that life would be worthless. He watched her now, bending over the cradle and murmuring to the child, *her child. Another man's child!* He visibly squirmed as he was made to imagine Scarlet locked in another man's arms. When the thought became tortuous, he deliberately smothered it, seizing on the desperate hope that soon she would agree to become his wife. Spurred on by this belief, he came to her side and, placing his hands on her shoulders, he turned her round to face him. 'No one will ever hurt you . . . or the child, not while I'm alive. I promise you that, Scarlet. Only . . . let me take you for my wife, that's all I ask.' When she raised her dark tempestuous eyes he was taken aback by their exquisite beauty. For a long agonising moment she stared at him, the blackness in her profound gaze seeming to glisten like the slivers of shattered glass. He never knew what she was thinking. It was unnerving.

'Please, Garrett.' There was desolation in her voice. 'I've told you . . . I will think about it. But not now, not yet.'

'Soon then.' There arose in him an overwhelming desire to hurt her. But then he was mortified by such thoughts. 'I love you, Scarlet. I need you.' His voice was a caress. 'You and the child. You need me also. All I want is to take care of you both.'

'I know, and I really *will* decide, soon . . . you have my word.' Her eyes were bright with pain and he hated himself for intimidating her. Slowly he bent his head towards her. He would have kissed her, but she lowered her eyes, remaining passive, unreceptive, yet not resisting. The temptation was lost, and he withdrew. 'Remember, Scarlet . . . I can give you a home, security, and a great deal of love. You have everything to gain, and nothing to lose.' His voice was harsh, but the entreaty was tinged with fear. 'I don't want to lose you, Scarlet. I'll make no demands on you,' he promised. And Scarlet knew he meant every word.

Later, when Garrett had departed the house to carry out the duties of the estate, Scarlet had a visitor. It was Shelagh.

'For a moment there, I didn't think that surly-faced housekeeper was going to let me in,' Shelagh laughed, embracing Scarlet and remarking how well she looked.

'I'm fine now,' Scarlet assured her. She was overjoyed to see the one who had so earnestly befriended her when she was at her lowest ebb. 'The housekeeper resents my being here,' she explained. 'She's ruled the roost for so long that another female in the house represents a threat to her authority.'

'*Two* females!' Shelagh reminded her, going to the crib and gazing on the sleeping child. 'Don't forget *this* little mite.' She made no attempt to take the child out, apologising, 'I'm so awkward with tiny babies. But, oh, she's lovely, Scarlet! What have you decided to call her?'

'Cassie.' Scarlet's pride was evident in her voice. 'It suits her,' Shelagh declared. Then, coyly, 'And will that be Cassie Pengally . . . or Cassie Summers?' When she saw Scarlet's expression darken, she was immediately penitent. 'Oh, Scarlet . . . take no notice of me. I was never one to be discreet. Of course, that's *your* business. Forgive me?'

Scarlet, however, was only too glad to have a friend in whom she could confide. She explained how Garrett was badgering her to name the day for their wedding, and how she was afraid to commit herself. 'I'm terrified of making a mistake,' she admitted.

'Do you love him?'

'*No*. Not in the way he wants me to love him.' Scarlet was bluntly truthful.

'But look what he's offering you, Scarlet.' Shelagh appeared distressed to see how Scarlet was so torn in her dilemma. 'A marriage *can* be successful . . . if one partner loves enough for two. Think about it before you say no,' she urged, 'be sure of what you're doing . . . there's little Cassie to think of as well.' She came to Scarlet and put a comforting arm round her neck. 'You've been through so much, Scarlet. Don't throw away the chance of a good life. And what's the alternative?'

'There's no alternative.' Scarlet was well aware of what Shelagh was so gently pointing out. Suddenly Greystone House and her father loomed in her mind, to darken her spirits. 'Tell me what's been happening with you,' she asked. At once the atmosphere changed, just as Scarlet knew it would. She felt Shelagh move away, her sudden silence unnerving. 'Is he well?' She could not bring herself to openly refer to him as her father.

'No, he is *not* well, Scarlet.' Shelagh had returned to the wicker chair now, as she met Scarlet's dark gaze with anxious brown eyes, her whole countenance appeared altered. The small round shoulders were slightly stooped and her short stocky fingers began nervously fidgeting with the folds of her sombre brown skirt. 'He's a strange man,' she said in quiet voice, 'since that night when he closed his door against you . . . he's gone from bad to worse. Sometimes he's almost out of his mind. He won't eat properly . . . and he locks himself in the cellar for days on end.' She shook her head, lowering her eyes to the floor and growing more agitated beneath Scarlet's curious gaze. 'Oh, I know I should leave him . . . I'm a fool *not* to leave him. But he's ill, you see . . . he *needs* me.' She raised her eyes and Scarlet was surprised to see that they were bright with tears. 'I can't leave him,' she said, 'you do understand? I've come to regard him as my responsibility . . . and Greystone House as my own.'

Scarlet was shocked by the startling revelations concerning her father, not only because he had always been so formidable and now was reported to be tragically punishing himself, but because of Shelagh's admission that she could not leave him. A startling thought crossed her mind and she had to put it to Shelagh. 'Are you saying you *love* him?' The idea shook her to the core.

'I don't know if I "love" him.' Shelagh also seemed

shaken by Scarlet's question. 'All I know is that Greystone House has become home to me. Your father is ill.' She smiled, and Scarlet's heart went out to her. 'It's so good to be needed, Scarlet . . . to have a purpose.'

'I think I understand.' Scarlet glanced towards the cradle. 'I, too, have a purpose now.' Even so, she found it hard to believe that anyone could willingly tie themselves to her father. Memories of her mother came into her thoughts. Was there *ever* love in Greystone House? If there was, she could not recall it. Yet there *was* something prevalent there. Some intangible essence that clung and sucked you into itself, making you want to belong. Even now, in spite of everything, she herself was not entirely free of the malevolence that lived and breathed in the house of her childhood. Often when the moon was unusually high in a black cloudless sky and the wind swept the moors with its mournful melody, she would hear the house calling her, wailing her name like a lost soul. It seemed to know that she was waiting, listening, and forever struggling with that part of her that craved to return. There was *evil* in Greystone House. *Vincent Pengally was that evil.* Scarlet knew that it was he who beckoned her back. He meant to punish her for the dreadful thing she had done. She had defied him, betrayed him, and because of it he would always haunt her. *He wanted her very soul.* Trembling inwardly, Scarlet went to the cradle. *Cassie was the sin her father would never forgive.* She was desperately afraid for Cassie. And for dear Shelagh, who seemed blind to Vincent Pengally's corrupt and predatory nature.

'What's the matter, Scarlet?' Shelagh saw the crippling fear in Scarlet's eyes when she brought her anxious gaze to bear on that kind homely face.

'Don't stay at Greystone House,' Scarlet pleaded. 'Get away from him . . . before he hurts you!'

For a moment, Shelagh appeared astonished, then her brown eyes crinkled into a warm disarming smile as she rose to collect her coat from the chairback. 'Bless you, Scarlet,' she laughed, 'your father won't hurt *me*. He relies on me too much.' She put on her coat and gloves, tucking her green and yellow scarf into the deep collar and coming to tickle the baby under the chin. 'You're so lucky, Scarlet . . . to have someone of your very own.' Suddenly her voice was serious. Turning to Scarlet she reminded her, 'I am not so lucky . . . all I have is your father. Like you, I have little alternative.' She offered her face for Scarlet to kiss. When the kiss was gladly given with a long loving embrace, she told Scarlet, 'The world is a cruel and frightening place, Scarlet. Would it be so difficult for you to let Garrett protect you from all that? I know he adores you . . . and I'm certain he'll treat little Cassie like his own flesh and blood.' She had never pressed Scarlet as to who was Cassie's father, although she had her own suspicions. For now, though, she wanted to save Scarlet from a worse fate than marrying Garrett Summers. Vincent Pengally was an unforgiving man, and only Shelagh knew how dangerously vengeful he felt towards his daughter and her child. 'Say yes to Garrett,' she urged Scarlet now. 'Who knows . . . you could well learn to love him dearly.' After playing with the child a moment longer and passing on John Blackwood's wish to be remembered to Scarlet, Shelagh reminded her, 'I'm not far away should you need me. I'll call whenever I can, you know that . . . but I do have my hands full, what with your father being so very difficult, and I still have to cope with the everyday running of the house.' She also revealed how the smithy was being allowed to run down. 'Your father doesn't seem to care that half his customers now take their horses to the blacksmith in Minehead.'

Scarlet was sorry to see Shelagh go because, for a short while, there had been real friendship to warm and guide her. She thought long and hard on Shelagh's wise words. Her mind was made up. When Garrett returned, she intended to tell him that yes, she would agree to become his wife, and they could begin making plans for the wedding in the spring of next year. In spite of her determination to see it through for Cassie's sake if for nothing else, there was an uneasy murmuring inside Scarlet, and a terrible sense of impending doom.

'Good lord, Silas . . . anybody'd think you'd seen a ghost!' Old Mr Turnbull was not surprised to find Silas already lighting up the forge. He had come to rely on him to be the first to work every morning, and today was no different, except that the young man's handsome face appeared ashen, and his manner was unusually strange. 'Are you alright, lad?'

Silas nodded, his black eyes seeming stark in his quiet face. He did not speak, but Mr Turnbull was not offended by this. He had long accepted that Silas was a man of few words. 'Looks like it's going to be a lovely day,' he remarked in an effort to draw Silas into conversation. 'The first day of May, eh? It's just as well it's coming summer . . . what with this blessed coal rationing. It does make life difficult and no mistake!' When Silas made no response, he too succumbed to a deep and thoughtful silence.

Several times throughout the morning Mr Turnbull surreptitiously watched Silas at his labours. As always, he was astonished at the young man's appetite for work. Silas had been here for almost a year now, and not once had he done anything that warranted reproach. He was a quiet brooding fellow, keeping himself to himself and offending no one. He lived a monotonous life, working each hour God sent and saving every penny he earned. During the one occasion when he had confided in another human being, Silas had revealed to Mr Turnbull how he intended to buy his own business, perhaps a smithy or a small farm where he would breed the finest hunters and sell them to the gentry hereabouts. Mr Turnbull had assured him that, with his knowledge of horses, he should do well. He also suspected that Silas had a young woman somewhere, and though he never mentioned her, there were times when he would fall into deep thought and a yearning far-away look would come into his eyes. There was no doubt as far as Mr Turnbull was concerned. The lad was haunted by love, and by something else besides; although Mr Turnbull couldn't say what exactly, only that it did seem on occasions as though Silas was deeply tormented.

In the early days, soon after he'd come to work at the Barnstaple smithy, Silas had a habit of disappearing for days on end, and then appearing just as suddenly. He had not done that for some time though. All the same, he was a difficult man to get to know. Mr Turnbull was convinced that Silas would make good, not only because he was the best worker ever seen at this forge and didn't squander his money like the others; but because he was driven by a raging passion to succeed, to become a man of property; to *be* somebody. He was different in that way, and in other ways. He was not one of the men, and was not treated as such. There was something about him that warned people off. He had suffered too; suffered badly at the hands of some devil. It was there, in his dark soulful eyes, and in the deep cutting scars on his wrist and arms. Almost as though he'd been strung up and tortured.

Throughout the long exacting day, Silas spoke not a word. His tormented mind kept returning to the article he had seen in the newspaper that morning, together with a picture. A picture of Scarlet, looking extraordinarily lovely in a pale shimmering dress and wearing a coronet of flowers, her arms closely linked with that of a man. The dress was a wedding gown, and the man was Garrett Summers.

Scarlet was married! The words echoed over and over in Silas's tortured thoughts, until he could think of nothing else. *Scarlet had betrayed him.* He cursed them both, cursing Scarlet more bitterly yet wanting her with every fibre of his being.

At day's end, weary and exhausted, Silas climbed into his bunk. His frantic thoughts had given way to a more orderly and calculating pattern. With clarity he saw what he must do. He must bide his time until he was a man of consequence. Then, and only then, could he dare to go back and claim what was his, what had *always* been his! *Scarlet was not lost to him.* For now, though, she could have her short freedom. But when the time was right, when he could return without guilt or fear, when the shadows that pursued him were finally dispersed and all the horrors from his past laid to rest for ever, he would return. He would have his Scarlet again, *or no other man would*! Nothing on this earth, or in the heavens beyond, would keep them apart for ever. Their lives were too irreversibly entwined.

PART FOUR

1923

TORMENT

> . . . The night is long
> That never finds the day
>
> Shakespeare

CHAPTER THIRTEEN

The maid thrust the poker through the bars and deep into the grate, agitating the dead coke ashes until they were all despatched into the lower tray. Withdrawing the tray, she laid a grimy cloth over it to prevent spillage, then on quick silent footsteps she departed, closing the door behind her, leaving Scarlet still seated at the far end of the room, thoughtfully gazing out of the window and down the long winding drive.

Wistfully, Scarlet looked up at the sky. Here and there were floating grey patches and the promise of rain, but in the far distance there was a vast stretch of bright blinding light. The breeze was gaining momentum. Soon the rain clouds would pass and the sun would break through. Sighing, Scarlet turned her gaze indoors, letting her dark eyes rove over the unquestionable grandeur of the drawing room, whose ornate expensive style and furnishing characterised every room throughout Selworthy Manor: deep plush carpets, velvet curtains, the smell of old leather and beeswax. *Scarlet loathed it all.* Some two years she had lived here, yet she could find no corner in which she belonged. She was uncomfortable in the presence of servants, and secretly awed by the invincible Ruth Taylor. Scarlet's stubborn refusal to be humbled by the housekeeper had only heightened the ill feeling between them, making them bitter enemies.

Garrett's father had reluctantly managed to come to terms with his son's choice of wife by ignoring her and staying out of her way at all times. There was resentment all round her, yet Scarlet was bitterly determined to hide her great unhappiness from them all. She made every effort to be polite and undemanding; she treated the housekeeper with respect and firmness and left her in no doubt that Scarlet Pengally could give as good as she got. She smiled and kept her dignity, exchanging pleasantries with Garrett's father whenever he inadvertently found himself in her company, even though her reward was an icy reception which might have frozen out a lesser woman. She suffered the touch of Garrett's probing hands on her and bore the grunting weight of his invading body in the dead of night when his appetite was roused. And always she gave the impression that his lovemaking was something good and exciting to her, when in reality the fusing of his bare flesh with hers made her inwardly cringe. Yet he was good to her, always kind and attentive, protecting her from the ill will of others and – his greatest endearing quality to Scarlet – treating Cassie as though she was his own. When Scarlet had borne him a son two years ago, she had been afraid that Garrett would favour his own flesh and blood in place of little Cassie. But he treated them both with equal love and attention. Scarlet was grateful for that. Garrett's father, however, went out of his way to cultivate the boy's affection, while ignoring Cassie as heartlessly as he did Scarlet. There were times when she wondered whether he might have somehow discovered that Cassie was not Garrett's. Yet she knew that could not be. The only two people who knew that for certain were herself and Garrett, and neither of them wanted the truth known. She consoled herself with the fact that Edward Summers was not partial to females, on top of which he had never forgiven Cassie for being born out of wedlock. He saw David as being his only grandchild and, as such, the only legitimate heir after Garrett. Although Scarlet abhorred the old man's rejection of Cassie, she was ashamed that her own maternal instincts towards David were not as they should be. She resented the fact that he was the favoured one, even doubted Garrett's impartiality sometimes. And the boy was the result of a long unbearable night when Garrett had returned, hungry for her, from one of his business trips. The memory was not a pleasant one. Neither was the birth itself, which was an agonising and prolonged experience.

In all of her loneliness and frustration there had been two beacons of light in Scarlet's life: one was her darling daughter; the other was Shelagh, who had kept in touch and proved to be a lifeline for Scarlet. She was a good listener, and seemed always ready with words of encouragement.

Suddenly, Scarlet was aware of a motor vehicle drawing up outside the front door. Quickly she crossed the room and came into the spacious hall. Here she paused on seeing the young maid coming towards her from the direction of the nursery. Cassie was toddling along beside her, wrapped in warm leggings and hooded coat. On seeing Scarlet, the child stumbled forward, excitedly calling, 'Mummy . . . Mummy!' Laughing, Scarlet swooped to pick her up. 'Hello darling,' she said, kissing her warmly. Then, turning to the young woman, she smiled, 'Thank you.' There it was again, that uneasiness she always felt when confronted by servants at her beck and call. Scarlet was reminded of the time soon after Cassie's birth, and the forceful way in which she had to persuade Garrett that *she* would care for her daughter; there was no need of the nanny he insisted she must have. The thought of someone else tending to her child, answering her cries in the night and watching her grow day by day in that intimate way

239

only a mother could enjoy, had filled her with dread. Cassie was *hers*. *She* would be the one to raise her! Seeing how adamant Scarlet was, Garrett had given in gracefully. But when his own son was born, his determination to employ a nanny was steadfast. Scarlet gave little resistance this time. Strangely enough, the prospect of Garrett's child being ministered to by another woman was not so painful to her.

After being assured that the boy was sleeping, Scarlet made her way out of the house. She was really looking forward to the trip to market – a rare pleasure.

'Well, I'm blessed!' John Blackwood took off his cap and thrust it under his armpit. 'It ain't so often *you* come into the market these days.' His smile was broad and full of delight. Scarlet was amused to see that he had two more gaps in his front teeth since she last saw him eight months ago.

'I couldn't stand being cooped up in that house a minute longer,' Scarlet told him, her attention suddenly caught by the sight of a little boy playing nearby: a handsome little fellow with light brown hair and laughing green eyes that were smiling at Cassie. 'Trent?' she asked.

'Aye. That's my young 'un . . . Trent. Growed a bit since you last seen him, ain't he, eh?' John was bursting with pride as he stooped to sweep the boy into his arms. Swinging him up onto the wagon, he pointed to Cassie, who was hiding shyly behind Scarlet's back. 'Pretty little thing, ain't she, boy?' he laughed, shaking the boy until he began loudly giggling. His laughter was infectious and soon Cassie also was laughing and peeking out from the folds of her mammy's skirt. 'The lass ain't much like *you*, is she?' John thoughtfully regarded the little girl's short fiery golden hair and dark eyes. 'She's got your eyes, though . . . dark and pretty. The fair hair's from her daddy's side, I expect?' He quietly observed Scarlet, thinking how lovely and prosperous she looked in that tweed coat with its fur collar and matching cuffs. Her long black tresses fell from beneath a brown beret that was placed on her head at an attractive jaunty angle.

'I expect so,' agreed Scarlet, wondering, not for the first time, how Cassie's hair *was* more like Garrett's than that of her father; Silas's hair was dark, so was hers. But then her own darling mother had hair the colour of Cassie's. Perhaps *Silas's mother* was fair also? It suddenly struck Scarlet that she knew nothing whatsoever of Silas's background. She knew only the awful things her own father had told her, and that Silas was just there; *all her life, he was just there*, skulking in the dark, silent and forbidding. She had never discovered who he was, or where he had come from. *Only that he would never leave her.* Suddenly she shivered, even though the cold February wind was subsiding and a surprisingly warm sun was beginning to peep through.

'Don't stand about too long, my girl . . . you'll catch a chill.' John put his son to the ground and, when Cassie began fidgeting, Scarlet eased her forward, but kept a firm hold on her hand. She was amused to see young Trent take hold of Cassie's other hand, determined that she would come and play. 'They'll be alright,' John assured Scarlet, 'Trent knows well enough that he's not to stray from the wagon. Boys is rascals, though . . . you'll see when your own lad gets a bit older . . . David, ain't it?' He kept on chattering.

'Stay close, darling.' Scarlet watched as the two children crawled into a large cardboard box, giggling and contented in each other's company. With a more serious face she turned to John, saying quietly, 'It seems my father is dying?' Since Shelagh had suggested that she ought to say her goodbyes and make peace with her father, Scarlet had suffered the most terrible nightmares. 'Shelagh thinks I ought to visit and make peace with him. I can't bring myself to do it.'

'And who can blame you if you refuse to see him?' John stridently remarked, his own expression forbidding. 'I know he's your father . . . your own flesh and blood, and the Lord says we must forgive. But, that devil caused you a lot of pain and suffering. He treated you badly . . . you and young Silas both. They allus say that we pay for our sins in the end, and, since he threw you out, your father seems to be paying his pound of flesh right enough. Did you know the smithy's closed down altogether?' When she nodded, he went on, 'Aye, no doubt Shelagh's kept you informed . . . just like she's kept *us* informed as to your own well-being. I don't mind telling you, my girl . . . I ain't never seen a man go so far downhill . . . like a crazy thing he's been! Ranting and raving one day, an' meek as a lamb the next. Bit by bit he's fallen apart . . . the doctors are baffled. They've given up on him . . . reckon it's all in his mind. Self-destruction, that's what *I* say!' He shook his head, adding, 'Shelagh called me in the other day . . . wanted me to move his bed by the window, where he could see out. He didn't even *know* me. Twenty years and more I've worked for Vincent Pengally at Greystone House . . . and he didn't even know me!' He lowered his gaze and continued to shake his head, his thoughts speeding back over the years, embracing the strange and wicked things that had occurred at Greystone House: the rapid deterioration of Vincent Pengally himself being only one in a long line. He lifted his gaze to Scarlet, his blue eyes troubled. 'It ain't my place to tell you what you should or shouldn't do.' He paused for a moment, seeming to think harder and his frown deepening until the tiny folds of skin between his eyebrows erupted into mountainous ridges. Presently he said, 'All I can tell you in good faith is this . . . if it were *my* father that were lying on his deathbed . . . no matter what pain he'd caused me in the past, I couldn't let him go to his maker without forgiveness. Me conscience wouldn't let me . . . I'd be haunted ever after if I let me own father die with bad blood 'atween us.'

John's words were an echo of what Shelagh had already told Scarlet. And, in truth, there was an unpleasant urge in her to see for herself how close to death's door her father was. For some reason she was disturbed by the possibility that maybe Shelagh, and now John, was exaggerating his illness. She needed to see for herself, to know that he would die soon. She craved to see the greyness of death in his eyes and be assured that before too long he would lie in a cold deep grave where he could never again hurt her. And even when it happened, when his breath was stopped and his vile body cold and stiff, she was still not sure whether the nightmares would end. In that painful dark corner of her mind that no one else must ever know he would live on, frightening her, touching, adoring, torturing her almost beyond endurance. *He and Silas. They were the cross she must bear until the end of her days!* And perhaps ever after. 'Will you go and see him?' John's voice filtered into her uneasy thoughts.

'No!' Her answer was swift. 'As you said, John . . . it's possible that I may be haunted ever after if I let him die with bad blood between us.' Again the fear. *Always the fear!* If she did go back to Greystone House, it would not be pity or compassion that took her back. It would not even be hatred. It would be that same paralysing fear. And an unpleasant curiosity to see the life draining from him. She was so close! So very close! 'Give my regards to your wife, John,' she said, beginning to look for Cassie. 'I must go . . . I promised Garrett I'd be waiting for him at the Yarn Market on the stroke of noon.'

Scarlet was the first to realise. *The children were gone!* Panic took hold of her. 'Cassie!' She searched frantically, in and amongst the boxes, calling her daughter's name, each time with increasing alarm. 'Cassie! . . . Where are you?'

Realising the seriousness of the situation, John also began desperately rummaging in the stock, throwing boxes aside and yelling out to the other stallholders, asking whether they had seen 'two young 'uns . . . playing nearby?' All but one shook their heads or replied, 'Sorry, mate . . . there's been no young 'uns round this way.' It was the flower lady who pointed out that she had seen two youngsters, a little lad and a toddler, 'hand in hand . . . going towards the shops. I had an idea they were with a plump lady who went into the butcher's,' she said.

Scarlet's footsteps sped over the cobbles, the rhythmic echo from beneath her boots reverberating in the sharp morning air. *Cassie!* Let her be alright, she prayed. At the entrance to the butcher's shop, she paused, gasping for breath, her black eyes wide and frantic as they combed the shop's interior. Then came John's voice, bursting with relief. 'There they are! . . . I oughtta smack you hard, you little tyke. Haven't I told you never to wander away!' He pushed into the shop, drawing Scarlet with him. What she saw in that instant struck horror to her senses. The butcher was smiling at her, tightly clutching the children one in each arm and there between them was the apron, *the same blood-spattered apron.* Surging forward she grasped the small girl, wrenching her from the butcher's grip. And all the while he kept smiling, staring, searching her face with those pleasant eyes. 'They just wandered in,' he told her, releasing the boy into his father's care. 'Children are so vulnerable,' he said, looking fondly on them, 'they need to be watched . . . all the time.'

'I can't think how they made off without us knowing it,' John was clearly relieved to find that young Trent had come to no harm. 'His mummy would have drawn and quartered me if anything had happened to the lad!'

Out of the corner of her eye, Scarlet saw the inner room and the bloody carcasses hanging there, nude, undignified, with patches of bright pink skin and dead grey muscle that created a weird gruesome chequer-work on the ravaged corpses. The awful smell of death permeated the air, a dry choking smell, sweetened with the irritating odour of dampened sawdust. The steady drip, drip of blood was magnified a thousand times in her ears; drip, DRIP, crimson splashes.

Scarlet blurted out her thanks and bade goodbye to John before hurrying from the shop. Her glance met that of the butcher. 'No doubt I'll see you again . . . Scarlet,' he murmured, his smile deepening. The small hairs bristled on the back of her neck. How dare he call her by her first name! She did not like that man. But he was charming. And she was foolish. Even as she went at a furious pace down the main thoroughfare and on to Church Street, Scarlet could still feel his gaze on her. To others, the butcher's ready smile might be warm and friendly; to *her*, it was lecherous and unsettling.

'Oh, what a little darling!' The voice sailed out from the newsagent's doorway. It was Ada Blackwood. 'My word, Scarlet . . . hasn't the child grown.' She came forward, halting Scarlet in her tracks and laughingly tousling Cassie's golden locks. 'D'you know, my dear . . . it must be what? . . . three years since I saw the child? And I've not even clapped eyes on the lad. You really should visit the cottage more often.' A look of caution entered her round homely face. 'But I expect you've done right . . . keeping a distance between you and Greystone House, after that *terrible* scene when your father put you on the street! I ask you . . . what kind of monster would do that to his only child? Mind you, me dear!' She wagged a finger in Scarlet's face. 'There's no doubt in *my* mind that you did wrong . . . getting yourself with child like that!' she said reproachfully. 'Still, that's all water under the bridge now, isn't it? Oh, but she really *is* a little sweetie . . . Cassie isn't it . . . if I remember rightly. Oh, yes, it must be close on three years since I last saw the little mite. It was very good of you to let Shelagh fetch me to Selworthy Manor.' There was no stopping her, thought Scarlet. 'Dreadful business . . . you being found like that on the moors. Goodness! If young Mr Summers and his men hadn't found you when they did and fetched a trap to carry you safely back . . . well! You might have given birth to Cassie there and then, in that frightful cottage!' She lowered her voice. 'O' course, *you* weren't to know as how that cottage was the *very same* where them two bodies were found . . . half-eaten by rats!' She shivered loudly. 'It don't bear thinking about, my dear. But, y'see . . . again, you brought it on yourself by being too impulsive and headstrong. You should never have gone out riding in your condition!'

'You're quite right, Mrs Blackwood.' Scarlet did not need a lecture just now. 'I really *must* go.'

'You do know your father's badly?' She swayed her head gravely. 'Won't last till summer, they say. And you're on your way to call on him, eh?' She smiled approvingly. 'That's a fine thing to do, after the way he's treated you, but like I said . . . you did bring some of it down on your own head! Still, you do well to pay your respects. You are his daughter after all, and his only kin.'

Not wishing to discourage her and at the risk of seeming impolite, Scarlet hastily excused herself and was quickly on her way. She wished now that she had not sent Mr Summers's motor vehicle back to the manor. She regretted having come out to the market altogether. She knew now that it had been a foolish thing to do. People never forgot. All this time, ever since first arriving at Selworthy Manor, she had resisted the insane desire to return to her father's house. Once Cassie was born, Scarlet had been content to busy herself with the child's upbringing and to while away her leisure hours in the magnificent grounds at the manor. Occasionally, when the moors had beckoned, as they always did, she had been satisfied with a ride in the back of the motor vehicle, gently pursuing the narrow meandering lanes that wound through the moors, following the safest routes. In truth, Scarlet would have preferred to saddle up the most spirited hunter in the Summers's stable and to gallop over the wild primitive landscape until she reached a place where no one would ever find her. She deliberately suppressed these feelings. Not for herself, but for Cassie, who was her only purpose in life. At Selworthy Manor Cassie had been blessed with all those things that Scarlet had never known – respect, social standing, wealth, a kind man to be her father – it was all hers for the taking. The only price would be exacted from Scarlet, who would never hesitate to sacrifice everything for her daughter's sake. Strange, how her son rarely came into her mind.

Deep in thought and drawn by instinct, Scarlet found that she was treading the footpath towards the moors. The experience was unpleasantly strange. In her mind, Scarlet had lived it over and over, but now that she was actually crossing Packhorse Bridge and coming closer to the path that would lead her right up to the door of Greystone House, she felt herself trembling. There was an uncanny, unreal quality about her slow determined steps, as though she was moving in a trance. At the curve of the bridge, she stopped, gazing up at the house and instinctively drawing her child closer to her.

She ventured towards the weed-strewn path. All round her were signs of neglect: the garden was wild and overgrown, green mildew and rampant vines had begun to climb over the smithy; there were gaping holes in the roof where the tiles had slipped away. The smithy was crumbling. *He* was crumbling. Scarlet smiled. That was why she was here. *To see him decaying!* She turned away, but was at once arrested by the homely figure of Shelagh, emerging from the house, a look of astonishment on her face on seeing Scarlet there.

'Must we huddle in here, Scarlet?' Shelagh gasped in the

cold damp air of the potting shed, where so often Scarlet and John had braved the elements in their work together. 'Come into the house, why don't you?' she asked for the third time. 'You needn't be afraid. Your father's sound asleep after his medicine. He can't hurt you any more.'

'I won't come into the house.' Scarlet was adamant. 'I can't do that, Shelagh . . . I told you.'

'I know, I know . . . but I do wish you would find the courage, my love . . . if he dies and there's bad blood between you, it could haunt you for the rest of your life. You wouldn't want that, would you, Scarlet?'

'No. I wouldn't want that!' Scarlet agreed. She would be haunted for the rest of her life in any event, she thought wryly; whether her father lived or died it made no difference. 'And the doctor really thinks there's little hope for him?' she asked now, praying with all her heart that it was so. In spite of the fact that she was struck with terror at the very thought of ever again entering Greystone House, and even more horrified by the awful prospect of looking on her father's face, she was also driven by an insane desire to witness for herself the shadowy mask of death creeping over his fearsome features. Yet even that would not temper the fear and hatred he had long fostered in her. She felt Shelagh's comforting hand on her arm, saw the homely face looking at her with concern, and Scarlet was moved to guilt. 'I'm sorry,' she murmured. 'I know you're only thinking to spare me pain.' She thought the young woman looked terribly worn. There were dark shadows beneath her eyes and a ghastly look about her. She had been such a friend. Oh, but Shelagh did not know all that had happened between the Pengallys of Greystone House! She was not there before, to protect the terrified child in the dead of night when the dark stranger came. She could not imagine how that monster had toyed with the child's gentle soul, tormenting it, shaping it with his rough probing hands, his cajoling evil tongue, and those unspeakable vile deeds, until that innocent child's soul was also black and wicked, twisted beyond repair and made to skulk from the daylight. *Hideous!* The loathing coursed through Scarlet's veins, engulfing every normal decent feeling. Oh! To gaze on that face now, just once more before it was too late! To see it emaciated. To bury that shame, that fear, along with him, and never again to suffer because of him. If only she had the courage! But death would never ease the horror; not *his* death, nor *hers*! Scarlet visibly shuddered.

'There!' Shelagh had seen her tremble. 'The pair of us will catch of our death lingering about in this damp air.' She glanced to where Cassie was engrossed in piling up the dozens of loose plant pots that had lain dormant in an apple crate. 'Won't you at least bring the child in for a hot drink?' Scarlet shook her head, her quiet expression belying turbulent thoughts. 'Do you want me to send for you if he gets worse?' Again Scarlet shook her head. Shelagh sighed noisily, drawing her woollen jacket tighter about her. 'John sent for the doctor, you know . . . while I was away for a few days, visiting friends in Taunton. Well! . . . I really thought he was much better, or I would never have left him. I was so tired though. And your father was up and about . . . even talking of going back to his work. He seemed much more like his cantankerous old self.' She smiled, and even her smile was weary. 'It really all began on the night he discovered you were with child . . . self-destruction the doctor says . . . all in his own mind.' Glittering with emotion, her brown eyes beseeched Scarlet. 'If only you could bring yourself to see him . . . talk with him. I'm sure there could be forgiveness between you. His health would quickly improve, I'm convinced of it.'

'*NO.*' Scarlet stooped to take hold of the child's hand. 'How can I ever forgive him?' Besides which, the thought that *she* should help to 'improve' his health was repugnant to her. She *wanted* him dead; *craved* him dead! Yet, in doing so, Scarlet knew that she was creating another nightmare for herself. No matter. It was already too late.

Long after Shelagh had gone into the house, Scarlet stood on Packhorse Bridge, gazing across at Greystone House, reliving memories and besieged by all the ghosts that were embalmed in the house for all time. Had she *really* escaped, she wondered? She knew instinctively that she was still inexplicably bound to the past: the house, her father and mother, Silas. They all rose up before her, taunting and enticing, beckoning, always beckoning. She wanted to run from that place. But something held her fast. Some compelling, intangible thing kept her there, owned her, body and soul. She reflected on Shelagh's words, 'He can't hurt you any more . . . haunt you for the rest of your life.' *And beyond*, Scarlet thought now; haunt me even beyond my life.

When the child began fidgeting, trying desperately to break free from her mammy's hold, and calling for her daddy, Scarlet lost no time in turning from the house, her frantic footsteps hurrying along West Street as though the devil himself was on her heels. Suddenly the wind was more fierce, cutting with spite against her face, piercing through the layers of her coat, causing her to tremble. Instinctively, she turned into St George's Church.

From a safe distance, Silas followed.

At the door Scarlet lingered awhile, her quiet gaze roving the church interior, and she thinking how beautiful it was – the high roof with its most exquisite fan vaulting, the magnificently carved rood-screen, then beyond, the altar . . . the heart of any church. 'Ssh, Cassie,' Scarlet bent to the restless child, putting a silencing finger to her lips and flashing a warning with her dark eyes. Together they went forward towards the altar, one with some reluctance, the other bathing in the aura of calm and tranquillity all around. The silence was complete. Nothing disturbed it.

When they knelt before the rood-screen, the child was distressed to see how freely the tears ran down her mammy's face. 'Don't cry, Mammy,' she whispered, gently shaking Scarlet's hand, being overwhelmed by the sight of such tears and made fearful by the awesome atmosphere. Quietly she snuggled into Scarlet, her wide eyes filled with wonder as they alighted on one grand ancient artefact after another.

Here in this beautiful church, where on so few occasions her own mammy had brought her as a child, Scarlet found a measure of peace. She recalled how Hannah had always been afraid that her husband might discover her forbidden rare visits to God's house; forbidden because Vincent Pengally fervently believed that there was no higher being. He denied all that was good and gentle, immersing himself in the darker, more evil elements of his existence. Hannah, therefore, was made to live by his beliefs. Yet there *were* times, though few, when she found the courage to defy him. Scarlet remembered. And among her heartfelt prayers the most profound was for Hannah. 'I know I have never really trusted you, Lord,' she murmured now, 'but . . . who else can I turn to?' Even so, she sensed that her tormented soul would never find sanctuary.

Outside, unaware that Silas was observing her from a distance, Scarlet took a moment to stand over the spot where Hannah was buried. Afterwards she meandered down the path, watching Cassie run playfully up and down the bank, and occasionally pausing to gaze at the many old granite headstones that marked the places where the dead were laid to rest. Scarlet was saddened by one in particular, where lay an infant of one year and seven months, by the name of Jane, also a lady called Ann. Scarlet could not read the inscription but was told the names by her mammy. She wondered, in passing, whether they were mother and child.

As she stood, slightly stooped towards the headstone,

her gaze lingering awhile, there came over Scarlet a creeping horror that she was being watched. The sound of her name, spoken in a whisper, struck fear to her heart. 'Scarlet . . . I've been looking for you.' She swung round.

SILAS! His name froze in her throat. She could hardly believe her eyes. Yet here he was, and it registered, even through her shock, how devilishly handsome he looked, in a long dark overcoat, his thick black hair loose and wayward about his face, and those intense violet eyes locking her to him just as they had always done.

'You!' Her black eyes were made brilliant by the horror that rose up in her. Instinctively she backed away, calling for Cassie. When the child ran to her, she clutched her tightly, until the blood was stopped in her tiny fingers. 'GO AWAY,' Scarlet implored him. When he still came towards her, calling her name, his gaze caressing her face, she swept the child up into her arms and, in her terrible panic, could only think to flee! Dark recesses were opened in her mind; her father's warnings all began murmuring in her senses. 'He eats little innocents . . . eats! . . . eats!' She was a child again, frightened and vulnerable. *But she loved Silas! NO!* He was no different from her father. *Why wouldn't they leave her be?* When his hands fell to her shoulders and her eyes were made to look on him, the words spat out. '*STAY AWAY FROM ME!*' Fear became loathing.

'*Never!* . . . I'll never stay away.' He would have taken the child and lowered it to the ground, but Scarlet had her so fast there was no parting them. Instead, he bent his head towards Scarlet, his voice but a whisper. 'I love you,' he told her, 'and you love me, Scarlet. You belong to no other man. Come with me now . . . you and the child.' When, unable to speak, she vehemently shook her head, he put his hand to her face, caressing her, awaking those feelings inside her that she believed to be long buried. 'I am my own man now, Scarlet . . . with a small business and fortune enough for us to lead a good life. I've worked hard for this day. Don't deny me now, Scarlet. I can't live without you. I *won't* live without you any longer!' There was such agony in his voice that, for a moment, Scarlet was stirred to compassion.

Suddenly, his mouth was on hers. In spite of herself, a small thrill ran through her. *But then she remembered.* She remembered and the spell was broken. Twisting away, she ran from him, on and on, his voice calling behind her in the distance, 'You'll never belong to any other man. I won't let you!' She dared not look back. Only forwards, to where the market traders loudly entreated and the people jostled each other, where she could be lost amongst them. Her head was pounding. He was back. *Silas was back.* Now the *other* things would be back. *THE BAD THINGS!*

From across the road, Garrett Summers had seen them together. He had seen Scarlet in Silas's arms; Silas, older and looking more prosperous, more handsome. He had seen how tenderly Silas had kissed Scarlet, and how she had melted in his arms. After that he could bear no more and had hurried away with a heavy heart, a broken spirit, and a terrible sense of outrage that threatened to consume him. For the first time in his life, he wanted to *kill* . . . Silas, Scarlet . . . *both* of them!

It was Sunday. The watery sunshine of the previous day had given way to gentle snow showers. Torn by the events that had cruelly shattered any peace of mind she might have gained, Scarlet had spent a sleepless night. She was restless, apprehensive, beset by all manner of crippling doubts and torment. *Garrett had not come home.* WHY NOT? Where was he? She had punished herself time and time again, until she thought she must go crazy. Was it possible that he *knew* how Silas had approached her? Was he somehow aware that they had spoken together? That he had kissed her and, God forgive her, that she had *wanted* him to? He *did* know. He must! If not, why was he not there to meet her at the Yarn Market? And why had he stayed out all night? . . . something he had never done!

In the back of her mind, Scarlet recalled a figure standing in the clockmaker's doorway when she fled from the church. Could *that* have been Garrett . . . watching? The idea did not even bear thinking about. She covered her face in her hands and remained huddled by the fire, unable to rid herself of the awful premonition that some terrible tragedy was brewing! Since their return yesterday, Cassie had been upset, crying and asking her mammy why 'the man wouldn't let you go?' This morning, when Scarlet had hoped the child might have forgotten, there had been a disturbing scene after the nanny had brought Cassie to Scarlet's bedroom, informing her that 'your daughter woke in a bad dream, Mrs Summers . . . she was very distressed . . . wet the bed. Who is this "man" she seems so afraid of?' Frantic, Scarlet had failed to pacify Cassie. Eventually she sent both her and the nanny away; the one still crying, the other in a black mood following a lashing with Scarlet's sharp tongue. Scarlet had felt deeply uncomfortable beneath the other woman's cold glare. With her mouth set in a thin angry line, the nanny had quickly retreated from the room, thankful to take the child with her and wondering whether the young Mrs Summers – the unusually unkempt and nervous, frightened Mrs Summers – had taken leave of her senses. But then, she had reminded herself, wasn't it common knowledge how the young master's wife had never really fitted into this household? Added to which, she was of Pengally stock. And weren't they all . . . somewhat strange?

Unable to settle and not yet ready to apologise, even though she was riddled with guilt over her unforgivable behaviour, Scarlet had washed and dressed, then gone downstairs with the intention of searching out any sign of Garrett. It was when she drew level with the library door that she heard the disgruntled voice of Ruth Taylor, the housekeeper. She was addressing Edward Summers, telling him, 'I'm not one to criticise, sir . . . but your daughter-in-law has caused a great deal of upset since coming to this house. She makes no attempt to fall in with normal routine . . . a routine I might add, that has been successful these many years . . . and she goes out of her way to antagonise both myself and the other members of this household. Why! Less than an hour ago, your grandson's nanny was all but forcibly ejected from Mrs Summers's room, after being spoken to most harshly! Really, Sir . . . I do think that you should have strong words with that young lady. She takes no notice of me.'

'I suggest that you petition my son with your complaints, Miss Taylor. If you recall, I have guests from America. Have Mr and Mrs Thornton been informed that I am waiting breakfast for them?' His manner was dismissive.

'Of course, sir. They will be down directly. But . . . about the other matter. I understand that your son did not come home last evening. The main door was left unbolted after I retired . . . on the express instructions of Mrs Summers. It was still unbolted this morning, and Nanny reports that Mrs Summers was alone in her room . . . greatly agitated by your son's absence, I believe.'

There was an awkward silence while this surprising information was considered. Outside the door, Scarlet wondered what Edward Summers's reaction would be. It was as she might have expected. There was undisguised pleasure in his sarcastic remark, 'Well! Well! So . . . my son left his "lovely" wife alone all night, did he?' There was another pause before, with irritation, he reminded her, 'I have told you before . . . don't bother me with domestic problems . . . I don't have time for such matters! As you so rightly pointed out . . . she is my son's wife, not mine! Thank God! Talk to *him* about it. It won't hurt Garrett to know how ill she fits in here. Now then. Kindly wheel me to the dining room.' Neither of them heard Scarlet slip quietly away.

As she retraced her steps across the hall and up the grand curving stairway, Scarlet's attention was drawn towards the nursery, which was situated some short way down the landing from the top of the stairs. She could hear a child's laughter over soft American voices and, amidst it all, the nanny's harsher tones. The door was open. Scarlet halted outside, looking in on the scene and regretting that she was not part of it. Beside the fireplace, the small pleasant figure of Mrs Thornton was stooped towards Cassie, the two of them playing some little game and every so often laughing out loud. Mr Thornton stood by the dresser, his tall authoritative presence seeming to fill the room, and overwhelming Nanny's slight form as she proceeded to outline in the smallest detail the unsettling events of the morning. Suddenly all were aware of Scarlet's presence and all eyes turned towards her; Nanny appeared to be suitably embarrassed though not repentant. Mr Thornton's stony glare told Scarlet of his outright disapproval of her, though he could not altogether disguise his certain appreciation of her charms and a lurking lust that outshone the contempt in his eyes. Cassie's gaze was the harshest, and the one which hurt Scarlet the most. The child had still not forgiven her for sending her away.

At once Mrs Thornton came forward, a warm genuine smile on her face, and her hands outstretched in welcome. 'Oh, Scarlet . . . what a delightful daughter you have in Cassie,' she said, catching hold of Scarlet's hand and drawing her into the room. 'We have to hurry down to breakfast now, but I'm sure you'll be glad to have Cassie to yourself.' Suddenly her voice was quieter, her soft eyes more wistful. 'I can't have children, you know. Oh, I can't tell you, Scarlet . . . what I would give for a child of my own . . . a daughter, like Cassie.'

'Don't burden others with your problems, Nancy,' reprimanded her husband. 'Just thank the Good Lord for the
many other blessings He's seen fit to bestow on you.' In a
moment he was at her side, his hand on her shoulder,
gently turning her away. 'Let's not keep our host waiting,'
he suggested. As they departed from the room, Mrs
Thornton glanced back to where Cassie was sitting, her
small face enveloped in a deep frown and her unhappy
gaze intent on Scarlet. Mr Thornton did not look back, but
Scarlet instinctively knew that his thoughts were on her.
The idea made her flesh crawl.

Getting down to her knees, Scarlet reached out to touch
her daughter's soft fair hair, twirling it round her fingertips
and smiling into those uplifted dark eyes. 'I'm sorry,
sweetheart,' she said lovingly, 'Mammy was wrong to
shout and send you away.' She was relieved to see the
warmth come flooding back into Cassie's tiny oval face.
'Can we be friends again?' she asked. 'Can we cuddle and
make up?' Soon there was no trace left of a frown, and the
child eagerly threw her small arms around Scarlet's neck,
hugging her close and declaring joyfully, 'Friends,
Mammy.' Scarlet held her tight. How easy it had seemed
for Cassie to forgive her. Would that *she* could forgive. But
there were things she could never forgive. Not now. Too
much had happened. Too much had been left to fester for
so very long.

After a while, she held the girl away and turned to the
nanny, who had been observing mother and child with
interest and a degree of envy. 'I really am sorry about my
behaviour earlier,' Scarlet told her, 'it won't happen
again.'

The woman nodded, her staid expression betraying
nothing of her feelings. 'Of course,' she replied. 'I understand.' She looked at Scarlet's troubled face and at the
dark shadows beneath her eyes. She recalled how young
Mr Summers had not been at home all night, and *still* she

felt no pity. Instead she would gladly have traded places with Scarlet, who she thought was very fortunate to be part of the respected Summers family, besides which she had two adorable children, and far too much beauty. Women like that seemed to think that the world owed them a living. Life was so unfair! However, she hid her feelings well, saying, 'Cassie has asked me whether she can go out in the snow . . . is that alright with you, Mrs Summers?'

Scarlet hesitated in her reply. But then a small excited voice piped in. 'Cassie . . . play in the snow!' Seeing that small face light up at the idea, how could Scarlet refuse? She embraced the child and kissed her tenderly. 'Well, alright, then,' she conceded, 'but only for a short while . . . just a walk round the drive and back again,' she informed Nanny, 'and make sure she's wrapped up warm.'

'Of course. But we won't be going just yet. I must see that David is settled first.' She went over to the cot. Scarlet followed. 'He's such a good baby,' Nanny added, 'so quiet. And isn't he the uncanny likeness of his grandfather?'

Scarlet reluctantly agreed. Even though the boy was barely eighteen months old, he was the image of Edward Summers, with his sharp angled features and vivid green eyes; he could have been made out of the same mould. She watched now, as the nanny collected the child into her arms, cooing and making baby noises that made him chuckle and gurgle, his podgy fingers reaching out to tug the frilly cap from her head. On impulse, Scarlet reached out to curl her fingers round his tiny hand. At once he began loudly crying, as though the touch of her hand was painful to him, and the more she attempted to console him, the harder he screamed. Scarlet felt rejected, humiliated by her own son. He had the power to do that to her and, because of it, her love for him had been smothered. She had given birth to him, a long, difficult process that still scarred her mind; but she had never truly felt that he was part of her – not like her darling Cassie. David had been kept from her; raised by another. He belonged to the Summers men, not her. It was a painful thing for Scarlet to admit, but she had no love for the boy. Often she wondered whether it was because he had not been *conceived* in love. She did not know. And now she had stopped fighting her coldness towards him, yet she could not fight the guilt she suffered. That would not go away. It was another cross to bear, another burden to weigh her down.

Leaving Cassie happily playing, Scarlet returned to her room. There she could close the door, shut out the harsh cruel world and be alone with her thoughts: thoughts of her father, of Garrett, and Silas. Thoughts that would not let her rest. During the next hour, she wandered aimlessly around the room, going from the long casement window to the fireplace, then back again to the window, where she gazed along the drive and into the distance, searching for Garrett. According to the stable-hand, Garrett had left Selworthy Manor in the carriage at about the time he had arranged to collect her and Cassie, then 'he returned the carriage and soon after rode out on his bay hunter'. Scarlet was at her wit's end. *Why* had he not been at the Yarn Market, then? It was true that her unexpected encounter with Silas had made her a few minutes late, but surely Garrett should have waited? Yet, according to what she had been able to discover since, he had arrived early and left the carriage waiting there while he himself set off on foot to scout for her. Shortly afterwards he had returned 'in an anxious state' and ordered the driver to take him back to the manor from where, soon after, he had ridden out across the moors. Since then, no one had any idea where he was. Scarlet might have consulted Edward Summers, but her instinct had warned her against it. And now, after the conversation she had overheard in the library this morning, she felt her instincts had been proved right. Garrett's father would have no regrets if anything untoward had brought a rift between his son and 'that damned Pengally woman'.

In the distance Scarlet could hear the church bells pealing out, calling parishioners of Dunster to early service. Suddenly she was engulfed by a tide of loneliness and despair. In that moment it seemed to Scarlet that, if there was a God, He had deserted her. There was no hope of love or laughter for her, no hope of peace or contentment; certainly not in *this* life. It seemed as though all of her life she had been immersed in darkness and fear, always struggling to reach for the light that would lead her out of that pit of Hell, yet, when she might glimpse the brink, something had dragged her down again. Surely death itself could be no worse. Then she thought of Cassie, and her heart was lighter. Cassie, who was fashioned from forbidden passion between Silas and herself; Cassie, who meant more than the whole world to Scarlet, more even than life. It was as though, on that night when she had given herself to Silas, when she had overcome the fear that marked her fascination of him, somehow there had been drawn from their passion all that was good and innocent; these elements alone had forged the unique creation that was Cassie. Now all that remained between Silas and herself was more sinister than it had ever been; a strong and forceful passion that could destroy them both. There was *evil* between them. She felt that in the churchyard yesterday, when he had held her close and kissed her. She felt it now. And she knew that she was not free of him.

After she had gazed out of the window for so long that the falling snowflakes made her eyes ache, Scarlet was suddenly aware of a horse and rider approaching. *It was Garrett!* She became agitated, not knowing whether to be relieved or apprehensive. As he drew nearer she was not surprised to find that she was both: relieved because, at long last, she would know the worst, and apprehensive because of the possible consequences of his return. She watched him veer off left towards the stables, and it struck Scarlet that there was something odd about the way he was astride his horse, something strange in his whole manner. He seemed to be falling sideways, swaying like a man wounded . . . or drunk! But no, how could he be drunk, she reproached herself. Garrett was not a drinking man.

A few moments later, Scarlet heard the sound of raised voices below. Going onto the landing, she leaned over the gallery, and was astonished to see Garrett and his father in the hall, angrily confronting each other. 'You're *drunk*, man . . . have you no pride? . . . behaving in such an undignified manner in front of our guests!' Edward Summers was struggling to get up from his wheelchair, his face red and furious. 'I never thought I'd see the day when I was ashamed of my own son!'

Without a word, Garrett lunged forward to grasp the arm of the chair. 'If you'd made her welcome in this house, things might have been different,' he yelled, angrily whipping the chair from him so that it careered wildly in a semi-circle, almost unbalancing and dislodging its astonished occupant. Mr Thornton stepped forward and quickly steadied it. 'Go easy there, son,' he said in a serious voice. 'Don't you think it might be an idea to go and get some shuteye . . . sleep off the booze, eh?'

Garrett made no reply. Instead he remained arrogant, his legs widely splayed and his confused bloodshot gaze going from his father to Jonathan Thornton, then resting on the petite Nancy Thornton, who had stayed by the dining room door, quietly observing the unseemly behaviour of the young man she had always seen to be a gentleman. She wondered what could have happened to bring him bursting into the dining room in that way, using such obscene language that she had never thought to hear in this house.

For the briefest moment a look of shame crossed Garrett's unhappy features. Then he looked up to see Scarlet there and the sight of her incensed him. With a growl, he turned away from the little group and stumbled up the stairway towards her. 'I should have listened to my father!' he shouted. 'He *said* you'd only bring heartbreak. He was right, wasn't he, eh? *He was right!* . . . I *saw* you, Scarlet . . . you and . . . him!'

So! *He knew.* She could do nothing else but face it. Aware of the three below, with all eyes looking to her, Scarlet retreated into the bedroom. She left the door open, and waited. His approaching footsteps were unsteady, shuffling. Not at all like her father's, which had been heavy and rhythmic. Yet even though the sound of their footsteps were different, the effect on Scarlet was exactly the same. They struck terror in her heart! She was a child again, waiting for the inevitable.

Suddenly, he was at the door, his arms outstretched and holding onto the door frame in order to keep his balance, staring at her in disgust as he demanded in a quiet voice, '*Why*, Scarlet? . . . aren't I good to you?' There were tears in his eyes. Scarlet was engulfed with shame; but then she was on the defensive as he went on more scornfully. 'Haven't I given you a good home? . . . You, *and* the girl . . . *his daughter*. Haven't I pretended all along that Cassie was mine? . . . Lied to my father and given her a respectable name?'

'Don't Garrett . . . please, don't.' Scarlet was horrified. She could imagine how Garrett's cruel revelation had been received by Edward Summers, who must have heard it all. She knew how thrilled he would be by the news that Cassie was *not* Garrett's child after all, just as he had always believed. But what of the American visitors, Scarlet thought with a new burst of shame, they must surely be appalled at such news? No doubt they would share the views of their host, that his daughter-in-law was nothing but a fortune-seeker, a social parasite, an opportunist, a woman of ill-repute who gave her favours freely! Scarlet was mortified. And furious. She could not forgive Garrett for bringing little Cassie into an argument that was not of the child's making. 'YES!' Her voice sailed across the room, startling him. '*Cassie is his* . . . as you say, you lied to give her a name.' Her dark eyes blazed into his. 'But she was *never* yours. *I* was never yours! So, we'll go. That's what your father would want. It's what *you* want, isn't it, Garrett? . . . ISN'T IT?'

'YES! GET OUT!' He staggered aside, the tears rolling down his face. 'If it's *him* you want, then get out. Go on! Go to him . . . and to Hell with the pair of you.' As she brushed past him, he caught her by the arm. 'Take the girl,' he told her, 'but the boy, he's *mine*. Leave him.'

Twisting from his grasp, she nodded. The boy would not come with her anyway; he was afraid of her. She was afraid of him! Quickly she made her way to the nursery. One look at the nanny's shocked face told Scarlet that she also had heard everything. Cassie was almost dressed for her 'walk in the snow'. White-faced and desperate now to be gone, Scarlet came into the room, feeling relieved that at least Cassie seemed unaware of what had transpired. She realised that she owed a debt of gratitude to the other woman, who had no doubt diverted the child's attention from the raging arguments. 'Please collect my coat,' she instructed the nanny, who faced her with a hostile and accusing look. 'I'll finish dressing Cassie.' Quickly the woman departed, slamming the door behind her.

In a surprisingly few moments the door was flung open wide. Scarlet fastened the ribbon under Cassie's bonnet, then looked up, holding out her arm to collect the coat she had sent for. She was shocked to see that the woman who had entered the room was not the nanny, but Ruth Taylor, the housekeeper. 'Don't come back to this house,' she told Scarlet, her face frozen in a malicious smile as, ignoring

Scarlet's outstretched arm, she flung the tweed coat at her feet. Without a word, Scarlet picked the coat up and hurriedly put it on. Then, sweeping Cassie up into her arms, she stormed past the housekeeper and out of the room. As she went speedily down the stairs, she could hear Garrett calling, 'Go on! Go to him . . . I never want to see you again!' She did not look back, but continued across the hall, her head held high when she passed within a painfully short distance of Edward Summers and the Thorntons. She could feel the animosity of the two men, but suddenly, when there was the gentle touch of a hand on her shoulder, she was made to pause. It was Nancy Thornton, her blue eyes filled with kindness. 'He doesn't mean what he says,' she murmured, 'he loves you, my dear.' Briefly, Scarlet touched her hand in gratitude, thinking how right the dear soul was. *And how very wrong.* She found herself wishing there had been more time to get to know Nancy Thornton. She was a good woman; unlike *me*, Scarlet tormented herself, *unlike me!*

As she went from the house, Scarlet was unsure of which way to go. Her first thoughts were to seek out Shelagh, dear kind Shelagh, who would help her decide for the best. But then she recoiled from the darker images of her father and Greystone House. She could not bring herself to go there. John Blackwood's cottage, then? His wife would not be pleased to see both Scarlet and her child appear on the doorstep, but Scarlet had nowhere else to turn. John would go for Shelagh, and together she and Scarlet could talk things through. It was settled. There was no alternative!

Choosing the most direct route to nearby Dunster, Scarlet headed towards the moors; she knew a short cut, and though it would bring them near the high cliffs, she was not deterred. She hurried on, her urgent footsteps noisily crunching the settling snow, and the sharp thin air whipping her face; the tiny frozen snowflakes penetrated her collar and settled in the crevice of her neck. 'Cuddle close to Mummy,' she told the child, but then was surprised to see Cassie's face uplifted to the skies, her small pink tongue catching the snowflakes and a look of sheer joy on her face. Scarlet smiled. As long as she had Cassie, nothing could hurt her any more. *Or so she thought!*

Back at the house, Garrett was torn with crippling remorse. What in God's name had he done? . . . taunting her about Silas and the child, when he had given his word that he would never use the past to hurt her! How could he have told Scarlet that he never wanted to see her again? And by what right did he order her to leave her son? . . . cruelly claiming that the boy was his alone! *He* was hurt, yes . . . and seeing her in Silas's arms had made him crazy. But what kind of man was he, to drown himself in drink? What kind of weak coward would do such a thing, instead of facing up to it and dealing with it all in a civilised manner? In the years they had been married Scarlet had never lied to him, never cheated him, yet she had not been happy, he knew that. What they had between them was a delicate strand of affection and companionship. It was all he could ever hope for. Scarlet was not like other women. He had never *wanted* other women. Now, through his blundering insensitivity, he had snapped that delicate thread between them and he was desolate! He must make amends. He had to go after her, take the boy to her, show her that they could be a family once more. He would even leave his father's house. *Nothing* mattered to him, except that he must chase after her, before it was too late, and beg her forgiveness. Blinded by his fear of losing Scarlet, and with his thinking dulled by the effects of prolonged drinking, Garrett staggered towards the nursery.

'Come back here, you bloody fool . . . you'll be the death

of the boy!' Edward Summers had been alerted by the frantic housekeeper and was horrified to see his son stumbling towards the outer door. He was clutching a thick woollen blanket, which all but covered the small sleeping child inside. 'Have you lost your senses?' the old man yelled.

At the door Garrett turned, a look of contempt on his face as he told his father, 'I *must* have lost my senses! . . . or I would never have let her go. Believe *this*, old man . . . as long as I'm alive, Scarlet will always come first. Before *you*, before all that you have planned for me. Without her, none of it means a damned thing. I wanted you to make her welcome in this house and you couldn't even do *that* for me! Well . . . to Hell with you. I'll get her back. *Don't fool yourself that it's ended!*' He saw the shock and pain on his father's face. And he was satisfied. With a last scathing glance he fled from the house towards the stables, where he quickly saddled and mounted the same dark hunter that had brought him home not two hours ago. Pressing the child into the curve of his loins, he held it fast and headed for the path which he knew Scarlet would take. He also was aware of the same short cut, which he had followed many times as a boy in his search for the black-eyed girl who had bewitched him.

Scarlet glanced up at the skies. Strange, she thought, how on the ground the snow lay like a sea of sparkling white, while the skies above became heavy and grey, seeming oppressed by the sheer weight that pressed them down. When the moors were cloaked in soft white snowflakes, there was an unusual beauty about them. And mortal danger! The snow had been falling steadily, disguising familiar landmarks and confusing the boundaries that guided the walkers. The little-used path along which Scarlet now trudged was narrow and precarious, having a wooded bank on one side that fell down to the brook, and a cliff edge on the other. Beyond that there was a sheer drop of some eighty feet into the rock-strewn valley below. Scarlet trod carefully, answering Cassie's constant pleas to 'play in the snow' with false assurances that 'we're almost at the cottage, sweetheart . . . soon you can play in the snow. Soon.' The truth was that the journey had become painstakingly slow and Cassie's slight form had begun to weigh heavily on Scarlet. Yet she dared not rest, nor ease her burden by putting the child to the ground. It was too dangerous. She began to wish she had kept to the road.

Looking into the distance, Scarlet was relieved to see the church spire piercing the skyline. Beyond that was the ridge above Greystone House. The skyline grew increasingly familiar and, seeing it, Scarlet smiled; thank God, she thought, holding the child closer to her. John Blackwood's cottage was not too far away now.

'Scarlet!' From behind, a little way from the bend in the path, there came a muffled sound of a horse's hooves, and a man's voice. 'Scarlet! . . . where are you?' It was Garrett, come to take her back, Scarlet left the path and hid behind a tree. 'Go away,' she murmured beneath her breath, 'it's over between us!' Still he called. 'I have our son . . . *your* son. Forgive me, Scarlet. We'll go away . . . make a new life. *Please*, Scarlet . . . answer me. *Talk to me*, PLEASE!' There were tears in his voice, and though she hated him for the coward he was, Scarlet was moved by his plea. She felt pity for him, and a measure of guilt for the part she had played in his misery. If she did not talk to him now, he would only seek her out later. It must be settled, She began inching her way through the bracken, towards the path.

Suddenly, everything happened at once! On emerging from the woods, Scarlet saw that Garrett was still some way off. The moment she appeared in his vision, he smiled and spurred the horse on. But then, without warning, the dark hooded figure sprang out, its arms raised wide towards the horse. Terrified, the poor creature whinnied in alarm, rearing up high on its back haunches as the sinister figure came at it again and again, forcing it back, relentlessly pursuing it on the cliff's edge. Surging forward, Scarlet began screaming, '*NO*, SILAS!' In the few frantic moments when she ran the short distance that seemed never-ending, the whole tragic scene unfolded with startling speed before her eyes. In her shocked mind the sound of laughter rang out: wild, insane laughter. She saw the horse fighting desperately for a foothold. She saw him slide over the precipice, and out of her sight to the depths below, taking with it the two souls on its back. For the rest of her life she would remember Garrett's shocked and disbelieving expression in the moment before he was gone, and the sound of naked horror in his voice as he stared into the shadowy evil face that was hidden from Scarlet's view. 'YOU!' His voice rang out like a death knell. Then the scream, the awful heart-piercing scream, as he fell headlong to his death, the tiny bundle torn from his grasp and plummeting with him. The scream went on, two seconds; longer; reverberating outwards, into and beyond the aftermath of unnerving silence. A silence that was like eternity.

Scarlet remembered screaming also. But there was nothing she could do. She was helpless, and they were dead. Garrett, her son . . . *both dead*. A grim warning in the back of her mind shone through the terror. NOW HE'LL KILL YOU, it said; and she knew she must hide. *Quickly!* The figure turned. '*WHY?* . . . who are you?' she asked, her tears blinding as she tried in vain to penetrate the shadows. It *was* Silas! Who *else*? Now the figure was moving towards her, and she asked again, 'WHY?' The silence clung like a fog. She was lost. And back came her own answer. *He was insane!* She felt the child trembling in her arms, quietly sobbing. The heart froze inside her. Fear pushed up into her throat. Suddenly she was running, gasping for breath as Cassie's arms clung round her throat. On and on, deeper into the woods, stumbling, tripping, desperation driving her blindly forwards. Behind her she could hear the footsteps, determined, rhythmic, *just as they had always been*, closing in, gaining ground. Cassie was like a dead weight on her. She could not go on; but she must. *She must! HIDE!* That was it! She would hide.

Quickly she wound her way into that part of the wood where the trees became dense, effectively forming a canopy overhead, a thick impenetrable blanket that kept out both snow and daylight. Here, pressed hard into the broad trunk of an ancient tree, she waited. In the distance, she could hear him, always pursuing, his footsteps crashing through the tangle of roots and shrub. Cassie's sobs filled the eerie silence. 'Don't cry, sweetheart. Be very quiet!' Scarlet turned the child until the sobs were smothered. 'You mustn't cry . . . *mustn't cry!*' Softly, she rocked her. 'Ssh.' The sobs broke; only the trembling went on. The child knew the danger and was terrified.

In a burst of stark realisation, Scarlet felt the blood trickling down her face. The wound on her temple was wide and jagged, the skin ripped apart by an intrusive branch as she had frantically made her way deeper, ever deeper into the woods. The left side of her coat was in tatters. Bits of twigs and leaf fragments were mingled with little Cassie's hair, and a long thorny spike hung from her shoulder, leaving in its wake a thin meandering bloodied scratch. With silent, deft movement, Scarlet tore the twig away, dropping it carefully to the ground. A grey wave of resentment swept over her. Why had he come back? Why couldn't he have left her alone? She knew why! Silas needed her. She needed him in the same way. NO! NO! She was transported back, over the years, a small haunted creature hunched and frightened in that attic. The past rose up to swamp her. It wouldn't let her go. The past, the future. NOW. It was all the same!

Dear God! He was so near she could reach out and touch him! *He had only to swing round and he would see her!* The sweat ran down her back. Don't let Cassie cry! She saw the child's big frightened eyes intent on that lone unearthly figure. *Don't let Cassie cry!* Her fearful heart was thumping so furiously, she was certain he must hear it. For what seemed like a lifetime, the figure stood motionless, staring round, peering deep between the trees. She could see its breath curling in the cold damp air. Her arms were breaking. Cassie was trembling against her. Dear God, don't let her cry.

The figure moved away, going slowly, searching, until it was swallowed up in the blackness. Scarlet waited a while, frozen with terror and loath to move, lest he was still within earshot. Even a tiny twig snapping underfoot would bring him down on her! The footsteps died away in the distance. NOW! 'Ssh, Cassie . . . don't make a sound,' she whispered. The way back was easier. Wet and bedraggled, she just followed the light at the rim of the trees.

She was almost there! *Suddenly, a hand descended on her, gripping her shoulder and swinging her round.* The piercing pain shot through her temple. She opened her mouth to scream, and when the shrill, broken sound shattered the air, the soothing voice told her, 'It's alright, Mrs Summers . . . you're safe.' At once, she recognised Garrett's foreman. She began laughing. And crying. He had seen the broken remains of her husband and son. He saw how bloody and torn were Scarlet and the girl; how shocked and terrified. He knew how treacherous the moors were, and he thought it fortunate that they had not *all* gone over the precipice. He took the small sobbing girl into his arms and helped Scarlet out of the woods. She was like a limp rag against him, deathly silent, then hysterical, talking about 'the devil' and how he meant to kill them *all*! She was demented by her loss. He understood.

CHAPTER FOURTEEN

It was midnight. Scarlet had lost count of the times she had climbed into bed and, unable to rest, had climbed out again to pace the floor, her broken mind trying frantically to fit together the pieces of a nightmarish jigsaw. Her thoughts were wild and incomprehensible. She couldn't breathe! Every breath of air caught thick in her throat, making her panic, causing her to gasp as though each one was her last. What should she do? Dear God, what should she do? There was no safe place, no haven where she might hide from him, from *them*. She could end it all, here and now, taking Cassie with her. Or she could run, and keep on running. Oh, but they would track her down. Nothing was surer! Her own life was nothing to her. *It had never been her own!* Why would it matter if it was ended in the next moment?

Who would miss her? Who would grieve? Shelagh perhaps. But not *them*! Because *they* would have won. They would have her soul, but still she would not be safe, because they would hound her beyond the grave. There was no sanctuary for her; nor did she deserve it. But Cassie, oh, innocent little Cassie, must not be corrupted or made to suffer what *she* had suffered. For Cassie there was still time. But *how*? What could she do to save the child? Scarlet was frantic. There must be a way; there *must* be!

Suddenly, it came to her. *The Thorntons.* They were

staying for the funerals in two days' time; after that they would return to America, thousands of miles away from here, from the evil that pursued her and Cassie. Scarlet became excited. The idea persisted. Nancy Thornton adored Cassie. She had said herself, 'I can't tell you what I would give for . . . a daughter like Cassie.' Scarlet had seen the desperate longing in the other woman's face. Now she saw the same longing as Cassie's only hope. Oh, but what of *Jonathan Thornton*? Scarlet's heart fell like a lead weight inside her. He would never agree.

Her hopes depleted, Scarlet crossed to the window, where she looked out into the black unyielding night. There must be a way, she murmured over and over; THERE MUST BE A WAY! It seemed as though there was *no* way. But then, like a flower opening in the dead of night, an idea blossomed in her fevered mind. Smiling, she crossed to the cot on the far side of the room, where at long last the child appeared to be peacefully sleeping. These past days since the awful events that had erupted round her. Cassie had suffered terrifying dreams, when she would wake screaming and sobbing, bathed in sweat and her dark eyes wide with horror. 'Don't cry,' her mammy would tell her softly, holding her close. 'Ssh, sweetheart . . . don't cry.' And soon the sobs would subside and the child slip back into uneasy dreams. Scarlet herself had moved Cassie's cot into her own room. She prayed the doctor was right when he told her, 'Soon, her nightmares will stop. Nature has a way of blocking them out.' Cassie's nightmares were the same as hers, thought Scarlet. Yet she believed that nature could *never* block from her mind the memory of that sinister figure, and the devastating sight of Garrett with the boy, falling into that terrifying empty space beyond the precipice. She could see Garrett's face now, shocked and wide-open in a scream that she would hear until her dying day. *He knew his murderer!* Scarlet had seen the look of recognition and disbelief on his face when he cried out 'YOU!' She inwardly shuddered. He knew *Silas*. But then, he knew her father also. In Scarlet's tortured mind, they were one and the same! Though one would have her love him in a way she could not. The other she loved. Only her *fear* of him was more compelling.

Going to the bedroom door, Scarlet drew it open and listened. They were still talking, consoling each other. She came out onto the landing and peered over the balustrade. The sound of voices drifted up, quiet, respectful, tinged with grief. The crying was done. Anger had set in. 'What in God's name possessed Garrett to take such a treacherous path . . . and with the boy?' They did not know that Garrett and the boy had been murdered. Scarlet knew they would never believe her. Instead they would look to *her* for the blame; and already there were people in this house who thought she was to be feared. Perhaps it *was* as they said. Yet she did not feel 'strange' or 'different'. Only doomed.

From some way along the landing, Scarlet heard the sound of sobbing. For Edward Summers, the crying was not over; his grief was too bitter. Since the news that two generations of the Summers family had been tragically killed, he had locked himself in his room, alone with the unbearable agony of his bitter quarrel with Garrett, and refusing to see even Jonathan Thornton.

It was Jonathan Thornton's voice that rang out now, telling his wife, 'I've got to see him . . . try at least one more time.'

'You go ahead,' came the reply. 'I'm not ready for bed yet . . . I'll stay awhile, to keep Miss Taylor company.' There was the soft sound of a door clicking shut, followed by the slow muffled tread of footsteps coming up the stairway.

Quickly Scarlet returned to her room, leaving the door open wide and throwing back the curtains so that the moonlight cascaded in. Slipping off her nightgown, she came forward, her naked form silhouetted between the light from the landing and the silvery glow of moonlight behind. He was drawing closer. Now he was almost at the door. She caught her breath, stiffening her body, aware of her own bewitching beauty. What if he went right by? She began to panic. No! He must see her there. He *wanted* her. She had known that all along.

Outside, the footsteps paused. He had seen the door was open. He started walking forward at a gentler pace, hesitant, curious. It was enough. Their eyes met: *his* opened in astonishment, *hers* sultry, dark, entrancing. She sensed the struggle in him, but she kept her gaze locked into his. She could not let him go. There was too much at stake. Slowly, tantalisingly, she came forward. He ventured into the room, his eyes greedily devouring the proud slim curves of her nakedness. His tongue came out, slithering over the rim of his lips and painting them dewy wet. Inside he was churning, fighting all that she awoke in him. *And losing.* For a moment everything was frozen in time, with her oval face and dark eyes the focus of his senses. He had known that this temptation would come, from the very first trembling moment when she had taunted him with her wild dark beauty, and those sullen moody black eyes. He was intimidated by her magnificence, rendered weak by the thought of his hands on her silken flesh. Softly he closed the door. With gentle deft fingers she undid the buckle of his belt. His own frantic fingers grabbed and clawed until there was no barrier between them. Groaning out loud he pulled her down, falling on her, smothering her with his hot sweating body and growing feverish with delight as their nakedness fused. He felt no tenderness; no romance. He stroked at her and laid his moist mouth over the nipples at her breast, licking, teasing, until she shivered and sent him into a frenzy.

Scarlet clung to him, surprised that she was also hungry

for love. His touch was shocking, awakening. A strange pleasure crept over her. She felt his fingers dig into the soft flesh of her thighs, pulling her into him and taking her along with the urgent rhythm of his body movements. She was aware of his tongue in her mouth and the weight of his body, pushing, thrusting, forcing her open, making her buck up to him and exciting her in spite of herself.

In a cruelly short time the tide burst, coursing through her and bringing with it a painful guilt. The thought of Cassie tempered that guilt. It was for *her*, for Cassie. To buy her peace.

'You're a witch,' he murmured, grappling with his clothes and evading her eyes. Jesus! *What a fool he was!* If Nancy should find out . . . The thought made his blood run cold. What he and Nancy had was special. After all these years, *she mustn't find out!*

'Nancy needn't know,' Scarlet slipped the nightgown over her head, lifting her black hair over it so that it spilled round her shoulders like a mantle. Her dark eyes were smiling, satisfied.

'What d'you mean?' He feared the worst and – hell! – it served him right!

'I want you to take my daughter back to America with you . . . raise her as your own.'

'*Never!*' His eyes were bright with loathing and disgust, of her, of himself.

'Very well.' She went to the door and opened it. 'You'd better go,' she softly laughed. 'Sleep well, Mr Thornton.'

Striding forward, he pushed her aside and closed the door. 'You little whore! You *want* Nancy to know! I could kill you . . . *right now.*'

'Go ahead.' There was no fear in her eyes, and he was taken aback. He was also beaten.

'What game are you playing?' he wanted to know. 'How can I be sure that if I do take the girl back . . . you won't keep coming at me . . . making me pay? What *other* reason could there be for you wanting to turn her over to strangers?'

'I have my reasons. And you have my word that you'll never hear from me again.'

'*Your word!*' His soft laugh was cynical.

'If you're not satisfied, I'll sign any paper you want me to. I don't like *you*, Mr Thornton . . . but your wife is a good woman. I know she will love my Cassie as though she was her own daughter.'

'You're a shrewd, cunning bitch!' He knew she was right about Nancy. It was her dearest wish to have a child, and she would idolise him all the more for it. A rush of love and guilt surged through him. But then it was swallowed by his hatred for this woman, and for the girl she had thrust on him. He had no choice. For a while he stared at her, hoping she could feel that hatred in him. Then, reluctantly, he nodded.

'You'll let Nancy take her?' For the first time in a long while, Scarlet experienced a burst of happiness. But it was tinged with regret. She loved Cassie so. How could she live without her?

'You leave me with no choice. I'm not about to let a conniving little whore like you destroy my marriage! But make no mistake . . . *you sign what I put in front of you, and you'll keep to it* . . . or rue the day!' After making sure that he would not be detected, he went quickly away down the corridor, his shoulders stooped and the spring gone from his step. He cursed himself bitterly for his own shameful weakness.

All traces of the recent snowfall had gone. In its place had come the bitter frost and sharp biting gales of March. On such a day, with the wind howling and shrieking, ravaging the treetops and buffeting the mourners as they filed into the churchyard, Garrett Summers and his son were laid to rest.

Throughout the service, and afterwards when the sombre figures encircled the yawning pit, sprinkling earth and flowers onto the splendid coffin below, Scarlet forced herself to think of those things that had given her pleasure. They were shockingly few. The 'pleasure' in her life had been as scarce as the peace she had known. Only two people had given her both. They were her mother and her daughter. Looking back over the years, she realised that the greatest source of her small contentment was the moors. Raising her cold dark gaze, she stared into the distance, beyond the churchyard and out over the low sweeping landscape beyond. An involuntary shiver ran through her, tempered with a thrill of excitement. The moors never changed. Their elusive and fascinating quality was timeless. It was a comforting thought amidst all the shifting elements of her life. The moors were in her blood. *Silas was, also*. His name seared her mind, painful, clinging. She thought of Cassie, his daughter, *their* daughter, and the tears rolled down her face, warm and salty against her chilled skin. Garrett was gone, and so was the boy. Soon, oh so very soon, Cassie also would be gone. Her departure would be just as devastating.

'You're doing fine, my love . . . just fine.' Shelagh was close by, watching Scarlet and thinking how pale and nervous was Vincent Pengally's daughter. Her gloved hand briefly touched Scarlet's arm. 'Come on . . . time to go,' she murmured, 'time to leave them.'

The black, bent shadows brushed by. Scarlet made no move. They did not look at her, nor she at them. They were Garrett's people, not hers. She could hear the wheels of Edward Summers's chair grinding down the hard nodules of earth as it passed her.

'You blame me, don't you?' she thought bitterly. And you're right. *I killed him!* On that day when he brought me to your house and I was heavy with another man's child . . . *Silas's child* . . . I signed his death warrant then.

My punishment is that now I must lose Cassie, or the same black vengeance that took my mother, that took *both* our sons, will seek her out. May God forgive me. May Cassie forgive me.

'No, Mammy!' Cassie's sobs were like knives to Scarlet's heart. 'Stay with *you* . . . Cassie . . . stay with you!'

'Ssh, sweetheart.' Thrusting the struggling child form her, Scarlet fought back her own tears, saying sternly, 'You mustn't cry. Big girls don't cry.' The big tearful eyes stared up at her and, beneath Scarlet's gentle touch, the small figure ceased its trembling. 'Oh, Cassie! . . . it'll be so wonderful . . . you're going to *America*, with Nancy. You *like* Nancy, don't you?' The fair tousled head slowly nodded. 'Well then! You're a lucky girl. Nancy will be your *new* mammy . . . and she'll show you such wonderful places. Has she told you about the big ship that will carry you across the great ocean?' Again the tiny head nodded, tears hovering and threatening to spill over. Encouraged, Scarlet injected a new note of enthusiasm into her voice. 'My, isn't that *exciting*? You'd better hurry, though, sweetheart, or it will sail away without you.' She flicked her sorrowful gaze towards the trim anxious figure of Nancy Thornton, who was standing some way off, her own eyes bright with tears. With a nod of her head, Scarlet suggested that Nancy should quickly take the child.

'My dear, *are you sure*?' Nancy Thornton stepped forward. She had witnessed the tender tragic scene between mother and daughter, and she wondered at the enormous sacrifice Scarlet had undertaken. Since Scarlet's intention was made known to her, she had been torn two ways. She desperately wanted the child. A child she could raise as her own, and who would call her 'Mommy'. With Cassie her life would be complete. But what of Scarlet? A tragic, tormented woman who could see no future for either herself or her daughter. 'I must go away . . . build a life for myself and do the best for Cassie,' she had told Nancy, 'and I could do no better for my child than to entrust her to your care. I know you will love and protect her always.' Only when Nancy had given such a promise to Scarlet did she sign the papers that Jonathan Thornton put before her. As she made her mark on the document, Scarlet did not reveal that she could not read. Instead, she looked deep and long into the other woman's candid green eyes and what she saw there gave her great courage. Afterwards, when Scarlet put down the pen, it was as though she had put down her own life.

'Take her . . . *please take her*!' Scarlet gave the child over. It was the hardest thing she had ever done, and she feared that now, in the final moment, her resolve would crumble. *Then she remembered!* To weaken now would mean danger for the girl.

At this point, Jonathan Thornton intervened. Impatient and quietly fuming at the manner in which he had been duped, he got from the motor vehicle and came towards his wife. 'Get her into the car,' he instructed, 'or leave her behind!' His contemptuous gaze fell on Scarlet's unhappy face. It gave him a rush of pleasure to see how she was suffering.

Distracting Cassie's attention with a large smiling teddy bear bought especially for the purpose of enticing Cassie away, Nancy lost no time in persuading her into the back of the vehicle. For a moment it seemed as though the child had forgotten Scarlet, who wisely hid in the shadows. But then the door was closed behind Nancy and the motor fired into life. Through a misty veil of tears, Scarlet glanced at the note which Nancy Thornton had earlier thrust into her hand, saying, 'Keep this safe, Scarlet. It's Cassie's new address.' The words written there meant nothing to Scarlet; they were just dark meaningless shapes. All the same, she would sew it safely into the lining of her coat as soon as Cassie was gone.

Too soon, the long black vehicle was pulling away, taking with it Scarlet's only source of joy. Now, when she realised the enormity of what she had done, Scarlet was tempted to run after Cassie, to bring her back. It took all of her courage to restrain herself. In the distance she would see the small white face at the rear window, the dark eyes searching for her. Through the mist of blinding tears, she saw Nancy Thornton reach up to take Cassie in her arms. She saw how the child took a moment to scan the drive and gardens for the familiar figure that was her mammy; when she saw nothing to comfort her, she turned to the woman and let herself fall into loving arms. Scarlet turned away. The pain was too much.

Night was falling. For hours Scarlet had wandered the moors, dazed and hurt. When Cassie had gone from her sight, she had gone back indoors. But she was restless and hopelessly lost. After a while she had sought refuge in the wild primitive haunts of her childhood. But, unlike then, she could find no solace there. No peace of mind, no contentment. Only memories that tore at her and made her fearful. She listened to the birds, watched the cold frothy waters of the brook as they rushed and tumbled headlong towards the river; she saw the creatures play and was spellbound by the fragments of scintillating light that peeped in and out of the overhead branches. But none of it brought joy to her heart. It was as though everything that had made life worth living was denied her. It haunted Scarlet to think that somewhere, somehow, she had committed a crime so heinous that God saw fit to punish her in such a cruel way.

After a seemingly endless while, when she had sat, hunched and dejected by the water's edge, Scarlet began making her way towards the churchyard. There she stood over the newly disturbed earth, her mind filled with images of the two who lay beneath. The man, Garrett, who had been her husband, yet had never known her. And the boy, David, who had struggled into this world from her own body, yet had never been a part of her. She had been a curse to them both. A curse to herself. Why was it, she wondered, that in the face of everything, she still clung to life? Was that all part of the punishment? And what now? Where did she belong? Scarlet answered her own question. *Nowhere!* She belonged nowhere.

The laughter rose in her, erupting with startling suddenness that shattered the solemn atmosphere of the churchyard. The laughter subsided, the tears fell and the gentle sobbing disturbed no one. Least of all the quiet souls now released from earthly pain.

Edward Summers's grief had turned to fury. It was betrayed in the thin gash that was his mouth and in the condemning eyes that bore into Scarlet. 'You *bewitched* my son!' he screamed, *'killed him as sure as if you'd pushed him over that cliff with your own hands! . . .* You blinded him to all reason.' From the library, where he was consumed by thoughts of his only son lying in the cold ground together with the grandson he had come to adore, Edward Summers had heard the knock on the door. When the maid went to answer it and Scarlet's voice came to his attention, the sum of his terrible grief hardened into hatred. Frantically wheeling himself to the other side of the room, he had grabbed the shotgun from its place on the wall. There was vengeance in his heart as he flung the door open wide, causing the maid to stumble. Startled to see the master almost out of his mind, she fled to summon the housekeeper.

'Get away from my house, or they'll bury you . . . like they buried him and the boy.' The shotgun had lain across his knee. In a swift, deliberate movement he swung it upwards, pointing the barrel at Scarlet's head, his hands trembling with emotion and the tears falling unheeded down his thin, stricken face.

Scarlet stood resolute and unimpassioned. His grief was no more crippling than was hers. He had lost a son; she a daughter. The boy was a tragic casualty of circumstances. 'I've come for Cassie's things,' her voice was cold, unafraid. 'Her toys . . . the clothes I knew her best in. Just *Cassie's* things. As for myself, I'll take nothing from this house but the clothes I stand up in. I came with only the garments on my back . . . I'll go the same way.' Her black eyes were like granite. Didn't he know that something had died in her also?

'Get away from here!' he yelled. 'You've taken enough from my house.' When she made no move, he cried out, struggling to cock the firearm. In his frenzy he unbalanced the wheelchair and was sent reeling sideways. The gun lodged fast between the wheel spokes and, as a shot rang out, splintering the top panel of the door, Ruth Taylor came running from the kitchen. At once she called the maid to assist her in making the chair upright and restoring the master to it. When she saw that he had suffered no real harm, but was deeply shocked, she came to the door, her glance scathing as she told Scarlet, 'I warned him from the start that you were trouble! Take your black heart from these parts, Scarlet Pengally.' Before she slammed the door shut, the housekeeper smiled. '*And may the devil go with you!*' she hissed. Scarlet smiled also, for she knew that he would.

'John . . . John Blackwood, open the door. It's Scarlet.' Stepping back a pace, Scarlet looked over the cottage for the umpteenth time. All was silent, the cottage remained in darkness. Scarlet's heart sank. Once more, she thought; she would try once more. 'John! . . . Ada, please come to the door. I need to talk.' No reply. The silence was eerie. Still, she could not accept that the Blackwoods were out so late, and with young Trent. Scarlet recalled how, some time ago, Shelagh had mentioned that Ada Blackwood's great-aunt in Barnstaple had been taken seriously ill. It was possible, then, that the old woman's health had deteriorated further and John had taken his wife over in the trap, and of course they would take the boy with them.

After she had twice more walked round the cottage and found no sign of life, Scarlet sat on the front doorstep. What now? She had hoped that John would be here, and that he would go to Greystone House to fetch Shelagh. She and Shelagh could talk things through, decide what was best. Only now, when she was so desperate and outcast, did Scarlet realise how very lonely and friendless she was. A glimmer of hope warmed her, though. There was still Shelagh. The hope was dashed. Shelagh was inside Greystone House. *Inside, with him.* Her father's face loomed into her mind, leering, beckoning. The image was superimposed with that of Silas. She closed her eyes and shook her head. Go away. GO AWAY! Shaken by the experience, she forced herself to think of more pleasant things: babbling brooks, the call of an owl, and a black sky dotted with twinkling stars. Still the images persisted, awesome, weaving in and out of her senses and flowing with her blood to every corner of her being. Clasping her hands to her throbbing temples, Scarlet thought *this* was how it felt. *Madness.* Was she insane? *Yes*, that was it. NO! It wasn't *her*. It was *them*! *They* were the insane ones. She had to believe that. *She had to believe that, or she was lost for ever.*

Coming to the foot of Packhorse Bridge, Scarlet looked across the bank and beyond, to Greystone House. Swathed in black night, and silhouetted against a silver-streaked sky, the house made a formidable sight, its tall gables reaching upwards and the slim fluted chimneys towering above like watchful sentries; there was something uniquely magnificent about the ancient house. And something chillingly sinister.

In spite of herself, Scarlet felt the magnetism of Grey-stone House, felt it tugging at her, drawing her nearer, into it. Slowly she went forward. The house held all of her secrets, *coveted* them with almost human possessiveness. Her mother was there still; Scarlet as a child; Vincent Pengally, fornication, the love of her mammy, Silas. Forbidden things . . . pain, fear, terror. *Nightmares*. Nightmares that would never end. They were all there, entombed in that house. They were all part of her. The essence of her existence. She belonged here. She could never belong anywhere else. Suddenly a lullaby came into her head, soft and caressing; her mammy used to sing it. Scarlet sang it now, her voice soft and plaintive, floating upwards and forwards, towards the house. The song soothed her, gave her a peculiar magical sense of well-being. In an instant they were all with her: Hannah, Garrett and the boy, David, Cassie. *Oh, Cassie!* The pain came back and the song was ended. *Shelagh*. She needed to talk with Shelagh. Yet she did not want to stay here a minute longer. *Run away!* Now was the time, she told herself. But where? She had no money and only the dress she wore. The coat was warm, though: best woollen cloth, with a deep fur collar to keep out the cold. The tears sprang to her eyes. Garrett bought it for her as a 'thank you' when she delivered him a son. Oh, God! What would become of her now, she wondered. The fear flooded her heart, but with it came a spiral of defiance. She could overcome the fear. She had done it before!

There were two lights burning in the house: one downstairs, in the drawing room; the other, a more subdued light like the glow of a candle, upstairs in *his* room. Scarlet thought of how Shelagh had described him. 'Too ill to hurt you . . . bedridden . . . dying.' The thought made her smile. She envisaged Shelagh now, sitting in the black horsehair armchair beside the fire-range, her homely brown head bent over one or another of her domestic duties. The thought was comforting. She went forward, needing the comfort that Shelagh could give.

Strange! *The front door was slightly ajar.* Scarlet stood on the step, hesitant, confused. It was not like Shelagh to leave the door open. Cautiously she went forward, up the step. Softly she inched open the door. Almost immediately the smell overwhelmed her: that familiar odour of damp and rotting wood, the camphor *he* always used to ease his aching back after a day's labour . . . all mingling with the pleasant tarry smell of burning peat. *And something else!* Something intangible, bitter and unpleasant to the senses. Scarlet wrinkled her nose in disgust, going into the hall and quietly pushing the door to behind her. She must remember to warn Shelagh of the danger in leaving the door open. The moors were a natural hiding-place that could harbour the most fearsome creatures.

Going deeper into the lamplit hall, Scarlet gave an involuntary shiver. *He was here.* His evil presence lay like a pall over the house. She glanced furtively towards the stairway, recalling Shelagh's words . . . 'can't hurt you . . . bedridden . . . dying.' She felt small comfort. STAY THERE AND DIE, YOU DEVIL. DIE HARD. Her black eyes glittered. On tiptoe she moved nearer the drawing room. The door was open wide; the teapot stood warming on its trestle in the hearth, the fire was brightly burning. But there was no sign of Shelagh! In the softest of whispers, Scarlet breathed her name. 'Shelagh . . . where are you?' The silence closed in on her. Even the sound of her own voice was unnerving. *'Shelagh.'* On swift quiet footsteps she went from room to room, searching the drawing room, the kitchen, across the hall to the best parlour. There was no sign of Shelagh. When Scarlet found herself standing beside the cellar door, it crossed her mind that maybe Shelagh was down there. But no! Only her father ever ventured into the cellar, only *he* kept the key. She brought herself up sharply. *That was when he was strong and well.* Gingerly, she raised her hand to the door knob. The cold forbidden touch sent ripples of horror down her back.

Suddenly there was a shuffling noise from upstairs. '*Shelagh!*' Relieved, Scarlet silently mounted the stairs. Of course! No doubt Shelagh had been attending to *him* before she retired for the night. A small bubble of warmth burst inside her at the thought of a few delightful hours sitting by the fireside and discussing events with her friend. Shelagh would know what to do for the best. She would advise her well.

It was in Scarlet's mind to leave Dunster, to go right away, perhaps to another country altogether. But there had to be a cohesive plan, and she needed money, a loan, that was all. Shelagh had money. She was thrifty. Also, for as long as Scarlet could remember, Vincent Pengally always kept a considerable cache of notes in the drawing room. In spite of his meanness, he was a wealthy man. In that same top drawer in the oak chest was her mother's jewellery. Hannah never wore the trinkets – 'where would I wear such fancy finery . . . when I'm doing the potatoes?' she would ask Scarlet with a shy smile. The jewellery had been her mother's, handed down through generations and reputed to be worth a small fortune. Maybe Scarlet would just take the two gold and bejewelled brooches. She would not sell them, but merely borrow against them, until such time when they could be recovered. But, by rights, they were hers anyway. Her mother had always promised her so; although her father had kept them from her, vowing, 'You'll not adorn yourself with things that might attract the scavengers to you . . . not while *I'm* alive!'

Scarlet waited at the top of the stairs, her wary gaze drawn towards the low shaft of light emanating from the room that was her father's. 'Well . . . you won't *be* alive for much longer, will you?' she murmured, leaning against the wall, listening and watching for the moving shadow that would tell her of Shelagh's departure from the room.

Patiently, Scarlet waited. *And waited.* Still, Shelagh did not come. Impatient, she toyed with the notion of returning downstairs to wait in comfort by the fire. She had grown chilled and slightly irritated. What in God's name was Shelagh *doing*? Curiosity getting the better of her, Scarlet crept noiselessly along the landing, until she was standing at the door to her father's bedroom. Not for the first time she was seized by an overwhelming compulsion to turn and run. But there were other, deeper, inexplicable instincts, telling her to stay. The house was sucking her back. It was an eerie sensation, yet strangely pleasant. She felt its smothering embrace, could feel the house breathing all around her, laughing, whispering, HANNAH . . . SCARLET . . . SILAS. In her head the whispers were like gentle soothing waves, splashing onto her like a caressing tide; surging, receding, each time taking with it a part of her. She gave no resistance; the experience was curiously satisfying.

Peering into the semi-dark room, Scarlet knew that she should escape the house before its embrace became a deathly stranglehold, yet she was loath to resist the warm, loving, hostile aura that held her there. She lingered a while in the gloom of the corridor, shivering with cold. Presently, with the tremulous fingers she pushed the door wide into the room. At once the smell assailed her nostrils; that unfamiliar distressing smell that she had noticed downstairs – a stinging vapour, hopelessness, the taste of death. He *was* dying! And she desperately needed to see the ugly truth of it. *She had to be sure.*

Driven by a morbid fascination, Scarlet went forward, her gaze fixed to the bedhead, searching him out. She trembled at the thought that he might sit up at any minute and see her there. The only sounds in the room were the soft tiptoeing of her feet on the carpet, and the harsh, uneven breathing that seemed to keep tempo with the fluttering of her heart. *There was no turning back.* She had to face the devil. *FACE THE DEVIL!* Fear became courage.

With painstaking slowness, she walked towards him, waves of panic engulfing her. For a long unnerving moment she stood by the foot of the bed, her quivering hand caressing the round brass sphere that decorated each of the four bedposts. Suddenly a strange thing happened. Her dark hesitant gaze alighted on his face and, astonishingly, all was calm inside her, deadly, shocking calm. Fascinated by his face, she could not tear her gaze away. It was not the face she knew. It was a long grey mask, gaunt, silent. Scarlet was drawn closer. Her eyes washed over his body; still a bulk of a man, pushing up from beneath the clothes, his chest rising and falling with that painful, rasping breathing, his long shapeless arms above the covers, heavy like dead hammers, the fingers involuntarily twitching. Scarlet was shocked rigid; relieved, quietly smiling as she dared to move nearer; peering into that strange face and hoping the breathing would stop. WILLING IT TO STOP. How easy it would be, she thought, how effortlessly she could trap that irritating, broken sound with the tips of her fingers; trap it in his throat; press her fingers into the grey parchment and squeeze – squeeze until the sound was no more. The thought became an urge; the urge became an insane compulsion. Oh, how easy it would be.

The long thick fingers twitched erratically. He was disturbed. Scarlet knew it was *her thoughts* that had disturbed him. Even as a child she was always terrified that he knew exactly what she was thinking. The fear flooded back. *Quickly! Get away!* BUT IT WAS TOO LATE. In a swift snake-like movement that almost stopped her heart, his fingers leapt out and locked around her wrist. The cold grey eyes flicked open, piercing her like hard glinting steel. '*I knew you'd come back.*' His voice was low, sinister, raising every nightmare she had ever known. His smile was a grimace, creeping over his face like slime. 'I've been waiting . . . waiting.' His fingers dug into her flesh, tugging her down to him. She could feel the arid stench of his breath on her face. His mouth opened to kiss her.

Suddenly she was screaming. Writhing to free herself, with her free hand striking him again and again until the skin on his forehead burst open in a shower of crimson spots. Still he clung to her, his long jagged nails snapping as they sliced deep into her flesh. When weakened by her onslaught, he relaxed his grip on her, Scarlet ran. She kept on running, her mind a whirl of confusion. Where was Shelagh? Why hadn't she come at the sound of her screaming? *Got to get away!* But what of the money? The jewels? How could she go without them? AND WHERE WAS SHELAGH? Her heart skipped a beat. *She was being pursued!* He was out of bed. *Following her!* She began running down the stairs two at a time. In her frantic haste she slipped, her ankle doubled up beneath her, the pain shooting through her body like knives. GET UP! GET UP! From the corner of her eye she saw the dark shadow looming above her. Quickly! There was no time to make it to the front door. *She must hide. HIDE!* But where? She was a child again, playing hide and seek and her mammy could never find her. *The kitchen. Dear God, help me.* Limping badly, with the pain dimming her senses, she found her way to the kitchen and into the old shaft where the disused dumb-waiter stood. Silently closing the hatch behind her, she curled up in a ball, afterwards remaining perfectly still and hardly daring to breathe. In the distance she could hear the approaching footsteps muffled and terrifying. When they came closer and filled her with such fear that the sweat trickled down her face, she held her breath, her big black eyes turned towards the shaft door, expecting any minute to see it flung open.

After what seemed like hours, Scarlet woke with a start.

Had she slept? All she could remember was hearing the footsteps come right up to the shaft door. Presently, when they had departed, she still dared not move. Supposing he was waiting, watching for her to leave her hiding-place? She *must* have slept. Her eyes were hot and gritty. Her body stiff and cramped. The sickness of fear had left her empty and weakened.

With painstaking slowness, and being careful not to make a sound, Scarlet climbed out of the old shaft. The lamp that had been lit on the mantelpiece was now out. She found herself in the same impregnable blackness as inside the shaft. But she knew her way. Every line and angle of this house was imprinted on her mind for ever.

After what seemed to be an excruciatingly long time, when even the noiseless press of her feet on the carpet appeared to echo from every wall, Scarlet came to the drawing room. Feeling her way round the familiar obstacles: the big polished table, the floral-covered armchair beside which was situated a tall plant-stand and jardiniere, the dull brass fender and the coal scuttle to its left; Scarlet remembered them all and skirted each one without difficulty. When at last she was standing before the dark oak dresser, her trembling fingers tracing the round bulky knobs either side of the top drawer, her heart was in her mouth, beating so furiously that she was certain it could be heard all over the house. With shaking hands and the blood in her body running cold with fear, she eased the drawer open. It creaked. *Wait!* She held her breath, her dark anxious eyes towards the direction of the door. The pitch blackness unnerved her. Had *he* heard? Was he on his way towards her even at this minute? She strained her ears, stretched her eyes wide, looking for the shaft of light that would herald his approach. WHERE IN GOD'S NAME WAS SHELAGH? The silence settled again, thick and suffocating. She dared not open the drawer any further. Instead she slipped long sensuous fingers beneath the drawer, probing, shifting, searching for the cord bag that held the money. A disturbing thought came to her. *Was the money spent?* After all, he had not worked in a long time. The jewellery then! Surely he would never let *that* go? She recalled how he would spend many hours seated by the fire with the sparkling gems spread out on his knee. He fawned over it, was fascinated by its exquisite flawless beauty, caressed it as a lover might caress his woman. No, she could not believe he would *ever* part with it, under any circumstances. Did he have it up there in his room, then? The thought made her search more desperately, until *there*! She had it in her grasp. The feel of the ribbed cord, the shapeless bulk caught between her fingers made her almost collapse with relief.

Quickly Scarlet tucked the cord bag inside her coat, lodging it securely beneath her ribs. Another minute and she had emerged into the hall. PANIC! There was a ray of subdued light ahead of her, coming from the open cellar door and illuminating the very spot where she would have to stand on opening the front door. Horrified, she flattened herself against the wall, gasping as the dampness struck cold to the back of her legs. *What to do!* She could go back, through the kitchen and out of the back door. But *no*. The door had heavy bolts at top and bottom and the big iron key was normally kept in the pantry. Even if she could quickly find the key, the rusted bolts were probably thrust home and the noise of jarring them back would alert whoever was in the cellar.

It suddenly occurred to her that the one in the cellar might well be Shelagh. She relaxed, then stiffened again as she recalled how, when she came to the house, Shelagh was not to be found. She thought of *him*, and of how he had looked at her, *through* her! A curdling shiver rippled over every inch of her being. She went forward hesitantly, coiled like a spring inside and ready to flee for her life at any minute.

The cellar door was open only so far; not far enough for Scarlet to see down the flight of wooden steps and beyond, to the flagged area; yet it was open wide enough for her to slide her body through without making any noise or disturbance. Frightened to her roots, yet curious as to whether it might be Shelagh down there after all, Scarlet paused by the door. All was silent below, deathly silent. She waited a second or two, the longing to see Shelagh and to talk with her almost overwhelming; even though her deeper instincts warned her to get away without delay.

Deciding to follow her instincts, Scarlet moved silently away. But then, as she drew back and passed the open door from a distance, something caught her eye. Lying across the top step and protruding into the hall was a long thin scarf, its green and yellow chequered pattern strangely muted by the yellow glow emanating from the cellar. Scarlet was abruptly halted in her tracks. *It was Shelagh's scarf!* Gingerly, she crept towards it; her stomach turning when, on looking closer, she saw how the chequered pattern was overlaid by a peculiar spreading patch which had dried into a dark violet hue. *Blood!* The word leapt into Scarlet's mind. THERE WAS BLOOD ON SHELAGH'S SCARF. Her stomach churned. Through her terror emerged the startling revelation that Shelagh was in danger! Her *own* safety seemed unimportant. Shelagh needed help. Scarlet was sure of it!

Stealthily, Scarlet descended the stairs, making not a sound that could draw attention to her approach. Below her the candles flickered. She drew closer, almost halfway down. *There was something there.* Someone! Suddenly she could see it all. A scene so grotesque, so macabre that for the rest of her days would haunt her! There in the arc of candleglow was a dark, sinister figure, cloaked and hooded, half-turned from her and its arms raised high. Now, Scarlet could hear the strange, high-pitched whisper, chanting, chanting. The figure swayed back and forth as though in a trance, spasmodically bending down to scoop from the long low table before it and lifting the hand-cupped offering upwards. Scarlet's horrified gaze was involuntarily drawn down, down to the table. The spreaded white cloth was a shroud, its limp folds following the lines of the corpse beneath, covering it from head to toe and betraying nothing of its identity.

The dark cloaked figure leaned forward to the mutilated chest cavity, dipping into the sea of whiteness that was now horribly blooded. Raising its cupped hands high, it grew excited, the chanting became ecstatic, the whisper increasingly distorted. Slowly the cupped hands opened to display the misshapen, fleshy mass which was bathed in a crimson sea. The sea broke away in gushing, meandering rivulets, trickling, dripping.

OH NO! *NO!* Scarlet backed away, her black eyes huge with fear. Instinctively she clamped the flat of her hand over her mouth, to stifle the scream, to quell the rising nausea. Strange twisted scenes tore through her turbulent mind, scenes of Garrett and of the figure which had sprung out, sending Garrett and the boy to their deaths. Footsteps, cold steel eyes. *Terror.* Blind, crippling terror! She was a child again and there was her father. 'He *eats* little innocents like you.' Silas, dead chickens. Her mother's face, floating, floating. SHELAGH! Dear God in heaven. *They've killed Shelagh. Who? Who killed her?* Who was that kneeling figure? *Her father? Silas? WHO?*

Half-crazed with grief and terror, Scarlet stumbled out of the front door and into the woods. Imagining every sound to be the dark figure pursuing her, she ran blindly on, not knowing in which direction, not caring. Desperate only to escape, she fled into the dawn of a new day, her mind assailed by phantoms that would destroy her, making her delicate sanity that much more fragile.

On seeing the bedraggled figure running out of the under-growth, the carriage-driver thought it must be a wild animal pursued by poachers. When two startled black eyes looked up into his coachlights, he was astonished to see that it was no animal, but a *woman*! White-faced and terrified, as though she had seen a ghost. For a moment, he hesitated to stop; there was always danger in picking up lone women, especially *frightened* women, barefoot women, and those who came out of nowhere like this one had done. He'd heard many a tale of how women deliber-ately laid charges against some innocent man, or they might *pretend* to be alone, then, when you were foolish enough to stop, a rogue or two would leap out from the hedges and rob you!

On this occasion, though, the carriage-driver had little choice. The frantic woman had positioned herself right in his path. He either had to grind to a halt and offer her a lift, or he had to keep going and let the horses' hooves trample over the top of her. Reluctantly he tugged the reins back, shouting and heaving until the startled horses came to a halt. 'What the bloody hell d'you think you're doing, woman?' he demanded, as Scarlet began climbing up beside him. 'Are you desperate to get yourself *killed*, or what?'

'Drive on . . . *please* drive on!' Scarlet glanced furtively about as, still cursing and moaning, the driver clicked the two cobs into motion. He felt nervous. *She* made him feel nervous. He cast a sly glance towards her. *Wild* she was. And magnificent. 'What're you doing . . . wandering the moors at such a God-forsaken hour?' He looked down, wincing at her torn legs and feet. 'Lost your shoes? Been running, have you?' His anger gave way to curiosity. 'Somebody *chasing* you, eh?' he chuckled. It was easy to see how a full-blooded man might want to chase such a primitive beauty.

When Scarlet gave no answer, but kept her gaze low-ered to the platform, he became bold enough to study her with a long, sweeping look. Still she made no move, so, being suitably encouraged, he reached out, touching his fingertips softly against her leg. She bristled and flashed her eyes on him; black, stabbing eyes, wild and murderous. Startled, he snatched away his hand, quickly returning his full attention to the road ahead.

Scarlet inched away, afterwards remaining motionless, her dark haunted gaze fixed on the place where her bruised feet rested. The driver also kept his gaze ahead. He had been shaken by the look she had given him. She was wild, alright, and magnificent, yes. But she was *trouble*! He could sense it. He could see it too, in her eyes. But there was something else in those haunted black eyes; something he wanted no part of. There was terror there. And madness!

'This is as far as I go. I'm waiting for two passengers . . . coming in on the next train.' The carriage pulled into the yard at Minehead Railway Station. 'You'll have to make your own way from here.' The driver watched Scarlet climb down. He was visibly relieved to be rid of her.

Some time later the train arrived, bringing with it his passengers. As they climbed into the carriage, the portly gentleman was heard to remark to his colleague, 'Poor dishevelled creature . . . a real beauty, though.' He shook his head and tutted. 'Shame . . . a terrible shame. I wonder why she was taking great pains to hide herself?'

'Don't be soft-hearted, you old fool,' chided the thin moustached fellow, 'no doubt she's brought her ill-fortune down on her own head! There *are* such women . . . and more often than not, it's the ones with the most striking looks that fall the furthest.' He waited patiently while the portly gentleman clambered into the carriage. 'Let that be a lesson to you . . . stay away from handsome females, or, like as not, they'll drag you down with them.' He chuckled. 'She probably didn't want to be seen because she's been up to no good. No doubt she's on her way to some unsuspecting man this very minute. Can't think why she would board a train headed for Weymouth, though . . . I should have thought there'd be better pickings in a livelier, rowdier place.'

'Nonsense, man. Are you blind? That young woman was not of the streets . . . too much quality about her. No! . . . if you ask me, the poor thing has suffered . . . probably at the hands of a callous bugger such as yourself! . . . I reckon she's been frightened. She *looked* frightened.'

'Deranged! That's what she looked, old man . . . *deranged*!'

As the driver eased the horses round to depart, he reflected on what the thin moustached fellow had said. And he agreed. The black-eyed beauty did look 'deranged'. He had been glad to be shut of her but, when all was said and done, he *was* a family man. And he couldn't help feeling a pang of sympathy for her. Weymouth, eh? He wondered what in the world would become of such a tragic soul.

PART FIVE

1930

SANCTUARY

Flesh perspires, I live on,
. . . Leaping from place to place
Over oblivion.
. . . That is I;
The eternal thing in man,
That heeds no call to die.

Thomas Hardy, from 'Heredity'

CHAPTER FIFTEEN

'It's a pity you never learned to read, Hannah.' The nurse stroked the brush through the woman's long black tresses for the twentieth time, the pleasure evident in her rosy face. Her own hair was quite mousy and fine, whereas her patient's magnificent locks were thick and luxuriant, bouncing beneath the brush and framing the pale lovely face in the most exquisite way. 'There's so much exciting news in the papers,' she went on, thinking how eagerly she herself would have taught this reluctant pupil the rudiments of reading and writing, if only she had shown the enthusiasm to learn. During the four years and more that she had been an inmate in the mental institution, the woman called Hannah had shown no such enthusiasm; and not only where elementary schooling was concerned. In the early years she had been a most unwilling patient, morose and withdrawn, prone to terrible nightmares and highly nervous of strangers. She had revealed almost nothing of her background or identity. More recently, however, she had begun to respond to long-term treatment and therapy, and the nightmares had become less persistent. About herself, though, she remained reticent, giving only the name Hannah. When she had first arrived here, via the hospital where she had been taken after collapsing in the street, it was evident that she had no real memory of either her own identity or of the reason as to why she should be wandering the back streets of Weymouth, barefoot, dishevelled and in an extreme state of distress.

'There!' Nurse Dixon patted the wayward tresses, her kindly face beaming. 'After you've had your breakfast, don't forget that Doctor Taylor has asked to see you. I'll be coming to collect you at ten forty-five . . . he will expect you in his office at eleven a.m. sharp!' She gave her patient a gentle nudge, bending sideways to peer into the quiet dark eyes. 'It's a special day today, Hannah,' she reminded her. 'If he thinks you're ready for the wide world, it's likely you could be released within the week.'

'Thank you.'

'Is that all you have to say? . . . "Thank you"? My goodness me! You should be dancing up and down this ward.' Realising that the other woman was in no mood for conversation, she placed the hairbrush on top of the bedside cabinet and went across the ward to the long narrow window. Here her smiling gaze wandered over the high-walled grounds below, and she thought how, though the wall was virtually unsurmountable, making the gardens a prison, it was a pleasant prison. And the sky promised another glorious July day. 'I hope it doesn't get uncomfortably hot,' she remarked, returning to her patient. 'I read in the newspaper this morning how *seventy-two people* died in a heatwave in Chicago!' She shuddered. 'Dreadful! . . . it doesn't bear thinking about.' For a few moments longer she bustled about, making the bed, refilling the water jug and plucking from a vase the dead flowers which had been left behind by another inmate, one who had a family and was fortunate enough to be cherished. She had especially requested that the flowers be given 'to that poor woman . . . so quiet . . . so alone'. She had tried hard to make friends, she explained, 'but she seems so afraid to let anyone near her'. Nurse Dixon knew exactly what she meant. 'Now then, Hannah . . . let me look at you.' She stood before the seated woman, eyeing her up and down, from the blue full-skirted dress, which had also been a gift, to the neat black patent shoes, crossed over at the ankle by a dainty strap. As usually she noticed how perfectly slim and attractive the dark-eyed woman was. 'It's not fair!' she said, good humouredly. 'You must have been at the *front* of the queue when they were giving out the beauty . . . I was at the *back*!' She chuckled, but it struck her how, if she could change places with this lovely-looking young woman, she would not. It would mean suffering loneliness and terror of a kind she herself could never envisage, and seeing into such a tortured mind that would make life too unbearable. No, she would not want to change places with the one who called herself Hannah.

'Can I go into the garden?'

'Of *course* you can. But not until you've had some breakfast. Good Lord! You never eat enough to keep a *bird* alive.' She pointed to the long table in the centre of the ward, and drew attention to the fact that, already, other patients were leaving their beds and seating themselves at the table. In the distance, the clatter of metal wheels on polished floor and the distinct tinkling of crockery indicated that the breakfast trolley was on its way. 'Off you go then, Hannah . . . have some breakfast, and afterwards I'll take you down to the gardens.' She wagged a finger. 'I shall ask Nurse Raymond whether you ate a hearty breakfast, mind you!' she warned.

As always the dark-haired woman known as Hannah seated herself at the corner of the table, as far away from the other women as possible. She listened to their aimless chatter and, when it was directed at her, she responded with a wan smile, reluctantly eating the boiled eggs and toast put before her. She said very little. She had nothing of value to add to their conversations. After a while they isolated her, regarding her with suspicion and disliking her for making them feel uncomfortable. One woman in particular, a small, bent creature with a serious mental affliction and a wicked disposition, scuttled round the table at one point, to grab a hank of Scarlet's hair, which she then spasmodically yanked and clung on to with such determination that it took two nurses and a ward orderly to pull her away.

Some short time later, Nurse Dixon arrived to collect her patient from the gardens where earlier she had escorted her, following the unfortunate experience at the breakfast table. From a distance she observed how deeply engrossed in thought was the dark-haired Hannah, and how sad she looked, sitting there by the fountain, her troubled black eyes following the flow of water as it tumbled down the cold marble status to the frothy pool below. She sensed the woman's great pain and she was also saddened, wondering what manner of thoughts were churning in that lovely head.

'Can't I stay here a while longer?' she asked the nurse. 'It's so beautiful . . . so tranquil.' When the answer had been no, and she was given the explanation, 'Doctor Taylor is waiting to see you,' there was no resistance. She followed the nurse out of the warm July sunshine, on up the open stairway and along the winding narrow corridor, the sound of their footsteps reverberating from the wood-block flooring and the smooth pale green walls that hemmed them in on both sides. *Footsteps!* FOOTSTEPS. The sound struck fear into one tremulous heart.

Doctor Taylor studied the dark eyes, cleared his throat and said with deliberation, 'There's nothing to be gained by containing you here any longer . . . we've done all we can. Your memory *is* impaired, of that there's no doubt. But otherwise you're recovered enough to cope in the outside world. Do you agree, Hannah?' He regarded her closely, the sunlight stemming through the window and flashing on the lenses of his spectacles. The patient glanced up, was temporarily blinded and quickly lowered her gaze. He shifted his position. 'I said . . . do you agree, Hannah?' he insisted.

The dark eyes became intense, searching for his eyes behind the reflection of his spectacles. *Hannah! . . .* Why did he call her Hannah, when her name was *Scarlet?* But then, he didn't know her, did he? *None* of them knew her. They were all strangers . . . enemies. She struggled to see the images in her mind. But always they hid from her, lost in a shifting fog that moved this way and that, allowing her only fleeting glimpses of people and places. The thick grey fog never cleared long enough for her to see whether the faces were those of friends or strangers. This man, this 'Doctor Taylor,' *he* was a stranger. They were *all* strangers here. She must not let them see how frightened she was. Nor must she give her name. What was he asking now?

'Hannah . . . do you feel able to cope with the outside world?' She smiled and nodded her acknowledgement. He was relieved. 'Good! . . . *We* feel you are well enough to leave this place, but of course you will need help to find somewhere to live. You do have a considerable sum of money. Hannah . . . the two thousand pounds you brought with you in the cord bag . . . together with the interest it has accumulated. And of course . . . there are the jewels, which must be worth a tidy sum.'

'They were my mother's.' *Now why did she say that?* She knew nothing of any jewels!

'Your *mother's*, eh?' Doctor Taylor smiled broadly and leaned forward to touch her on the shoulder. That was the very first time she had revealed anything of her background. 'You see . . . you're already beginning to remember. It *will* all come back to you . . . piece by piece, like just now, or overnight . . . when your entire past will flood into your mind. Believe me, Hannah, it could happen.' His voice grew more serious. 'Or you may *never* really get total recall. It would have been more satisfactory if all our efforts to trace your identity had thrown up some positive results. They did not. And now there's little more we can do.' He sighed, declaring abruptly, 'But we *can* help to get you settled . . . keep an eye on you, so to speak. Do you feel happy about that, Hannah?'

He was calling her by that name again. Well, *let him*! She would keep her secret. 'I'll be fine,' she told him, adding, with a warm glance at Nurse Dixon who was waiting to take her back, 'And thank you for all you've done.'

'That's what we're here for, my dear.'

'When can I leave?' She had been impatient to depart this place for many weeks now. Something told her that she must keep moving. *Keep moving*. Fool them. Then they would never find her! But *who*? Who 'would never find her'? And how would she know those who would harm her, even if she came face to face with them? Icy fingers touched her heart. She shuddered, praying she would always stay one step ahead of her pursuers. She had no real memory, no roots, no past or future. But one thing she *did* have. *And that was a deep murmuring sense of terror!*

'Wait here, my dear. The almoner will see you shortly.' Nurse Dixon placed a small brown suitcase on the wooden bench, at the same time leaning forward to do up the top button of her patient's pretty blue dress. 'I know it's a lovely day, Hannah . . . but you've spent most of your time indoors. We don't want you catching a chill now, do we?' She lifted the fob watch that was pinned to her breast pocket. 'Goodness! I should be taking Mrs Clayton for her bath.' She looked down at the bent, dark head and a wave of compassion washed through her. 'Look after yourself, my dear,' she said softly, easing her ample posterior onto the seat and laying her podgy hand over the long elegant fingers. She was surprised to feel the other woman's hand stiffen beneath her touch.

'I don't want to see the almoner!' The black eyes swivelled

upwards towards the glass-panelled door opposite.

'Oh, now Hannah! . . . She's here to *help* you. After all, you need somewhere to stay . . . perhaps a job? Well . . . the almoner has many contacts. Trust her.'

'Thank you for the suitcase.'

'You're very welcome. I've put your other dress in there . . . with your hairbrush and toiletries.' She leaned forward and lowered her voice. 'I think you were very foolish to insist on *cash*, my dear. But of course, it *is* your money. You'll find it's all there . . . together with the jewellery. Be very careful. Guard the case at all times!' She sighed and drew closer. 'Are you sure you wouldn't rather deposit the money in the bank?'

'I'm sure.' The voice was impatient.

'Very well, my dear.' She eased herself up from the bench. 'I must go, or there'll be all hell let loose,' she laughed. It was a pleasant sound. 'But do take care, Hannah . . . look after yourself. And don't forget your appointment with Doctor Taylor in a month's time. The card is in your coat pocket . . . see?' She raised the tweed coat from the bench and dipped into the pocket. Drawing out a small yellow card, she pointed to the date: 20 August 1930. 'Don't lose it!'

'Goodbye, Nurse Dixon . . . and thank you again.' The dark gaze bathed the nurse's face. She smiled in return, but gave no reply. For a moment longer Nurse Dixon studied the other woman's magnificent eyes, thinking how quiet they seemed. In her experience she had witnessed much sorrow and tragedy; she had seen how cruelly a mind might be twisted and hopelessly deranged. The cases were many: shock, grief, persecution, or something so deeply inherent and cruelly destructive in the mind itself that it could not be recognised or treated. She saw that elusive quality now, in those quiet dark eyes. She knew instinctively that, beneath the quietness, there was so much suffering that even to look on it was to *feel* it also.

In spite of the conscious effort to disguise it, the torture was there, always there, lurking beneath the surface.

'You mustn't worry about me. I'll be fine . . . really.' Nurse Dixon's anxiety had conveyed itself. The dark eyes smiled. The long elegant fingers reached out to enfold the podgy hand. 'Please go.'

Impulsively, the nurse bent forward to kiss the pale gaunt face. She would have muttered a word of affection, but it stuck fast in her throat. Instead she merely nodded her head and turned away quickly, reminding herself of the fallacy that nurses should never submit to emotion.

The mirror in the washroom was grimy and criss-crossed with fine ancient lines. The dark eyes were strangely distorted, the lovely face split into fragments, like the pieces of a jigsaw. The reflection was not true, but frightening. *Unnerving.* Still, the dark brooding gaze searched and shifted, intent on finding itself. When it could not, the bitter tears fell, blurring the image even more. 'SCARLET? . . . *'I am Scarlet.'* The voice was like that of a child.

'Alright, are you, dearie?' The stranger bustled into the washroom, surprised to find such a strikingly handsome lady actually *talking* to herself in that awful mirror, and softly crying.

'Yes . . . I'm alright.' Gathering up her suitcase, she quickly departed the washroom and, a few moments later, was out on the street, leaving the almoner puzzled and annoyed as to why the woman known as Hannah should not have attended the appointment made for her. Still, for every ungrateful soul, there were others who would be *glad* of her help!

'Who the devil's that, at this late hour?' Edward Summers snatched the tumbler of whisky from the housekeeper's outstretched hand. 'Send them away!' he grumbled, incoherently muttering after her as she went on hurried footsteps towards the front door.

'Yes?' Ruth Taylor was intrigued to see a tall, dark-haired and exceptionally handsome young man waiting at the door. She was old enough to be his mother. Yet beneath his smiling violet eyes she felt like a young girl again, even softly blushing as she opened the door wider to let the light shine more fully on him. She calculated that he must be the better side of thirty years.

'My apologies for disturbing you so late in the evening.' He inclined his head politely.

'Are you from the police? They've *already* paid us a visit . . . *we know nothing of any murder*, I can assure you!' The smile faded. In its place was a look of irritation.

'Murder?' There was shock in his voice. And fear. 'I'm not from the police. I'm looking for . . . a friend. She was married to the late Garrett Summers. Scarlet Pengally.'

'That woman!' The housekeeper bristled at the name. At once she retreated into the house and would have slammed shut the door if only he had not placed his hand against it. *'Please.'* His voice trembled. *'I must find her!'*

'Then search where *all* of her kind seek refuge . . . GO TO HELL!'

On her return to the library, Ruth Taylor found her master in a drunken stupor. The sight was not a pleasant one, nor was it unfamiliar. Since the tragic deaths of his son Garrett and the boy several years ago he had gone steadily downhill. To her mind, there was only one creature to blame. SCARLET PENGALLY! *A witch without a heart.*

'Who was it?' Edward Summers lifted heavy eyelids and turned in his wheelchair. 'Was it the police again?' His voice was slurred, matter-of-fact.

'No, no . . . it wasn't the police, sir.' Ruth Taylor came forward, gently taking the empty tumbler from his hand. 'It was a stranger . . . come to ask directions.'

'Oh. Not the police . . . bloody fools! What do they think

we know of mutilated bodies found buried on the moors?'
Suddenly, the tears were running down the wrinkled folds
of his face. *'Wicked!'* he murmured, 'wicked, wicked! . . .
What devil would do such a thing?' He shook his head and
closed his eyes, quietly mumbling to himself.

'Devil indeed,' agreed the housekeeper, tucking the rug
about his knees. The image of Scarlet Pengally rose in her
mind. *There was a 'devil'.* One who deserved no peace. One
who should be tortured till the end of her days . . . just as
this poor old man was being tortured.

The moon was high; its soft glow disturbed by scurrying
clouds that created gyrating shadows over the moors. The
breeze had whipped up to a spiteful wind that played
weird laments in the treetops, and the air struck suddenly
chilly. It was a forbidding evening, more reminiscent of
winter than July. An evening to match Silas's mood as he
wended his way across the moors towards Dunster, and
Greystone House. All this time and endless searching; all
in vain. It was as though she had vanished from the face
of the earth. *Somebody* must know where Scarlet had gone!
He was now convinced that they were all lying to him.
But he would not be beaten.

The unusually cold air clung to him. Shivering, he drew
the long black coat tighter about his lithe figure. Bending
into the wind he made a grim sight. *Scarlet was his!* She
would not escape him. Not now, when he had made so
many sacrifices and achieved all he had set out to do. *He
would find her.* Even if it took him a lifetime and he was
made to search every dark corner of the earth!

CHAPTER SIXTEEN

'Take your grubby hands off my daughter!' The prim middle-aged woman was horrified to see the vagrant actually offering her small daughter a dubious-looking parcel.

'It's only a sandwich,' protested the down-and-out, a look of pain and confusion in her large dark eyes, 'But . . . *she's my daughter, not yours*!' Scarlet gazed at the child in the perambulator. She was a pretty little thing, about two years of age, fair-haired and friendly. She *looked* like Cassie, yet the *eyes* were different somehow . . . vivid blue they were, not dark like those of the child who came alive in Scarlet's deepest dreams. 'Her name is *Cassie*,' she insisted, '*my* daughter . . . Cassie.' She reached down to stroke the fair hair with cold, chapped hands.

At once, the woman sprang forward, striking the paper parcel to the pavement and hurrying the bemused child away. 'I shall make it my business to inform the first constable I meet!' she warned. 'Tramps shouldn't be allowed amongst decent folk!' As she made her way along the street, which was already thronging with Christmas shoppers, the woman began to tell all and sundry about the 'scruffy wild-eyed creature who might have abducted my baby if I hadn't come out of the shop in time!'

Finding herself the subject of great curiosity and sensing

the anger that was quickly brewing, Scarlet stared at the onlookers with scorn. '*I made a mistake*!' she told them, at the same time moving discreetly away. 'I thought it was my *own* little girl . . . my Cassie. Anybody can make a mistake, can't they?' As she hurried away, quickly ramming the sandwiches back into her hessian bag and safely tucking the battered suitcase under her arm, Scarlet felt the crowd's resentment. She also felt their fear. It made her smile. They were afraid of her. She was wary of them. People were strange. She must never forget that they were not to be trusted!

Caught in the surging push of people, all eager to make their festive purchases before hurrying home to a cheery fireside, Scarlet was not surprised to find herself given a wide berth, her approach even prompting some people to walk over to the other side of the road in order to avoid contact with her. She didn't mind. It was unnerving to be surrounded by people and, as a rule, she did her best to keep away from the shops and busier area of Weymouth centre. Her favourite haunt was the beach. There she would find a quiet corner where she could sit and watch the incoming waves gently lapping over the sand. There was a timeless quality about the ocean. It soothed her troubled mind, creating in her a unique sense of peace and a deep-rooted belief that she belonged. Somewhere in her past the sea had been a source of contentment to her. She felt that above all else.

In the summer, when she had left the institution, the sea had seemed to call her, and she had gladly spent many hours just sitting and watching from the beach. All through that long sultry summer and the mild winter that followed, she had never wandered far from the comforting roar of the ocean. Her needs were few and her appetite meagre. The small fortune she carried with her was barely disturbed. Money meant nothing to her, though she knew she could not survive without it. The jewels, however, intrigued and fascinated her. Not because of their exceptional beauty, nor because of their obvious value. But because they represented something in the past. They were like a key which might unlock a door that was closed to her.

Time and again, when she felt safe and unobserved, Scarlet had taken the two brooches and matching necklace from the small cord bag in the suitcase and, for long searching moments, she would gaze on the sparkling gems. One of the brooches was of oblong shape, encrusted with a border of diamonds and bearing a large sapphire in the centre; the gold necklace was of matching design. The smaller brooch was of oval shape, made up of gold filigree and overlaid with small emerald clusters. Often, if she stared into them long enough, Scarlet would imagine the stones merging to become a face. A small, quiet face with anxious china-blue eyes. *Its name was Hannah.* Scarlet knew that instinctively. She knew also that Hannah was her mother. *And Hannah was dead.* But *Cassie,* wasn't dead. WHY? Why would Cassie be sent away? But, of course . . . she *knew* why! *Because Cassie was in danger. She* was in danger also. Someone meant to kill them. Why? WHY? What dreadful thing had she, or little Cassie, ever done that made someone want to kill them? When the persistent questions tormented her, Scarlet would pacify herself with the constant belief that Cassie was safe now. CASSIE. She remembered the golden hair and the sound of laughter. She saw Cassie in every child who passed her on the streets. Little by little the jigsaw pieces were sliding into place. As the emerging picture grew stronger, so did Scarlet's inexplicable terror. A terror that kept her constantly hiding behind the dirt and rags of a vagabond. A terror that urged her to look continually over her shoulder, and drove her deeper into herself. To those who could not know her, Scarlet was a woman of the streets, unkempt and unclean, someone to be suspicious of and who must be avoided. What they could not even *begin* to know was that beneath that grime and tattered garments was a young woman of exceptional beauty, a woman living in fear for her very life, haunted beyond endurance and suffering all the more because, while the memory was still sleeping, the horror of her past was very much alive.

Leaving the bright lights and Christmas decorations behind, Scarlet crossed to the promenade, pausing for a moment beside the statue of Queen Victoria. Here Scarlet gathered her thoughts. She was disturbed. That business with the girl had been most distressing. Not for the first time the paralysing fear squeezed her heart. It was always there. So was the loneliness. But the greatest loneliness was in not remembering it all, not seeing the full revealing picture that was always submerged beneath the surface. Sighing, Scarlet tramped across the beach, feeling curiously excited as the fine sand gave way beneath her footsteps, piling up around the imprints of her shoes, like miniature dunes. There was something oddly satisfying about the way a body sank into the shifting sand, when it sucked at you, drawing you in deeper. Suffocating.

Placing the suitcase down, Scarlet draped the hessian bag over it and sat cross-legged beside them, her dark, thoughtful gaze concentrating on the vast stretch of ocean before her. 'Hannah . . . my mother.' Her voice was velvet soft in the cold night air. *Hannah*. Scarlet knew the face. She had seen it so many times. 'Cassie . . . my little girl. *Not my little girl!*' There was confusion still. Frustration. Scarlet wondered whether it would *always* be that way. The thought was unbearable.

'Scarlet!' The voice came from behind her. She slewed round, wary, suspicious.

'What do you want?' It was *her* again. At once, Scarlet was on her guard. Her black eyes were hostile.

'I knew I'd find you here . . . huddled in a corner and staring out to sea like a lost soul.' The ragged woman chuckled, her mouth loosely opened and displaying a line of blackened teeth with wide gaps between. Folding her tall wiry figure she drooped to the sands beside Scarlet. 'Here . . . this'll warm you up.' She dug into her holey bag and withdrew from it a pork pie, which she thrust at Scarlet. 'A Christmas present,' she laughed, winking one bloodshot eye and keeping the other wickedly on Scarlet's unwelcome expression. 'An' it didn't cost me a single penny!'

'Where did you get it, then?' Scarlet knew the woman only briefly. They had first met last Christmas on this very spot. And only twice since then. She was a woman of unpredictable moods, with unattractive appearance and possessed of pale shifty eyes. Scarlet felt uncomfortable. The woman made her nervous. She pushed the pie away.

'*Stole* it! . . . Had to.' Her eyes bored into Scarlet. '*It's either steal . . . or starve!*' The voice quickened with anger. '*You* don't steal though. No! . . . I ain't never seen *you* steal.' She leaned closer, her bad breath fanning Scarlet's face. 'Got money, 'ave yer?' Her gnarled fingers reached out, touching, lingering. *Intimate*.

'That's *my* business!' Scarlet recoiled from her touch and began gathering together her belongings.

'Share an' share alike . . . that's what *we* should do . . . folks like us.' She scrambled to her knees, agitated by Scarlet's impending departure. 'Show old Meg what yer got in that there suitcase.' She made a snatch at it. Scarlet was quicker. The woman fell back into the sand, laughing and crying. 'Go on then . . . run off with yer money . . . see if I care!' Her voice became a whine. 'Oh, look 'ere Scarlet . . . old Meg don't want much. Yer a bad 'un . . . keeping it all to yerself!' As Scarlet hurried away, the obscenities intensified. 'Piss off then! . . . Yer money won't do yer no good! You'll see. *You'll see!*'

All was quiet. The shoppers had long dispersed and the

back streets were empty. Shivering, Scarlet quickened her steps. Here in the dark unlit alleys that led towards the old railway station and the derelict house, there was a sense of danger. The house, though, where Scarlet had found shelter on many a cold night, was not too far. Scarlet was heartened by the thought. Drawing her tattered tweed coat more securely about her thin figure, she pressed on. In a moment the house was in sight: a severe Victorian monstrosity, it stood close to the railway lines, surrounded by debris and with its many small windows shattered. Yet it was sturdy, and the roof remained intact. Many a homeless soul had found refuge within its walls.

Carefully wending her way through the broken glass and brickbats that littered the ground floor, Scarlet found her way into a corner of what might once have been the parlour. Here she made herself comfortable, and settled down to sleep, her coat pulled over her bent knees, and her belongings wedged against the wall for a pillow. The silence was eerie, broken only by the occasion echo of engines being shunted along the nearby railway line. The tiredness weighed heavily. She drifted in and out of sleep. The walls seemed to close in on her. The house was *another*, from the shadows that were her past. The room was a prison and she was captured there, a child, small and afraid. 'No, Daddy . . . don't leave me here!' Her voice startled the still air, frightening her. Suddenly she was sitting bolt upright, cold, trembling, with the beads of sweat clammy on her skin; she was intensely aware of her isolation, her vulnerability.

For a long, desperately uncomfortable moment, Scarlet made no move. She dared not. *All of her instincts told her there was someone else here, in this room.* Skulking in the dark. *Watching her.* Her flesh tingled. She kept every muscle still, and listened. Nothing stirred. Only her fearful imagination. Relieved, she leaned back against the wall, wincing as the sharp, jagged protrusions dug into the arc of her shoulders. Fatigued, she closed her eyes, letting the weariness wash over her in dizzy waves. Sleep eluded her. Through the gap where the window had been, Scarlet could see the moon, wintery and cold to the eye; it stared back at her like a pale, dead face. *Her mother's face!* 'Hannah.' The name was uttered like the cry of a child. Gripped by a terrible sadness, Scarlet bowed her head. The tears coursed down her face, warm and comforting. 'Hannah . . . Mammy.' She whispered the words over and over and was strangely relieved. Moved by a deep inexplicable compulsion, she began feverishly delving into the suitcase; she had a great need to feel the jewels between her fingers. They comforted her. As did the memory of the name Shelagh.

In the light of the moon, the gems lay in her hands like grey matter. The longer she gazed on them, the sharper became the image in Scarlet's mind; of *someone else*, bent over the trinkets, caressing them. The image shifted. *Smooth, dark hair. Piercing grey eyes!* Terror flooded her heart. IT WAS HIM! *The maggot at the core of her existence.* Her heart folded into itself, as the image became real. Warm and close. She opened her mouth to scream and, suddenly, *he was on her*! Tearing at her, ripping the gems from her hand. Fingers thrust into her coat, seeking the warmth of her breasts, the foul, rancid mouth covering hers. She pushed and fought, fists flailing. Her assailant was too strong, too determined. Her hand felt the sharp angled shape of a brickbat. Instinctively, she clutched it into her groping fingers. But then, just as quickly, it was wrenched from her. Then a voice, whispering, laughing, a voice she knew. *The woman's voice!*

'Always knew you were a beauty underneath them rags. It's a pity you don't like ol' Meg . . . you an' me, we could a' been good pals . . . *real good pals*!' Again the lewd laughter, quickly subsiding when there came the sound of footsteps picking their way through the debris. The last thing Scarlet saw before the brickbat thudded into her temple, was the vagrant's face, leering, taunting, superimposed by *his* face. The penetrating grey eyes mocked her, even through her dying senses.

The layers of fog began to peel away. Like the spasmodic burst of candlelight in the instant before the flame splutters and dies, the images flickered clear and sharp in her mind. Deep-rooted terror pressed her down. One after the other, the faces sought her out. Hannah, Cassie. Just as she had imagined. But they were disembodied. Without substance. The pain was unendurable. Her father. Silas, SILAS! HER FATHER! A white, blood-spattered shroud; and the kneeling figure. Cloaked and hooded. STEEPED IN DEATH. MURDER. Who? WHO? The horror filled her soul, growing until there was no place for it to go but outwards. Like a tidal wave the awful scream burst from her. 'NO! NO!' Her hands flew to her temples. Hot, sticky blood. Staining her fingers. Crimson splashes on a white background. *Mutilated!* Spiralling through the maelstrom in her mind came a friendly face with round brown eyes. 'Shelagh!' The name left Scarlet's lips as a cry for help.

'Ssh, child. Put your arm round my neck.' Scarlet felt herself being tenderly lifted. Soft, comforting hands tended her wound and the face that bent over her was kind, concerned. The vision was an angel, all in white, soft, flowing. *Smudged with blood.* 'Can you stand, my dear? . . . lean on me.' The voice gentled into Scarlet's mind. Dazed, trusting, she pushed herself up. Crumbling legs folded beneath her. 'Alright, don't worry . . . I'll get help.' The words echoed down a long black tunnel. The room was spinning. In the shifting grey sky, the moon remained passive, its yellow luminance casting a weird glow on Scarlet's pallid face. Unseeing, she slithered into a cradle of darkness.

Outside, the nuns dispensed mugs of hot broth to the

waiting vagrants. The sight of Sister Ellen rushing from the derelict house, her long white habit sullied and a look of alarm on her face, did not disturb them. Someone was hurt. *Dying*, maybe.

But then, there were worse things than death!

CHAPTER SEVENTEEN

'Where d'you reckon she is . . . after all this time?'
John Blackwood threw the remainder of his sandwich to the birds, his blue eyes fixed in a thoughtful gaze, as he asked his wife, 'What's become of her, d'you think?' He slurped the remaining dregs from his cup and wiped the back of his hand over his mouth, 'You'd a' thought Scarlet might a' kept in touch with *Shelagh*, at least. They were friends when all's said and done.'

'Humph!' Ada Blackwood snorted and shifted beside him. 'Dunno about "friends".' She stretched her neck to see what her son was doing. Satisfied that he was busily mending his fishing line, she returned her attention to her husband. 'If you ask *me*, I'd say they were more "strange bedfellows" than friends. *I* certainly wouldn't want them for friends. Neither of 'em! . . . and that's a fact.'

'That don't surprise me at all, Ada Blackwood!' John laughed. 'You're one o' them rare women who prefers her own company. You never did like Scarlet anyway . . . not when she were a little girl, an' not in all the years since.'

'I don't deny it.' She half-turned her head, quietly regarding him and thinking, sadly, how the passage of time was beginning to show: in the hair that was streaked with grey, in the growing stoop of his shoulders and the lines that lately were etched deeper into his lean face. The mirror showed *her* the same truths. But life was good.

They had a fine young son, tall and strong, not far off his sixteenth birthday. But already a man in the making.

'I allus thought you were harsh in your judgement of Scarlet. *Life* was harsh on her . . . giving her up to a man like Vincent Pengally.' He laughed, a tight cruel sound, 'They say the devil looks after his own. Well! . . . it seems he's looking after *that one* alright!' He raised his condemning eyes to Greystone House. 'Almost eight years since that wicked man drove his own daughter away. They reckoned 'e were on his deathbed *then*.' He shook his head slowly. 'The bugger *still* ain't dead, is he?'

'He might as well be . . . from what you tell me,' remarked Ada, her gaze also drawn to the upper window of that darkened room where she knew Vincent Pengally to be wasting away. 'Although, I do believe you could be too harsh on Pengally.' She gave a small chuckle. But then it died on her lips when she saw the seriousness of her husband's face.

'I ain't being "too harsh", Ada,' he murmured, 'an' I'll tell you some'at else . . . you'll not get me setting foot in that house again. *Not as long as I live!* I couldn't rightly refuse my help when Shelagh found him collapsed outside the bedroom . . . she would never a' got him back in bed on her own, that's for sure.' He shivered. 'But, oh, I'm telling you, gall . . . if I ever saw the living dead . . . it were on that day, in the form o' Vincent Pengally!'

'Illness is never a pretty sight.'

'I know that. But it weren't just the "illness" I saw in his face. There were some'at else . . . *a worse disease.* Ugly and terrible, like a mad hunger.' He would have said 'it were eating away his very soul'. But he had said enough. Talking of Vincent Pengally was repugnant to him. It brought back the effigy to his mind. Not of a man. But of a thing so awful that he had suffered many a sleepless night because of it.

'Aye, well . . . he's been ill a long time. I do marvel at

the way Shelagh devotes herself to him.' She smiled knowingly. 'Mind you . . . I heard in the butcher's shop that Vincent Pengally has changed his will in her favour.'

'So if Scarlet *was* to come back, there'd be nothing to call her own, eh?'

'Huh! . . . She gave up all right to anything from her father when she got herself with child . . . an' her little more than a child herself!' Her expression became one of disgust. 'An' to think she led us all to believe that young Garrett Summers were the father. Dear God, what terrible heartache she caused old Edward Summers. *No wonder he died a broken man.* That woman has a lot to answer for. I'm not surprised she daren't show her face round these parts.'

'Ada Blackwood, you're a hard woman, that you are.' His voice grew stern. 'But I'll not have you putting all the blame on Scarlet's shoulders . . . not when you don't know . . . *you don't know.*' He fell silent, his thoughts carrying him back over the years, rearing images that made him shudder: images of a boy, made to suffer the harshest brutality, and a girl whose vulnerable mind was warped by the foulest creature that God ever saw fit to put on this earth. In his mind's eye he saw the formidable figure of a man, shadowy in the glow of candlelight, and gazing on his own child with eyes that glittered evil thoughts. If Scarlet had gone wrong along the way, then who could condemn her? Certainly not him! And not anyone who knew the truth. There were those who said that Scarlet Pengally was a monster. He did not deny that she *had* been the cause of some heartache. But her *own* pain was no doubt much greater. She was no monster. Scarlet Pengally was an innocent victim, created by another monster who was her father. She was to be pitied. Not blamed.

'What d'you mean . . . "I don't know".' Ada had long suspected that her husband had seen and heard things at Greystone House that he had never revealed. 'What are you trying to tell me?' she insisted, resting the darning on her lap and looking up with quizzical eyes. 'What's playing on your mind?'

For a seemingly endless time he gave no answer. Instead he stared up at Greystone House, hurt by the deterioration that had taken place over the years. Twice he had offered to put the garden and smithy to rights. But Shelagh had brought back Vincent Pengally's express instructions that 'no stranger will set foot on Pengally land . . . not while *I'm* alive!' On many occasions afterwards, he had appeared at the bedroom, his searching grey eyes raking over what was his. Watching. Suspicious. And always with a murderous expression on his wasting features. Only the orchards and the outer fields were kept tended. John Blackwood was grateful at least that he was allowed to carry on with the market gardening. But then, as Shelagh reminded him, 'it's the only income we have now.' He recalled that there had been talk of money and Hannah's jewellery. But he supposed it was probably gone by now, what with the smithy having been closed for so long. After all, when his own wage was paid, there was precious little left from the fruit and vegetable trade. Suddenly John felt his wife's anxious gaze on him. 'Sorry, love . . . what were you saying?' he asked quietly.

'By! . . . you're a million miles away these days. It's alright. I weren't saying nothing that can't wait.'

'I wonder if Silas has found her. D'you think he'd let us know?'

'He might . . . it depends. Mind you, it were quite a shock when he turned up on the doorstep again last summer . . . *still* searching for her. *Haunted he looked. HAUNTED!*'

'Aye, that's the right word, I'm thinking.' He smiled, but it was a smile without mirth. '*He'll find her, though*. Or she'll find him.'

'You sound very sure.'

'Oh, I am. I've never been more sure of anything in me life.'

A dark silence settled between them, before Ada remarked, 'He's done well, though . . . what with owning his own smithy, *and* going into the buying and selling of horses.'

'Don't mean a thing to him, though . . . not without her to share it with. He told us that much. But . . . I would 'a guessed it anyway.' John knew that Silas would go on searching for Scarlet. *He had to.*

In the instant before he followed his wife into the cottage, John's troubled gaze was drawn once more to the upper window of Greystone House. His thoughts darkened as they dwelt on the wickedness of the man lying beyond. 'You're an evil man, Pengally,' he muttered, 'and if there's any justice in this world . . . you'll be made to suffer the same terror you caused them two innocent souls.' For a moment his kindly eyes were stiff with hatred. Then, ashamed and shocked by the vehemence of his own feelings, he bowed his head and went inside.

In the warm sultry air John's words lingered on. From a short distance away Trent Blackwood's handsome green eyes were raised to the spot where his father had stood a moment earlier. He knew little of the true history surrounding Greystone House and its inhabitants. His parents were loath to satisfy his curiosity, and the village gossip was always contradictory. But he had heard things: strange, incomprehensible things, such as the unnatural relationship between father and daughter; the drowning of gentle Hannah Pengally; and the series of sinister incidents, including the wanton massacre of an entire flock of fowl. How much of it was true he did not know, for it seemed that, over the years, Greystone House and the man Pengally had become a legend where truth and imagination ran riot. Yet there was no imagining the condemning look on his father's face just now, when he had stared up at the house. And there was no imagining the animosity of his words, 'You're an evil man, Pengally.' That was all Trent had heard. It was enough to tell him what whatever had taken place over the years had touched his father deeply; too deeply for him to discuss it openly.

Ada Blackwood had also heard her husband's words, and was made thoughtful by them. 'You should be made to suffer,' he had said. Unkind words from a gentle man. Yet no one could have foreseen how strangely prophetic were John's harshly uttered words!

It was evening. The room was filled with shadows whipped alive by candlelight. There was a smell of death in the air, dallying, sempiternal. A sense of fear. Torture.

The cries were low and muted, permeating the gloom, like the tormented wail of an outcast soul. 'You . . . WITCH . . .' The voice was feeble, ancient, the grey eyes dulled with pain, and marbled with terror.

'Ssh, old man. You're not ready to die . . . not yet.' Shelagh worked quickly, dabbing the treated cottonwool to the network of small deep cuts that criss-crossed the man's torso in a weird, bloody pattern. 'You're a fool!' Her small brown eyes blazed down at him. '*I* was a fool to have left the tray behind . . . with the knife in such easy reach. God almighty! . . . *look at you*! And the *pain* . . . the pain must be unbearable.'

'No . . . NO.' His stricken eyes were raised to hers. They grew until they were like scrubbed pebbles protruding from his gaunt face. Half-smiling, she stroked his thin grey hair and talked softly to him. When he cried out again, and shook his head slowly from side to side, she deliberately looked away, wiping his wounds with unusual tenderness and ignoring his pitiful moans until finally he was silent and still, a frame of bones against the mattress.

'Foolish man!' she chided. '*I won't let you die . . . you*

should know that.' With painstaking deliberation, she dressed the weeping scars and drew the bedclothes over his emaciated body, her eyes hard and condemning as she stared down on his face. Reaching down to the tray beside her feet, she whispered, raising his head and putting the cup to his sagging mouth. Only when the last drop of the foul-smelling liquid was gone and the frantic spluttering had ceased, did she seem satisfied. For a long while, she continued to stare at his seemingly lifeless form, when only the laboured rhythm of his breathing disturbed the silence. Then, collecting the bowl and other paraphernalia, she went from the room, taking great care to lock the door behind her. 'I'll be back,' she murmured, 'you must have broth to keep up your strength. Later, of course, *you will have to be punished.'*

PART SIX

1936

JOURNEY'S END

. . . Long is the way
And hard, that out of hell leads up to light.

> John Milton, *Paradise Lost*

CHAPTER EIGHTEEN

'Goodbye, Scarlet. May God go with you.' Sister Ellen kissed the small wooden cross and held it out. 'Take it, child.' She waited until Scarlet had the cross in her grasp and was thoughtfully regarding it, before she added, 'Remember what you have learned here. Trust in the Lord and He will guide you.' She smiled, and her face was lit with love. 'Keep the crucifix with you at all times. It will comfort and protect you.'

Scarlet's exquisite dark eyes encountered the nun's serene gaze. For a long time she gazed on that old unblemished face, her own expression betraying little of the turmoil within her. She had not yet come to believe wholly in a God who could help her. She returned the cross, saying, 'I won't forget your kindness. You have given me so much . . . yet you've never sought anything in return, or asked me of myself.'

'Is there anything you *want* to tell me?'

'No. There is nothing to tell.' Except fragmented memories and instinctive dread, she thought. And how could she speak of such things when she didn't understand them herself?

'Is there no one? No relative, or friend?'

Scarlet thought for a moment before shaking her head. 'No one,' she murmured. Except the faces that fill me with panic and make me want to flee the dark, she recalled.

Suddenly her fears were tempered with the emergence of a particular face, round and kindly, with small brown eyes. It was the only friendly image amongst those that constantly assailed her. *Shelagh*. The face had no real substance. But it had a name.

'If you should need us . . . this is God's house. The doors are always open.'

'I know.' Scarlet had experienced a certain degree of peace here in the Convent of All Saints. Yet she knew that never again would she cross its threshold. *What she craved was not here.*

At the foot of the wide, meandering path, Scarlet paused. From here, the convent looked magnificent: a creation of huge gables and splendid bow windows, crisscrossed with leaded diamonds, the ancient brickwork festooned with rambling plants already bursting with glorious May blossoms. The air was heady with their powerful scent. Scarlet walked away; the sunshine felt warm on her face, yet her heart was cold.

At the gate she was tempted to look back once more, but she forced herself to go on. It was not good to dwell too much on the past, she told herself. We are all travelling towards our destiny. And that must always take us *forward*, however uncertain or frightening is the journey. All the same, she longed to know of her roots.

An hour later, Scarlet was seated in a café opposite the promenade, quietly sipping her tea and ruminating on the haven she had just left. The nuns had been both patient and kind with her, and she would never forget them. At first she had loathed the work in the laundry, but later it had seemed to give her a sense of purpose. Her stay there had seemed all too short, although in truth she had seen four summers come and go. Time had passed. It meant nothing to her. She was older, but not wiser.

This morning, when she had looked at herself in the

mirror, she realised with a shock that her youth had gone. Staring back at her was a woman now in her thirties. Yet beneath the maturity of that familiar face was something that had not changed with the years. A certain spectral essence, a loitering shadow that marred the beauty and scarred the dark tragic eyes. Always the fear was there, lurking, swamping her heart and punishing her soul.

'Is there anything else you want?' The waitress placed the bill on the table. She was a young cockney woman possessed of a bright cheerful personality and endowed with that fortunate ability to put people at their ease. 'Ain't I seen you in 'ere before, lady?' she asked, eyeing Scarlet in a quizzical manner and thinking how strikingly handsome she was. The girl prided herself on never forgetting a face. She struggled to recall where she had seen those elegant features, and the unusually lovely dark eyes that held a world of pain and secrets. There was a strange quietness about the lady. And a disturbing sense of wildness. Even in her ordinary blue summer dress and with her rich black hair tied back into the nape of her neck, there was something different about her. Some uniqueness that made her stand out in a crowd. 'Been in 'ere before, 'ave yer?' It bothered her when she couldn't place a face precisely.

Scarlet smiled. How clever of the young woman to remember her. The last time they had spoken was when the cockney waitress had lectured a colleague for threatening to turn a vagrant onto the streets. That was close on five years ago. The 'vagrant' was Scarlet. 'It's been a long time since I was in here,' Scarlet told her now. 'I remember you also.'

'There!' The young woman was relieved to be proved right. 'I *knew* I'd seen you somewhere.' She frowned. Funny, but somehow she still couldn't recall their exact meeting. 'Just arrived . . . or just going?' she asked, her attention caught by the small suitcase at Scarlet's feet.

'Just arrived.' There was a surge of confidence in Scarlet's voice, and a reassurance in her smile that belied the truth.

'Thought you'd get 'ere before the summer crush, eh?' When Scarlet merely nodded, she went on, 'Where yer staying?'

'Oh, I haven't booked anywhere. I'll find a quiet place, off the main promenade, I expect.'

'I know the very place! . . . Mrs Grady's boarding-house on Victoria Street. She keeps a clean respectable establishment, and her terms are very good, so I'm told.' When Scarlet hesitated, she suspected the reason why, and was quick to assure her, 'She's not a busybody neither, by all accounts . . . allows the boarders their privacy.'

'Is it a busy place?' Scarlet dreaded the thought of being hemmed in by people.

'I don't think so. Happen no more than half a dozen boarders altogether.'

'I don't know. Perhaps I'll look round first . . . take my time and find the right place.' Scarlet was loath to admit that this 'Mrs Grady's boarding-house' seemed exactly what she was looking for. She had learned to be cautious, and though this cockney woman was friendly enough, it wouldn't do for too many strangers to know her whereabouts.

'Please yerself, lady.' The waitress shrugged her shoulders and scurried away. Scarlet looked about. Apart from an elderly gentleman seated in the far corner, she was the only customer.

Resisting the urge to stroll along the promenade and watch the children at play on the beaches, Scarlet hurried towards Victoria Street. She was most anxious to secure a room. She had much to think about. She *had* to think, to pry and delve into that part of her subconsciousness that sought to drive her insane. It was all there, the secrets, the past, even the future. *If there was one.*

'Amy will show you to your room.' As she opened the

register, Mrs Grady glanced at Scarlet's hand. Seeing no ring there, she collected the pen from the desk and held it towards Scarlet. 'If you would just fill in your name and the date, miss,' she suggested, 'your room number is four . . . a nice spacious room at the top of the stairs.'

Suppressing the shame and the panic that suddenly threatened to overwhelm her, Scarlet gripped her suitcase with both hands. 'Can I leave *you* to fill in the register?' she entreated, beginning to move away. 'I've been travelling . . . need to lie down a while.' She drew a trembling hand across her brow, indicating that she had a headache. She could not bring herself to admit that she had never learned to read or write.

'Of course.' Mrs Grady began writing, murmuring the details aloud. 'May the twenty-ninth, 1936 . . . Room Four. How long will you be staying, dearie?'

'I haven't decided.'

'In . . . def . . . in . . . itely,' Scarlet smiled to see Mrs Grady struggling to spell the word. Somehow, it eased her own shame. 'And what did you say your name was?' the genial woman enquired.

'Scarlet.' She felt the suitcase being taken from her grip by the girl Mrs Grady had referred to as Amy; a small being in dark dress and white apron. She had the merriest brown eyes.

'Miss . . . Scarlet.' Mrs Grady looked up, waiting. Her curious gaze met Scarlet's anxious frown. 'Yes, dearie? . . . your *surname*, if you please?'

The name sprang to Scarlet's lips of its own accord. 'Pengally.' She was visibly shocked. SCARLET PENGALLY. *That was her name!*

Mrs Grady had seen the colour drain from Scarlet's face. 'Don't hang about there, Amy!' she reprimanded the girl. 'Take Miss Pengally up to her room at once.' Addressing herself to Scarlet, she said, 'You look exhausted, dearie. You go with Amy. Let me know if there's anything you need.' She watched as Amy led their new guest upstairs. Shaking her head, she wondered whether this 'Scarlet Pengally' would be trouble. She hoped not. This was a respectable house!

Scarlet wished Amy would go. She was a pleasant little thing, bright and cheerful, but her incessant chattering jarred on Scarlet's already frayed nerves. The name of 'Pengally' throbbed in her mind like the ticking of a clock . . . Pengally – Pengally; SCARLET PENGALLY. That was her name, yet it belonged to an era she did not know. It should have comforted her to find that another fragment of the jigsaw had fallen into place. Instead it greatly disturbed her. She had the eerie sensation of going down a dark narrow tunnel, always travelling towards the light in the far distance, a light that was the tiniest speck, yet now was beginning to grow, illuminating isolated patches in the darkness, until soon the darkness would be swallowed and the whole picture would emerge. Scarlet was excited. She was also petrified. She remembered the piece of paper sewn into the lining of her coat, and which had worked its way through the broken stitches. The paper was safe in her suitcase now. Thanks to Sister Mary, Scarlet knew exactly what was written there. It bore the names 'Cassie' and 'Nancy Thornton,' together with an address in America. Scarlet was comforted. Later, if the nightmare persisted, she might ask the woman at the post office to send a message to this 'Nancy Thornton'.

'This is the best room in the house . . . my favourite.' Amy swung down the case onto the chequered eiderdown. 'Do you want me to unpack, miss?' she asked, patiently tucking a stray lock of hair beneath her frilly cap, and wondering about the one small suitcase.

'No, thank you. I'll see to it.' Holding out the coat which she had carried over her arm, Scarlet felt in the pocket and drew out her purse. Taking from it a shilling piece, she handed it to Amy. 'I'll call if I need anything.' Suddenly she felt weary.

'You do that, miss,' remarked the girl. She then proceeded to open all the drawers and cupboards, checking the linen and commenting on the news that was sweeping the land. 'It's all in the papers,' she chirped, completely oblivious to Scarlet's preoccupation with her own thoughts. 'King Edward VIII's coronation is set for May of next year. If you ask *me*, it's a good thing too . . . I honestly thought he'd end up and marry that Mrs Simpson. It's a shame though, don't you think, Miss Pengally? . . . I mean them two do love each other, don't they?' She seemed astonished that the new guest was not hanging on her every word. Somewhat peeved, she closed the drawer and hurried to the door. 'If that's all, then?' she asked.

'Thank you . . . Amy.' Scarlet was pleased when finally the girl departed. At last she was alone. With time to think. Twice she lay back on the bed and closed her eyes to sleep; but there was no sleep in her. Agitated, she began pacing up and down the room, thinking, searching for the answer. *Scarlet Pengally!* There must now be a way to trace her origins. But where? How? Inside her skull the fire raged, her eyes felt like lead weights. She was so tired. So very tired. She made her thoughts pause before they pushed her sanity over the edge. Her gaze was lifted out of the tiny side window that overlooked the promenade. A sense of desolation swamped her. Out there were ordinary people, with ordinary lives. Ordered. Fulfilled. She was neither. It was a beautiful day. A lazy tranquil day, when everything was bathed in glorious sunshine, and lovers strolled arm in arm along the edge of the white, glistening sands. *Lovers*, Silas, SILAS. 'Where are you now?' Her voice sounded like a death knell in the silence of her room.

Suddenly, it came to her. She would go and see Reverend Arnold. *He* would help her, she knew. Hadn't he said as much on his visits to the hospital where first she had been taken? 'If there's ever anything I can do for you, Scarlet,' he had promised, 'you have only to ask.' Well, now there *was* something he could do. He could find her past; *Scarlet Pengally's past.* She could go to the police, but her every instinct warned her not to. Yet why should she fear what might be unearthed? She did not know. She only knew the awful nightmares that would not let her be. And the final premonition that had become like another sense. Sadness and frustration threatened to overwhelm her. She drew her gaze from the horizon, from the 'ordinary' people and the brilliant sunshine. Yes, she would go to Reverend Arnold and beg him to ask his God for guidance. Because, whatever the consequences, she had to know what lay behind her before she could go on. And perhaps, while he was praying, the man of God might save one small prayer for her wretched soul. In her moment of darkest desolation, Scarlet regretted having returned the cross to the nun. 'It will comfort and protect you always,' she had said. And that was what Scarlet craved. *'Comfort and protection.'*

'If you know where she is . . . for mercy's sake, Shelagh, have pity. *Tell me!*' Silas raised his stricken violet eyes. *'You must know!*' he pleaded. Something in the timbre of his voice made her turn away. 'She's not dead. I know it.' He bowed his head to the fire's glow, becoming mesmerised by the brilliant colours there. He had a sudden image of Scarlet: the chiselled contours of her lovely face, the long rich hair as black as night, the dark bewitching eyes that melted his very soul. Black cruelty spiralled through the image. Would she never stop hurting him? He shuddered. His life was meaningless without her. *His death, the same.*

'No, Silas . . . I've heard nothing of Scarlet in all this time. Who knows *where* she might be . . . since Garrett and the boy.' She paused. They both remembered and the air became still. 'I don't know. I can only imagine how it must have torn her apart to give away the girl she adored . . . to "make a new life for herself", as they say.' She smiled. A secret smile. 'Believe me, there was much more to it than that. Cassie was all she had left.' Shelagh leaned forward from her chair. 'Let me take that.' She wrapped her stocky fingers round the cup and drew it from his grasp. His hands dropped to his knees as he fell back, exhausted, into the tall horsehair chair that was Vincent Pengally's. 'You're driving yourself insane . . . you know that?' She was astonished to see how well he fitted the chair, almost as well as Pengally himself. It suited him. *It set her thinking!*

'You're wrong, Shelagh! Cassie was not "all that Scarlet had left". She had *me. She will always have me.*' He lapsed into a strange silence.

Engrossed in thought, Shelagh watched him. The sight of his long lean form occupying that particular chair with such ease and naturalness troubled her. It was almost as though he was set in the same mould as Pengally. At first, she was gazing on Silas. Then, as she stared all the longer, he was *not* Silas. He *became* Vincent Pengally! Suddenly they were back. All those unsettling currents and dangerous undertows that left her helpless in their grip. She did not like them. She could never control them. 'You'd better go,' she said frostily, rising from the chair, 'It's getting late.'

At the door, he turned to tell her, 'She will come back . . . I know it.'

'Yes, Silas. I believe it also.' She did not tell him that *she* had made many attempts to track Scarlet after her untimely departure from the area. She did not reveal her reasons. But, like him, she knew that Scarlet would return to Greystone House. *It was the only way they would all find peace!*

'I don't know where else to look, Shelagh. I've exhausted so many avenues. All the same, when she returns, I'll be here, waiting. Now that I've sold my business and moved into Dunster, she won't escape me so easily next time.'

'Goodnight, Silas.'

'Forgive me for haunting Greystone House. It's just that I feel closer to Scarlet here.'

'You know what the consequences would be if Vincent Pengally were to find you under this roof?'

He nodded. 'He's a devil. Or he would have died long ago.' A look of hatred darkened his eyes.

'He has unusual strength. No doubt he will linger a while yet.' She smiled, raising her face to the night sky. 'Looks like a bad storm brewing.' This month of November had been a strange one.

'Will you attend Ada Blackwood's funeral tomorrow?'

'No. I don't like seeing the dead put into the ground. It's too final. You can't see them any more.' Her voice faltered.

'I understand.' He thought of Scarlet, and his heart was heavy.

While Silas hurried into the night, his crazed mind intent on Scarlet, Greystone House was plunged into darkness, save for one small candle burning in an upper room. Inside, the rocking chair made a weird melodic sound as it was thrust back and forth. Soft laughter disturbed the air. Deft fingers moved swiftly, purposefully. *The noose began to take shape.* An insane whisper permeated the silence. *'Soon . . . soon it will be over. Justice will be done, and the spirit will rest!'*

CHAPTER NINETEEN

'Why couldn't Mr Arnold come with us?' Scarlet glanced at the vicar. She felt uncomfortable in his presence. Strange, she thought, how he claimed to have known her since birth. Yet she could not recall him at all.

'I told you, Scarlet . . . parish duties would not allow him the time.' The Reverend Mr Lacy sighed and half-turned his head towards her. 'Weymouth is a big responsibility, my dear. But you needn't concern yourself about things . . . I can only imagine your father will give thanks to God for your safe return.' He concentrated his attention on the road ahead. At least the recent snowfall had not settled as was feared; in fact there was hardly any sign left of it at all. He shook his grey head at his own thoughts. It had been the worst January he could ever remember.

'Mr Lacy?'

'Yes, child?'

There was a moment during which Scarlet resented being referred to as a 'child'. 'Tell me again . . . about my father . . . about "Greystone House".' Oh, how she wished that her urgent message to America had brought a reply. But it had not, and now she had given up hope of receiving one. But soon she could ask her father to satisfy all of her questions.

'Goodness me! . . . I must have told you a dozen times already.' He was instantly mortified at the impatience in his tone. After all, was he not doing God's work? Hadn't Mr Arnold been guided by the hand of the Almighty when, on one of the rare occasions they found themselves in each other's company, he had mentioned his search for relatives of a woman called Scarlet Pengally. 'Well, of course, Mr Arnold only had to tell me how you were able to recall certain names. What convinced me that you were the one and the same Scarlet Pengally was when he told me that you remembered the name of *Hannah*. After that, of course . . . I was impatient to see you for myself.' His long congenial face broke into a self-satisfied smile. 'You always had the most beautiful dark eyes. Not the sort of eyes that a man might forget . . . even a *man of God*.' He chuckled. 'They haven't changed, Scarlet . . . only grown *more* beautiful.'

'Were my mother's eyes dark?'

'Heavens, child! . . . I can't remember *that*. In fact, I hardly knew your family, you understand . . . your father was not a church-going man, and I only spoke to your mother twice. Once when she came to the church and asked me to pray for you both. And once when I called at Greystone House.'

'Why would she want you to pray for us both?'

'She gave no reason. On that day, she brought you with her to the church.' He paused, remembering. Hannah Pengally had struck him as being a very sad woman who could not bring herself to confide in him. One of his failures, he always remembered, to his shame. 'You were very small,' he said quietly, 'and the loveliest child I had ever seen . . . I remember that.'

'Was *she* lovely? . . . my mother?'

'As I recall, she was a quiet, gentle woman.'

'And my father?'

For a moment, Mr Lacy was quiet, his aged mind reaching back over the years. 'I'm sorry, child . . . it was a long time ago . . . too long for an old man of my sixty-five years. I was only in Dunster for about eighteen months. Soon after, I was sent to Bournemouth, and I've been here ever since.' He laughed. 'Now, they've put me out to pasture. You know my dear . . . you have provided me with the opportunity to return to Dunster and look up old familiar haunts.'

'Did you *never* see my father?'

'Only on the occasion when I called at Greystone House. It seems I must have called at a bad moment, because, as I recall, he furiously ordered me off his property.' He chuckled and slapped his hand against the steering wheel. He was a big fellow, I can tell you that! I'm afraid that was the first and last time I met him.' He then went on to outline the details he had already explained when the Reverend Mr Arnold had brought the two of them together. It was little enough. All he knew was that Scarlet Pengally was an only child; her father was the village blacksmith and the family resided at Greystone House, a monstrous place that had been in the Pengally family for many generations. Apparently, under previous ancestors it had seen far better days. There were certain facts which Mr Arnold thought wise to keep from this obviously troubled and unfortunate woman: such as the drowning of her mother and the altogether disagreeable character for which her father was known. There were *other* things also, disturbing things that came to his knowledge during his short time in Dunster. But they were only rumours that cast a dangerous slur on Vincent Pengally's relationship with his daughter. As a man of the cloth, he was expected to love all God's children, but he had not been sorry when the Pengally man had ostracised himself from all matters concerned with the Church. *Sometimes, there was an evil so strong, so wanton that no amount of prayer could purge the soul of it.* All the same, he had felt great compassion for the one called Hannah, and only wished that, somehow, he might have been more of a comfort to her;

when the news reached him of her drowning, he had been greatly saddened. All of these things he kept from the anxious woman beside him. It saddened him also that Scarlet had suffered some accident or other, resulting in loss of memory. And that, having seemingly struck out on her own, she was now compelled to return to Dunster, to Greystone House. It was not a happy place, he recalled.

'Is the journey much farther?' Scarlet was not comfortable being cooped up in a motor vehicle. It was an unpleasant experience.

'Be patient, my dear . . . we've covered some thirty miles, with the same distance still to go. Hopefully, we'll arrive before dark. Close your eyes . . . see if you can sleep.'

Sleep was a comfort that Scarlet had never enjoyed. But she closed her eyes and relaxed into the soft leather, shivering as it struck cold against her neck. This long and tedious journey was like a trip into the unknown. She wondered with apprehension what awaited her at the end of it. Not her mother, for Hannah was dead. That much she knew. She thought of the name Vincent Pengally, and she desperately tried to give it an identity. *None of the faces fitted.* She felt more alone now than at any time she could remember. When Mr Lacey had first spoken of her father, she had searched her heart for a loving response. There had been none. But then, that was not surprising, she thought. Perhaps when she came face to face with him, perhaps *then* she would know. She smiled. Or perhaps even when she gazed on his features he would still remain a stranger. Suddenly Scarlet felt herself trembling. Why had she chosen to put herself through such an ordeal? The answer came back. She had no choice. Fate moved in mysterious and unpredictable ways. Fate was guiding her now, *urging* her back to the roots from which she had strayed. Back to the past, the future. *Her destiny.*

Surprisingly, Scarlet slept. Not a deep and restful sleep, but shallow and fretful, quickened by inherent fears and gyrating images. Soon, she thought, soon she would belong. Strangely, the thought brought little solace to her trembling heart.

'The road ends here, child.'

The words pressed into Scarlet's mind. *'The road ends here.'* Foreboding words that seemed to find an echo deep inside her. In the space of a single heartbeat his utterance had triggered in her a latent, instinctive terror. Yet if only Scarlet had known how fortuitous were the words spoken by Mr Lacey, her terror might have been tenfold.

'Well, at least we made it in daylight.' Mr Lacey sighed contentedly and climbed from the vehicle. Scarlet came to stand beside him, her dark brooding gaze drawn towards the lane ahead; her thoughts taking her far beyond. 'The road narrows down to a path,' he went on, pointing the way. 'The footpath will take us past the thatched cottage and on to Packhorse Bridge.' His face broke into a warm smile. 'Your father's house is on the other side of the river,' he said reassuringly, 'I don't mind telling you, my dear . . . I'm looking forward to stretching my legs and perhaps warming myself before a cheery fire.' He was *not* looking forward to meeting Vincent Pengally again, although, on contacting the local vicar with regard to Scarlet Pengally, he had been informed that the master of Greystone House had been bedridden these many years. 'No doubt Miss Williams, the housekeeper, has been told of your imminent arrival.' Scarlet wondered how this Miss Williams would greet her.

'Would you mind if I went on alone?' She was loath to ask such a thing when he had brought her so far. By the same token, she could not bear the thought of his being beside her when the door of Greystone House was opened. It was something she must do alone. She had prepared herself for it. It was not an experience to be shared.

'Whatever you say, child.' He sensed the loneliness in her; and the strength. She made him feel humble. 'If you're really sure?' Scarlet's dark eyes were bright with pain. 'Very well,' he conceded, 'If you need me, I'll be at the vicarage. I intend to make an early start in the morning, so . . . if I don't hear from you, I will assume that all is well. God bless you, child.' He cast an anxious glance to the greying skies. 'But hurry. *Soon it will be dark.*'

Scarlet did not look back; not even when she heard the car engine splutter into life, then gradually die out as the vehicle drove away. She expected to feel lonely, cast out on a strange road that drew her even closer to her heart of darkness. But somehow she did not feel lonely. Only exhilarated. Every step she took made her tremble. How had she come to wander from this place? Soon she would know all there was to know.

At the bend in the path, Scarlet paused, her probing gaze travelling the landscape; a strange almost primeval landscape that was unknown to her and yet which filled her with a peculiar sense of belonging. There was magic in the air. An inexplicable and bewitching ambience that seemed to caress and bathe her troubled soul. At the same moment there was a delicate conflict created in her: all of her being craved to go on, yet there were other murmuring doubts, persuading her to leave. Leave *now*. Before it was too late.

Suddenly it was twilight. Scarlet pressed on, her eyes scanning the way ahead as she recalled what Mr Lacey had said. She must keep alert for the landmarks: a thatched cottage and a bridge. Beyond the river was Greystone House. *And home!* A sense of terror fluttered through her, and she chided herself.

Intent on her destination and alienated by the increasing darkness, Scarlet gave a sigh of relief as she hurried past the thatched cottage. Inside, John Blackwood was drawing the curtains against the cold grey evening. Scarlet did not see him, but he saw her and was visibly shocked. Had his old eyes deceived him? Or was that slim dark figure the same tragic creature that had long ago fled these parts? He peered after her. He could not be sure; so much time had passed. Yet hadn't Trent mentioned something only that very morning? Hadn't there been rumours that Scarlet Pengally was on her way back? Dear God! *He hoped not*. Many a time he had given thanks that Scarlet had escaped the wickedness, the terrible evil in that house; evil that had spanned too many years and touched too many souls. *And Scarlet's most of all*. Why would she want to return? *Why?* His heart grew cold.

Suddenly he was shivering, though the fire blazed cheerily in the hearth and a moment ago he had felt cosy and warm. Agitated, he closed the curtains and shuffled to his armchair. 'You were free, Scarlet Pengally,' he muttered, huddling nearer to the fire's glow, 'now ... *he'll never let you go*!' He was afraid. Just as he had been afraid all these years; afraid to look across at the house; afraid to glance towards the ridge on a grey, ominous evening such as this. *Afraid to remember*. But when you grow old and your darling has gone forever, memories are all that remain. You kept them close, cherished them, always loath to let them go. He and his Ada had spent all of their married life in this cottage. Man and boy, he had toiled on the land of Greystone House and had been a living part of all that had transpired within its walls. He had seen things that would haunt him to his grave; wicked things, cruel and sinister things. *Things that he had never told anyone!* He could not separate the good memories from the bad. They were forever intermingled. If he must keep some, then he must keep them all. He thought again of the woman who had passed by his cottage. If he was anything of a man he would go after Scarlet Pengally and beg her to stay away, warn her of the inhuman monster who had awaited her return all these years; and he would terrify her with the things he had seen. *Things that no man should see.* But then, he was no longer a man. He was old and decrepit, wizened by his grief and paralysed by things he did not dare to understand. Frantic, he bent forward, losing his churning thoughts in the leaping flames. 'Come home, Trent,' he muttered, beginning to rock back and forth and occasionally glancing furtively towards the door. 'Hurry home, son. *Don't leave me alone too long!'*

As she crossed Packhorse Bridge, Scarlet was gripped by the strangest sensation: the path she was now following seemed familiar to her! She had been over this bridge many times before. Relief flooded her heart. In a moment she was standing on the far bank, her searching gaze reaching out to the house which was only a few steps away. She crushed down the insane desire to turn from it; to go back the way she had come. 'Don't be foolish, Scarlet Pengally!' she told herself in a frightened whisper. 'This is your home . . . *here, your father awaits to embrace you.'* She took a step forward, but could not go on. Something about the house made her feel uncertain, fearful. She was shocked by its appearance. Somehow she had not expected the house to look so forbidding, so grim and oppressive against a skyline that was too incredibly beautiful. The moors rose and fell almost like a beating heart, stretching away as far as the eye could see. Above the ridge, day and night fought for supremacy over the skies, splitting the light into weird and wonderful patterns. Slowly the skies darkened, causing strange shadows over the land. Somewhere in the depths of the wild heathland a night bird cried. The sound was like the call of a kindred spirit, striking a cord in Scarlet's trembling heart. She was familiar with the sound; she was part of the moors. The moors called her. *The house cried out to her.* Softly, she went forward, through the rampant untended garden where rapacious plants had smothered all that was gentle and yielding.

At the door, Shelagh waited: a small homely figure in a dark skirt and startlingly white blouse; her brown hair unkempt, like the garden. Scarlet knew her face: that kindly face which had haunted her dreams, the wise brown eyes the very same that gazed at her now with compassion. She remembered. And she was not afraid. 'My father? . . . is he here?' There was so much she must know.

'Soon . . . you will see him. First enjoy the meal I've provided for you, Scarlet . . . we'll talk a while.' She touched Scarlet on the arm. 'He'll be so delighted that you're home again. Oh, Scarlet . . . you've been gone so long. Too long. *You must never go away again.*' She took the suitcase from Scarlet's hand. The sound of the door closing caused Scarlet to look around, a feeling of panic rising in her. As they went deeper into the house, the panic subsided. Outside the night was cold and hostile; the wind moaned gently, like a tortured soul. In here it was warm and welcoming. Even the house itself seemed to enfold her. She followed the one called Shelagh; a friend. *At last she was home!*

She was astonished to find herself wondering whether the man named Silas would be here. The prospect filled her with inexplicable longing.

On the peak of the ridge, where the spinney was steeped in darkness, Silas stepped from the shadows. The bitter January air bit into him, numbing his face and causing him to shiver. But he did not feel the cold, only the chilling sensation that Scarlet's appearance had wrought in him. He had waited so long. Now, at last, the waiting was finally over. This woman, who was as much a part of him as was his own soul, had brought with her a new lease of life for him. From the vantage point where he had hidden himself some two hours earlier, the view down the valley was unrestricted. When at last he had seen the shadowy figure moving towards Greystone House, he knew instinctively that it was Scarlet. As she drew closer to the lighted window of Greystone House, his lonely heart had skipped a beat. There was no mistaking her slim loveliness, the long black hair that was loose about her shoulders, and that special ethereal way she had of moving. He imagined her dark lustrous eyes, ablaze with passion as they had been on the night when Scarlet had made glorious love. He had never forgotten; he never could. He wanted her again in that way. *In every way!* His elation was cruelly pierced, as he wondered whether she might not feel the same towards him. But she must! Surely to God, she would not spurn him again. Not now. *Not ever.* He recalled their last meeting, when she had been so cruelly hostile. He smiled secretly. But then, hadn't she always fought against the fierce and magnificent love that bound them together? In his heart he knew that Scarlet had never loved any other. Right from when they were children, it had been decreed that they belonged together. Their souls were one. They had grown irrevocably entwined, played in the shadows, laughed and cried in each other's arms, and always found a way to belong, even though it was forbidden and dangerous. Scarlet was his. Nothing mattered but her. Destiny had parted them. *Destiny had drawn them together again.* The years between had been too long and unbearable. Now he would claim her, take her far away from all that reminded her of the past. Together they would build a new life, create a family. Love each other in the way it was always intended. Now, at last, they were both free.

Quickly, Silas began his descent into the valley. *He must hurry!* For even at this moment, Vincent Pengally might be weaving the same malevolent spell that had kept her under his influence for too long!

★ ★ ★

'So now, Scarlet . . . you know as much as I can tell you. Don't worry if you can remember little of it. I'm sure it will all come back to you. Meanwhile, *I'll* take care of you.' She laughed softly. To Scarlet it was a disturbing sound. 'After all, Scarlet, we must never forget . . . *you are a Pengally*.' The quick smile returned. 'But then you were gone so long that I almost *did* forget. That was unforgivable. Your father has every right to scold you.'

'From what you tell me, you've had all your time taken up with caring for my father.' In spite of Shelagh's reassurances, Scarlet could not still the uneasiness inside her.

'I can't deny it. Your father *has* been a trial.' Her voice fell to a whisper.

'There were times when I feared it would never end.' Suddenly her plain, worn features broke into a surprisingly bright smile. 'But of course, now that you're home where you belong . . . *we can all sleep soundly.'*

'I would like to go to him.' Scarlet was impatient. In spite of the sketchy details outlined by Shelagh, she had learned no more than what Mr Lacy had told her. There were still many questions she must ask. What was the truth about her marriage to Garrett Summers? And the 'tragedy' that had taken both her husband and son? Why were Shelagh and the vicar so loath to elaborate on the details, except to assure her that 'you must not blame yourself'? And why in God's name would she allow the Thorntons to take away her only remaining child? What had led to her leaving the area? How had she come to be found so many miles away, apparently in a state of shock and devoid of all memories regarding her past? No one had the answers. Maybe her father was the only one who could help now.

'I can understand your anxiety.' Shelagh put the bowl of broth on the table. 'It's only to be expected, after all you've been through.' She put the spoon in Scarlet's hand.

'You'll need your strength for the ordeal ahead. Your father has waited for you these many years. He can wait a while longer.' Her gentle smile bathed Scarlet's black, troubled eyes. 'You're unhappy. Please . . . don't be. Not now.' Her smile deepened when she saw how hungry Scarlet seemed. 'Good!' she exclaimed, seating herself opposite and watching every mouthful disappear. 'You see . . . I don't suppose you realised just how hungry you were?'

Placing the spoon into the empty bowl, Scarlet rose from her chair. 'Thank you, Shelagh,' she said, 'and you're right . . . I really didn't know how hungry I was. These past few days, I'm afraid I've eaten very little.' The rich aroma of the broth lingered in the air: mutton, all manner of vegetables and herbs. And something undefinable.

'The broth is an old, cherished recipe.' The smile froze on Shelagh's face and her eyes glittered like those of an artful fox. 'It was one of the few things my mother taught me.' Each word seemed to cut the air like a knife. 'Are you content, Scarlet?'

'More than I have been for a very long time. It's a wonderful thing, Shelagh . . . to know that you belong.' A wave of weariness engulfed her. 'But there is still so much I need to know. Where is my father's room?'

'Go to the top of the stairs. The room is lit by candle-light. You won't go astray.' In a moment she had lit a small oil lamp, which she handed to Scarlet. 'Hurry, my dear. Your father has waited so long. Go to him . . . stay with him. You two have much to talk about . . . I promise I won't disturb you.'

At the top of the stairs, Scarlet glanced towards the sheaf of soft yellow which emanated from a room some way along the landing. Her stomach was churning. She felt strange – as though her senses were slipping away. 'Calm yourself,' she murmured, going stealthily towards the light, her hands trembling and her whole body bathed in a film of sweat. Suddenly she found herself wishing that she had never returned. She was shocked by the thought. With each step, the high dark walls of the corridor seemed to close in on her. *She couldn't breathe.* The gloom enveloped her, becoming darker as she groped her way nearer to the light; the light flickered, first it was blinding, then it was not there at all. Exhausted, she leaned against the wall, eyes closed, waiting for her strength to recover. Her eyelids were like lead weights pressing against the eyeballs beneath; her head was pounding in keeping with a frantic heartbeat. Somewhere in the distance she could hear a voice, a woman's voice, softly singing. Thoughts of her mother invaded her mind. 'Hannah . . . Mammy, is that you?' She knew it was not. Agony wormed up inside her. Stubbornly, she dragged herself onwards, towards the quivering beacon that taunted her, beckoning her, confusing her.

Suddenly, the whole corridor was bathed in a brilliant hue. She was travelling down an avenue, a long, meandering tunnel where faces from the past leapt out at her: Shelagh . . . Hannah, *Silas*. They were all there, leering and tormenting. 'I love you, Scarlet . . . Silas loves you . . . *loves* you.' His voice was soft in her ear. She felt the frightening strength of his passion inside her. Holding onto his image she looked deep and long into those beseeching violet eyes. They were a mirror, reflecting everything that had gone before; the whole of her life played out in his eyes. *'Oh please . . . leave me alone!'* Her voice cried out, broken, terrified. *She saw it all!* Like a terrifying spectacle it paraded through her senses: all the evil, the horror, the sinister bondage of her past. She was a child again. *He was there.* Touching and molesting. John knew! Her mother knew! *Pain. Helplessness.* Panic rampaged through her. 'Cassie, CASSIE!' But Cassie was gone. Garrett and the boy, they were gone too – over the cliff, dead, MURDERED! It was

SILAS. NO! NOT SILAS. Realisation paralysed her. *Silas loved her.* SHE LOVED HIM.

Suddenly the solid wall gave way beneath her, and Scarlet found herself inside the room where the soft light played tricks in her fevered mind. Now she could hardly see for the pain and darkness that invaded every corner of her being. Stumbling towards the dresser, she put down the oil lamp, her senses swimming as she glanced around the room. Horror gripped her. *It was his room!* SHE HAD TO GET AWAY. *But she could not move.* 'Help me, oh please . . . Shelagh, help me!' The sound of her own voice startled her. She clawed at the dresser, feeling her way back towards the door. Her legs were like jelly beneath her, and her life was ebbing away. Don't give in! DON'T GIVE IN. She slithered to the floor, the tears rolling down her face, bringing with them a strange sense of relief and contentment. In that instant, Scarlet looked up. HE WAS THERE! *Vincent Pengally looked down on her*: a grisly corpse hanging from the beams, his bulbous eyes staring fixedly in a piercing look of astonishment. The smell of his wasting form enveloped her; a scream rose like torment from her soul, echoing against the walls, and Silas's name shaped itself on her lips. There was no one to hear. *Only him.* ONLY THE DEVIL.

Shelagh was still softly singing when the knock came on the door. It was Silas. 'I've come for Scarlet.' His voice was ragged. 'Don't send me away, Shelagh. I know she's here.'

'What makes you think Scarlet's here?'

'You can't deny it. I saw her arrive. I've been waiting, you see. Watching from the ridge these two hours and more.' He took a step forward.

'Oh, then I *can't* deny it, can I?' She stepped aside, beckoning him into the hall. 'You're right, of course, Silas.' She was composed, her thoughts racing ahead. 'Scarlet is upstairs with her father. They have a great deal to talk over. *Must you disturb them?'*

'I'm taking Scarlet away from this house . . . *from him.* You don't know, Shelagh. You *can't* know how he's crippled her since the day she was born.' Awful visions of the cellar loomed in his mind: of two babies. Of blood and . . . he stopped himself. He must not dwell on such things. 'You can't know how *evil* he is.'

'*You think I don't know?'* Her voice sliced through him like a knife. He shuddered. But then she was charming again. 'Come in, Silas. You can see her, if you insist. But you won't take her from Greystone House . . . from her father. *I can't let you do that.* She belongs here . . . with him.'

'We'll have to see what *Scarlet* has to say about that, Shelagh! Which is Vincent Pengally's room?' He had a distant memory of it, but that was long ago. And yet, wasn't it only yesterday?

'At the top of the stairs . . . first to your right. Please . . . go up, Silas. I'll be along shortly.' She watched him go, a man in his prime, handsome, desperate in his love for Scarlet. She sighed, murmuring after him, *'You just won't let her go, will you, Silas?* How unfortunate that you also were touched by him . . . that you crave after a Pengally.' *Slowly, she turned and withdrew the axe from the stair cupboard.* 'Scarlet will be pleased to see you,' she called out in a weird, shrill voice. 'Why! . . . only just now, she was calling your name.' An insane look twisted her features. *She started after him.*

His gentle tap on the door seemed to echo like thunder over the eerie silence of the house. He waited, then when no sound came from within, he tremulously pushed open the door. At first he could see nothing in the half-light. Over on the window ledge a candle flame was wafted by the spasmodic breeze that forced itself in through the warped and ancient window frame. The oil lamp on the dresser cast a subdued glow that fell in shadow all around. Slowly his vision adjusted to the semi-darkness. The bed was empty; neatly made up. *Like a coffin.* Had he come to the wrong room? Irritated, he began to withdraw. Suddenly, he swung his gaze downwards. What in God's name was that? There was a groan, low and pitiful. He fell to his knees, his heart stiffening with fear as he came to recognise the misshapen bundle. 'SCARLET!' *He could not believe what his eyes were telling him.* Swiftly, he cradled her into his arms. In that moment, she opened her eyes; dark spears of pain tearing him apart. He saw the colour of death in them. 'Silas . . . forgive me,' she whispered.

He heard the soft tread of footsteps behind him. Clinging to Scarlet, he looked up, preparing to lift his precious burden; even though he had seen the mantle of death cover her eyes, dulling the brilliance there.

The axe came down with astonishing swiftness, slicing into his shoulder and felling him to the ground. His scream mingled with her laughter. Through a sea of pain, he glanced up to see the blade glinting in the lamp's orange glow. The flickering light made a sinister pattern of his own scarlet blood on her white blouse. He made a desperate effort to recover, before he heard the curiously melodic whistle as the axe sped through the air, embedding itself in his screaming skull. The last thing he saw was Scarlet's wide-open eyes. Familiar. BECKONING. Lovingly, he sank into them.

PART SEVEN

1937

THE CIRCLE CLOSES

Life is an imprisoned thing.
Only death can give it wings.

J.C.

CHAPTER TWENTY

'So there you have it, miss.' John Blackwood leaned back in his chair, exhausted and unsettled by the dark tale he had recounted to the young American girl. 'Every word I've told you is God's truth.'

'A cruel tale, Mr Blackwood.' Cassie was subdued by what she had heard. 'My heart goes out to Scarlet Pengally . . . to have such a heartless man for a father. Then to lose her mother in such a shocking way.' She shook her head, turning her forlorn gaze towards the window, then beyond, to the house. Its shadowed limbs were almost lost to the darkness. Only the rising moon betrayed its grey, formidable presence. 'You say she loved Silas . . . and that the daughter she gave to the American couple might well have been conceived in that love. Yet she married another, and even then happiness eluded her.' She was lost for a moment, tortured as she imagined Scarlet to have been. 'How terrible that she should lose both her husband and her son in such a tragic way. No wonder she felt compelled to leave the area, where she had known such great sorrow.'

'Scarlet Pengally was born to sorrow.' There were tears in his voice.

'But from what you say she had one friend at least . . . Shelagh Williams?'

'I thought so . . . for a long time. Now, I don't know.' He

shook his head. 'Shelagh Williams is reckoned by some to be no better than a fortune-hunter. There are those who say that Vincent Pengally has a tidy sum hidden away, and that his will has been changed to favour her . . . then o' course there's Greystone House.' He shuddered. 'But *I* wouldn't want it, I can tell you!'

'Surely, she deserves whatever comes to her, Mr Blackwood. Especially since, according to you, she's cared for Vincent Pengally these many years.'

'Aye,' he looked at her with sharp, quizzical blue eyes, 'and *why* would any woman want to do that for a stranger, eh? Oh, I've often asked myself the very same question. Moved into Greystone House, she did . . . with one purpose in mind. To get her claws into Vincent Pengally. But in God's name, *why*? Y'know . . . there's something about that woman,' he murmured, gazing out at the house again, 'some strange quality that I haven't yet been able to fathom. *Who is she*? Where did she come from afore she turned up in Dunster? Nobody seems to know.' He raised his brows and threw out his hands in exasperation. 'I dare say there's things to do with that house, and that family, we'll never know.'

'You say that Scarlet Pengally returned some eight weeks ago?'

'Aye, that's what I said. Went right past the cottage without even glancing its way. I weren't sure at the time, what with it being dark an' all, *but it were Scarlet alright*. In no time at all, it were all over the village . . . as how she'd come back poorly. Folks reckon she's med off again, with Silas.' A look of sadness crept into his lined face. 'All the while she were gone, that poor soul pined. Broke your heart to see it. *Demented*, he was.'

The news was disturbing to Cassie. It would be cruel if she had come so far, only to find that Scarlet had eluded her again. 'Do *you* think she and Silas have gone away together?'

'I don't know, miss . . . I ain't set eyes on Scarlet since the night she came back, and I ain't seen Silas in a longer while. But I'll tell you this! I hope to God the two of 'em *have* found each other, because they'll never know happiness with anybody else, *that's* for sure!'

'Don't you ever visit the house?'

Her question shocked him. He turned to look at her, his eyes round with fear. 'Visit? *Not me!* Decent God-fearing folk don't "visit" the devil's lair.' He straightened his back, groaning a little as he regarded her with impatience. 'Trent's late home tonight,' he said absent-mindedly, quickly adding, 'It's pitch black outside. Best if you don't venture out on your own . . . sit tight till my son comes. He'll see you safely back to the inn.' When she made no response he went on, 'I don't expect you'll be staying round these parts, eh? Back to America soon, is it? Or have you got other places to see afore you end your travels?'

'Mr Blackwood, you've been very honest with me.' Cassie felt the time had come to explain the real reason for her being here. 'I think it only fair that I'm just as honest with you.' She watched him closely, gauging his reaction as she told him, 'I did not come here out of idle curiosity. My name is Cassie . . . *Cassie Thornton*.' She saw the light kindle in his eyes. 'Yes. The child that was given to the American couple. Scarlet Pengally is my mother, and if what you say is true . . . Silas is my father.' She was astonished to see him turn away, his whole attention gripped by what he had glimpsed outside. Suddenly, he was making the sign of the cross on himself; at the same time shouting for her to 'Look out of the window! Jesus, Mary and Joseph . . . what in God's name?' He rose from his chair, blundering backwards and pointing a quivering finger into the darkness beyond; strange noises emitting from his throat and his cracked blue eyes staring ahead.

Caught up in the old man's fear, Cassie tore back the

curtain. Her frantic gaze was instantly drawn to the flickering halo of light in the upper window of Greystone House. At first she could not understand what had so terrified the old man, but then she saw the dark sombre shape that was silhouetted in the light; a hooded figure, swaying from side to side, its arms raised high as though in a posture of prayer. Cupped in its hands was a lit candle, the hazy glow drawing an arc high up in the window as it went from side to side. Suddenly the figure was still. It seemed to Cassie as though the sinister hidden face was staring directly at her. She watched, mesmerised, as the arm reached out to touch the naked flame against the curtains. She heard the old man gasp, saw him clutch his chest. *'Pengally!'* The word was a cry of horror. She heard him calling after her as she ran, 'Come back, you little fool!'

Cassie was halfway over the bridge when she heard the running footsteps behind her. 'My father will raise the alarm.' Trent Blackwood raced ahead, his long, lean legs quickly covering the ground. 'You go back,' he screamed, 'Go BACK!' His words fell on deaf ears. Cassie sped after him, her heart bursting. Above her the flames licked at the window, paling the moon with their red brilliance. She could hear the glass panes splitting in the heat. They made a weird squealing sound. *As if the house were screaming!*

The scene of carnage that she witnessed that night would stay with Cassie for ever. It was strange how the house seemed to be waiting for them. The front door was wide open. Cassie followed Trent into the darkness, aware of the eerie silence all around. Rushing deeper into the bowls of the house they could hear a low, rhythmic chanting permeating the air. It sent a chill down Cassie's spine. As they fled up the stairs, the smoke clung to them, choking, blinding. She ignored Trent's frantic instruction for her to 'Go back'. The only thing on her mind was that Scarlet might be trapped here. *Her mother.* The smoke was drifting, surrounding them. Cassie convinced herself that there was no immediate danger.

'Stay back I tell you!' At the bottom, Trent lunged his arm outwards, barring Cassie's entrance. For a moment her vision was impaired by the brilliance of the flames and the spasmodic coils of grey smoke that billowed outwards from the window. The heat was intense. She was suddenly aware that the wailing chant had stopped. Trent stood rigid, staring frantically into the room, uncertain as to whether anyone was in there. Cassie pushed forward, the thick dry air causing her to gasp. There was pain now, and a feeling of panic. Pulling the neck of his jumper over his mouth, Trent moved forward. Cassie's hand touched his back and she felt it stiffen. *'Jesus Christ!'* His cry struck dread into her heart. She felt him pressing her backwards; groaning when she resisted. He was staring at the far side of the room, at the hooded figure bent to its knees, head bowed, hands joined together in prayer. The chanting started again and the head swung upwards, its eyes raised to the figure hanging above: a grisly, rotting carcass, naked, its bones dripping with flesh. Only the eyes were preserved. Bulging, colourless eyes, fixed in a dead, piercing stare. *Looking at me*, Cassie thought. AT ME! Terror rolled up inside her. She heard her own scream echoing round the room. The chanting stopped and into the awful silence that followed there crept the sound of laughter: *wild, insane laughter.*

What happened next took place so swiftly that, even many years after, Cassie could not recall every detail. Suddenly the figure leapt forward, snatching the oil lamp from the dresser and rushing to the window, where in the same instant the ravaged tapestry curtains fell to the floor in a crush of dust and flame. Directly above the window the ceiling was alight, the spreading fire fanned by the incoming breeze. Raising the oil lamp high into the air, the figure snatched the hood from its face. Trent's whisper was a shock of disbelief. 'SHELAGH!' The flames licked across the room as he started forward. 'NO! *Stay away.* It's too late . . . they're dead. ALL DEAD!' Her mad eyes danced in the light as the flames played all round her. The maniacal laughter reached a terrifying pitch as she looked across the room to where the two figures lay huddled together. 'It's done at last,' she screamed. *'The devil is hanged and all that he touched will burn in Hell beside him!'*

A swear of terror seized hold of Cassie when she heard Trent's horrified cry, 'God above! *It's Silas . . . and . . . Scarlet?'* He burst forward, but then began reeling backwards when the lamp came hurtling through the air, gushing oil in its trail, and exploding in a fireball at his feet. The laughter reached a crescendo, before erupting into agonised screams as the flames licked her body.

Cassie recoiled from the raging heat that scorched her eyeballs. Suddenly there were hands clutching her, wrenching her away; pandemonium everywhere.

In that split second before she and Trent were plucked from the creeping flames, Cassie saw the two figures. They made a pitiful sight huddled together; Silas, with his arm flung protectively over the woman's shoulder and his broken, bloodied head pressed to her breast. Scarlet's magnificent opaque eyes seemed to gaze on his face, her long black hair entwined with his and the two of them locked forever in each other's embrace. There was no pain in Scarlet's quiet eyes. Only contentment, and a look of serenity that cut Cassie to the heart.

Long after it was swallowed in the ferocious inferno, and the charred blackened corpses were brought from its heart, the house struggled in its death throes, emitting a weird lament that merged with the night, like long-ago witchcraft.

The tragic news spread far and wide, sweeping through

the quaint old town of Dunster like an invading plague, affecting every man, woman and child who knew the name of Pengally. Some expected such a violent end, had foretold it over the years. Others were shocked to their roots, hurrying away with bowed heads and frantically making a sign of the cross on their brows, lest the evil should seek *them* out!

Greystone House was reduced to ashes. *Madness had taken place there. And murder!* Vincent Pengally was not killed by the fire; nor was his tragic daughter, Scarlet. As for Silas, whose lifelong obsession with the bewitching Scarlet was well known, it seemed as though he too had met a bloody and violent end at the hands of some insane creature. Rumour had it that Shelagh Williams had murdered all three. *But why?* Questions were raised. Did anyone really know her? Or where she hailed from originally? No one had been able to ascertain her identity or the reasons for her apparent madness. She had come to the Luttrell Arms as a young girl not yet twenty years of age. That was almost twenty years ago. No one knew her then. No one knew her now. She had avoided friendships and strictly kept her own counsel. Always the stranger. A private soul. A MAD SOUL.

No one regretted the destruction of Greystone House, nor of its sinister master. But what of Silas? *Another stranger.* A child who came from nowhere: darkly handsome, surly, morose, fashioned in the mould of the devil who brought him to Greystone House? And Scarlet, whose whole life had been a purgatory beneath her father's ominous shadow. No one doubted that the hand of the devil had touched these two unfortunate souls, tormenting them beyond human endurance. The only comfort they had found was in each other, yet it was forbidden. Torture, suspicion and fear had torn them apart. But something else, a far more powerful force, had emerged to unite them. *Passion. Love. Death.* There were things of the secret heart that could never be smothered. They blossomed and grew beyond all else, spanning a lifetime. *Released beyond.* Immortal.

'Be patient with him.' The matron ushered Inspector Farrell into the cubicle, softly closing the curtains behind them as she whispered, 'He has very little time. And I have already told you the full story.'

The Inspector nodded, his loose pale eyes sympathetic, his features set in a stern expression. '*I must be sure,*' he murmured, 'you do understand?' She lowered her gaze and stepped away, discreetly placing herself where she was least conspicuous.

'I need to confess . . . *please.* I need to confess before I meet my maker.' The voice was almost inaudible. The mask of death was already grey in the old man's protruding, frightened eyes.

'That's why I'm here, sir . . . to listen.' The Inspector eased his bulky frame onto the bed edge, leaning forward so as not to miss a single word. 'Now then . . . don't be afraid. No one is going to punish you. Just tell me everything you know.'

The man sighed, a long weary sound that seemed to drain him. He closed his eyes. When at last he opened them to gaze unseeing into the Inspector's face, they were glazed with tears.

'May God forgive me,' he cried, clutching the Inspector's hand with trembling fingers. 'My sins have found me out.'

CHAPTER TWENTY-ONE

'*Eight people?*' John Blackwood gripped the arms of his chair, his face a study in astonishment, as he stared at the Inspector. '*Are you telling us that Shelagh Williams murdered eight people?*' The colour drained from his face and he felt a sharp pang of guilt. But he could not have known. Even he could not have prevented it. All the same. *All the same.* He turned away.

'Hannah Pengally . . . my grandmother . . . was *she* murdered also?' Cassie's voice trembled. Trent leaned over the back of the chair, reaching his two hands down, caressing her. 'I'm fine,' she murmured, touching her fingers to his. He had been her strength. She bowed her head, unable to say any more. Her heart was too heavy and there were no words to describe her desolation. In that all too fleeting tragic moment when she had seen the face of Scarlet Pengally something was triggered inside her: a long-lost memory of a young and beautiful woman with tears running down her face and her desperate love spilling over with the words, 'Ssh, sweetheart . . . *you mustn't cry.* Nancy will be your new mammy.' Now, as the picture emerged clearer in her mind, Cassie could not hold back the sobs that racked her sore heart. The years sped away. She was a child again, safe in her mammy's arms. Then she was screaming, as tender loving hands wrenched her away. Oh, how desperately she, had scanned the driveway through the back window of the car. Searching. Calling for her mammy. Loving her so much that the pain had stayed with her all these years. *Now it was too late!* Too late to tell Scarlet how she had forgiven her and how very much she had longed for her during those early days in America. Now she would never be able to talk with Scarlet, to laugh with her, or cry with her. *Scarlet Pengally was gone.* And yet Cassie knew that her mother would live on, in the legend that was already in the making. The thought gave her a degree of solace. She prayed that people would speak of Scarlet Pengally with kind understanding tongues. Cassie had to know. 'Inspector Farrell . . . *why* did Shelagh Williams murder my family?'

'*For no other reason than that they were Pengallys.*' He looked at her in a kindly manner, for she had suffered so much, and he had a daughter of the same age. '*You* were in grave danger from the moment of your birth, Cassie . . . Scarlet Pengally knew that. That was why she made the greatest sacrifice any mother could ever make . . . she sent you away where she felt you would be safe. Unfortunately she believed Shelagh Williams to be a friend . . . over the years your mother confided in this demented woman.' He shook his head and momentarily lowered his gaze. 'Scarlet Pengally was cruelly lured to her death . . . just as the others were.'

'*Who was she?*' Trent came to sit beside Cassie, taking her hand in his and all the while his dark green eyes intent on the Inspector. 'The others who died . . . they surely could not *all* have been Pengallys? And why did she hate that family so much?'

For a long, poignant moment the Inspector made no reply. Instead, he sank back into the chair, stroking his finger and thumb across his chin and staring upwards with a far wider look in his eyes, as though struggling to make order out of the chaos in his mind. Suddenly he sat forward in his chair, stiffened his shoulders and began to address the three anxious beings before him in a more quiet sober voice. *'It's a strange and sinister story.'* He looked from one to the other, his face unyielding. 'The roots of it go back nigh on forty years . . . beginning and ending with the man known as Vincent Pengally. Shelagh Williams's entire life was eaten up with hatred and revenge because of what he did. She was driven insane . . . no one could have realised.' He glanced reassuringly at the old man. *'You* were the only one she did not entirely convince. She knew you were wary of her. But you couldn't have known . . . you have nothing to reproach yourself for. Remember that. The more insane the mind is, the more devious and calculating.' He waited. When John slowly nodded his head, he went on. 'About forty years ago, a young woman was besotted with her lover . . . left her husband and small child for him. That lover was Vincent Pengally. The woman was Evelyn Walters . . . mother of Shelagh. *Mister* Walters was a gentle, kind man, heartbroken by the break-up of his marriage; he did everything he could to persuade Evelyn to forget this other man. She couldn't . . . *or wouldn't*! Distraught, he left the area, taking the girl with him. From that day on, they never knew any peace . . . wandering from place to place like gypsies. He tried to kill himself . . . three times. Each time it was the girl who found him and ran for help. Each time her hatred grew, and the idea of revenge became a terrible obsession. Gradually, cunningly, she began delving for information . . . reasons, the truth, a name; hoarding every little snippet until the time and opportunity when she could exact revenge for herself and for the father she adored. Day by day she watched him destroy himself . . . drink, loose women. He became possessed of extreme moods . . . on one occasion he was made to serve a prison term. During this time the girl was sent to a grim establishment. When her father was released, he was a broken man . . . the bitterness was gone, and with it his feeling for the girl.

But she stood by him . . . watching over him, caring for him, when he was suffering from a crippling nervous disorder that slowly began to rob him of his faculties. The girl idolised him.' Here he paused, turning his head to the window and gazing out at the ruins of Greystone House. Presently he resumed his story. 'Shelagh Walters was a girl . . . *just a girl*. But her young heart was already black with hatred . . . for the mother who had deserted them, for the 'devil' who had taken her away. As her father grew weaker, so the awful hatred grew stronger. Finally, when Shelagh was fourteen years of age, her father was pronounced mentally unstable. Soon after, he was committed. The girl was devastated. She wanted to go with him . . . work at the institution . . . help to provide and care for him. She was turned away. Undaunted, she applied for work at a nearby home for the decrepit and seriously afflicted, a place similar to the one where her father was kept . . . but containing a certain element in society that was far more unpredictable, and considered to be extremely dangerous. She found no difficulty in obtaining work here. It was a harrowing experience for her. Yet she saved every penny of her meagre wages . . . determined to find a better place for her father. Never a day went by when she didn't visit him. Finally she did manage to have her father transferred to a more congenial place, but there was never any hope of him making a full recovery. The money she was earning never seemed enough, so when she saw advertised the position of chambermaid at the Luttrell Arms in Dunster, she set her heart on acquiring the post. Over the years she had ferreted out enough information to know that the man who lured her mother away was a man by the name of Vincent Pengally. She knew also that he had lived in a place near Minehead . . . a place called *Dunster*. She changed her name, cajoled someone into forging a reference and consequently she was installed in the Luttrell Arms from where she kept track of Vincent Pengally's every movement, frustrated by the fact that he was a man who ferociously defended his privacy and scorned any outside influence. So she did the next best thing . . . she struck up a friendship of sorts with Ada Blackwood. It was through her that she heard the rumours of a woman called Evelyn . . . buried in a pauper's grave. She knew the woman must be her mother. She still couldn't forgive her. When Hannah Pengally fell ill, Shelagh seized her opportunity.' Inspector Farrell looked at Cassie, his face compassionate as he told her gently, 'Soon after, she urged your grandmother to her death.'

'What kind of monster could harm a timid, frail creature like Hannah Pengally?' John Blackwood had closely followed the Inspector's tragic tale, quietly blaming himself, for *he* was the one who had persuaded Vincent Pengally to hire Shelagh Williams as housekeeper.

'*Shelagh Williams was seen that night.* She was wearing the cloak and hood that had been the only thing belonging to her mother, Evelyn. All these years she had kept it with her . . . a remnant from the past that she couldn't let go. There was a young pot-girl who lived in at the Luttrell Arms . . . a brash creature who had taken an instant dislike to Shelagh Williams when she had arrived as the new chambermaid. She became suspicious when Shelagh took to haunting the moors at all hours of the night. Suspecting Shelagh Williams of having an affair with *her* young man, the pot-girl took to following Shelagh. On a certain night *she saw her murder Hannah Pengally*. The result was years of blackmail. The financial drain on Shelagh Pengally was crippling . . . what with the expense of keeping her father cared for, and catering to the pot-girl's demands . . . demands that increased tenfold over the years. She also knew how deeply the pot-girl hated her, and she lived in fear of being betrayed. She finally decided she had to get rid of her.'

'Of course!' John Blackwood recalled the girl. He grew excited. 'The mutilated body found on the moors . . . *was that the girl?*'

The Inspector nodded.

'But you said there had been *eight* murders?'

'That's right.' The Inspector reached into his waistcoat pocket. Taking out a small clay pipe, he stuffed it with tobacco. Making no attempt to light it, he rolled it thoughtfully between his fingers. '*Eight murders.* Hannah Pengally drowned and the witness to it viciously mutilated some years later. Vincent Pengally horribly tortured, slowly poisoned, then hanged. Scarlet poisoned. The man, Silas, bludgeoned to death. Scarlet's son and her husband, Garrett Summers, might have stood in the way of luring Scarlet back to Greystone House . . . and so, they too were murdered . . . dashed to their deaths after being forced over a cliff.' He glanced at John, saying, 'Do you recall the discovery of the two bodies at the herb-gatherer's cottage?' When John thought for a moment, then nodded, he went on, 'That was the strangest of all. The old woman died at the hands of a twisted cripple boy . . . horribly deformed he was. It seems that Shelagh Williams was there when the old woman was crushed to death in the boy's arms. *She turned it to her advantage.* The boy was terrified of her. She used him . . . used the cottage, and got to know the poisons which the old herb-gatherer kept. When the crippled boy was of no further use to her, Shelagh Williams fed him a paralysing substance, secured him to the outhouse, and left him to starve to death. Later, when she was satisfied he was dead, she left the cottage as she had found it . . . and only ever returned once.'

'Good God!' John Blackwood was bolt upright in his chair. '*Scarlet was right!* She swore there was somebody there when she was forced to take shelter in the cottage . . . when Cassie here was struggling to be born. "*A dark, hooded figure,*" she said. Folks thought she were imagining things.'

'Scarlet Pengally was *not* "imagining things". If Garrett Summers and his men had not arrived, there is no doubt she would have been murdered there and then.' He looked at Cassie, whose face was chalk-white, 'and you with her, I'm afraid.' Suddenly he rose from the chair. 'Forgive me if all this has been too distressing for you, my dear . . . but it will all be public knowledge soon enough. It's best that you are armed with the facts. I'll trouble you no longer.'

'How were you able to find all this out . . . so many killings . . . so many years?' John Blackwood also got from his chair.

'The truth found *us*, Mr Blackwood. As you know, there was considerable newspaper coverage of the tragic events at Greystone House. Consequently we were called to an old gentlefolks' home in Taunton. It seemed that Mr Walters . . . Shelagh Williams' father, was fast slipping away. He learned of the events and felt he had to make a confession before being called to meet his maker. Apparently Shelagh Williams confided *everything* to him . . . *every gory detail as it took place. He knew she was insane.* He blamed himself . . . tried to shut it all out of his mind. Mr Walters died soon after we left.' He half-turned away, but then a strange look came over his face. 'The crippled boy . . . now, *there's* a weird and sinister thing. Shelagh Williams never knew it, but when she killed that unfortunate creature . . . *she killed a Pengally!*'

'What do you mean?' Cassie's heart turned over.

'During our investigations, we tracked down the herb-gatherer's husband. In his wanderings, he had met up with Silas. It seems that Silas had this haunting fixation that, on the night when he first came to Greystone House, he had witnessed the birth of *two* babies . . . one was Scarlet; the other a grotesquely deformed thing, that was later shut in the cellar with him. Terrified by the child's screams, he tried to comfort it. Some time later, when Silas was weak and confused from his imprisonment, he thought some terrible demon of the night had torn the child from his arms. All of this he revealed one evening to an inn full of people . . . he had been driven to drink . . . was nearly out of his mind with his obsession for Scarlet Pengally. His strange story was scoffed at. Nobody paid much attention, with the exception of one man . . . the herb-gatherer's husband. He took Silas on one side, questioned him thoroughly, and realised that the 'demon of the night' who had torn the deformed creature from the boy's arms was his own black dog. He had taken the crippled boy home to his childless wife, and over the years had come to bitterly regret it. The boy became a monster . . . *that "monster" was Vincent Pengally's own son.'*

In the ensuing shocked silence, Inspector Farrell quickly left.

'Oh, look there!' Cassie pointed to a tiny yellow bud that was pushing its way up through the scorched ground near the entrance to Greystone House.

'A daffodil,' Trent told her, affectionately placing his arm round her shoulders and smiling into the luxuriant dark eyes that John had commented were *'Scarlet Pengally all over again.'* 'It is *spring*, you know,' he laughed.

'Oh, but to bloom *here*.' She stooped to uncover the debris from around it. *'A new life beginning . . . where so many ended in tragedy.'*

'Roots go deep,' he said softly, pulling her to him, *'life will go on.'* He began walking her away. 'It's time we made our way back, Cassie. I'm glad you accepted Father's offer for you to stay at the cottage.' Already he felt the murmurings of love for her.

'So am I,' she smiled up at him. 'You and your father have been very kind to me, Trent. I don't know what I would have done without you.' *And I don't know how I can ever leave you*, she thought sadly.

'Cassie . . . must you go away tomorrow? Is there so much more for you in America than I can offer you?' He bent his head to kiss her. She did not resist. The kiss was gentle, reassuring, and filled with the promise of wonderful things. *She loved him!*

'How can I leave?' she asked, suddenly bursting with childish joy, 'when all my past is here?'

'And your future.'

In the brilliant April sunshine, with the song of birds overhead, they strolled the path back to the cottage, content in each other, their love spilling over.

At the cottage door, Cassie glanced back to the dismembered ruins of Greystone House. She thought of Silas and Scarlet. She cried inside for the love they might have known. Yes, she would stay. And she would rebuild Greystone House to its former glory. Together, she and Trent would bring happiness and love to warm its grey sombre walls. One day. *One glorious day in the not too distant future!*